The Return of the Soul & Other Curious Tales

ROBERT HICHENS

Edited by Gregory Shepard

Introduction by S.T. Joshi

Stark House Press • Eureka California

THE RETURN OF THE SOUL & OTHER CURIOUS TALES

Published by Stark House Press
1315 H Street
Eureka, CA 95501, USA
griffinskye3@sbcglobal.net
www.starkhousepress.com

"The Return of the Soul" from *The Folly of Eustace and Other Stories* (originally published and copyright © 1896 by D. Appleton, New York).

"William Foster" and "The Cry of the Child" from *Tongues of Conscience* (originally published and copyright © 1900 by Methuen & Company, London, and Frederick A. Stokes, New York).

"The Villa by the Sea" from *The Last Time and Other Stories* (originally published 1924 by Hutchinson & Co., London)

"Abdullah Ben Brahim" from *The Streets and Other Stories* (originally published 1928 by Hutchinson & Co., London)

"Saturday Night," "The Inn" and "The Address Book" from *The Gates of Paradise and Other Stories* (originally published 1930 by Cassell and Company, Ltd., London)

"Introduction" copyright 2025 © by S. T. Joshi

ISBN: 979-8-88601-118-0

Book design by Mark Shepard, shepgraphics.com
Proofreading by Bill Kelly
Cover art by C. B. Williams

First Stark House Press Edition: January 2025

The Return of the Soul & Other Curious Tales

The Return of the Soul: Ronald is a cruel young man, forced to live with his grandmother to gain his inheritance. When she dies, he spitefully kills her white cat. Now, years later, a kinder, gentler man, he falls in love and marries. But gradually his young wife begins to fear him, showing all the characteristics of the murdered cat.

"William Foster": When Catherine marries Mark Sirrett she considers him the kindest, most considerate husband in the world. But beneath his benign intentions lurks the soul of an artist who wants to write about the world the way it *really* is. Mark becomes "William Foster" and writes a dangerous book that becomes immensely popular. But popularity has its price…

The Villa by the Sea—The Pierces—Arthur and Elaine—find themselves curiously attracted to a villa by the sea while travelling in Northern Africa. They rent it, and soon discover that the previous tenants, another couple, left separately. However, their emotional battle still haunts the villa.

Cry of the Child: Maurice Dale is a haunted man. Years ago he had had a child out of wedlock, and after the mother's death, he had taken over responsibility for the baby. But driven by his egotist desires to be the best in his medical profession, he had ignored the child's cries one night, and it had died. Now he hears the child's cry almost every day. Then he marries Lily, the Canon's daughter, and everything changes.

**Enter the intriguing world of Robert Hichens.
These stories plus four more tales of murder,
duplicity and betrayal await you.**

Contents

FIRST PUBLICATIONS

The Return of the Soul (*The Pall Mall Magazine*,
   August 1895, as "A Re-incarnation")
The Villa by the Sea (*Hutchinson's Magazine*, August 1922)
The Inn (*Cosmopolitan*, May 1924)
The Address Book (*Harper's Bazar*, September 1927)
Saturday Night (*Liberty*, April 13 1929)

Introduction

By S. T. Joshi

This volume contains stories from more than three decades of writing by Robert Hichens, demonstrating the themes, settings, and motifs that the author found so obsessively compelling that he returned to them over and over again—but always with innovative variations that render them fresh and distinctive.

"The Return of the Soul" (1895) is the earliest of the eight tales in this book, and is one of Hichens's earliest treatments of the metempsychosis motif—the notion of the transmigration of souls, which entered into such memorable narratives as "A Tribute of Souls," "The Charmer of Snakes," and "The Black Spaniel." In this story—presented as the diary of a man who provides only his first name, Ronald—we see how Hichens skillfully uses the supernatural to enhance a moral conception. It is one thing to decry a boy's irrational killing of a cat that had done him no harm; it is a very different thing to portray that boy, the young Ronald, doing the deed and then, nearly two decades later, finding himself married to a woman who uncannily appears to be endowed with the soul of that dead animal. Hichens is well aware that the very idea that animals have souls is a religiously radical one; the Catholic church has long rejected such a notion, and other religions have not been far behind. (The question as to whether there is even such a thing as the soul, human or otherwise, does not seem to concern them.) Hichens deliberately makes no secret of the basic thrust of the tale. We learn that Ronald's wife, Margot, is able to see in the dark; she then exhibits fear of her husband—"a fear such as an animal might feel towards the master who had beaten it." Ronald himself develops a fear that "the animal's soul within her no longer merely shrinks away in fear of me. It has grown sinister. It lies in ambush, full of a cold, a stealthy intention." In this subtle way Hichens has transformed the scenario whereby the erstwhile victim becomes the pursuer, and Ronald inexorably becomes its prey.

A similar moral undercurrent, ending in tragedy, is the focus of "The Cry of the Child," one of several long tales in *Tongues of Conscience* (1900)—including "Sea Change" and "How Love Came to Professor

Guildea"—that generate an almost unbearable degree of emotional torment in the reader. Hichens chose the title of his book by design, and it presumably echoes the memorable words of King Richard III in Shakespeare's play: "My conscience hath a thousand several tongues, / And every tongue brings in a several tale, / And every tale condemns me for a villain." In "The Cry of the Child" the "villain," as it were, is the protagonist, Maurice Dale, a physician who admits to his beloved, Lily Alston, that he had caused the death of his infant child when he neglected it while pursuing his medical studies. (Dale's wife had died soon after childbirth.) "I'm a haunted man," he states, for he now hears an ineffable crying—the crying of his dead child, "full of pain and of eternal reproach"—wherever he goes. To the extent that Maurice expresses remorse at his heedless actions, he is shown to be morally redeemable; it is that quality that attracts Lily to him, in spite of Maurice's worry that she "may be haunted as I am." He desperately hopes that their marriage will put an end to the crying—but it doesn't, and he upbraids his new wife: "You cannot help me." At the last Lily does help him—but the end result is hardly one that we, or Maurice, can consider a happy outcome.

Another tale in *Tongues of Conscience,* "'William Foster,'" generates a different type of terror, for all that it is non-supernatural. It was written at a time when the scandal over the sexual irregularities of Oscar Wilde—whom Hichens had parodied in his first book, *The Green Carnation* (1894)—were still fresh in people's minds. It could well be that the protagonist, the writer Mark Sirrett, is a stand-in for Wilde: he adopts the pseudonym "William Foster" for a work that will express "the terrors that trooped in his imagination." His wife Catherine, raised by a religiously devout mother (although her father is a freethinker like her husband), hopes that he might write about "the beauty, the joy, the purity, the goodness of life"—but he refuses to write didactic literature of this sort. This conflict encapsulates the battle between "moral" and "immoral" literature that was dominant at the time, with Wilde and his allies promoting an "art for art's sake" attitude that scorned bourgeois morality and sought to portray the world as it was, warts and all. Sure enough, the book by "William Foster" is condemned as "dangerous, morbidly imaginative, horrible in subject, and likely to do great mischief because of its undoubted power and charm"—perhaps like Wilde's own weird novella, *The Picture of Dorian Gray* (1890). And since we know at the outset that Catherine Sirrett is a murderess— the story opens with a man who sees a model of her at Madame

Tussaud's—we similarly know the outcome of this grim tale.

A trio of stories set in North Africa—a favorite vacation destination of Hichens—are similarly only on the borderline of the weird, but their emotional resonance is nonetheless intense. "The Villa by the Sea" (1922) is the most expansive of these tales, as Arthur Pierce and his wife Elaine alternatively tell the story of how they came upon a charming villa near Sidi Barka (an obscure locale in Morocco) formerly occupied by a John and Evelyn Eardsley. In one room of the villa, Arthur believes that "Here, in this small enclosed space . . . something extraordinary has happened in the past." Indeed, he feels "a moral fear, a fear of soul." And yet, it is fairly clear from the start that nothing supernatural has occurred in this baleful room. Elaine, taking the room as her bedroom, senses "the mental anguish of a woman." Could John Eardsley have been a fugitive from justice who had come to this remote place to hide from the law? Had his wife only discovered his dereliction while they were living there, and is that why she had fled from the villa and from her husband? Hichens expounds the tale in a somewhat leisurely manner, but the spectacular revelation of what John Eardsley had done is well worth the wait.

"The Inn" (1924) is set in Tunisia, where the narrator, an elderly man, meets a young woman who announces herself as Mrs. Colegate. Plunged in gloom, cynicism, and despair, she eventually reveals that she had married an Australian and had stayed at the inn years before. Her husband had gone hunting for several days, but never returned; and when she learned of his fate, she took actions that exhibit her disdain for the man she had married. "Abdullah Ben Brahim" is set in Biskra (a city in Algeria), where again a male narrator meets a married woman, Mrs. Van Brandt. The metempsychosis element recurs here, as she thinks she is the reincarnation of an Arab woman and thereby becomes infatuated with a native guide, Abdullah Ben Brahim. When it is revealed that Abdullah is married, and in addition has a mistress, we know that the outcome for all concerned cannot be good.

Two lighter tales, "The Address Book" (1927) and "Saturday Night" (1929), nevertheless underscore Hichens's focus on human psychology, especially in social contexts. The former is an overtly comic story about class distinctions in England—an issue that Americans (who purportedly live in a "classless" society, even if there are in fact radical distinctions based on wealth, education, and other factors) may have trouble relating to, but which remain central to the English mentality. "Saturday Night" is another moral fable, exhibiting the weakness of a struggling playwright who allows himself to be seduced by a heartless actress.

The wealth of impressive work—in the novel, the novella, and the short story—produced by Robert Hichens should make him a notable literary figure; but it is a sad fact that, in his mainstream work, he found himself out of step with the times. The avant-garde work of James Joyce, Virginia Woolf, and others in the 1920s and thereafter rendered much of his writing outmoded and passé, for all its great virtues in character portrayal, vibrancy of setting, and intensity of emotional impact. But his weird tales—whether they be of supernatural or psychological horror—will continue to live, and deserve to live. It is abundantly clear that he scorned the notion of writing stories merely to evoke a shudder; he always infused his work with an element of "conscience," whereby terror is designed to underscore the psychological troubles and traumas faced by his sensitive protagonists. And his deft narrative skills allow his readers to gain a sense of cumulative horror and unease until the climax explodes with cataclysmic power. Hichens's elegance of diction is a refreshing change from the slovenliness of contemporary writing, and any one of his novels and tales is worth reading solely for the sensuous pleasure inherent in a compelling tale finely told.

—June 2024

....

S. T. Joshi is a freelance writer and editor. He has prepared comprehensive editions of H. P. Lovecraft's collected fiction, essays, poetry, and letters, including an annotated edition of *The Case of Charles Dexter Ward* (2010). He is the author of *The Weird Tale* (1990), *The Modern Weird Tale* (2001), *I Am Providence: The Life and Times of H. P. Lovecraft* (2010), and *Unutterable Horror: A History of Supernatural Fiction* (2012), and has edited *the anthology American Supernatural Tales* (2007).

The Return of the Soul & Other Curious Tales

....

ROBERT HICHENS

THE RETURN OF THE SOUL

"I have been here before,
But when, or how, I cannot tell!"
ROSSETTI.

I.

Tuesday Night, *November 3rd*.

Theories! What is the good of theories? They are the scourges that lash our minds in modern days, lash them into confusion, perplexity, despair. I have never been troubled by them before. Why should I be troubled by them now? And the absurdity of Professor Black's is surely obvious. A child would laugh at it. Yes, a child! I have never been a diary writer. I have never been able to understand the amusement of sitting down late at night and scrawling minutely in some hidden book every paltry incident of one's paltry days. People say it is so interesting to read the entries years afterwards. To read, as a man, the menu that I ate through as a boy, the love-story that I was actor in, the tragedy that I brought about, the debt that I have never paid—how could it profit me? To keep a diary has always seemed to me merely an addition to the ills of life. Yet now I have a hidden book, like the rest of the world, and I am scrawling in it today. Yes, but for a reason.

I want to make things clear to myself, and I find, as others, that my mind works more easily with the assistance of the pen. The actual tracing of words on paper dispels the clouds that cluster round my thoughts. I shall recall events to set my mind at ease, to prove to myself how absurd a man who could believe in Professor Black would be. "Little Dry-as-dust" I used to call him. Dry? He is full of wild romance, rubbish that a school-girl would be ashamed to believe in. Yet he is abnormally clever; his record proves that. Still, clever men are the first to be led astray, they say. It is the searcher who follows the wandering light. What he says can't be true. When I have filled these pages, and read what I have written dispassionately, as one of the outside public might read, I shall have done, once for all, with the ridiculous fancies that are beginning to make my life a burden. To put my thoughts in order will make a music. The evil spirit within me will sleep, will die. I shall be cured. It must be so—it shall be so.

To go back to the beginning. Ah! what a long time ago that seems! As a child I was cruel. Most boys are cruel, I think. My school companions were a merciless set—merciless to one another, to their masters when they had a chance, to animals, to birds. The desire to torture was in nearly all of them. They loved to bully, and if they bullied only mildly, it was from fear, not from love. They did not wish their boomerang to return and slay them. If a boy were deformed, they twitted him. If a master were kind, or gentle, or shy, they made his life as intolerable as they could. If an animal or a bird came into their power, they had no pity. I was like the rest; indeed, I think that I was worse. Cruelty is horrible. I have enough imagination to do more than know that—to feel it.

Some say that it is lack of imagination which makes men and women brutes. May it not be power of imagination? The interest of torturing is lessened, is almost lost, if we cannot be the tortured as well as the torturer.

As a child I was cruel by nature, by instinct. I was a handsome, well-bred, gentlemanlike, gentle-looking little brute. My parents adored me, and I was good to them. They were so kind to me that I was almost fond of them. Why not? It seemed to me as politic to be fond of them as of anyone else. I did what I pleased, but I did not always let them know it; so I pleased them. The wise child will take care to foster the ignorance of its parents. My people were pretty well off, and I was their only child; but my chief chances of future pleasure in life were centred in my grandmother, my mother's mother. She was immensely rich, and she lived here. This room in which I am writing now was her favourite sitting room. On that hearth, before a log fire, such as is burning at this moment, used to sit that wonderful cat of hers—that horrible cat! Why did I ever play my childish cards to win this house, this place? Sometimes, lately—very lately only—I have wondered, like a fool perhaps. Yet would Professor Black say so? I remember, as a boy of sixteen, paying my last visit here to my grandmother. It bored me very much to come. But she was said to be near death, and death leaves great houses vacant for others to fill. So when my mother said that I had better come, and my father added that he thought my grandmother was fonder of me than of my other relations, I gave up all my boyish plans for the holidays with apparent willingness. Though almost a child, I was not shortsighted. I knew every boy had a future as well as a present. I gave up my plans, and came here with a smile; but in my heart I hated my grandmother for having power, and so bending me to relinquish pleasure for boredom. I hated her, and I came to her and kissed her, and saw her beautiful white Persian cat sitting before the fire in this room, and thought of the fellow who was my bosom friend, and with whom I longed to be, shooting, or fishing, or riding. And I looked at the cat again. I remember it began to purr when I went near to it. It sat quite still, with its blue eyes fixed upon the fire, but when I approached it I heard it purr complacently. I longed to kick it. The limitations of its ridiculous life satisfied it completely. It seemed to reproduce in an absurd, diminished way my grandmother in her white lace cap, with her white face and hands. She sat in her chair all day and looked at the fire. The cat sat on the hearthrug and did the same. The cat seemed to me the animal personification of the human being who kept me chained from all the sports and pleasures I had promised myself for the holidays. When I went near to the cat, and heard it calmly purring at me, I longed to do it an injury. It seemed to me as if it understood what my grandmother did not, and was complacently triumphing at my voluntary imprisonment with age, and laughing to itself at the pains men—and boys—will undergo for the sake of money. Brute! I did not love my grandmother, and she had money. I hated the cat utterly. It hadn't a *sou!*

This beautiful house is not old. My grandfather built it himself. He had no love for the life of towns, I believe, but was passionately in touch with nature, and, when a young man, he set out on a strange tour through England. His object was to find a perfect view, and in front of that view he intended to build himself a habitation. For nearly a year, so I have been told, he wandered through Scotland and England, and at last he came to this place in Cumberland, to this village, to this very spot. Here his wanderings ceased. Standing on the terrace—then uncultivated forest—that runs in front of these windows, he found at last what he desired. He bought the forest. He bought the windings of the river, the fields upon its banks, and on the extreme edge of the steep gorge through which it runs he built the lovely dwelling that today is mine.

This place is no ordinary place. It is characteristic in the highest degree. The house is wonderfully situated, with the ground falling abruptly in front of it, the river forming almost a horseshoe round it. The woods are lovely. The garden, curiously, almost wildly, laid out, is like no other garden I ever saw. And the house, though not old, is full of little surprises, curiously shaped rooms, remarkable staircases, quaint recesses. The place is a place to remember. The house is a house to fix itself in the memory. Nothing that had once lived here could ever come back and forget that it had been here. Not even an animal—not even an animal.

I wish I had never gone to that dinner party and met the Professor. There was a horror coming upon me then. He has hastened its steps. He has put my fears into shape, my vague wondering into words. Why cannot men leave life alone? Why will they catch it by the throat and wring its secrets from it? To respect reserve is one of the first instincts of the gentleman; and life is full of reserve.

It is getting very late. I thought I heard a step in the house just now. I wonder—I wonder if *she* is asleep. I wish I knew.

Day after day passed by. My grandmother seemed to be failing, but almost imperceptibly. She evidently loved to have me near to her. Like most old dying people, in her mind she frantically clutched at life, that could give to her nothing more; and I believe she grew to regard me as the personification of all that was leaving her. My vitality warmed her. She extended her hands to my flaming hearth fire. She seemed trying to live in my life, and at length became afraid to let me out of her sight. One day she said to me, in her quavering, ugly voice—old voices are so ugly, like hideous echoes:

"Ronald, I could never die while you were in the room. So long as you are with me, where I can touch you, I shall live."

And she put out her white, corrugated hand, and fondled my warm boy's hand.

How I longed to push her hand away, and get out into the sunlight and the air, and hear young voices, the voices of the morning, not of the twilight, and be away from wrinkled Death, that seemed sitting on the doorstep of that house huddled up like a beggar, waiting for the door to be opened!

I was bored till I grew malignant. I confess it. And, feeling malignant, I began to long more and more passionately to vent myself on someone or something. I looked at the cat, which, as usual, was sitting before the fire.

Animals have intuitions as keen as those of a woman, keener than those of a man. They inherit an instinct of fear of those who hate them from a long line of ancestors who have suffered at the hands of cruel men. They can tell by a look, by a motion, by the tone of a voice, whether to expect from anyone kindness or malignity. The cat had purred complacently on the first day of my arrival, and had hunched up her white, furry back towards my hand, and had smiled with her calm, light-blue eyes. Now, when I approached her, she seemed to gather herself together and to make herself small. She shrank from me. There was—as I fancied—a dawning comprehension, a dawning terror in her blue eyes. She always sat very close to my grandmother now, as if she sought protection, and she watched me as if she were watching for an intention which she apprehended to grow in my mind.

And the intention came.

For, as the days went on, and my grandmother still lived, I began to grow desperate. My holiday time was over now, but my parents wrote telling me to stay where I was, and not to think of returning to school. My grandmother had caused a letter to be sent to them in which she said that she could not part from me, and added that my parents would never have cause to regret interrupting my education for a time. "He will be paid in full for every moment he loses," she wrote, referring to me.

It seemed a strange taste in her to care so much for a boy, but she had never loved women, and I was handsome, and she liked handsome faces. The brutality in my nature was not written upon my features. I had smiling, frank brown eyes, a lithe young figure, a gay boy's voice. My movements were quick, and I have always been told that my gestures were never awkward, my demeanour was never unfinished, as is the case so often with lads at school. Outwardly I was attractive; and the old woman, who had married two husbands merely for their looks, delighted in feeling that she had the power to retain me by her side at an age when most boys avoid old people as if they were the pestilence.

And then I pretended to love her, and obeyed all her insufferably tiresome behests. But I longed to wreak vengeance upon her all the same. My dearest friend, the fellow with whom I was to have spent my holidays, was leaving at the end of this term which I was missing. He wrote to me furious letters, urging me to come back, and reproaching me for my selfishness and lack of affection.

Each time I received one I looked at the cat, and the cat shrank nearer to my grandmother's chair.

It never purred now, and nothing would induce it to leave the room where she sat. One day the servant said to me:

"I believe the poor dumb thing knows my mistress can't last very much longer, sir. The way that cat looks up at her goes to my heart. Ah!

them beasts understand things as well as we do, I believe."

I think the cat understood quite well. It did watch my grandmother in a very strange way, gazing up into her face, as if to mark the changing contours, the increasing lines, the down-droop of the features, that bespoke the gradual soft approach of death. It listened to the sound of her voice; and as, each day, the voice grew more vague, more weak and toneless, an anxiety that made me exult dawned and deepened in its blue eyes. Or so I thought.

I had a great deal of morbid imagination at that age, and loved to weave a web of fancies, mostly horrible, around almost everything that entered into my life. It pleased me to believe that the cat understood each new intention that came into my mind, read me silently from its place near the fire, tracked my thoughts, and was terror-stricken as they concentrated themselves round a definite resolve, which hardened and toughened day by day.

It pleased me to believe, do I say? I did really believe, and do believe now, that the cat understood all, and grew haggard with fear as my grandmother failed visibly. For it knew what the end would mean for it.

That first day of my arrival, when I saw my grandmother in her white cap, with her white face and hands, and the big white cat sitting near to her, I had thought there was a similarity between them. That similarity struck me more forcibly, grew upon me, as my time in the house grew longer, until the latter seemed almost a reproduction of the former, and after each letter from my friend my hate for the two increased. But my hate for my grandmother was impotent, and would always be so. I could never repay her for the *ennui*, the furious, forced inactivity which made my life a burden, and spurred my bad passions while they lulled me in a terrible, enforced repose. I could repay her favourite, the thing she had always cherished, her feline confidant, who lived in safety under the shadow of her protection. I could wreak my fury on that when the protection was withdrawn, as it must be at last. It seemed to my brutal, imaginative, unfinished boy's mind that the murder of her pet must hurt and wound my grandmother even after she was dead. I would make her suffer then, when she was impotent to wreak a vengeance upon me. I would kill the cat.

The creature knew my resolve the day I made it, and had even, I should say, anticipated it.

As I sat day after day beside my grandmother's armchair in the dim room, with the blinds drawn to shut out the summer sunlight, and talked to her in a subdued and reverent voice, agreeing with all the old banalities she uttered, all the preposterous opinions she propounded, all the commands she laid upon me, I gazed beyond her at the cat, and the creature was haggard with apprehension.

It knew, as I knew, that its day was coming. Sometimes I bent down and took it up on my lap to please my grandmother, and praised its beauty and its gentleness to her. And all the time I felt its warm, furry body trembling with horror between my hands. This pleased me, and I pretended that I was never happy unless it was on my knees. I kept it there for hours, stroking it so tenderly, smoothing its thick white coat, which was always in the most perfect order, talking to it, caressing it.

And sometimes I took its head between my two hands, turned its face to mine, and stared into its large blue eyes. Then I could read all its agony, all its torture of apprehension: and in spite of my friend's letters, and the dullness of my days, I was almost happy.

The summer was deepening, the glow of the roses flushed the garden ways, the skies were clear above Scawfell, when the end at last drew near. My grandmother's face was now scarcely recognizable. The eyes were sunk deep in her head. All expression seemed to fade gradually away. Her cheeks were no longer fine ivory white; a dull, sickening, yellow pallor overspread them. She seldom looked at me now, but rested entombed in her great armchair, her shrunken limbs seeming to tend downwards, as if she were inclined to slide to the floor and die there. Her lips were thin and dry, and moved perpetually in a silent chattering, as if her mind were talking and her voice were already dead. The tide of life was retreating from her body. I could almost see it visibly ebb away. The failing waves made no sound upon the shore. Death is uncanny, like all silent things.

Her maid wished her to stay entirely in bed, but she would get up, muttering that she was well; and the doctor said it was useless to hinder her. She had no specific disease. Only the years were taking their last toll of her. So she was placed in her chair each day by the fire, and sat there till evening, muttering with those dry lips. The stiff folds of her silken skirts formed an angle, and there the cat crouched hour after hour, a silent, white, waiting thing.

And the waves ebbed and ebbed away, and I waited too.

One afternoon, as I sat by my grandmother, the servant entered with a letter for me just arrived by the post. I took it up. It was from Willoughby, my school friend. He said the term was over, that he had left school, and his father had decided to send him out to America to start in business in New York, instead of entering him at Oxford as he had hoped. He bade me goodbye, and said he supposed we should not meet again for years; "but," he added, "no doubt you won't care a straw, so long as you get the confounded money you're after. You've taught me one of the lessons of life, young Ronald—never to believe in friendship."

As I read the letter I set my teeth. All that was good in my nature centred round Willoughby. He was a really fine fellow. I honestly and truly loved him. His news gave me a bitter shock, and turned my heart to iron and to fire. Perhaps I should never see him again; even if I did, time would have changed him, seared him—my friend, in his wonderful youth, with the morning in his eyes, would be no more. I hated myself in that moment for having stayed; I hated still more her who had kept me. For the moment I was carried out of myself. I crushed the letter up in my burning hand. I turned fiercely round upon that yellow, enigmatic, dying figure in the great chair. All the fury, locked within my heart for so long, rose to the surface, and drove self-interest away. I turned upon my grandmother with blazing eyes and trembling limbs. I opened my mouth to utter a torrent of reproachful words, when—what was it?— what slight change had stolen into the wrinkled, yellow face? I bent over her. The eyes gazed at me, but so horribly! She sat so low in her chair; she looked so fearful, so very strange. I put my fingers on her eyelids; I drew them down over the eyeballs: they did not open again. I felt her withered hands: they were ice. Then I knew, and I felt myself smiling. I leaned over the dead woman. There, on the far side of her, crouched the cat. Its white fur was all bristling; its blue eyes were dilated; on its jaws there were flecks of foam.

I leaned over the dead woman and took it in my arms.

That was nearly twenty years ago, and yet tonight the memory of that moment, and what followed it, bring a fear to my heart which I must combat. I have read of men who lived for long spaces of time haunted by demons created by their imagination, and I have laughed at them and pitied them. Surely I am not going to join in their folly, in their madness, led to the gates of terror by my own fancies, half-confirmed, apparently, by the chance utterances of a conceited Professor—a man of fads, although a man of science.

That was twenty years ago. After tonight let me forget it. After tonight, do I say? Hark! the birds are twittering in the dew outside. The pale, early sun-shafts strike over the moors. And I am tired.

Tomorrow night I will finish this wrestle with my own folly; I will give the *coup de grâce* to my imagination. But no more now. My brain is not calm, and I will not write in excitement.

II.

Wednesday Night, *November 4th.*

Margot has gone to bed at last, and I am alone. This has been a horrible day—horrible; but I will not dwell upon it.

After the death of my grandmother, I went back to school again. But Willoughby was gone, and he could not forgive me. He wrote to me once or twice from New York, and then I ceased to hear from him. He died out of my life. His affection for me had evidently declined from the day when he took it into his head that I was only a money-grubber, like the rest of the world, and that the Jew instinct had developed in me at an abnormally early age. I let him go. What did it matter? But I was always glad that I had been cruel on the day my grandmother died. I never repented of what I did—never. If I had, I might be happier now.

I went back to school. I studied, played, got into mischief and out of it again, like other boys; but in my life there seemed to be an eternal coldness, that I alone, perhaps, was conscious of. My deed of cruelty, of brutal revenge on the thing that had never done me injury, had seared my soul. I was not sorry, but I could not forget; and sometimes I thought—how ridiculous it looks written down!—that there was a power hidden somewhere which could not forget either, and that a penalty might have to be paid. Because a creature is dumb, must its soul die when it dies? Is not the soul, perhaps—as he said—a wanderer through many bodies?

But if I did not kill a soul, as I killed a body, the day my grandmother died, where is that soul now? That is what I want to arrive at, that is what I must arrive at, if I am to be happy.

I went back to school, and I passed to Oxford. I tasted the strange, unique life of a university, narrow, yet pulsating, where the youth, that is so green and springing, tries to arm itself for the battle with the weapons forged by the dead and sharpened by the more elderly among the living. I did well there, and I passed on into the world. And then at last I began to understand the value of my inheritance; for all that had been my grandmother's was now mine. My people wished me to marry, but I had no desire to fetter myself. So I took the sponge in my strong, young hands, and tried to squeeze it dry. And I did not know that I was sad—I did not know it until, at the age of thirty-three, just seventeen years after my grandmother died, I understood the sort of thing happiness is. Of course, it was love that brought to me understanding. I need not explain that. I had often played on love; now love began to play on me. I trembled at the harmonies his hands evoked.

I met a young girl, very young, just on the verge of life and of womanhood. She was seventeen when I first saw her, and she was valsing at a big ball in London—her first ball. She passed me in the crowd of dancers, and I noticed her. As she was a debutante her dress was naturally snow-white. There was no touch of colour about it—not a flower, not a jewel. Her hair was the palest yellow I had almost ever seen—the colour of an early primrose. Naturally fluffy, it nearly concealed the white riband that ran through it, and clustered in tendrils and tiny natural curls upon her neck. Her skin was whiter than ivory— a clear, luminous white. Her eyes were very large and china-blue in colour.

This young girl dancing passed and repassed me, and my glance rested on her idly, even cynically. For she seemed so happy, and at that time happiness won my languid wonder, if ingenuously exhibited. To be happy seemed almost to be mindless. But by degrees I found myself watching this girl, and more closely. Another dance began. She joined it with another partner. But she seemed just as pleased with him as with her former one. She would not let him pause to rest; she kept him dancing all the time, her youth and freshness spoken in that gentle compelling. I grew interested in her, even acutely so. She seemed to me like the spirit of youth dancing over the body of Time. I resolved to know her. I felt weary; I thought she might revive me. The dance drew to an end, and I approached my hostess, pointed the girl out, and asked for an introduction. Her name was Margot Magendie, I found, and she was an heiress as well as a beauty.

I did not care. It was her humanity that drew me, nothing else.

But, strange to say, when the moment for the introduction arrived, and I stood face to face with Miss Magendie, I felt an extraordinary shrinking from her. I have never been able to understand it, but my blood ran cold, and my pulses almost ceased to beat. I would have avoided her; an instinct within me seemed suddenly to cry out against her. But it was too late: the introduction was effected; her hand rested on my arm.

I was actually trembling. She did not appear to notice it. The band played a valse, and the inexplicable horror that had seized me lost itself in the gay music. It never returned until lately.

I seldom enjoyed a valse more. Our steps suited so perfectly, and her obvious childish pleasure communicated itself to me. The spirit of youth in her knocked on my rather jaded heart, and I opened to it. That was beautiful and strange. I talked with her, and I felt myself younger, ingenuous rather than cynical, inclined even to a radiant, though foolish, optimism. She was very natural, very imperfect in worldly education, full of fragmentary but decisive views on life, quite unabashed in giving them forth, quite inconsiderate in summoning my adherence to them.

And then, presently, as we sat in a dim corridor under a rosy hanging lamp, in saying something she looked, with her great blue eyes, right into my face. Some very faint recollection awoke and stirred in my mind.

"Surely," I said hesitatingly—"surely I have seen you before? It seems to me that I remember your eyes."

As I spoke I was thinking hard, chasing the vagrant recollection that eluded me.

She smiled.

"You don't remember my face?"

"No, not at all."

"Nor I yours. If we had seen each other, surely we should recollect it."

Then she blushed, suddenly realizing that her words implied, perhaps, more than she had meant. I did not pay the obvious compliment. Those blue eyes and something in their expression moved me strangely; but I could not tell why. When I said goodbye to her that night, I asked to be allowed to call.

She assented.

That was the beginning of a very beautiful courtship, which gave a colour to life, a music to existence, a meaning to every slightest sensation.

And was it love that laid to sleep recollection, that sang a lullaby to awakening horror, and strewed poppies over it till it sighed itself into slumber? Was it love that drowned my mind in deep and charmed waters, binding the strange powers that every mind possesses in flowery garlands stronger than any fetters of iron? Was it love that, calling up dreams, alienated my thoughts from their search after reality?

I hardly know. I only know that I grew to love Margot, and only looked for love in her blue eyes, not for any deed of the past that might be mirrored there.

And I made her love me.

She gave her child's heart to my keeping with a perfect confidence that only a perfect affection could engender. She did love me then. No circumstances of today can break that fact under their hammers. She did love me, and it is the knowledge that she did which gives so much of fear to me now.

For great changes in the human mind are terrible. As we realize them we realize the limitless possibilities of sinister deeds that lie hidden in every human being. A little child that loves a doll can become an old, crafty, secret murderer. How horrible!

And perhaps it is still more horrible to think that, while the human envelope remains totally unchanged, every word of the letter within may become altered, and a message of peace fade into a sentence of death.

Margot's face is the same face now as it was when I married her— scarcely older, certainly not less beautiful. Only the expression of the eyes has changed.

For we were married. After a year of lovemaking, which never tired either of us, we elected to bind ourselves, to fuse the two into one.

We went abroad for the honeymoon, and, instead of shortening it to the fashionable fortnight, we travelled for nearly six months, and were happy all the time.

Boredom never set in. Margot had a beautiful mind as well as a beautiful face. She softened me through my affection. The current of my life began to set in a different direction. I turned the pages of a book of pity and of death more beautiful than that of Pierre Loti. I could hear at last the great cry for sympathy, which is the music of this strange suffering world, and, listening to it, in my heart there rang an echo. The cruelty in my nature seemed to shrivel up. I was more gentle than I had been, more gentle than I had thought I could ever be.

At last, in the late spring, we started for home. We stayed for a week in London, and then we travelled north. Margot had never seen her future home, had never even been in Cumberland before. She was full of excitement and happiness, a veritable child in the ready and ardent expression of her feelings. The station is several miles from the house, and is on the edge of the sea. When the train pulled up at the wayside platform the day drew towards sunset, and the flat levels of the beach shone with a rich, liquid, amber light. In the distance the sea was tossing and tumbling, whipped into foam by a fresh wind. The Isle of Man lay far away, dark, mysterious, under a stack of bellying white clouds, just beginning to be tinged with the faintest rose.

Margot found the scene beautiful, the wind life-giving, the flat sandbanks, the shining levels, even the dry, spiky grass that fluttered in the breeze, fascinating and refreshing.

"I feel near the heart of Nature in a place like this," she said, looking up at a seagull that hovered over the little platform, crying to the wind on which it hung.

The train stole off along the edge of the sands, till we could see only the white streamer of its smoke trailing towards the sun. We turned away from the sea, got into the carriage that was waiting for us, and set our faces inland. The ocean was blotted out by the low grass and heather-covered banks that divided the fields. Presently we plunged into woods. The road descended sharply. A village, an abruptly winding river sprang into sight.

We were on my land. We passed the inn, the Rainwood Arms, named after my grandfather's family. The people whom we met stared curiously and saluted in rustic fashion.

Margot was full of excitement and pleasure, and talked incessantly, holding my hand tightly in hers and asking a thousand questions. Passing through the village, we mounted a hill towards a thick grove of trees.

"The house stands among them," I said, pointing.

She sprang up eagerly in the carriage to find it, but it was hidden.

We dashed through the gate into the momentary darkness of the drive, emerged between great green lawns, and drew up before the big doorway of the hall. I looked into her eyes, and said "Welcome!"

She only smiled in answer.

I would not let her enter the house immediately, but made her come with me to the terrace above the river, to see the view over the Cumbrian mountains and the moors of Eskdale.

The sky was very clear and pale, but over Styhead the clouds were boiling up. The Screes that guard ebon Wastwater looked grim and sad.

Margot stood beside me on the terrace, but her chatter had been succeeded by silence. And I, too, was silent for the moment, absorbed in contemplation. But presently I turned to her, wishing to see how she was impressed by her new domain.

She was not looking towards the river and the hills, but at the terrace walk itself, the band of emerald turf that bordered it, the stone pots full of flowers, the winding way that led into the shrubbery.

She was looking at these intently, and with a strangely puzzled, almost startled expression.

"Hush! Don't speak to me for a moment," she said, as I opened my lips. "Don't; I want to— How odd this is!"

And she gazed up at the windows of the house, at the creepers that climbed its walls, at the sloping roof and the irregular chimney-stacks.

Her lips were slightly parted, and her eyes were full of an inward expression that told me she was struggling with forgetfulness and desired recollection.

I was silent, wondering.

At last she said: "Ronald, I have never been in the North of England before, never set foot in Cumberland; yet I seem to know this terrace walk, those very flower pots, the garden, the look of that roof, those chimneys, even the slanting way in which that great creeper climbs. Is it not—is it not very strange?"

She gazed up at me, and in her blue eyes there was an expression almost of fear.

I smiled down on her. "It must be your fancy," I said.

"It does not seem so," she replied. "I feel as if I had been here before, and often, or for a long time." She paused; then she said: "Do let me go into the house. There ought to be a room there—a room—I seem almost to see it. Come! Let us go in."

She took my hand and drew me towards the hall door. The servants were carrying in the luggage, and there was a certain amount of confusion and noise, but she did not seem to notice it. She was intent on something; I could not tell what.

"Do show me the house, Ronald—the drawing room, and—and— there is another room I wish to see."

"You shall see them all, dear," I said. "You are excited. It is natural enough. This is the drawing room."

She glanced round it hastily.

"And now the others!" she exclaimed.

I took her to the dining room, the library, and the various apartments on the ground floor.

She scarcely looked at them. When we had finished exploring, "Are these all?" she asked, with a wavering accent of disappointment.

"All," I answered.

"Then—show me the rooms upstairs."

We ascended the shallow oak steps, and passed first into the apartment in which my grandmother had died.

It had been done up since then, refurnished, and almost completely altered. Only the wide fireplace, with its brass dogs and its heavy oaken mantelpiece, had been left untouched.

Margot glanced hastily round. Then she walked up to the fireplace, and drew a long breath.

"There ought to be a fire here," she said.

"But it is summer," I answered, wondering.

"And a chair there," she went on, in a curious low voice, indicating— I think now, or is it my imagination?—the very spot where my grandmother was wont to sit. "Yes—I seem to remember, and yet not to remember."

She looked at me, and her white brows were knit.

Suddenly she said: "Ronald, I don't think I like this room. There is something—I don't know—I don't think I could sit here; and I seem to remember—something about it, as I did about the terrace. What can it mean?"

"It means that you are tired and overexcited, darling. Your nerves are too highly strung, and nerves play us strange tricks. Come to your own room and take off your things, and when you have had some tea, you will be all right again."

Yes, I was fool enough to believe that tea was the panacea for an undreamed-of, a then unimaginable, evil.

I thought Margot was simply an overtired and imaginative child that evening. If I could believe so now!

We went up into her boudoir and had tea, and she grew more like herself; but several times that night I observed her looking puzzled and thoughtful, and a certain expression of anxiety shone in her blue eyes that was new to them then.

But I thought nothing of it, and I was happy. Two or three days passed, and Margot did not again refer to her curious sensation of preknowledge of the house and garden. I fancied there was a slight alteration in her manner; that was all. She seemed a little restless. Her vivacity flagged now and then. She was more willing to be alone than she had been. But we were old married folk now, and could not be always in each other's sight. I had a great many people connected with the estate to see, and had to gather up the tangled threads of many affairs.

The honeymoon was over. Of course we could not always be together.

Still, I should have wished Margot to desire it, and I could not hide from myself that now and then she scarcely concealed a slight impatience to be left in solitude. This troubled me, but only a little, for she was generally as fond as ever. That evening, however, an incident occurred which rendered me decidedly uneasy, and made me wonder if my wife were not inclined to that curse of highly-strung women—hysteria!

I had been riding over the moors to visit a tenant farmer who lived at some distance, and did not return until twilight. Dismounting, I let myself into the house, traversed the hall, and ascended the stairs. As I wore spurs, and the steps were of polished oak and uncarpeted, I walked noisily enough to warn anyone of my approach. I was passing the door of the room that had been my grandmother's sitting room, when I noticed that it stood open. The house was rather dark, and the interior was dim enough, but I could see a figure in a white dress moving about inside. I recognised Margot, and wondered what she was doing, but her movements were so singular that, instead of speaking to her, I stood in the doorway and watched her.

She was walking, with a very peculiar, stealthy step, around the room, not as if she were looking for anything, but merely as if she were restless or ill at ease. But what struck me forcibly was this, that there was something curiously animal in her movements, seen thus in a dim half-light that only partially revealed her to me. I had never seen a woman walk in that strangely wild yet soft way before. There was something uncanny about it, that rendered me extremely discomforted; yet I was quite fascinated, and rooted to the ground.

I cannot tell how long I stood there. I was so completely absorbed in the passion of the gazer that the passage of time did not concern me in the least. I was as one assisting at a strange spectacle. This white thing moving in the dark did not suggest my wife to me, although it was she. I might have been watching an animal, vague, yet purposeful of mind, tracing out some hidden thing, following out some instinct quite foreign to humanity. I remember that presently I involuntarily clasped my hands together, and felt that they were very cold. Perspiration broke out on my face. I was painfully, unnaturally moved, and a violent desire to be away from this white moving thing came over me. Walking as softly as I could, I went to my dressing room, shut the door, and sat down on a chair. I never remember to have felt thoroughly unnerved before, but now I found myself actually shaken, palsied. I could understand how deadly a thing fear is. I lit a candle hastily, and as I did so a knock came to the door.

Margot's voice said, "May I come in?"

I felt unable to reply, so I got up and admitted her.

She entered smiling, and looking such a child, so innocent, so tender, that I almost laughed aloud. That I, a man, should have been frightened by a child in a white dress, just because the twilight cast a phantom atmosphere around her! I held her in my arms, and I gazed into her blue eyes.

She looked down, but still smiled.

"Where have you been, and what have you been doing?" I asked gaily.

She answered that she had been in the drawing room since tea-time.

"You came here straight from the drawing room?" I said.

She replied, "Yes."

Then, with an indifferent air which hid real anxiety, I said:

"By the way, Margot, have you been into that room again—the room you fancied you recollected?"

"No, never," she answered, withdrawing herself from my arms. "I don't wish to go there. Make haste, Ronald, and dress. It is nearly dinnertime, and I am ready." And she turned and left me.

She had told me a lie. All my feelings of uneasiness and discomfort returned tenfold.

That evening was the most wretched one, the only wretched one, I had ever spent with her.

I am tired of writing. I will continue my task tomorrow. It takes me longer than I anticipated. Yet even to tell everything to myself brings me some comfort. Man must express himself; and despair must find a voice.

III.

Thursday Night, *December 5th*.

That lie awoke in me suspicion of the child I had married. I began to doubt her, yet never ceased to love her. She had all my heart, and must have it till the end. But the calm of love was to be succeeded by love's tumult and agony. A strangeness was creeping over Margot. It was as if she took a thin veil in her hands, and drew it over and all around her, till the outlines I had known were slightly blurred. Her disposition, which had been so clear cut, so sharply, beautifully defined, standing out in its innocent glory for all men to see, seemed to withdraw itself, as if a dawning necessity for secrecy had arisen. A thin crust of reserve began to subtly overspread her every act and expression. She thought now before she spoke; she thought before she looked. It seemed to me that she was becoming a slightly different person.

The change I mean to imply is very difficult to describe. It was not abrupt enough to startle, but I could feel it, slight though it was. Have you seen the first flat film of waveless water, sent by the incoming tides of the sea, crawling silently up over the wrinkled brown sand, and filling the tiny ruts, till diminutive hills and valleys are all one smooth surface? So it was with Margot. A tide flowed over her character, a waveless tide of reserve. The hills and valleys which I loved disappeared from my ken. Behind the old sweet smile, the old frank expression, my wife was shrinking down to hide herself, as one escaping from pursuit hides behind a barrier. When one human being knows another very intimately, and all the barricades that divide soul from soul have been broken down, it is difficult to set them up again without noise and dust, and the sound of thrust-in bolts, and the tap of the hammer that drives in the nails. It is difficult, but not impossible. Barricades can be raised noiselessly, soundless bolts—that keep out the soul—be pushed home. The black gauze veil that blots out the scene drops, and when it is raised—if ever—the scene is changed.

The real Margot was receding from me. I felt it with an impotence of despair that was benumbing. Yet I could not speak of it, for at first I could hardly tell if she knew of what was taking place. Indeed, at this moment, in thinking it over, I do not believe that for some time she had any definite cognisance of the fact that she was growing to love me less passionately than of old. In acts she was not changed. That was the strange part of the matter. Her kisses were warm, but I believed them premeditated. She clasped my hand in hers, but now there was more mechanism than magic in that act of tenderness. Impulse failed within her; and she had been all impulse? Did she know it? At that time I wondered. Believing that she did not know she was changing, I was at the greatest pains to guard my conduct, lest I should implant the suspicion that might hasten what I feared. I remained, desperately, the same as ever, and so, of course, was not the same, for a deed done defiantly bears little resemblance to a deed done naturally. I was always considering what I should say, how I should act, even how I should look. To live now was sedulous instead of easy. Effort took the place of simplicity. My wife and I were gazing furtively at each other through the eyeholes of masks. I knew it. Did she?

At that time I never ceased to wonder. Of one thing I was certain, however—that Margot began to devise excuses for being left alone. When we first came home she could hardly endure me out of her sight. Now she grew to appreciate solitude. This was a terrible danger signal, and I could not fail to so regard it.

Yet something within me held me back from speaking out. I made no comment on the change that deepened day by day, but I watched my wife furtively, with a concentration of attention that sometimes left me physically exhausted. I felt, too, at length, that I was growing morbid, that suspicion coloured my mind and caused me, perhaps, to put a wrong interpretation on many of her actions, to exaggerate and misconstrue the most simple things she did. I began to believe her every look premeditated. Even if she kissed me, I thought she did it with a purpose; if she smiled up at me as of old, I fancied the smile to be only a concealment of its opposite. By degrees we became shy of each other. We were like uncongenial intimates, forced to occupy the same house, forced into a fearful knowledge of each other's personal habits, while we knew nothing of the thoughts that make up the true lives of individuals.

And then another incident occurred, a pendant to the incident of Margot's strange denied visit to the room she affected to fear. It was one night, one deep dark night of the autumn—a season to affect even a cheerful mind and incline it towards melancholy. Margot and I were now often silent when we were together. That evening, towards nine, a dull steady rain set in. I remember I heard it on the windowpanes as we sat in the drawing room after dinner, and remarked on it, saying to her that if it continued for two or three days she might chance to see the floods out, and that fishermen would descend upon us by the score.

I did not obtain much response from her. The dreariness of the weather seemed to affect her spirits. She took up a book presently, and appeared to read; but, once in glancing up suddenly from my newspaper, I thought I caught her gaze fixed fearfully upon me. It seemed to me that she was looking furtively at me with an absolute terror. I was so much affected that I made some excuse for leaving the room, went down to my den, lit a cigar, and walked uneasily up and down, listening to the rain on the window. At ten Margot came in to tell me she was going to bed. I wished her good night tenderly, but as I held her slim body a moment in my arms I felt that she began to tremble. I let her go, and she slipped from the room with the soft, cushioned step that was habitual with her. And, strangely enough, my thoughts recurred to the day, long ago, when I first held the great white cat on my knees, and felt its body shrink from my touch with a nameless horror. The uneasy movement of the woman recalled to me so strongly and so strangely the uneasy movement of the animal.

I lit a second cigar. It was near midnight when it was smoked out, and I turned down the lamp and went softly up to bed. I undressed in the room adjoining my wife's, and then stole into hers. She was sleeping in the wide white bed rather uneasily, and as I leaned over her, shading the candle flame with my outspread hand, she muttered some broken words that I could not catch. I had never heard her talk in her dreams before. I lay down gently at her side and extinguished the candle.

But sleep did not come to me. The dull, dead silence weighed upon instead of soothing me. My mind was terribly alive, in a ferment; and the contrast between my own excitement and the hushed peace of my environment was painful, was almost unbearable. I wished that a wind from the mountains were beating against the windowpanes, and the rain lashing the house in fury. The black calm around was horrible, unnatural. The drizzling rain was now so small that I could not even hear its patter when I strained my ears. Margot had ceased to mutter, and lay perfectly still. How I longed to be able to read the soul hidden in her sleeping body, to unravel the mystery of the mind which I had once understood so perfectly! It is so horrible that we can never open the human envelope, take out the letter, and seize with our eyes upon its every word. Margot slept with all her secrets safeguarded, although she was unconscious, no longer watchful, on the alert. She was so silent, even her quiet breathing not reaching my ear, that I felt impelled to stretch out my hand beneath the coverlet and touch hers ever so softly. I did so.

Her hand was instantly and silently withdrawn. She was awake, then.

"Margot," I said, "did I disturb you?"

There was no answer.

The movement, followed by the silence, affected me very disagreeably.

I lit the candle and looked at her. She was lying on the extreme edge of the bed, with her blue eyes closed. Her lips were slightly parted. I could hear her steady breathing. Yet was she really sleeping?

I bent lower over her, and as I did so a slight, involuntary movement, akin to what we call a shudder, ran through her body. I recoiled from the bed. An impotent anger seized me. Could it be that my presence was becoming so hateful to my wife that even in sleep her body trembled when I drew near it? Or was this slumber feigned? I could not tell, but I felt it impossible at that moment to remain in the room. I returned to my own, dressed, and descended the stairs to the door opening on to the terrace. I felt a longing to be out in the air. The atmosphere of the house was stifling.

Was it coming to this, then? Did I, a man, shrink with a fantastic cowardice from a woman I loved? The latent cruelty began to stir within me, the tyrant spirit which a strong love sometimes evokes. I had been Margot's slave almost. My affection had brought me to her feet, had kept me there. So long as she loved me I was content to be her captive, knowing she was mine. But a change in her attitude toward me might rouse the master. In my nature there was a certain brutality, a savagery, which I had never wholly slain, although Margot had softened me wonderfully by her softness, had brought me to gentleness by her tenderness. The boy of years ago had developed toward better things, but he was not dead in me. I felt that as I walked up and down the terrace through the night in a wild meditation. If my love could not hold Margot, my strength should.

I drew in a long breath of the wet night air, and I opened my shoulders as if shaking off an oppression. My passion for Margot had not yet drawn me down to weakness; it had raised me up to strength. The faint fear of her, which I had felt almost without knowing it more than once, died within me. The desire of the conqueror elevated me. There was something for me to win. My paralysis passed away, and I turned toward the house.

And now a strange thing happened. I walked into the dark hall, closed the outer door, shutting out the dull murmur of the night, and felt in my pocket for my matchbox. It was not there. I must inadvertently have laid it down in my dressing room and left it. I searched about in the darkness on the hall table, but could find no light. There was nothing for it, then, but to feel my way upstairs as best I could.

I started, keeping my hand against the wall to guide me. I gained the top of the stairs, and began to traverse the landing, still with my hand upon the wall. To reach my dressing room I had to pass the apartment which had been my grandmother's sitting room.

When I reached it, instead of sliding along a closed door, as I had anticipated, my hand dropped into vacancy.

The door was wide open. It had been shut, like all the other doors in the house, when I had descended the stairs—shut and locked, as it always was at night-time. Why was it open now?

I paused in the darkness. And then an impulse seized me to walk forward into the room. I advanced a step; but, as I did so, a horrible low cry broke upon my ears out of the darkness. It came from immediately in front of me, and sounded like an expression of the most abject fear.

My feet rooted themselves to the ground.

"Who's there?" I asked.

There came no answer.

I listened for a moment, but did not hear the minutest sound. The desire for light was overpowering. I generally did my writing in this room, and knew the exact whereabouts of everything in it. I knew that on the writing table there was a silver box containing wax matches. It lay on the left of my desk. I moved another step forward.

There was the sound of a slight rustle, as if someone shrank back as I advanced.

I laid my hand quickly on the box, opened it, and struck a light. The room was vaguely illuminated. I saw something white at the far end, against the wall. I put the match to a candle.

The white thing was Margot. She was in her dressing gown, and was crouched up in an angle of the wall as far away from where I stood as possible. Her blue eyes were wide open, and fixed upon me with an expression of such intense and hideous fear in them that I almost cried out.

"Margot, what is the matter?" I said. "Are you ill?"

She made no reply. Her face terrified me.

"What is it, Margot?" I cried in a loud, almost harsh voice, determined to rouse her from this horrible, unnatural silence. "What are you doing here?"

I moved towards her. I stretched out my hands and seized her. As I did so, a sort of sob burst from her. Her hands were cold and trembling.

"What is it? What has frightened you?" I reiterated.

At last she spoke in a low voice.

"You—you looked so strange, so—so cruel as you came in," she said.

"Strange! Cruel! But you could not see me. It was dark," I answered.

"Dark!" she said.

"Yes, until I lit the candle. And you cried out when I was only in the doorway. You could not see me there."

"Why not? What has that got to do with it?" she murmured, still trembling violently.

"You can see me in the dark?"

"Of course," she said. "I don't understand what you mean. Of course I can see you when you are there before my eyes."

"But—" I began; and then her obvious and complete surprise at my questions stopped them. I still held her hands in mine, and their extreme coldness roused me to the remembrance that she was unclothed.

"You will be ill if you stay here," I said. "Come back to your room."

She said nothing, and I led her back, waited while she got into bed, and then, placing the candle on the dressing table, sat down in a chair by her side.

The strong determination to take prompt action, to come to an explanation, to end these dreary mysteries of mind and conduct, was still upon me.

I did not think of the strange hour; I did not care that the night was gliding on towards dawn. I was self-absorbed. I was beyond ordinary considerations.

Yet I did not speak immediately. I was trying to be quite calm, trying to think of the best line for me to take. So much might depend upon our mere words now. At length I said, laying my hand upon hers, which was outside the coverlet:

"Margot, what were you doing in that room at such a strange hour? Why were you there?"

She hesitated obviously. Then she answered, not looking at me:

"I missed you. I thought you might be there—writing."

"But you were in the dark."

"I thought you would have a light."

I knew by her manner that she was not telling me the truth, but I went on quietly:

"If you expected me, why did you cry out when I came to the door?"

She tried to draw her hand away, but I held it fast, closing, my fingers upon it with even brutal strength.

"Why did you cry out?"

"You—you looked so strange, so cruel."

"So cruel!"

"Yes. You frightened me—you frightened me horribly."

She began suddenly to sob, like one completely overstrained. I lifted her up in the bed, put my arms round her, and made her lean against me. I was strangely moved.

"I frightened you! How can that be?" I said, trying to control a passion of mingled love and anger that filled my breast. "You know that I love you. You must know that. In all our short married life have I ever been even momentarily unkind to you? Let us be frank with one another. Our lives have changed lately. One of us has altered. You cannot say that it is I."

She only continued to sob bitterly in my arms. I held her closer.

"Let us be frank with one another," I went on. "For God's sake let us have no barriers between us. Margot, look into my eyes and tell me— are you growing tired of me?"

She turned her head away, but I spoke more sternly:

"You shall be truthful. I will have no more subterfuge. Look me in the face. You did love me once?"

"Yes, yes," she whispered in a choked voice.

"What have I done, then, to alienate you? Have I ever hurt you, ever shown a lack of sympathy, ever neglected you?"

"Never—never."

"Yet you have changed to me since—since—" I paused a moment, trying to recall when I had first noticed her altered demeanour.

She interrupted me.

"It has all come upon me in this house," she sobbed. "Oh! what is it? What does it all mean? If I could understand a little—only a little—it would not be so bad. But this nightmare, this thing that seems such a madness of the intellect—"

Her voice broke and ceased. Her tears burst forth afresh. Such mingled fear, passion, and a sort of strange latent irritation, I had never seen before.

"It is a madness indeed," I said, and a sense almost of outrage made my voice hard and cold. "I have not deserved such treatment at your hands."

"I will not yield to it," she said, with a sort of desperation, suddenly throwing her arms around me. "I will not—I will not!"

I was strangely puzzled. I was torn with conflicting feelings. Love and anger grappled at my heart. But I only held her, and did not speak until she grew obviously calmer. The paroxysm seemed passing away. Then I said:

"I cannot understand."

"Nor I," she answered, with a directness that had been foreign to her of late, but that was part and parcel of her real, beautiful nature. "I cannot understand. I only know there is a change in me, or in you to me, and that I cannot help it, or that I have not been able to help it. Sometimes I feel—do not be angry, I will try to tell you—a physical fear of you, of your touch, of your clasp, a fear such as an animal might feel towards the master who had beaten it. I tremble then at your approach. When you are near me I feel cold, oh! so cold and—and anxious; perhaps I ought to say apprehensive. Oh, I am hurting you!"

I suppose I must have winced at her words, and she is quick to observe.

"Go on," I said; "do not spare me. Tell me everything. It is madness indeed; but we may kill it, when we both know it."

"Oh, if we could!" she cried, with a poignancy which was heartbreaking to hear. "If we could!"

"Do you doubt our ability?" I said, trying to be patient and calm. "You are unreasoning, like all women. Be sensible for a moment. You do me a wrong in cherishing these feelings. I have the capacity for cruelty in me. I may have been—I have been—cruel in the past, but never to you. You have no right to treat me as you have done lately. If you examine your feelings, and compare them with facts, you will see their absurdity."

"But," she interposed, with a woman's fatal quickness, "that will not do away with their reality."

"It must. Look into their faces until they fade like ghosts, seen only between light and darkness. They are founded upon nothing; they are bred without father or mother; they are hysterical; they are wicked. Think a little of me. You are not going to be conquered by a chimera, to allow a phantom created by your imagination to ruin the happiness that has been so beautiful. You will not do that! You dare not!"

She only answered:

"If I can help it."

A passionate anger seized me, a fury at my impotence against this child. I pushed her almost roughly from my arms.

"And I have married this woman!" I cried bitterly. I got up.

Margot had ceased crying now, and her face was very white and calm; it looked rigid in the faint candlelight that shone across the bed.

"Do not be angry," she said. "We are controlled by something inside of us; there are powers in us that we cannot fight against."

"There is nothing we cannot fight against," I said passionately. "The doctrine of predestination is the devil's own doctrine. It is the doctrine set up by the sinner to excuse his sin; it is the coward's doctrine. Understand me, Margot, I love you, but I am not a weak fool. There must be an end of this folly. Perhaps you are playing with me, acting like a girl, testing me. Let us have no more of it."

She said:

"I only do what I must."

Her tone turned me cold. Her set face frightened me, and angered me, for there was a curious obstinacy in it. I left the room abruptly, and did not return. That night I had no sleep.

I am not a coward, but I find that I am inclined to fear that which fears me. I dread an animal that always avoids me silently more than an animal that actually attacks me. The thing that runs from me makes me shiver, the thing that creeps away when I come near wakes my uneasiness. At this time there rose up in me a strange feeling towards Margot. The white, fair child I had married was at moments— only at moments—horrible to me. I felt disposed to shun her. Something within cried out against her. Long ago, at the instant of our introduction, an unreasoning sensation that could only be called dread had laid hold upon me. That dread returned from the night of our explanation, returned deepened and added to. It prompted me to a suggestion which I had no sooner made than I regretted it. On the morning following I told Margot that in future we had better occupy separate rooms. She assented quietly, but I thought a furtive expression of relief stole for a moment into her face.

I was deeply angered with her and with myself; yet, now that I knew beyond question my wife's physical terror of me, I was half afraid of her. I felt as if I could not bring myself to lie long hours by her side in the darkness, by the side of a woman who was shrinking from me, who was watching me when I could not see her. The idea made my very flesh creep.

Yet I hated myself for this shrinking of the body, and sometimes hated her for rousing it. A hideous struggle was going on within me— a struggle between love and impotent anger and despair, between the lover and the master. For I am one of the old-fashioned men who think that a husband ought to be master of his wife as well as of his house.

How could I be master of a woman I secretly feared? My knowledge of myself spurred me through acute irritation almost to the verge of madness.

All calm was gone. I was alternately gentle to my wife and almost ferocious towards her, ready to fall at her feet and worship her or to seize her and treat her with physical violence. I only restrained myself by an effort.

My variations of manner did not seem to affect her. Indeed, it sometimes struck me that she feared me more when I was kind to her than when I was harsh.

And I knew, by a thousand furtive indications, that her horror of me was deepening day by day. I believe she could hardly bring herself to be in a room alone with me, especially after nightfall.

One evening, when we were dining, the butler, after placing dessert upon the table, moved to leave us. She turned white, and, as he reached the door, half rose, and called him back in a sharp voice.

"Symonds!" she said.

"Yes, ma'am?"

"You are going?"

The fellow looked surprised.

"Can I get you anything, ma'am?"

She glanced at me with an indescribable uneasiness. Then she leaned back in her chair with an effort, and pressed her lips together.

"No," she said.

As the man went out and shut the door, she looked at me again from under her eyelids; and finally her eyes travelled from me to a small, thin-bladed knife, used for cutting oranges, that lay near her plate, and fixed themselves on it. She put out her hand stealthily, drew it towards her, and kept her hand over it on the table. I took an orange from a dish in front of me.

"Margot," I said, "will you pass me that fruit-knife?"

She obviously hesitated.

"Give me that knife," I repeated roughly, stretching out my hand.

She lifted her hand, left the knife upon the table, and at the same time, springing up, glided softly out of the room and closed the door behind her.

That evening I spent alone in the smoking room, and, for the first time, she did not come to bid me good night.

I sat smoking my cigar in a tumult of furious despair and love. The situation was becoming intolerable. It could not be endured. I longed for a crisis, even for a violent one. I could have cried aloud that night for a veritable tragedy. There were moments when I would almost have killed the child who mysteriously eluded and defied me. I could have wreaked a cruel vengeance upon the body for the sin of the mind. I was terribly, mortally distressed.

After a long and painful self-communion, I resolved to make another wild effort to set things right before it was too late; and when the clock chimed the half-hour after ten I went upstairs softly to her bedroom and turned the handle of the door, meaning to enter, to catch Margot in my arms, tell her how deep my love for her was, how she injured me by her base fears, and how she was driving me back from the gentleness she had given me to the cruelty, to the brutality, of my first nature.

The door resisted me: it was locked. I paused a moment, and then tapped gently. I heard a sudden rustle within, as if someone hurried across the floor away from the door, and then Margot's voice cried sharply:

"Who's that? Who is there?"

Margot, it is I. I wish to speak to you—to say good night."

"Good night," she said.

"But let me in for a moment."

There was a silence—it seemed to me a long one; then she answered:

"Not now, dear; I—I am so tired."

"Open the door for a moment."

"I am very tired. Good night."

The cold, level tone of her voice—for the anxiety had left it after that first sudden cry—roused me to a sudden fury of action. I seized the handle of the door and pressed with all my strength. Physically I am a very powerful man—my anger and despair gave me a giant's might. I burst the lock, and sprang into the room. My impulse was to seize Margot in my arms and crush her to death, it might be, in an embrace she could not struggle against. The blood coursed like molten fire through my veins. The lust of love, the lust of murder even, perhaps, was upon me. I sprang impetuously into the room.

No candles were alight in it. The blinds were up, and the chill moonbeams filtered through the small lattice panes. By the farthest window, in the yellowish radiance, was huddled a white thing.

A sudden cold took hold upon me. All the warmth in me froze up.

I stopped where I was and held my breath.

That white thing, seen thus uncertainly, had no semblance to humanity. It was animal wholly. I could have believed for the moment that a white cat crouched from me there by the curtain, waiting to spring.

What a strange illusion that was! I tried to laugh at it afterwards, but at the moment horror stole through me—horror, and almost awe.

All desire of violence left me. Heat was dead; I felt cold as stone. I could not even speak a word.

Suddenly the white thing moved. The curtain was drawn sharply;

the moonlight was blotted out; the room was plunged in darkness—a darkness in which that thing could see!

I turned and stole out of the room. I could have fled, driven by the nameless fear that was upon me.

Only when the morning dawned did the man in me awake, and I cursed myself for my cowardice.

The following evening we were asked to dine out with some neighbours, who lived a few miles off in a wonderful old Norman castle near the sea. During the day neither of us had made the slightest allusion to the incidents of the previous night. We both felt it a relief to go into society, I think. The friends to whom we went—Lord and Lady Melchester—had a large party staying with them, and we were, I believe, the only outsiders who lived in the neighbourhood. One of their guests was Professor Black, whose name I have already mentioned—a little, dry, thin, acrid man, with thick black hair, innocent of the comb, and pursed, straight lips. I had met him two or three times in London, and as he had only just arrived at the castle, and scarcely knew his fellow-visitors there, he brought his wine over to me when the ladies left the dining room, and entered into conversation. At the moment I was glad, but before we followed the women I would have given a year—I might say years—of my life not to have spoken to him, not to have heard him speak that night.

How did we drift into that fatal conversation? I hardly remember. We talked first of the neighbourhood, then swayed away to books, then to people. Yes, that was how it came about. The Professor was speaking of a man whom we both knew in town, a curiously effeminate man, whose every thought and feeling seemed that of a woman. I said I disliked him, and condemned him for his woman's demeanour, his woman's mind; but the Professor thereupon joined issue with me.

"Pity the fellow, if you like," he uttered, in his rather strident voice; "but as to condemning him, I would as soon condemn a tadpole for not being a full-grown frog. His soul is beyond his power to manage, or even to coerce, you may depend upon it."

Having sipped his port, he drew a little nearer to me, and slightly dropped his voice.

"There would be less censure of individuals in this world," he said, "if people were only a little more thoughtful. These souls are like letters, and sometimes they are sealed up in the wrong envelope. For instance, a man's soul may be put into a woman's body, or *vice versa*. It has been so in D——'s case. A mistake has been made."

"By Providence?" I interrupted, with, perhaps, just a *soupçon* of sarcasm in my voice.

The Professor smiled.

"Suppose we imitate Thomas Hardy, and say by the President of the Immortals, who makes sport with more humans than Tess," he answered. "Mistakes may be deliberate, just as their reverse may be accidental. Even a mighty power may condescend sometimes to a very practical joke. To a thinker the world is full of apple-pie beds, and cold wet sponges fall on us from at least half the doors we push open. The soul-juggleries of the before-mentioned President are very curious, but people will not realize that soul transference from body to body is as much a plain fact as the daily rising of the sun on one half of the world and its nightly setting on the other."

"Do you mean that souls pass on into the world again on the death of the particular body in which they have been for the moment confined?" I asked.

"Precisely: I have no doubt of it. Sometimes a woman's soul goes into a man's body; then the man acts woman, and people cry against him for effeminacy. The soul colours the body with actions, the body does not colour the soul, or not in the same degree."

"But we are not irresponsible. We can command ourselves."

The Professor smiled dryly.

"You think so?" he said. "I sometimes doubt it."

"And I doubt your theory of soul transference."

"That shows me—pardon the apparent impertinence—that you have never really examined the soul question with any close attention. Do you suppose that D—— really likes being so noticeably different from other men? Depend upon it, he has noticed in himself what we have noticed in him. Depend upon it, he has tried to be ordinary, and found it impossible. His soul manages him as a strong nature manages a weak one, and his soul is a female, not a male. For souls have sexes, otherwise what would be the sense of talking about wedded souls? I have no doubt whatever of the truth of reincarnation on earth. Souls go on and on following out their object of development."

"You believe that every soul is reincarnated?"

"A certain number of times."

"That even in the animal world the soul of one animal passes into the body of another?"

"Wait a minute. Now we are coming to something that tends to prove my theory true. Animals have souls, as you imply. Who can know them intimately and doubt it for an instant? Souls as immortal—or as mortal—as ours. And their souls, too, pass on."

"Into other animals?"

"Possibly. And eventually, in the process of development, into human beings."

I laughed, perhaps a little rudely. "My dear Professor, I thought that old notion was quite exploded in these modern scientific days."

"I found my beliefs upon my own minute observations," he said rather frigidly. "I notice certain animals masquerading—to some extent—as human beings, and I draw my own conclusions. If they happen to fit in at all with the conclusions of Pythagoras—or anyone else, for that matter—well and good. If not, I am not much concerned. Surely you notice the animal—and not merely the animal, but definite animals— reproduced in man. There are men whose whole demeanour suggests the monkey. I have met women who in manner, appearance, and even character, were intensely like cats."

I uttered a slight exclamation, which did not interrupt him.

"Now, I have made a minute study of cats. Of all animals they interest me the most. They have less apparent intensity, less uttered passion, than dogs, but in my opinion more character. Their subtlety is extraordinary, their sensitiveness wonderful. Will you understand me when I say that all dogs are men, all cats women? That remark expresses the difference between them."

He paused a moment.

"Go on—go on," I said, leaning forward, with my eyes fixed upon his keen, puckered face.

He seemed pleased with my suddenly aroused interest.

"Cats are as subtle and as difficult to understand as the most complex woman, and almost as full of intuitions. If they have been well treated, there is often a certain gracious, condescending suavity in their demeanour at first, even towards a total stranger; but if that stranger is ill disposed toward them, they seem instinctively to read his soul, and they are in arms directly. Yet they dissemble their fears in a cold indifference and reserve. They do not take action: they merely abstain from action. They withdraw the soul that has peeped out, as they can withdraw their claws into the pads upon their feet. They do not show fight as a dog might, they do not become aggressive, nor do they whine and put their tails between their legs. They are simply on guard, watchful, mistrustful. Is not all this woman?"

"Possibly," I answered, with a painful effort to assume indifference.

"A woman intuitively knows who is her friend and who is her enemy—so long, at least, as her heart is not engaged; then she runs wild, I allow. A woman— But I need not pursue the parallel. Besides, perhaps it is scarcely to the point, for my object is not to bolster up an absurd contention that all women have the souls of cats. No; but I have met women so strangely like cats that their souls have, as I said before souls do, coloured their bodies in actions. They have had the very look of cats in their faces. They have moved like them. Their demeanour has been patently and strongly feline. Now, I see nothing ridiculous in the assumption that such women's bodies may contain souls—in process of development, of course—that formerly were merely cat souls, but that are now gaining humanity gradually, are working their way upwards in the scale. After all, we are not so much above the animals, and in our lapses we often become merely animals. The soul retrogrades for the moment."

He paused again and looked at me. I was biting my lips, and my glass of wine was untouched. He took my agitation as a compliment, I suppose, for he smiled and said:

"Are you in process of conversion?"

I half shook my head. Then I said, with an effort: "It is a curious and interesting idea, of course. But there is much to explain. Now, I should like to ask you this: Do you—do you believe that a soul, if it passes on as you think, carries its memory with it, its memory of former loves and—and hates? Say that a cat's soul goes to a woman's body, and that the cat has been—has been—well, tortured—possibly killed, by someone—say some man, long ago, would the woman, meeting that man, remember and shrink from him?"

"That is a very interesting and curious problem, and one which I do not pretend to have solved. I can, therefore, only suggest what might be, what seems to me reasonable.

"I do not believe that the woman would remember positively, but I think she might have an intuition about the man. Our intuitions are, perhaps, sometimes only the fragmentary recollections of our souls, of what formerly happened to them when in other bodies. Why, otherwise, should we sometimes conceive an ardent dislike of some stranger—charming to all appearance—of whom we know no evil, whom we have never heard of nor met before? Intuitions, so called, are often only tattered memories. And these intuitions might, I should fancy, be strengthened, given body, robustness, by associations—of place, for example. Cats become intensely attached to localities, to certain spots, a particular house or garden, a particular fireside, apart from the people who may be there. Possibly, if the man and the woman of whom you speak could be brought together in the very place where the torture and death occurred, the dislike of the woman might deepen into positive hatred. It would, however, be always unreasoning hatred, I think, and even quite unaccountable to herself. Still—"

But here Lord Melchester rose from the table. The conversations broke into fragments. I felt that I was pale to the lips.

We passed into the drawing room. The ladies were grouped together at one end, near the piano. Margot was among them. She was, as usual, dressed in white, and round the bottom of her gown there was an edging of snow-white fur. As we came in, she moved away from the piano to a sofa at some distance, and sank down upon it. Professor Black, who had entered the room at my side, seized my arm gently.

"Now, that lady," he whispered in my ear—"I don't know who she may be, but she is intensely catlike. I observed it before dinner. Did you notice the way she moved just then—the soft, yielding, easy manner in which she sat down, falling at once, quite naturally, into a charming pose? And her china-blue eyes are—"

"She is my wife, Professor," I interrupted harshly.

He looked decidedly taken aback.

"I beg your pardon; I had no idea. I did not enter the drawing room tonight till after you arrived. I believed that lady was one of my fellow guests in the house. Let me congratulate you. She is very beautiful."

And then he mingled rather hastily in the group near the piano.

The man is mad, I know—mad as a hatter on one point, like so many clever men. He sees the animal in every person he meets just because his preposterous theory inclines him to do so. Having given in his adherence to it, he sees facts not as they are, but as he wishes them to be; but he shall not carry me with him. The theory is his, not mine. It does not hold water for a moment. I can laugh at it now, but that night I confess it did seize me for the time being. I could scarcely talk; I found myself watching Margot with a terrible intentness, and I found myself agreeing with the Professor to an extent that made me marvel at my own previous blindness.

There was something strangely feline about the girl I had married— the soft, white girl who was becoming terrible to me, dear though she still was and must always be. Her movements had the subtle, instinctive and certain grace of a cat's. Her cushioned step, which had often struck me before, was like the step of a cat. And those china-blue eyes! A sudden cold seemed to pass over me as I understood why I had recognised them when I first met Margot. They were the eyes of the animal I had tortured, the animal I had killed. Yes, but that proved nothing, absolutely nothing. Many people had the eyes of animals—the soft eyes of dogs, the furtive, cruel eyes of tigers. I had known such people. I had even once had an affair with a girl who was always called the shot partridge, because her eyes were supposed to be like those of a dying bird. I tried to laugh to myself as I remembered this. But I felt cold, and my senses seemed benumbed as by a great horror. I sat like a stone, with my eyes fixed upon Margot, trying painfully to read into her all that the words of Professor Black had suggested to me—trying, but with the wish not to succeed. I was roused by Lady Melchester, who came toward me asking me to do something, I forget now what. I forced myself to be cheerful, to join in the conversation, to seem at my ease; but I felt like one oppressed with nightmare, and I could scarcely withdraw my eyes from the sofa where my wife was sitting. She was talking now to Professor Black, who had just been introduced to her; and I felt a sudden fury in my heart as I thought that he was perhaps dryly, coldly, studying her, little knowing what issues—far-reaching, it might be, in their consequences—hung upon the truth or falsehood of his strange theory. They were talking earnestly, and presently it occurred to me that he might be imbuing Margot with his pernicious doctrines, that he might be giving her a knowledge of her own soul which now she lacked. The idea was insupportable. I broke off abruptly the conversation in which I was taking part, and hurried over to them with an impulse which must have astonished anyone who took note of me. I sat down on a chair, drew it forward almost violently, and thrust myself in between them.

"What are you two talking about?" I said, roughly, with a suspicious glance at Margot.

The Professor looked at me in surprise.

"I was instructing your wife in some of the mysteries of salmon fishing," he said. "She tells me you have a salmon river running through your grounds."

I laughed uneasily.

"So you are a fisherman as well as a romantic theorist!" I said, rather rudely. "How I wish I were as versatile! Come, Margot, we must be going now. The carriage ought to be here."

She rose quietly and bade the Professor good night; but as she glanced up at me, in rising, I fancied I caught a new expression in her eyes. A ray of determination, of set purpose, mingled with the gloomy fire of their despair.

As soon as we were in the carriage I spoke, with a strained effort at ease and the haphazard tone which should mask furtive cross-examination.

"Professor Black is an interesting man," I said.

"Do you think so?" she answered from her dark corner.

"Surely. His intellect is really alive. Yet, with all his scientific knowledge and his power of eliciting facts and elucidating them, he is but a featherheaded man." I paused, but she made no answer. "Do you not think so?"

"How can I tell?" she replied. "We only talked about fishing. He managed to make that topic a pleasant one."

Her tone was frank. I felt relieved.

"He is exceedingly clever," I said, heartily, and we relapsed into silence.

When we reached home, and Margot had removed her cloak, she came up to me and laid her hand on my arm.

So unaccustomed was her touch now that I was startled. She was looking at me with a curious, steady smile—an unwavering smile that chilled instead of warming me.

"Ronald," she said, "there has been a breach between us. I have been the cause of it. I should like to—to heal it. Do you still love me as you did?"

I did not answer immediately; I could not. Her voice, schooled as it was, seemed somehow at issue with the words she uttered. There was a desperate, hard note in it that accorded with that enigmatic smile of the mouth.

It roused a cold suspicion within me that I was close to a masked battery. I shrank physically from the touch of her hand.

She waited with her eyes upon me. Our faces were lit tremblingly by the flames of the two candles we held.

At last I found a voice.

"Can you doubt it?" I asked.

She drew a step nearer.

"Then let us resume our old relations," she said.

"Our old relations?"

"Yes."

I shuddered as if a phantom stole by me. I was seized with horror.

"Tonight? It is not possible!"

"Why?" she said, still with that steady smile of the mouth.

"Because—because I don't know—I— Tomorrow it shall be as of old, Margot—tomorrow. I promise you."

"Very well. Kiss me, dear."

I forced myself to touch her lips with mine.

Which mouth was the colder?

Then, with that soft, stealthy step of hers, she vanished towards her room. I heard the door close gently.

I listened. The key was not turned in the lock.

This sudden abandonment by Margot of the fantastic precautions I had almost become accustomed to filled me with a nameless dread.

That night I fastened my door for the first time.

IV.

Friday Night, *November 6th.*

I fastened my door, and when I went to bed lay awake for hours listening. A horror was upon me then which has not left me since for a moment, which may never leave me. I shivered with cold that night, the cold born of sheer physical terror. I knew that I was shut up in the house with a soul bent on unreasoning vengeance, the soul of the animal which I had killed prisoned in the body of the woman I had married. I was sick with fear then. I am sick with fear now.

Tonight I am so tired. My eyes are heavy and my head aches. No wonder. I have not slept for three nights. I have not dared to sleep.

This strange revolution in my wife's conduct, this passionless change—for I felt instinctively that warm humanity had nothing to do with the transformation—took place three nights ago. These three last days Margot has been playing a part. With what object?

When I sat down to this gray record of two souls—at once dreary and fantastic as it would seem, perhaps, to many—I desired to reassure myself, to write myself into sweet reason, into peace.

I have tried to accomplish the impossible. I feel that the wildest theory may be the truest, after all—that on the borderland of what seems madness, actuality paces.

Every remembrance of my mind confirms the truth first suggested to me by Professor Black.

I know Margot's object now.

The soul of the creature that I tortured, that I killed, has passed into the body of the woman whom I love; and that soul, which once slept in its new cage, is awake now, watching, plotting perhaps. Unconsciously to itself, it recognises me. It stares out upon me with eyes in which the dull terror deepens to hate; but it does not understand why it fears— why, in its fear, it hates. Intuition has taken the place of memory. The change of environment has killed recollection, and has left instinct in its place.

Why did I ever sit down to write? The recalling of facts has set the seal upon my despair.

Instinct only woke in Margot when I brought her to the place the soul had known in the years when it looked out upon the world from the body of an animal.

That first day on the terrace instinct stirred in its sleep, opened its eyes, gazed forth upon me wonderingly, inquiringly.

Margot's faint remembrance of the terrace walk, of the flowerpots, of the grass borders where the cat had often stretched itself in the sun, her eagerness to see the chamber of death, her stealthy visits to that chamber, her growing uneasiness, deepening to acute apprehension, and finally to a deadly malignity—all lead me irresistibly to one conclusion.

The animal's soul within her no longer merely shrinks away in fear of me. It has grown sinister. It lies in ambush, full of a cold, a stealthy intention.

That curious, abrupt change in Margot's demeanour from avoidance to invitation marked the subtle, inward development of feeling, the silent passage from sensation only towards action.

Formerly she feared me. Now I must fear her.

The soul, crouching in its cage, shows its teeth. It is compassing my destruction.

The woman's body twitches with desire to avenge the death of the animal's.

I feel that it is only waiting the moment to spring; and the inherent love of life breeds in me a physical fear of it as of a subtle enemy. For even if the soul is brave, the body dreads to die, and seems at moments to possess a second soul, purely physical, that cries out childishly against pain, against death.

Then, too, there is a cowardice of the imagination that can shake the strongest heart, and this resurrection from the dead, from the murdered, appalls my imagination. That what I thought I had long since slain should have companioned me so closely when I knew it not!

I am sick with fear, physical and mental.

Two days ago, when I unlocked my bedroom door in the morning, and saw the autumn sunlight streaming in through the leaded panes of the hall windows, and heard the river dancing merrily down the gully among the trees that will soon be quite bare and naked, I said to myself: "You have been mad. Your mind has been filled with horrible dreams, that have transformed you into a coward and your wife into a demon. Put them away from you."

I looked across the gully. A clear, cold, thin light shone upon the distant mountains. The cloud stacks lay piled above the Scawfell range. The sky was a sheet of faded turquoise. I opened the window for a moment. The air was dry and keen. How sweet it was to feel it on my face!

I went down to the breakfast room. Margot was moving about it softly, awaiting me. In her white hands were letters. They dropped upon the table as she stole up to greet me. Her lips were set tightly together, but she lifted them to kiss me.

How close I came to my enemy as our mouths touched! Her lips were colder than the wind.

Now that I was with her, my momentary sensation of acute relief deserted me. The horror that oppressed me returned.

I could not eat—I could only make a pretence of doing so; and my hand trembled so excessively that I could scarcely raise my cup from the table.

She noticed this, and gently asked me if I was ill.

I shook my head.

When breakfast was over, she said in a low, level voice:

"Ronald, have you thought over what I said last night?"

"Last night?" I answered, with an effort.

"Yes, about the coldness between us. I think I have been unwell, unhappy, out of sorts. You know that—that women are more subject to moods than men, moods they cannot always account for even to themselves. I have hurt you lately, I know. I am sorry. I want you to forgive me, to—to"—she paused a moment, and I heard her draw in her breath sharply—"to take me back into your heart again."

Every word, as she said it, sounded to me like a sinister threat, and the last sentence made my blood literally go cold in my veins.

I met her eyes. She did not withdraw hers; they looked into mine. They were the blue eyes of the cat which I had held upon my knees years ago. I had gazed into them as a boy, and watched the horror and the fear dawn in them with a malignant triumph.

"I have nothing to forgive," I said in a broken, husky voice.

"You have much," she answered firmly. "But do not—pray do not bear malice."

"There is no malice in my heart—now," I said; and the words seemed like a cowardly plea for mercy to the victim of the past.

She lifted one of her soft white hands to my breast.

"Then it shall all be as it was before? And tonight you will come back to me?"

I hesitated, looking down. But how could I refuse? What excuse could I make for denying the request? Then I repeated mechanically:

"Tonight I will come back to you."

A terrible, slight smile travelled over her face. She turned and left me.

I sat down immediately. I felt too unnerved to remain standing. I was giving way utterly to an imaginative horror that seemed to threaten my reason. In vain I tried to pull myself together. My body was in a cold sweat. All mastery of my nerves seemed gone.

I do not know how long I remained there, but I was aroused by the entrance of the butler. He glanced towards me in some obvious surprise, and this astonishment of a servant acted upon me almost like a scourge. I sprang up hastily.

"Tell the groom to saddle the mare," I said. "I am going for a ride immediately."

Air, action, were what I needed to drive this stupor away. I must get away from this house of tears. I must be alone. I must wrestle with myself, regain my courage, kill the coward in me.

I threw myself upon the mare, and rode out at a gallop towards the moors of Eskdale along the lonely country roads.

All day I rode, and all day I thought of that dark house, of that white creature awaiting my return, peering from the windows, perhaps, listening for my horse's hoofs on the gravel, keeping still the long vigil of vengeance.

My imagination sickened, fainted, as my wearied horse stumbled along the shadowy roads. My terror was too great now to be physical. It was a terror purely of the spirit, and indescribable.

To sleep with that white thing that waited me! To lie in the dark by it! To know that it was there, close to me!

If it killed me, what matter? It was to live and to be near it, with it, that appalled me.

The lights of the house gleamed out through the trees. I heard the sound of the river.

I got off my horse and walked furtively into the hall, looking round me.

Margot glided up to me immediately, and took my whip and hat from me with her soft, velvety white hands. I shivered at her touch.

At dinner her blue eyes watched me.

I could not eat, but I drank more wine than usual.

When I turned to go down to the smoking room, she said: "Don't be very long, Ronald."

I muttered I scarcely know what words in reply. It was close on midnight before I went to bed. When I entered her room, shielding the light of the candle with my hand, she was still awake.

Nestling against the pillows, she stretched herself curiously and smiled up at me.

"I thought you were never coming, dear," she said.

I knew that I was very pale, but she did not remark it. I got into bed, but left the candle still burning.

Presently she said:

"Why don't you put the candle out?"

I looked at her furtively. Her face seemed to me carved in stone, it was so rigid, so expressionless. She lay away from me at the extreme edge of the bed, sideways, with her hands toward me.

"Why don't you?" she repeated, with her blue eyes on me.

"I don't feel sleepy," I answered slowly.

"You never will while there is a light in the room," she said.

"You wish me to put it out?"

"Yes. How odd you are tonight, Ronald! Is anything the matter?"

"No," I answered; and I blew the light out.

How ghastly the darkness was!

I believed she meant to smother me in my sleep. I knew it. I determined to keep awake.

It was horrible to think that, as we lay there, she could see me all the time as if it were daylight.

The night wore on. She was quite silent and motionless. I lay listening.

It must have been towards morning when I closed my eyes, not because I was sleepy, but because I was so tired of gazing at blackness.

Soon after I had done this there was a stealthy movement in the bed.

"Margot, are you awake?" I instantly cried out sharply.

The movement immediately ceased. There was no reply.

When the light of dawn stole in at the window she seemed to be sleeping.

Last night I did not close my eyes once. She did not move.

She means to tire me out, and she has the strength to do it. Tonight I feel so intensely heavy. Soon I must sleep, and then—

Shall I seek any longer to defend myself? Everything seems so inevitable, so beyond my power, like the working of an inexorable justice bent on visiting the sin of the father upon the child. For was not the cruel boy the father of the man?

And yet, is this tragedy inevitable? It cannot be. I will be a man. I will rise up and combat it. I will take Margot away from this house that her soul remembers, in which its body so long ago was tortured and slain, and she will—she must forget.

Instinct will sleep once more. It shall be so. I will have it so. I will strew poppies over her soul. I will take her far away from here, far away, to places where she will be once more as she has been.

Tomorrow we will go. Tomorrow—

Ah, that cry! Was it my own? I am suffocating! What was that? The horror of it! The pen has fallen from my hand. I must have slept; and I have dreamed. In my dream she stole upon me, that white thing! Her velvety hands were on my throat. The soul stared out from her eyes, the soul of the cat! Even her body, her woman's body, seemed to change at the moment of vengeance. She slowly strangled me, and as the breath died from me, and my failing eyes gazed at her, she was no longer woman at all, but something lithe and white and soft. Fur enveloped my throat. Those hands were claws. That breath on my face was the breath of an animal. The body had come back to companion the soul in its vengeance, the body of—

Ah, it was too horrible!

Can vengeance for the dead bring with it resurrection of the dead?

Hark! There is a voice calling to me from upstairs.

"Ronald, are you never coming? I am tired of waiting for you. Ronald!"

"Yes."

"Come to me!"

"And I must go."

Just at the glimmer of dawn the first pale shaft of the sun struck across a bed upon which lay the huddled and distorted corpse of a man. His head was sunk down in the pillows. His eyes, that could not see, stared towards the rising light. And from the open window of the chamber of death a woman in a white wrapper leaned out, watching eagerly with wide blue eyes the birds as they darted to and fro, rested on the climbing creepers, or circled above the gorge through which the river ran. Her set lips smiled. She looked like one calm, easy, and at peace. Presently an unwary sparrow perched on the trellis beneath the window just within her reach. Her white hand darted down softly, closed on the bird. She vanished from the window.

Can the dead hear? Did he catch the sound of her faint, continuous purring as she crouched with her prey upon the floor?

ABDULLAH BEN BRAHIM

I

I was walking alone in the Count's garden at the edge of the desert in Biskra, when I saw a small, slight and very pretty woman with long green earrings strolling among the great trees, protected from the burning sun partly by the trees, partly by a green and white sun-umbrella. She was followed by a little black boy dressed in a thin blue robe, a little boy who might have stepped out of a picture by Manet. It was the month of October and the palm trees were loaded with their burdens of golden dates. The Jew merchants were already over from France. The rich Arabs who owned vast plantations of palm trees were talking business and reckoning up their probable gains. And as I walked in that lovely garden I often heard the dry little sound of a date dropping on the warm sand of the narrow winding paths, the dry little sound which belongs to the Saharan autumn.

The pretty woman with the long earrings and the tiny black boy in the blue robe were only seen by me for a moment. Then they vanished among the trees. But not before I had glanced at the woman curiously, and she, not curiously, I thought, had glanced hack at me. She had unusually large hazel eyes I believed, though I had not been near enough to her to be quite certain about that. And in those eyes I had surprised a look of startled uneasiness, as if her mind had said at that moment, "Who is this man? Why does he come here? I don't want him here."

Yet surely I had as much right to be in the garden as she had. I had known and loved it for at least thirty years; before she was born, in fact. For I judged her to be not more than twenty-five or so, little more than a girl.

As I wandered on under the densely-growing trees, hearing the voices of the birds which sing in that desert paradise, the voices of the rills of running water spanned here and there by tiny bridges of palm-wood covered with beaten sand, I wondered who the woman was. For this was no time for travellers in Biskra. And I knew most of the residents, not many, by sight. Perhaps she was the newly-wedded wife of an officer and had just arrived at the walled in barracks which stands near the mill and the public gardens. But she was surely not French. In the brief glimpse I had had of her I had guessed her to be an American.

That garden in Biskra is not unlike a maze, turning and turning upon itself, and presently, rounding a corner, I came face to face with the pretty woman and the little black boy. The path there was very narrow and overshadowed by the fans of close growing palms. We confronted each other and instinctively I took off my hat. Her eyes— they were hazel—looked into mine, and I saw in them an expression which seemed to me mingled of willfulness and helplessness. It was as if they appealed for and at the same time refused something.

The narrow path we were on sloped down on each side to the lower ground where the trees were planted. I had to stand sideways to let the woman pass. It seemed unnatural not to say something, and I made the banal remark, "There's not much room on this path, is there!"

"No," she said.

She slipped by. (She was very slim.) The little black boy followed after, his long robe floating out with an absurd sort of majesty from his minute body. She slipped by—and stopped. And after an instant of hesitation she said

"Do you know Abdullah Ben Brahim?"

"Yes," I said. "I've known him for years."

"Then I think perhaps I know who you are."

She mentioned my name and I said it was mine. And she added:

"He told me you were expected."

"I arrived from Europe yesterday."

"I have been in North Africa all the summer," she said.

And then we were walking on, at first one behind the other, then, when we turned into a wider path, side by side.

She was an American. I knew that by her voice, a soft Southern voice, and by something in her manner, her way of holding herself, her way of putting on her clothes. (She was dressed in khaki colour. I couldn't give a name to the material.) There was an extraordinary delicacy about her. When you looked at her the first word that came in your mind having reference to her was "refinement." Her body was exquisitely thin. Her wrists and ankles were fine. Her features were small, clear cut, beautifully proportioned. She had light brown hair that looked very soft and individual. Her eyebrows were narrow and slanted slightly downwards from above the nose towards the cheeks. Her mouth was small, and she had tiny little gleaming white teeth.

She was extraordinarily pretty in a thistledown sort of way. And there was meaning in her, too. She looked earnest, intelligent and seeking. But there was wistfulness in her eyes.

"This charming creature from over the seas has an obstinate will," I said to myself. "When I first saw you," I said to her. "I felt that you were startled at seeing me and not at all pleased at my venturing into this garden."

"That's true. I've become accustomed to having it all to myself. But I can't resent your being here."

She looked up at me.

"I know how you love it and how long you have known it."

"Yes; before you were born."

And then I told her of my first coming to Biskra before the crowd of tourists had found it out, in the time when it seemed a very remote place, very far away, and of the fascination it had cast over me, and of my wanderings in the desert beyond it, to Touggourt and the great dunes that stretch towards El-Oued. And she listened, keeping her big eyes upon me, and when I had done she said:

"Abdullah wasn't born then!"

"No. But I remember him later as a small boy, then as a tall boy, then as a man. He knows the desert well. His father knew it before him."

"Yes; he knows the desert well," she agreed.

And when she said that there was a fatal sound in her delicate voice that made it seem heavy for a moment.

"Do you know it well?" I asked.

"I was in it all summer," she said.

I was amazed.

"You could stand the heat!"

"Yes. But a good part of the time I was fairly high up."

"In the Aures?"

"For a while. And I was at Bou Saada, and Laghouat, and Tozeur, and Nefta, and Kairouan, and up in the hills not far from El-Kantara. But I call it the desert. For it all seemed the desert to me."

Again the heavy sound came in her delicate voice.

"Then you camped a good deal, I suppose?" I said.

"Yes. I camped quite a lot. Abdullah managed things for me."

She glanced at me, then added:

"I've been over in North Africa for nearly two years now."

"So long as that!"

"Yes. We came because of my husband's health."

"Oh, your husband's here!" I said.

And I remember that I felt a sense of relief.

"No. He got cured, and he's gone back to America to business. But I felt I must stay over here."

She paused, then she said.

"For a time."

And my sense of relief died out of me.

II

Abdullah Ben Brahim was what they call in Egypt a dragoman and in Biskra a guide. During the season, he was attached to a hotel. Out of the season he exercised mysterious functions in liberty. Once when I inquired of him what he did for a living when the big Royal Hotel closed its doors, he said in French—he talked French fluently, but with a very peculiar accent: "I make little business."

What exactly that little business was I never found out. But at the time I am writing of he had started a café Maure in the village, a place where the natives went to drink coffee, mint tea or lemonade, to gossip, and to play backgammon, dominoes, and their favourite "ladies' game." He had put in a *homme de confiance* to look after it for him, but he was there every day when in Biskra, and be sure he went over the "takings" each night with scrupulous sharpness.

On the evening of the day when I first met Mrs. Van Brandt—that wasn't her real name, which for reasons any reader can guess I can't give—after dining in my hotel, the Hotel des Zibans which faces the public gardens near the Catholic Church, I lit a cigar and strolled towards Abdullah's café. I hadn't seen him yet since I had arrived in Biskra. I thought I should like to have a word with him.

The night was deliciously warm. The purple blue sky did not show the vestige of a cloud. The mimosa trees in the long alleys which stretch towards the station were absolutely motionless. A breathless hush seemed to hold the oasis. But in the distance dogs were barking persistently under the stars, and nearer at hand I could just hear a very faint sound of native music. In the open space before the Café Glacier a few people were sitting, sipping iced drinks and talking. Two or three French soldiers strolled towards the Barracks. A little boy from Morocco, in bizarre red and white clothes, with bare arms and legs, and long, rusty-black hair, was making a monkey do tricks at the end of a cord.

Biskra! I was back once more in Biskra. How familiar it seemed to me in its out-of-season dress, lying cradled in warmth hidden among its palms in the windless night. Its old fascination was upon me despite my intimate knowledge of it. And the tourists wouldn't come for a long time yet. For nearly three months more Biskra would still be Biskra. I tried to recall my first visit there as a young man, my very first visit to an oasis. Everything in Biskra had seemed very strange to me then. I knew it all now as well as I knew Piccadilly, the Rue de la Paix, the Corso in Rome. Yet that night I captured again for a little while the faraway feeling which the facilities of modern travel are making more and more rare. And I was able to imagine the effect which the very peculiar region in which Biskra lies might have on a romantic temperament. (And even in our unsentimental times, romantic temperaments exist, however carefully they try to conceal that fact.)

I crossed the Rue Berthe and walked towards the Cardinal's statue. The music from the street of the dancers was thinly audible to me the old familiar drumming, the old familiar crying, vehement and fragile, of the pipes. Always the sameness of North Africa, sameness of music, sameness of monotonous dancing, sameness of shrouded listeners, shrouded starers. Can a desert man tire of anything?

Yes; he can tire of a woman.

A rather thick voice, sensuous and heavy, a voice which sounded dark to me in the night, said in my ear:

"*Bon soir*, Monsieur Robert."

And against my khaki riding-suit brushed the dark blue embroidered burnous of Abdullah Ben Brahim.

Abdullah Ben Brahim was at that time about twenty-eight years old, and he looked his full age. What exactly his origin was I don't know. But though he called himself an Arab he must, I think, have had some other strain of blood in him, His skin was so dark that most Europeans would have called it black. But there were tints of deep brown in it. It wasn't a blue-black skin, such as you see on the faces of the Senegalese. He was very tall and muscular, with large heavy black eyes showing a pale-yellow tint in their "whites," a curved nose, rather large, and with a curious bend in it near the tip, thick, black eyebrows, and a large black moustache spreading out on his cheeks. Some Arabs have a great deal of charm. I couldn't see charm in Abdullah. He wasn't at all an ugly man. He was stalwart, powerful and carried a suggestion of great spaces and fierce, fiery heat with him. But his expression was unsmiling, sulky almost as a rule. There was no lightness, no gaiety in his manner. To me there was something grim in his personality. One thing I always specially noticed about him. He didn't seem observant of you, or very conscious of you when he was with you. To me he suggested a man self-concentrated, wrapped up in himself. He was always extremely well dressed, and his snow-white turban bound with camel's hair was a triumph.

After the usual greetings I told Abdullah that I was on the way to his café. He replied that I must take coffee or whatever I liked there at his expense. I didn't refuse. It wouldn't have been etiquette to do so as we were old acquaintances, and I had never been to his café before.

Abdullah's café was quite near to the street where the Ouled Nails dance in Biskra. It was well situated, and had a big open space in front of it giving plenty of room for going and coming. Some rugs were spread out on the sun-dried earth. There were the usual tables and chairs. Within the café burned oil lamps. The coffee niche glowed. One could see turbaned heads bent over games. Some Spahis were taking coffee. A little madman in white was being teased by two painted girls covered with barbaric ornaments of gold set with heavy jewels.

And alone by a table set on a rug sat Mrs. Van Brandt smoking a cigarette.

III

That evening my real acquaintance with the pretty little American woman began. Abdullah led me up to her table and placed a chair for me by it, and in due time my coffee was brought there.

"I told him I met you in the garden," she said to me, as if in explanation of Abdullah's calm and insouciant doings.

And we sat there and talked in the windless night, just hearing now and then the voices of the pipes from the dancing-houses, and having as background to our talk—and our lives—the dull and persistent murmur of the tom-toms. We talked about lovers of the East, about Burton, and Kinglake, and Loti, and Farrère, and Blunt, and Lafcadio Hearn. And of course we talked about Eberhardt, the woman who loved a desert man, and who died in trying to save him from a flood. And while we talked we could see Abdullah going slowly, with his nonchalant and half-sulky air, slowly to and fro among his guests, greeting some of them in the dignified Arab fashion ceremoniously, sitting for a while among the Spahis, watching, but without apparent interest, a game of backgammon played by a notable from Chetma with an elderly sheikh from Sidi-Okba, conferring mysteriously in a corner with a Negro from the household of the great chieftain Bou Aziz Ben Gana, and presently having an apparently violent quarrel with a man in tattered garments, who looked to me like a nomad, and who was probably trying to "get away" with two coffees at the price of one.

Abdullah Ben Brahim!

As I watched, through our talk about men, women, thoughts and deeds, certainly never dreamed of by Abdullah—apart from Loti and the Eberhardt—I felt, as I had felt many times before, the almost irritating apartness of myself from the Biskris whom I had known for so many years, who all called me "Monsieur Robert," and who invariably welcomed me on my return to their village with genuine cordiality. I felt it and I spoke of it to Mrs. Van Brandt.

"And the reason of it," I said. "Lies not in me, not in us,"—I included her with a smile—" but in them."

"What do you mean?" she asked.

And her hazel eyes, I thought, had a look of fear in them.

"I mean that they put us in their thoughts right away from themselves. We never really touch their lives. Our nearest approach to their lives—I'm speaking now of Abdullah and his kind, not of the great Arab notables—is when we are paying over money to them."

"You can say that after all this country has meant to you!" she said. And the soft Southern voice vibrated with surprise and, I fancied, resentment.

"I say it because I believe it is true. I don't want it to be true."

"I don't believe it! I don't believe it!" she said. " If I believed it I wouldn't go on living here. I would go back—" she paused, then she added with a quite indescribable intonation—"to Cambridge, Mass."

She sat silent, looking towards the dim lights in the café, looking towards Abdullah, who at that moment was standing in the doorway quite still with his arms folded under his burnous.

"But I don't believe it!" she said again, almost passionately.

"Well, who knows? Perhaps I'm wrong," I said gently. "But—"

"Of course you've been in this country many times," she interrupted me. "And I never came here till two years ago. But in those two years I've never left Africa. And, in Africa, I've ignored Europe and—and America."

"Oh!" I said.

"Yes. I haven't lived like the ordinary tourist. I've lived for Africa. Do you believe in reincarnation?"

When she said that, I knew at once what was coming.

"I can't say I do. There are undoubtedly curious happenings, curious instincts, desires, satisfactions, longings, which one could understand if one was certain that one had lived already in such and such a way, but which—"

"Yes, yes—exactly!" she again interrupted. "Well, I do believe in reincarnation absolutely, and I know that in some former life I was an Arab woman."

Of course! Exactly what I was waiting for! Poor little thing! I felt so sorry for her, and so anxious about her, and so afraid for her. But what was I to do?

Just then I saw Abdullah Ben Brahim's large heavy-lidded eyes turned towards us, and for once they looked to me observant.

"How do you know?" I said, lowering my voice, and looking casual, disinterested.

"By a great many things. I feel far more at home here than I have ever done in America. I felt at home directly I got here. My husband hated it. He hated the place and he hated the people. He only stayed here till his lung healed up, and he was always abusing everything. I resented his abuse as if I had been an Arab. I was an Arab once. I have known it for a long time."

"No one can prove a negative," I said. "And I shall not try to."

"But you're out of sympathy with me! Of course! Everyone is. But I don't care. I always follow my instincts and they always lead me right."

"And they lead you to Abdullah Ben Brahim!" I said to myself. "A married desert Arab, who waits at the doors of hotels to catch tourists, and who thinks of Americans in terms of Algerian paper money, a man of no education, though of undoubted astuteness, who can barely write his name but who has complete self-assurance. Woman's instincts! Woman's madness rather! And the theory of reincarnation to explain and excuse the whole monstrosity."

Aloud I said:

"It must be wonderful to be so self-confident. I'm afraid I'm not."

And then I got up to go.

Seeing this, Abdullah came slowly up to us.

"I hope the coffee was good, Monsieur Robert."

"Excellent! Thank you for your hospitality. I shall come again as a client."

"*Inshallah!*"

I took off my hat to Mrs. Van Brandt.

"Good night. Unless I can walk with you to your hotel?"

"Oh," she said. "I don't live in a hotel. No! I've got an apartment. Abdullah found it for me. And it's such a lovely night. I'm not going yet."

I left her among the natives lighting a fresh cigarette from a vesta held by Abdullah's black hand with its light-coloured palm.

IV

I thought as I walked home that Mrs. Van Brandt wouldn't take much more notice of me. I knew that my view of the Biskris had upset her, that she was disappointed in me. Probably the only reason which had led her to wish to know me a European, was her conviction that I was not as other Europeans, that I was obsessed by Africa and things African as they were not. The fact of my seeing clearly in spite of the glory of the Saharan sun had obviously distressed her. And my remark about money had roused acute resentment in her. She wouldn't forgive me for that easily. Poor little thing! I saw her lying awake that night turning and turning that cruel remark of mine over and over in her mind, and hating me for having made it. Such a remark applied to such a romance! It had been very cruel. It had been like the surgeon's knife applied to a cancerous growth. But who can cut out a cancerous growth from the imagination and the soul of a woman?

I was unhappy that night. I felt as if I had a duty to do. I felt as if I ought to push ruthlessly into Mrs. Van Brandt's life and hack away her illusions, the illusions a strange land had brought her. But my conventionality whispered: "You can't. You're a stranger. You've no right to interfere with her. She's free to do what she chooses. Her life is no business of yours. Don't be a fool. Don't imagine that you can lift the veil from her eyes."

I resolved to go my way in Biskra and, if possible, to see no more of Mrs. Van Brandt.

But Biskra is small, though the desert is vast and she sought me out. I could hardly say why. She was complex, and she was in a very strange condition of body and mind. I suppose a fashionable doctor would have said that she was highly neurotic. I think in her heart she was afraid, afraid of herself, afraid of life, afraid of the future, afraid of the dark domination under which she lay, incomprehensibly. Perhaps she sought me as the last European who might be able to do something for her, in spite of her crazy willfulness. Or, perhaps she sought me as another romantic who, in spite of a cruel debut, would presently give her right. Who can say? Anyhow she sought me. We became in a sort of way, and in spite of innumerable reticences, intimate.

One day the Catholic priest of Biskra spoke to me near the church. After the usual politenesses, he said:

"Excuse me, Monsieur, for what I am going to say. But I have lived for over twenty-five years in North Africa. I speak Arabic fluently, and I think I know the natives pretty well. That American lady, your friend, is making a terrible mistake which may easily have consequences one doesn't care to think of."

He stopped and pulled his big beard.

"Yes?" I said.

"You know what I mean, Monsieur—Abdullah Ben Brahim!"

"He's her guide, I know. Why shouldn't he be?"

"Ah, Monsieur!"

He threw up his large pale hands.

"We are men who know something of human nature! We may not understand it, but we can see what happens before our eyes. The little lady—you are the only white man she lets know her. Tell her!"

"Tell her what?"

"Tell her that she is nothing to Abdullah but a thing to use, to get pleasure from, and, before all, profit from. Tell her that not only is he married—she knows that, of course—but that he has a mistress in the dancers' street, the woman who dances with a bottle on her head."

"That Jewess!" I exclaimed.

"Is she a Jewess? I daresay. I have nothing to do with those women. But anyhow, Abdullah is madly in love with that woman. Tell your friend! Tell her! All the French people here they are saying dreadful things about her."

"That wouldn't affect her. When a woman is obstinate—" I paused.

"I know, I know," he said. "She will lift her little foot and kick at all creation. But you—do what you can."

"You've suggested a difficult job to me."

"Has she seen the Jewess?"

"I don't know."

"If she hasn't, take her to the dancing-house and tell her."

After thinking the whole matter over on a seat near the mill I resolved to do this.

V

In the evening I found Mrs. Van Brandt at Abdullah's café and asked her in a very casual way whether she wouldn't come with me to the dancers' street. It was nearly full moon, and I said the effect of the silvery light on the white-robed crowd, mingling with the lights from the dancing-houses and the stairways of the Ouled Nails, would be curious and charming.

"I don't care much for that street," she said.

"Then I'll go alone," I said carelessly.

I fancied I had detected suspicion in her. Now, perhaps I had laid it to rest. For she got up from her chair on the rug and said:

"I'll come with you."

"You are going, Madame?" said Abdullah's thick voice as we passed before the lighted café.

"Just for a little. With Monsieur Robert to the dancers' street."

She looked up at his almost black face anxiously.

"It's all right for me, isn't it?"

"Monsieur Robert will take care of you," he replied.

But he looked sulky as he swung his blue burnous up over his left shoulder, and suddenly shouted to one of his coffee boys.

"Perhaps I'd better not go" Mrs. Van Brandt said, hesitating almost piteously.

"Don't if you'd rather not," I said.

That decided her. I had spoken with a faint smile, a slight touch of sarcasm.

"I'll come. There's no harm in it."

But I could see that her natural willfulness was almost smothered by uneasiness. And I felt a sudden, useless hatred of Abdullah.

We stood at the door of a dancing-house under the moon, and saw fluttering painted figures, veils spotted with silver, glittering headdresses. We heard through the noisy music the barbaric chink of moving bracelets. In the distance near the musicians I saw the long-nosed Jewess from Setif who danced with a bottle on her head.

"Shall we go in?" I asked Mrs. Van Brandt.

"Do you want to?"

"I hear there's a woman who dances very cleverly balancing a bottle on her head."

"Is there?"

She had evidently never heard of the woman before. I could tell that by the tone of her voice.

"I don't mind going in for a moment if you want to."

The Arabs round the door made way, and we passed in, brushing against their garments. We found a bench and sat down. I saw the Jewess's heavily-painted eyes fixed upon us. A fat girl in bunched-up muslin was posturing.

"What dreadful women they are!" murmured Mrs. Van Brandt in my ear.

"The Arabs don't think so."

I saw a quick look of fear in her eyes.

"They can't really like them!" she whispered.

"Look round you," I answered.

All about us the Biskris, and men from the Zibans and the farther desert, were sitting, dressed in white, still, silent, watching the women.

"Why do they come here?" I asked Mrs. Van Brandt. "It's habit. They've nowhere else to go."

"From whom do the women get those strings of gold coins, those cataracts of bracelets, those golden, or gilded, headdresses, those jewels?"

She was silent.

"Look at this woman!" I added.

The Jewess from Setif was rising to her feet, and with henna-dyed hands was posing a bottle nearly full of water on her head covered with gaudy silk handkerchiefs.

"But she's frightful! Look at her nose! She hasn't a single good feature. And she's dirty. Her hands are dirty."

"The Arabs don't mind that," I said.

Holding her narrow head sideways the thin Jewess moved about the floor, between the walls of men dressed in white. "She's the star here," I said.

"Because she's clever with the bottle. That's a trick of balancing. But otherwise—she's hideous."

"Abdullah Ben Brahim doesn't think so," I murmured.

Mrs. Van Brandt made a sudden movement which upset the blue glass of mint tea on the little table beside her. I saw an ugly flood of red surge over her delicate little face. The Jewess, looking sideways, came near to her, posing for money. Mrs. Van Brandt leaned back as if trying to get away. The piper held a long angry note. Mrs. Van Brandt sprang up and went out, pushing her way between the standing Arabs round the door.

When I had paid and joined her in the alley outside she turned on me.

"You did it on purpose! You took me there on purpose. I—I think it was vile of you. But it isn't true! I don't believe it. I will never believe it."

"The woman with the bottle is Abdullah Ben Brahim's mistress," I said. "Why shouldn't she be? What does it matter if she is?"

I shall never forget the look in the big hazel eyes as I asked that question.

VI

After that evening Mrs. Van Brandt avoided me and I made no attempt to see anything of her. She had told me I was vile. She had parted from me in front of Abdullah's café without a word of goodbye. It wasn't for me to seek her out. I had done what I had felt it was right to do. And there I must leave the matter. It wasn't my affair. I kept telling myself that. But I had become almost painfully interested in the fate of the little delicate creature whom I had first seen among the trees in the Count's garden with the tiny attendant in blue.

And hasn't one a duty to one's neighbour?

But I had done what I could. I had even forced myself to be cruel. I couldn't, I said to myself, do anything more.

What had happened, if anything had happened, between Mrs. Van Brandt and Abdullah I didn't know. But I knew that no definite breach had been made between them by my information so brutally conveyed in the dancing-house. Mrs. Van Brandt still went to Abdullah's café at night. I didn't go there anymore, but I knew this from Abdullah himself. He inquired of me jealously why I had deserted his receipt of custom, and urged me to return, adding in his heavy voice:

"*Madam Van Brandt elle rient toujours chez moi comme autrefois.*"

Not a word, not the least hint, about my having given him away. Arabs know when to be silent. But I realised that besides Abdullah's silence I had had Abdullah's bit of deliberate information. He had discreetly let me know my own impotence.

"I'll come back one night," I said.

But, nevertheless, I didn't go. And I knew that Abdullah was put out at losing my custom. He liked me to be seen in his café.

The weather wasn't quite so hot now, and I had taken to the sands. Nearly every day I motored out, with my Arab friend Laala, on the desert route to Tolga, left the motor at the foot of a big sandhill on the right of the road, and spent the day there, being fetched by the motor towards sunset.

Directly the motor had crawled away, like a black insect over the pale-yellow desert, towards Biskra, Laala and I were alone in the vastness, alone in the sun-smitten silence. We made our way up the sandhill—almost a mountain it was—till we got to the summit. There, in a sort of huge cup of sand, we lay down on the Eastern rug we had brought with us, and we sank into our desert day, into its air, its warmth, its peace, its glorious remoteness and separation from the cries and the darkness and the hubbub of ordinary life.

From our sand-mountain we could see over an immense stretch of desert beyond the rough *piste* leading to Tolga, and now and then, though not often, we perceived desert travellers moving slowly, mysteriously, upon their mystical business. (Mystical it seemed to me, looked at from a height and afar.) We saw a solitary camel, a horseman, an Arab man on a donkey followed by his woman on foot, sometimes a string of camels passing across the waste and eventually fading into the glitter of the distance. Now and then the sound of human voices reached us. I remember a boy, alone, holding a wand, and singing passionately to the sun as he went barefoot in tattered garments towards the horizon. He sang like a conqueror and possessed, I suppose, nothing. But mostly we were alone, heard nothing, saw only the desert. And our day slipped by with the gliding stealthiness of desert days, shining, silent, enchanted.

But there came a day when, towards afternoon but long before the time for our motor to return to us, Laala and I saw coming from the direction of Biskra a little blackness that moved fast and had nothing mystical about it.

"*C'est une Ford!*" said Laala.

It stopped at the foot of our sand-mountain and we saw a woman getting out.

Laala was on his feet, with his brown hands held up, like blinkers, near his eyes.

"It is Madame, the American!" he said.

The woman stood still in the sand and looked up. Instinctively I waved my hand. She did not wave in reply, but she began slowly mounting towards us, holding a sun-umbrella over her head.

"I'll go down to meet her," I said to Laala.

And I started at a run. Laala, I believe, made a movement to come with me, then stopped. Mrs. Van Brandt and I met alone in the sand.

"You were looking for me?" I asked.

I was surprised, anxious. It seemed to me that something extraordinary must have happened to induce her to seek me out, considering the coldness there was between us.

"Yes. I knew you came here. I—I wanted to speak to you."

"Shall we—do you wish to climb to the top?"

She looked up, then at the desert.

"Yes, please."

We walked up slowly in the sand. And not another word was said between us. When we reached the top of the hill Laala saluted her. He had dusted the rug and was laying it down. She thanked him—I suppose for the dusting.

"May I sit down?"

"Of course," I said.

I looked at Laala. He returned my look with understanding eyes, and went away from us. In the distance, at the edge of a steep slope he sat down on his haunches and gazed out over the desert. I lay down on the rug near Mrs. Van Brandt and waited for her to speak. But she didn't speak immediately. She was looking out over the desert and there was, I thought, a strange severity in her small, delicate face, the severity that often comes from an interior intensity. For a moment, as I watched her, I thought:

"Is she—can she be saying goodbye to all this?"

At last she turned and looked at me.

"You wonder why I've come," she said, in her soft Southern voice. "And I almost wonder, too. But I suppose it's because you took me to the dancing-house. Your doing that showed me that you—that you were bothering about me. And besides, I really came here because of you."

"Because—you told me it was your husband's health."

"Yes. He was ill. But we might have gone to Arizona. He had a choice of places. Something I read made me choose—Biskra."

I said nothing. I felt very uncomfortable.

"You have a certain interest in me, haven't you?"

"Indeed I have," I said.

"Well, I've got to decide something. I heard from my husband today. "

"Yes?"

"He says that if I don't go back to him he will try to divorce me."

"Go back to him!" I said.

"You sincerely advise me to do that, to go back to Cambridge, Mass., and to a man who hasn't the power to interest me, to hold me, to make me obey him, to frighten me, who hasn't the power even to disturb me? I thought you were rather romantic. I thought you had emotion. I even sometimes thought you understood women."

I looked into her hazel eyes and hesitated.

"This is what I care for," she said, putting out a small hand towards the desert. "Since I came to this country I have suffered a lot—oh yes, a lot! But I have been awake all the time, awake to the meaning of living."

I saw that she had a letter in her left hand. She looked down at it.

"Being what you must be, and living as I suppose you have lived—not a dull life, do you really advise me to give all this up and to go back to Cambridge, and my husband, who hates all this, and who talks of, expresses his hatred? Shall I do that?"

"If you don't, what will become of you?" I said.

"I don't know exactly. But—" her soft voice sank almost to a whisper—"but at least I shall never be dull."

She looked up at me steadily, and there was a really dreadful pathos in her eyes as she said:

"And if I go back I shall always be dull, always. Could you live a dull life?"

"I don't know. I don't want to."

"Nor I!"

"Tell me something," I said. "And don't be angry. Wasn't I right about the Jewess?"

Her face flushed quickly, but she said without a tremor of the voice:

"Yes, you were right."

"Well then—you see! What's—what's the good?"

"Although I'm an American I feel that a man has an absolute right to do what he chooses about women. I must have been an Arab woman once. I feel it so strongly in my blood."

Suddenly I said in a voice that I felt to be harsh:

"Mrs. Van Brandt, I advise you to leave Biskra at once, to leave North Africa, to go back to your husband. Dullness—I hate it. But isn't it better than destruction?"

"I'm not sure. But I don't believe it is."

I felt at that moment that she was deeply disappointed in me.

"My life here is at any rate an adventure," she said, again looking out over the desert. "My life in Cambridge—it's like one of those hymns with no meaning that a village choir sings lustily—lustily—on a Sunday evening in Autumn when rain's coming down. I believe I'd rather be destroyed here than exist for long years over there."

She got up. Again she was looking at me.

"D'you know you're not really a bit like the man I imagined you to be?"

"I can't help wanting to protect you, to safeguard you."

"That's kind."

There was a faint, extraordinary sarcasm in her way of saying "that's kind."

"I don't quite know why I've come to disturb you," she added.

"I do. You wanted me to tell you to continue the adventurous life you are leading out here. But I can't. I simply can't. I know too much about conditions over here."

"You are imaginative," she said. "Very! But you have a lot of caution in you."

I watched the insect-like Ford creep away on the desert track. Then I heard the voice of Laala beside me.

"Abdullah Ben Brahim does not love the American lady, Monsieur Robert. It is the Jewess from Setif that he loves, she who dances with a bottle on her head."

He lit a cigarette.

"The American ladies—they are all very rich, Monsieur Robert."

When the tourists began to arrive in force I went away from Biskra. I did not return to North Africa from Europe until the following year, in November. And then, happening to be in Sicily, I crossed by boat from Trapani to Tunis.

In Tunis I had an old friend called Nataff, and on the morning of my arrival I went with him into the Souks. Nataff is a great talker and he told me all the "news." When we were going back to the Tunisia Palace Hotel, he said:

"You have heard of the suicide of the American lady, Monsieur Robert?"

"No," I said. "What American lady?"

"Madame Van Brandt, Monsieur Robert. She has been living here lately. She took a little house in the native quarter. But it was quite clean. Yes, it was clean. But they say she had very little money. Most American ladies are rich, but not this one."

"Whom did she live with?" I asked, trying to speak in an unconcerned voice.

"All alone, Monsieur Robert. That is she had one servant, a Sicilian woman, in the house with her."

"No one else? No—no guide to show her round, to look after her?"

"No, Monsieur Robert. She was alone. They say she came to the end of her money, and about two weeks ago she poisoned herself."

"Poor woman!"

"Yes, Monsieur Robert. She had been over in this country a long time. They say she came with her husband, but when he went back to America she preferred to stay here. She used to be in Biskra. There she had always a guide called Abdullah Ben Brahim. Perhaps you know him. They went into the desert together."

"I have seen him. Well, au revoir, Nataff! Come back at three o'clock and we'll go to Sidi-Bou-Saïd."

"*Bien*, Monsieur Robert."

Three days later, in the train between Constantine and Biskra, I went into the restaurant car to have lunch. There I found Abdullah Ben Brahim, in a snow-white turban bound with camel's hair and a mauve burnous embroidered in gold, seated alone at a table eating his way through a mound of risotto. He got up on seeing me.

"Monsieur Robert! *Bon jour!*"

We spoke a few words.

"You are coming to Biskra, Monsieur Robert?"

"Yes."

"You must come to my café."

"By the way," I said, looking at his heavy-lidded eyes. "I hear that Madame Van Brandt has just killed herself in Tunis."

"*Oui, pauvre femme elle est morte!*" said Abdullah Ben Brahim. "If you wish to make a desert excursion this winter, Monsieur Robert, I have now a fine camp equipment. It has all come from London. The beds are beautiful, and there are no tents like mine. You will give me the first chance, Monsieur Robert?"

I forget exactly what I answered. But it must have been something quite non-committal.

SATURDAY NIGHT

I

It seemed to John Arkrite that the whole world was waiting, not perhaps breathless but exceedingly attentive, to know whether his play "The Last Throw," would be a success or not. And by success he understood not merely a success in any limited literary sense, not merely a success with coteries, with finicking critics or disdainful highbrows, but a solid success with the great public, the sort of success that brings in plenty of money. He knew of course that his feeling was absurd, that no great world issues hung upon the triumph or failure of his play, yet he could not get rid of it.

"Fact is," he said to himself, "that if a man lives long in the world behind the scenes he gets everything out of focus."

And he had been living almost perpetually in that world for just over six weeks, during rehearsals at the Blue Theatre. The other world, *the* world, had been almost entirely shut out. He had nearly forgotten it. It had sunk away into the mists that enshroud the vague. What was happening there didn't matter. What did matter, tremendously, was whether the final act of "The Last Throw," was powerful enough, whether the play sagged or was sufficiently swift, the dialogue sufficiently witty, the characterisation sufficiently cynical, to satisfy present-day requirements.

The management of the Blue Theatre talked a great deal about what the "present-day public" demanded. In fact, Arkrite thought, they talked of the present-day public as if it were a new phenomenon, like a new beast appearing for the first time out of the depths of the jungle, bringing brand new appetites with it, appetites that Arkrite and the company must satisfy or be devoured—by failure.

This new beast—would it like the food that was going to be set before it on Saturday night?

Then there was Esmé Banks to think about. She presented a problem to Arkrite. He was of course marvellously lucky to have her in his play, for she was a young actress who had an immense "following." It was an understood thing in London that any play in which Miss Banks appeared *must* run for at least six weeks before that "following," which insisted on seeing its idol in every new part she undertook, was what the management described as "exhausted." Six weeks the minimum required to "exhaust" Miss Banks's public. What an asset!

But Arkrite didn't like Miss Banks, couldn't see exactly where her great attraction lay. Probably it was mainly physical. She was pretty, but in a peculiar way that he didn't care for, though in London it was a way greatly admired, the very smooth, very clear, very unchanging, very disdainful type, that never wrinkles and never looks soft or appealing, but always superior. Whatever was happening Miss Banks looked disdainful and superior, and carried her sickle-moon eyebrows slightly raised. Arkrite was sure that if the Trumpet sounded and she was ushered before the Judgment Seat she would walk in languidly, with her eyebrows raised and her Cupid's bow of a mouth drawn down in an expression of faint disdain.

An extraordinary type! He couldn't understand it. But he was told that Miss Banks was ultramodern and he read in the newspapers paeans of praise of her beauty, her "insolent charm," and her "alluring talent."

He was certain she didn't like him. But then it was quite possible that she liked nobody but herself. That at any rate was what her fixed expression suggested.

She was said to be very clever, but he couldn't get anything out of her. He found her monosyllabic. She seemed to have no conversation, yet he had the impression that she was exceedingly wide-awake. To him she looked vicious. But he was always hearing her spoken of as not Medusa but Madonna. At rehearsal the company talked of her "angel face." He must surely be all wrong about her. But then obviously she thought very little of him. Instead of petting him as "the author" Miss Banks practically ignored him. She had never consulted him about her part. From the beginning it was given out that Miss Banks would of course play the part "in her own way," and must on no account be interfered with.

The management was on its knees to her. Of course there was her "following"!

Arkrite hoped to heaven they'd follow.

It was terribly important to him to bring off a real money success this time, because if he did he would be able to marry Madge, and if he didn't the marriage couldn't take place perhaps for a very long time. For, though talented, he was miserably poor, impossibly poor really, for London life in after the war conditions with everything so disgustingly expensive. And though Madge declared herself ready to face abject poverty with him he was hardheaded enough to know that a shared penury is apt to bring about destruction of sentiment. He had been witness of such destruction more than once in the cases of friends. One of those loves had perished miserably in the wilds of Brixton. Another had died the death in a dreadful semi-detached house in Balham. A back slum in Brighton had killed a third. And though Madge loved him with an enthusiastic fidelity, which he never for a moment doubted, she didn't love squalor. What pretty girl of today did? It was the silk-stocking age. That had to be faced.

How utterly different Madge was from Miss Banks! Arkrite had had that driven in upon him at rehearsal. (For owing entirely to his influence Madge had been given a tiny part in his play.) Madge was all changefulness and fire. The little wrinkles round her lively dark eyes were expressive of her mobility. They seemed often to have a life of their own. Sometimes when Arkrite looked at their movement he felt as if he were looking at thoughts in motion. Madge was very quick-minded, very intelligent, perhaps far more intelligent than Miss Banks. One felt that she was full of sparks. She was eager, talked well, was what Americans call "quick on the uptake." And she would do her small part very well, would put all her heart into it. For it was his play. Faithful, keen, enthusiastic was Madge.

Surely some day she would have a "following" as Miss Banks had?

Why was it that that expressionless, unchanging, monosyllabic amazingly smooth type had such an effect on the public?

"It's beyond me!" Arkrite said to himself, as he thrust his long hands deep down in his pockets.

He went to the window and stared out into London.

Darkness was coming on. It was early spring and the days were still short—and when is not London inclined to darkness?

Arkrite lived in a tiny flat of two small rooms and a bathroom on the fourth floor of a building at the top of Shaftesbury Avenue, close to where the Avenue leads into Oxford Street. Not far off on the opposite side of the way was the Prince's Theatre.

He had just come back from the last rehearsal but one of his play, which was being produced at the Blue Theatre, near the Piccadilly Circus end of the Avenue. He had wanted Madge to come with him to have tea, or a cocktail, in his tiny green and red sitting room. She had been prevented prosaically by an obligatory visit to the dentist. During rehearsal a back tooth had been grumbling.

Arkrite was young, just thirty, tall, very lean, very freckled, with thick generally rough red hair, a very white skin, a plain, but faun-like face, slightly pointed ears, and brown eyes with red lights shining in them, or behind them. His body was so supple that it seemed made of elastic. There was in his appearance something slightly animal, but amiably animal, that women found very attractive.

"Will it succeed?"

That was the question in his mind as he stared into the humid twilight roaring with traffic.

"Will it succeed and what about Miss Banks?"

She had been, he thought, extraordinarily listless at rehearsal that day. Her indifference—considering that the management was paying her two hundred a week—had really been insolent. But she was insolent. Her whole personality suggested insolence. An insolent Madonna! What a contradiction in terms! But that connection of adjective and substantive fitted her.

Really it was extraordinary to be so entirely ignored by your "leading lady"! Miss Banks had never consulted him about her part. Certainly she had listened politely to a few suggestions that he had ventured to make, but he had felt that she didn't consider them of value. She had of course "her own way" of doing things. And evidently it paid. But still—

What would Madge have made of the part? Surely something vital and interesting. She was so tremendously vivid! She would have poured vitality, fire into it. It must have come alive in her hands. But of course no management would have entrusted it to her. She hadn't a "name." She hadn't a following. She hadn't made good. The question was how were you ever to make good unless you were given a big chance. Well at any rate, Arkrite thought, he had his chance now. But would Miss Banks spoil it for him? She had been so dreadfully listless at rehearsal that day. Madge, in the tiny part, had been acting for all she was worth, and Miss Banks, in the "lead," had just walked through like an insolent Madonna. As he looked out into the damp evening from the window of his little flat on the fourth floor in Shaftesbury Avenue, John Arkrite was on thorns—gnawed by anxiety. He wanted so terribly to marry little Madge and she wanted so terribly to marry him. And unless he had a success this time they couldn't marry with any chance of comfort. And discomfort, whatever the sentimentalists may say, does make the wings of love droop, until they are covered with the mire of the gutter—in this silk-stocking age.

In the narrow passage, papered blue, of the flat the telephone sounded. Madge, perhaps, speaking from the dentist's!

Yes, it was Madge. She would be kept quite a time, but could meet him later. They settled through the telephone to dine together at a cheap Soho restaurant called Belloni's. Arkrite went back to the window. But almost directly the telephone sounded again. Madge must have forgotten something she had meant to say and rung up once more.

"Yes, Madge? Is that you, dear?"

"I beg your pardon!" said a voice with a strong foreign accent.

Arkrite felt himself redden.

"Who is it speaking?" continued the foreign voice.

"John Arkrite."

"Monsieur Arkrite—*bien!* I speak for Mademoiselle Banks."

"Miss Banks! "

"Yes, sair."

"What is it, please?"

"Mademoiselle Banks wishes to see you, sair, about the play. You hear?"

"Yes, I hear!"

"Will you please come to her—number four ell, Sout Audley Street?"

"She wants me to come at once?"

"Yes, please—number four ell, Sout Audley Street."

"I'll come."

"*Bien*, monsieur."

Arkrite left the telephone, feeling oddly excited.

II

When he got to "Sout" Audley Street he found that number 4L was a building that had been converted into evidently very superior flats. There were only three of them. Number 3 was occupied by Miss Esmé Banks. A man in livery took Arkrite up in a very superior lift that seemed really to smell of money. (There was no lift where Arkrite lived in Shaftesbury Avenue.)

"If the play really succeeds Madge and I might live in a place like this!" Arkrite thought, as he looked at the liftman's brass buttons.

He stood on a very thick blue and red carpet and pushed an ivory bell knob. Immediately the shining mahogany door of the flat was opened by a very smart maid and Arkrite was confronted—that was how he felt it—was confronted by a marvellous smell of heliotrope, jasmine, and, as it seemed to him, all scented flowers. He gave his name.

"Mademoiselle Banks is expecting you, sair."

He stepped in among a maze of flowering plants and laid his soft hat on an ebony stool inlaid with ivory.

"This way, sair."

The maid led him across the square hall, carpeted with a one-colour carpet that looked to him like velvet tinted café-au-lait, into a large room in which a log fire was burning on an open hearth with brass dogs. Again there was a very thick carpet, this time primrose yellow. There were long primrose yellow curtains at the tall windows. The ceiling was apparently made of silver. In silver tubs blossomed yellow azaleas. An enormous divan, grass green with primrose cushions, and three huge low grass green armchairs, a green lacquer cocktail table, and an easel of green lacquer on which stood a Japanese picture of a flowering almond tree, completed the furnishing of this room, which looked extremely spacious yet temptingly comfortable.

"Please to sit down, sair," said the maid, and she went away.

Arkrite sat down in an armchair by the cocktail table, which held various bottles, a shaker, a silver pail full of ice, and some plates of salted almonds, olives, etc. The armchair engulfed him. It seemed to him that his head with its rather rough red hair merely peeped out above it.

"How Madge would love this room!" he said to himself, as he stared at it. "If I get a success this time and if she makes good presently we might manage to—"

And then the shining red brown door opened and Miss Banks strolled into the room, with her sickle-moon eyebrows raised and her Cupid's bow mouth turned down, looking as always disdainful, and astoundingly smooth and clear and snow white and rose. She certainly had a most marvellous skin.

When she saw Arkrite her expression did not change in the least. She came to him, as he got up out of the enormous armchair, holding out a bare white arm languidly, and said:

"How are you? I'll just mix you a cocktail."

"Oh, thanks awfully," he said.

He never knew how to deal with Miss Banks, and so up to now he had never really dealt with her at all.

She stood by him in silence mixing the cocktail in a cool and masterly manner, presently poured it into two extra-large cocktail glasses, gave him one, took up the other, and saying, in the cool, lazy voice, which was apparently characteristic of her, "Here's luck to the play!" emptied her glass slowly but completely. Then she gave him a cigarette, took one herself, struck a match, held it to his cigarette and to hers, and sat down on the huge divan. In silence she banked herself up with cushions. Then she looked full at Arkrite and he noticed what very large yellow-grey eyes she had. And while he was noticing that she said,

"You didn't like my performance at rehearsal today."

Arkrite felt himself redden to the roots of his rough red hair, even to the pointed tips of his faun-like ears.

"But I assure you, Miss Banks—" he began in a hurry.

"I've no doubt your conception of the way to play that role and mine are quite different," she pursued, with inflexible calmness. "Yours may be right—you are the author—and mine wrong, but mine is the one that will please the public. I have my own way of doing things. I never give in to the conceptions and ideas of other people and I invariably have the public on my side."

"That's true. I consider I'm very lucky to have you in my play."

"Really you are," she said, with such cool conviction that it seemed somehow to bar out conceit.

She looked steadily at him for a moment; then she said, "Have another cocktail."

"The last was pretty strong, wasn't it?" he said.

"Very. A cocktail should be strong. You will have another."

It was a simple statement of fact apparently. At any rate he proved it to be so in another moment, and she joined him. Then, once more on the divan, she said:

"I shall make this play a success."

Again obviously a statement of fact. He seemed ruled out of the whole matter, did not come into it at all apparently.

"You needn't be nervous," she added, rather like one addressing a child. "They will like the way I shall do it. I am exactly right for my day. That is why I am such a success."

Against his will almost, perhaps even totally against his will, Arkrite felt tremendously impressed.

"Yesterday—no. Tomorrow—perhaps no again! One can't be sure. But today—yes. And it is all intentional."

"Intentional?" he said, leaning forward in the engulfing green grass armchair towards the immense divan.

"I choose it all. I make it so. There is nothing casual, nothing chancy about it."

He was amazed. Was she then going to let him in abruptly to a strange intimacy? It seemed incredible, and yet here she was making a sort of confession—with the utmost languid coolness.

"Eagerness is no good. It doesn't take with the public of today. You should tell that to the little dark girl to whom, so they tell me, you are engaged."

Arkrite felt himself redden again to the roots of his hair. This young woman astounded him.

"What is her name? I forget."

"I suppose you mean Miss Linfield?"

"I mean the little dark girl you are engaged to."

Why did he at that moment feel that it was rather "cheap" to be engaged to Madge?

"Yes," he said, unevenly, "Madge Linfield."

"Is it? She is too eager, too anxious to get there. That is a mistake. If you show the public you want them you will never get them. Since the war even children are sophisticated. It is the old who are sentimentalists while the young are cynics. Everything is reversed. A Sarah Bernhardt wouldn't have a chance in these days."

She put her round white chin on her upturned palm and gazed at him without changing her curious fixed expression of an insolent Madonna.

"Yes. She *does* look vicious!" he thought.

"Perhaps not," he said. "But why did you kindly ask me to come here today?"

"I saw you were afraid at the rehearsal."

"Oh—afraid!"

"Yes, you were; afraid I might let you down."

Another cool statement of fact. He couldn't somehow dispute it.

"I thought I would tell you it was all right."

"Thank you very much."

After lighting another cigarette very slowly Miss Banks said, "This is not an age that likes wrinkles."

"Wrinkles!" said Arkrite, completely at a loss.

"Except in Rembrandt pictures. If that little dark girl of yours goes on trying to be so tremendously expressive do you know what will happen? Before she is near forty she will have a face like a motor map. You ought to tell her so."

"I couldn't really!"

"Why not? Don't you care for her enough?"

"Of course I—I care for her."

"People don't care very much nowadays as a rule. But since you do! She has lines round her eyes already. How old is she?"

"Twenty-four."

"By the time she is thirty those lines will spray far down on her cheeks. She is not going to be a success as an actress."

"I consider she has talent."

"She smiles and frowns far too much to impress the people of today. But after all that's her affair. You will never marry her."

Arkrite's blood seemed to give a bound in his veins.

"But I'm going to!" he said, with an attempt at her rigid firmness in stating a fact.

"I don't think so. She has an old-fashioned soul. One can see that."

"Then perhaps I have an old-fashioned soul too!"

"Not entirely. No. You know something about music?"

"Something—yes. I'm intensely fond of music."

"You know the *Après-midi d'un Faune?*"

"Yes, of course."

She looked at him with her large yellow grey eyes, which he was beginning to think enormous.

"Well, you could never know *la nuit d'un faun*—with her. Useless to try!"

Almost immediately after that Arkrite got up to go. It seemed to him as if the huge green armchair didn't want to release him, as if he had to struggle to get out of it, and out of that room. But Miss Banks made no effort to keep him. She did not move from the divan, but just stretched up a cool hand to his, looked up at him with her curiously disdainful eyes and said,

"Come in again directly after the dress rehearsal, will you?"

"But that's at night, tomorrow night," he said.

"Yes, I know. And don't be frightened about me. The public will love my performance. The critics will praise me. And the Box Office will satisfy you. Be sure of that. Whether you will like the way I act is another thing. I don't think you will. Not for a moment. But it will be all right. I know exactly what they want—today, and I don't believe you do. And I'm quite sure that little dark girl doesn't and never will. What did you say her name was?"

"Miss Linfield, Madge Linfield."

"She shouldn't be so eager. That's a great mistake."

The smart maid let him out. She was dark, and looked as if she knew infallibly every secret a man wished to hide.

"Thank you," he said, as she opened the shining mahogany door.

"Goodbye, sair," she replied with a smile.

III

Belloni's, Arkrite thought, was looking rather squalid that night. It was the favourite restaurant of Madge and himself. The food, Italian cooking, seemed good to both of them and the prices were astonishingly reasonable. Then you could always get ravioli, and Madge loved ravioli.

"It's so cosy and homey here!" she said, as they sat down in a corner.

And she began to tell him about the dentist, while the

Italian waiter, with a good many grease spots scattered about him and a face which had—perhaps—been rather badly shaved on the previous day, poured them out Chianti and planted their food in front of them on the tiny table.

Madge was eager about the dentist, made a narrative of her visit to him. The little lines near her eyes worked expressively as she talked. She smiled quickly, from time to time looking up for response into Arkrite's eyes with the red lights in or behind them. Then she came to the play—of course—and said:

"Oh, Jack darling, wasn't Miss Banks disappointing today?"

"Disappointing!"

He pulled himself up. His supple body felt suddenly tense. "Why disappointing?"

"So cold, so listless! No fire! Her face never changes. It's like a mask. There's no soul in it."

"The public love her."

"I suppose they do. Of course she's a great favourite. I know that. But *you*? Are *you* satisfied?"

She looked at him over the ravioli. A little spark she was. Fire showed in her dark eyes. A pageant of expressions kept changing her small dark face.

"Surely you thought her listless at rehearsal today?"

"Listless? But that's her way, Madge."

"I call it indifference."

"No. Indifference is a lack. Miss Banks's manner is intentional."

"Intentional?"

"Yes. There's nothing casual, nothing chancy about it."

"Chancy?"

She frowned slightly, intent on what he was saying, and he thought, "What a pity it is she makes those lines! They'll become fixed presently."

"How d'you mean, Jack?"

"That Miss Banks is an actress with a method of her own,
and behind that method an intention. And by that intention resulting in that method she is earning a couple of hundred pounds a week."

"Oh, I know she gets a splendid salary. But do you think there's anything interesting in the way she acts?"

"Our public of today doesn't want Sarah Bernhardts."

"But surely—"

"It's a great mistake to be too emphatic nowadays. The time for that has passed. No one should act to please old people."

"I don't understand."

"It's like this. Since the war everything is reversed. The old may be sentimentalists but the young are cynics, and one must act for the young if one wants to succeed on the stage."

"But we are young!"

"We? What's that got to do with it?"

"We have sentiment, haven't we?"

How earnest, how ardent her eyes were! But it was a pity those lines—

"*We* are not cynics."

"Oh, I don't know. Don't let's worry about all that. The great thing is not to be too eager. One mustn't show—I'm talking of the stage—the public that one is longing to get hold of them. One must hold back, appear to disdain them. That's the way to impress people. Then they think that you are superior to them."

"But if you aren't?"

"It's no use arguing merely for the sake of arguing, Madge."

"But—"

"I'm telling you my opinion. Don't frown! Why do you frown?"

"Am I frowning?"

"Yes. And you often do. It's a pity. It gives you lines, and nobody likes to see lines on a woman's face."

"I'm sorry. I'll try not to."

Her little face became rigid. During the rest of the meal she was actually self-conscious, she who was usually so perfectly natural. When the grease-spotted waiter came with their coffee she said, after a silence, "What did you do after rehearsal today, Jack?"

"Went home. But you know I did! I was tired out. I wanted a rest."

Immediately she melted. The little lines at the corners of her eyes moved, and she touched his hand softly, "Poor old Jack!" she murmured.

But he was looking at those tiny telltale wrinkles, and saying to himself, "If she doesn't look out they'll become fixed!"

IV

It had been an understood thing between Madge Linfield and Arkrite that they would go out to supper together after the dress rehearsal, unless it ended too late, which was unlikely, and that he would see her home afterwards. (She lived in Bloomsbury quite near to him.) But a greater festivity than this had been arranged for the night of the first performance—Saturday night. This was a supper party to be given by Madge for her *fiancé*, the first she had ever given for him. It had been her idea, and when of course Arkrite gratefully and gladly accepted she had gone to work enthusiastically to prepare a wonderful finish to this important first night, which would probably mark the first big step in the career to fame and fortune. She was not at all rich, but she had saved enough money to pay for a noble feast, of course with champagne of the best quality. (No other wine could be thought of on such an occasion.) As restaurants close too early, and as Madge belonged to no supper clubs, a friend of hers who had a house in Bedford Square, but was now wintering abroad, lent the house to Madge for the night. Madge had arranged for the supper, waiters, flowers, etc., to be supplied from Gunters' for a fixed sum. (It would leave her "cleaned out," but no matter!) The number of guests, and who they were to be, had been arranged between her and Arkrite after anxious consideration. There would be in all twenty guests, ten men and ten women. Madge and Arkrite would bring the number up to twenty-two.

At the meeting after the dress rehearsal the last little details of this unique festivity were to be discussed and finally settled between hostess and guest of honour.

But now Arkrite had to explain to Madge that he couldn't come after the dress rehearsal as Miss Banks had invited him and of course he simply couldn't refuse her. He might have told Madge at the dinner at Belloni's, but somehow he didn't. In fact he put the matter off until he met Madge behind the scenes at the Blue Theatre, dressed and made up for her small, rather unimportant part, and glowing with excitement and the desire to do justice to her lover's inspiration. For to her the part seemed of most vital import.

"Oh Madge, I say!" he began, in a hurried and casual manner. "I wanted to tell you. I can't get away tonight."

"Jack! Why not? But it's so important! We've got to settle—"

"Oh everything's settled all right. Fact is Miss Banks has invited me."

"Miss Banks!"

"Yes. I believe she wants to discuss something in her part with me."

"But surely it's too late to do that after the dress rehearsal!"

"Oh, no! I'm awfully sorry. But of course I couldn't refuse her."

Madge said nothing, but stood in the narrow corridor looking intensely expressive; aggravatingly expressive, he thought.

"I say, Madge, don't forget about not frowning so much, will you?"

And then he hurried off to say something to the stage manager. The curtain was just going to be rung up on the first act.

Madge's part finished in the second act. Arkrite expected her to go into the auditorium after she had changed, to watch the rest of the play. During the third and fourth acts he supposed she was there though he didn't happen to see her. But he was mostly in the stalls and she might easily be hidden away in the dress circle. She would probably come round at the end to say good night to him and to tell him how she thought it had gone.

When the last curtain fell he didn't see her, and had no time to look for her as he was surrounded by people saying what they thought about the way his piece had "panned out." And when they had done with him it was time to seek Miss Banks, who had acted in her usual cool, unimpassioned but perfectly competent way, and had certainly looked remarkable, "like a statue come to life" as the assistant stage manager said more than once.

Arkrite hurried to her dressing room and tapped. Miss Banks's dresser came.

"Oh, it's you, sir. Come in, please. Miss Banks particularly wants to see you."

Arkrite went in and found Miss Banks, wrapped up in furs, standing with a tall pretty girl who had her kind of expression, disdainful and detached, but coolly observant.

"Oh, Mr. Arkrite," she said. "I wanted to tell you—do you know Lady Marcia Vinsent? Marcia this is Mr. Arkrite.— I wanted to tell you that I'm sorry I can't manage tonight after all. I forgot that I had an engagement. But our supper is only postponed—till tomorrow. I shall expect you tomorrow. I'm going to make a great success of your play. He's rather frightened about me, Marcia, but he'll see tomorrow night."

"I should think so, darling. But you're simply too marvellous in the part."

"Yes, it's all right. I know what I'm doing. Good night, Mr. Arkrite. Tomorrow—at my flat. You can come and drive there with me after the performance. I'll expect you. Oh, by the way, if you thought of sending me flowers tomorrow let it be orchids. Good night. Come along, Marcia."

As Lady Marcia went down the passage indolently with Miss Banks she said, "He looked pretty sick, Esmé. I suppose he's in love with you?"

"Oh, I don't know. I fancy he's *en route*."

"Where are you going to supper?"

"Nowhere. I'm going to bed to have plenty of beauty sleep."

"But then why—"

"He mustn't think I'm keen on him."

"Are you?"

"I shall know tomorrow—and so will he."

"But are you sure he'll come? He looked pretty grim and I thought he was going to refuse if you'd given him time."

"I thought so too. But he'll come all right. Get in. I'll drive you home."

V

Arkrite didn't follow Miss Banks and her friend to the stage door. After they had gone out of the dressing room he stood for a moment alone. Then the dresser came and began putting things away in the room and looking at him in a particular manner that dressers have with visiting "gentlemen."

"Here please—good night!" said Arkrite, giving the lady half a crown.

"Thank you, sir. Miss Banks did look lovely in the part, didn't she?"

"Lovely?"

"Yes, sir."

"I suppose she did."

And then he went out leaving the dresser with a "Well, I'm sure!" on her lips.

Madge had evidently gone. Almost everyone had gone. But he didn't want to see Madge just then. He took a taxi and drove home to his flat in Shaftesbury Avenue. There was no supper for him there, but he didn't want supper. He only wanted a stiff drink and to be quite alone.

He got the stiff drink, a pipe, and sat down in his armchair by the grate in which there was a fading out fire with still a few red sparks left among the ashes.

"I'll not go! I'm damned if I'll go!" he said to himself.

He was angry, very angry; but with his anger another feeling mingled, of horrible disappointment. He must have been looking forward eagerly to the night visit which had been so casually cancelled before that disdainful girlfriend. If *she* hadn't been there—but she had been there to see his startled discomfiture. Intolerable pair of women with their clear cool eyes and disdainful red mouths! He thought of them as his enemies, as enemies of men, laughing at them, playing with them, despising them.

But anyhow he wouldn't go with Miss Banks tomorrow. He couldn't. He was engaged to Madge's supper party. So that settled it. He would tell Miss Banks so—after the performance was over. She had left her cool rejection until the last moment, and so would he leave his. When he went round to pay her the usual compliments and to see how she liked her orchids—for of course he would have to send her some orchids—he would tell her how awfully sorry he was that he was engaged for supper to the "little dark girl" who frowned and smiled too much, and who would be like a motor map before she was forty.

No; perhaps he wouldn't tell her all that. No need to explain. He wouldn't explain. He would just say, as she had, that unluckily he had another engagement.

What would she look like then?

He poured out another drink.

Girls like that deserved a thorough good taking-down. Their cheek and their indifference to the feelings of others were intolerable. He would read Miss Banks a lesson tomorrow night. And then he would go to dear little Madge's supper party, where he would be among friends, where he would be fêted, made much of, where he would be the great man. Madge was a darling.

But it really was a pity she was so intense, so eager, so mobile. Miss Banks was right there. All that did make the lines come in a woman's face, and besides nowadays people didn't want all that eagerness. It didn't impress them.

Dear little Madge! How she would love that room with the primrose-coloured carpet and curtains and the grass green divan and armchairs—buttercups-in-a-meadow colour. She would love it. But would she suit it? Somehow Miss Banks did suit it—or it suited her.

Dear little Madge! She was so excitable. That was why the lines came in her face. Miss Banks was never excited. But couldn't she be? There must surely be moments when her almost inhuman calm and detachment gave place to something else. It would be rather wonderful to see her when that something else got the upper hand—if it ever did. It would be an experience—even perhaps a great experience.

There was something vicious about her.

That night Arkrite found out that Miss Banks had a very definite power, the power to present herself to a man as a problem.

Dear little Madge wasn't a problem.

But he was going to have supper with Madge.

VI

As, of course, Arkrite was going to "turn down" Miss Banks it was quite unnecessary to mention her invitation to Madge, and Arkrite did not say anything about it, though he saw Madge for a very few minutes on the Saturday afternoon before his first night. Their meeting was not arranged but fortuitous, and it took place in the Shaftesbury Avenue not far from Piccadilly Circus. Madge was hurrying home from Gunters' in Berkeley Square where she had been to say some last urgent words about her supper. Arkrite was about to look in at the Blue Theatre. He was in a state of acute nervous tension. Madge was excited and anxious. They only spoke for a few minutes.

"Did you enjoy yourself—with Miss Banks?" asked Madge, looking terribly expressive.

"Oh, it was all right," said Arkrite.

"Well, good luck for tonight, Jack."

"Thanks awfully."

"I shall just stay to hear the reception at the end from the back of the house—the pit, I think. And then I must hurry to Bedford Square to make sure everything's all right. Come as soon as you possibly can, won't you. We shall all be waiting for you."

"Yes—thank you, Madge."

"I *do* wish you luck, Jack!"

She squeezed his hand and was gone. He couldn't forget the expression in her dark eyes as they looked up into his just before she went. Why hadn't he told her that he hadn't been with Miss Banks on the previous night? Her eyes had been asking about that. How quickly a girl becomes anxious about her lover, the Madge type of girl! But he hadn't cared to tell Madge that he had been thrown over. He would tell her when he had thrown over Miss Banks. Then it would be all right.

He turned in at the stage door.

The play went exceedingly well. Miss Banks in the principal part seemed to make no special effort. Arkrite had vaguely expected her to "come out strong" when she found herself before a smart and critical audience. But not a bit of it! She acted just as she had at rehearsal. She was, in fact, just Esmé Banks perfectly gowned, perfectly *coiffée*, absolutely mistress of herself and her emotions, if she had any, entirely at her ease, if anything just a shade more disdainful than usual. And everyone, the critics included, found her marvellous.

"She strikes," said one, in a high dictatorial voice, "the exact centre of the modern note."

When everything was over, and he had answered his "calls," and had received behind the scenes congratulations from the management and from heaps of people whose names he didn't know and whose faces he had forgotten, if he had ever seen them before, Arkrite braced himself up for the ordeal. He had to "turn down" Miss Banks, and get away with all speed to Madge's supper party in Bedford Square. Quickly he got hat and coat and hurried down the corridor in which the "star's" dressing room was situated. Miss Banks's dresser was standing outside the door and smiled when she saw him.

"Good evening, sir. Miss Banks is expecting you. She'll be out in one moment. She's got rid of them all. No easy job, sir, I can tell you on a night like this. She *has* had a success this time and no mistake. They're all wild about her. But she's sent them off, sir. I'll just tell her you're waiting and ready."

And before Arkrite could say anything she slipped into the dressing room and he heard her say, in a fawning voice, "Your gentleman's here, Madam. He's quite ready."

"Coming!" said Miss Banks's cool voice inside. "Give me the orchids, Briggs. That's right. And just spray me."

There was an instant of silence; then Miss Banks appeared, wrapped up in white furs, and carrying Arkrite's big bouquet of orchids.

"Oh, here you are! Well it went all right, didn't it? I didn't let you down, did I? Everyone says it will run till we're all sick of it—except of course *you*. That will give you time to write me another. Thanks for the orchids. Just carry them for me, will you? I've got the car. We'll have supper at home. No one but you and me."

She walked in front down the corridor, the steps, through the stage door. There was a crowd outside gathered about her big car.

"Here she comes!" cried a voice.

"Here she is!" cried another.

"Ain't she lovely?" exclaimed a third.

"Now I must tell her! I've got to tell her!" Arkrite said to himself.

Miss Banks nodded airily to the crowd without smiling and got into the car. Arkrite handed in his orchids.

"D'you know I'm awfully—" he began, standing by the door of the car.

"So am I!" said Miss Banks from inside. "But a couple of cocktails will soon put us right. Get in!"

"I can't say it before this crowd!" Arkrite thought, desperately.

"My dear man, don't keep me here! Get in!" He got in.

Miss Banks didn't trouble to talk anymore as they drove across the Circus and down Piccadilly, but Arkrite saw her large coolly observant eyes regarding him steadily, and he had an absurd idea that more than once those eyes looked hard at the tips of his faun-like ears. His heart began to beat rather fast. But he went on thinking of Madge, bothering about Madge. He still thought he meant to go to the supper in Bedford Square. He still thought he intended to explain why he must go to Miss Banks on the doorstep of number 4L "Sout" Audley Street. But when they got there and she said, "Come along in! I'm dying for some food and a cocktail!" he couldn't.

How could he?

But up in the hall with the thick café-au-lait carpet that looked as if it were velvet, while the smart maid was helping him to take off his coat, and was saying " Good evening, sair!" in a soft significant voice, he felt that he must do something. He simply couldn't let Madge's supper party wait for him into the small hours of the morning. Miss Banks had vanished behind a shining mahogany door in the distance beyond a cloud of flowering shrubs. He was alone with the maid.

"Can I use the telephone?" he said desperately.

The maid smiled.

"The telephone is in mademoiselle's bedroom, sair," she answered serenely. "Perhaps you would kindly ask mademoiselle about the telephone."

"Oh—God!" Arkrite said to himself.

And just at this moment he saw Miss Banks coming back. She must have had very acute ears for she said to the maid, "What's that about the telephone, Reine?"

"Monsieur asked me if he could telephone, mademoiselle, and I said the telephone was in mademoiselle's bedroom."

Arkrite was scarlet.

"It's all right. It doesn't matter in the least. I only—"

Miss Banks's large eyes held a flicker of apparent amusement.

"Don't let us bother about telephoning the success till we've had something."

She laid a cool hand on his arm.

"Try and think about *me* for five minutes. Do you realise you are *made* from tonight? And I've made you. Let the others go hang—for tonight. Come along."

And they went into the room with the primrose-coloured carpet and the grass-green divan and armchairs. There was a supper table there set by the fire. Miss Banks went to the cocktail table.

"We'll only have one each tonight—and then supper." Calmly she mixed the strange liquids and languidly manipulated the shaker, while Arkrite watched her and grew hot all over thinking of Bedford Square. He must, simply must, do something.

"Here is yours! We won't drink success to the play, because the play is a success already. We'll drink," she fixed her eyes on the tips of his ears, "to the night of a faun."

He stared at her.

"I don't believe in afternoon," she said, putting her empty glass down. "Now for supper!"

The maid was coming in with some covered dishes. Miss Banks went to sit down by the table, in a round-backed green-and-gold lacquered chair.

"Come along!"

And she pointed to a similar chair put for him.

"Miss Banks!" he said desperately.

"Yes? What is it?"

"I was engaged tonight to a supper party in Bedford Square."

"Never mind," she said, without changing her expression. "It's much nicer here."

"Yes, ever so much. But I ought really to let them know."

"Them! Who is it?"

"Well it's—well there'll be quite a lot of people."

"Who's giving it?"

"Well it's—"

"I know. It's the little dark girl! What's the number?"

He gave it.

"Reine," said Miss Banks, repeating the number slowly in an insouciant voice. "Go to the telephone. Call up that number. Ask for Miss—what's her name."

"Miss Linfield."

"Miss Linfield, and just explain that Mr. Arkrite is here having supper with me. They are not to wait."

"*Bien*, mademoiselle. Mees Leenfield."

"That's it."

The maid went away.

"And now, Mr. Faun," said Miss Banks, half closing her attentive eyes. "Forget the afternoon world. This is the world of night."

John Arkrite obeyed her. He forgot the afternoon world.

It was between four and five o'clock in the morning when he opened the front door of the building in which his flat was. As he shut it he saw something white in the letter box. Was it for him? He couldn't see the name on the envelope but he felt that it was, and he went upstairs, got his key to the letter box, opened it and took out a note which hadn't been through the post. It was addressed to him in Madge's handwriting. He carried it upstairs and into his sitting room.

A letter from Madge!

He tore it open and read:

"I had your message. This is mine—Finished. Madge."

Short and to the point. But there was a postscript, one sentence underlined.

"*From the first rehearsal I knew she would try to do it.*"

"That's a lie!" muttered Arkrite, crushing the note in his hot hand. "But women always accuse each other of things like that."

Did he feel sick at heart?

He didn't know. At any rate he was "made" as a playwright, and that night he had learnt a lot as a lover.

If Miss Banks's *béguin* for him lasted he felt just then as if perhaps he could forget "the little dark girl."

But if it didn't?

With his finger tips he touched the tips of his faun-like ears.

"It will last! It will! I'll make it!" he muttered.

And he threw little Madge's note into the wastepaper basket.

"WILLIAM FOSTER"

One sad cold day in London, city of sad cold days, a man in a Club had nothing on earth to do. He had glanced through the morning papers and found them full of adjectives and empty of news. He had smoked several cigarettes. He had exchanged a word or two of gossip with two or three acquaintances. And he had stared moodily out of a bow window, and had been rewarded by a vision of wet paving stones, wet beggars and wet sparrows. He felt depressed and inclined to wonder why he existed. Turning from the window to the long room at his back he saw an elderly Colonel yawning, with a sherry and bitters in one hand and a toothpick in the other. He decided not to remain in the Club. So he took his hat and went out into the street. It was raining in the street and he had no umbrella. He hailed a hansom and got in.

"Where to, sir?" asked the cabby through the trap door.

"What?" said the man.

"Where to, sir?"

"Oh! go to—to—"

He tried to think of some place where he might contrive to pass an hour or two agreeably.

"Sir?" said the cabby.

"Go to Madame Tussaud's," said the man.

It was the only place he could think of at the moment. He had lived in London for years but he had never been there. He had never had the smallest desire to go there. Wax and glass eyes did not attract him. Dresses that hung from corpses, which had never been alive, did not appeal to him. Nor did he care for buns. He had never been to Tussaud's. He was only going there now because literally, at the moment, he knew not where to go. He leaned back in the cab and looked at the wet pedestrians, and at the puddles.

When the cab stopped he got out and entered a large building. He paid money at a turnstile and drifted aimlessly into a waxen world. Some fat men in strange costumes, with bulging eyes like black velvet, and varying expressions of heavy lethargy, played Hungarian music on violins. It was evident that they did not thrill themselves. Their aspect was at the same time fierce and dull, they looked like volcanoes that had been drenched with water. The man passed on, the music grew softer and the waxen world pressed more closely round. Kings, cricketers, actresses, and statesmen beset him in vistas. He trod a maze of death that had not lived. There were very few school treats about, for the fashionable school treat season had not yet fully set in. So the man had the wax almost entirely to himself. He spread his wings to it like a bird to the air. By degrees, as he wandered—pursued by the distant music from the drenched volcanoes—a feeling of suffocation overtook him. All these men and women about him stared and smiled, but all were breathless. They wore their gaudy clothes with an air, no doubt. The Kings struck regal attitudes. The cricketers had a set manner of bringing off dreamy, difficult catches. The actresses were properly made up to charm, and the statesmen must surely have brought plenty of empires to ruin, if insipidity has power to cause such wreckage. But they were all decisively breathless. They seemed caught by some ghastly physical spell. And this spell was laid also upon the man who wandered among them. The breath of life withdrew from him to a long, long distance—he fancied. He felt as one who, taken by a trance, is bereft of power though not of knowledge. The staring silence was as the silence of a tomb, whose walls were full of eyes, intent and fatigued. He started when a person in uniform, hitherto apparently waxen, said in a cockney voice,

"See the Chamber of Horrors, sir?" But he recovered in time to acquiesce.

He descended towards a subterranean vault: as if to a lower circle of this inferno full of breathless demons. Here there were no rustic strangers, no clergymen with their choirs, no elderly ladies in command of "Bands of Hope." The silence was great, and the murderers stood together in companies, looking this way and that as if in search of victims. Some sat on chairs or stools. Some crouched in the dock. Some prepared for a mock expiation in their best clothes. One was at work in his house, digging in quicklime a hole the length of a human body. His waxen visage gleamed pale in the dim light, and he appeared to pause in his digging and to listen for sounds above his head. For he was in the cellar of his house.

The man stood still and looked at him. He had a mean face. All the features were squeezed and venomous, and expressive of criminal desires and of extreme cruelty. And so it was with most of his comrades. They varied in height, in age, in social status and in colouring. But upon all their faces was the same frigid expression, a sort of thin hatefulness touched with sarcasm. The man wandered on among them and saw it everywhere, on the lips of a youth in rags, in the eyes of an old woman in a bonnet, lurking in the wrinkles of a labourer, at rest upon the narrow brow of a doctor, alive in the puffed-out wax of an attorney's bloated features. Yes, it was easy to recognise the Devil's hallmark on them all, he thought. And he wondered a little how it came about that they had been able, in so many cases, to gain the confidence of their unhappy victims. Here, for instance, were the man and woman who had lured servant girls into the depths of a forest and there murdered them for the sake of their boxes. Even the silliest girl, one would have supposed, must have fled in terror from the ape-like cunning of those wicked faces. Here was the housekeeper who had made away with her aged mistress. Surely any one with the smallest power of observation would have refused to sit in the evening, to sleep at night, in company with so horrible a countenance. Here was the man who killed his paramour with a knife. How came he to have a paramour? The desire to kill lurked in his bony cheeks, his small, intent eyes, his narrow slit of a mouth, but no desire to love. God seemed to have set his warning to humanity upon each of these creatures of the Devil. Yet they had deceived mankind to mankind's undoing. They had won confidence, respect, even love.

The man was confused by this knowledge, as he moved among them in the dimness and the silence, brushing the sleeve of one, the skirt of another, looking into the curiously expressive eyes of all. But presently his wondering recognition of the world's fatuous and frantic gullibility ceased. For at the end of an alley of murderers he stood before a woman. She was young, pretty and distinguished in appearance. Her features were small and delicate. Her brow was noble. Her painted mouth was tender and saintly; and, though her eyes were sightless, truth and nobility surely gazed out of them. For a moment the man was seized by a conviction that a mistake had been made by the proprietors of the establishment, and that some being, famous for charitable deeds, or intellect, or heroic accomplishment had been put in penance among these tragic effigies. He glanced at her number, consulted his catalogue, and found that this woman was named Catherine Sirrett, and that she had been convicted of the murder of her husband by poison some few years before. Then he looked at her again and, before this criminal, he felt that she might, nay, must, have deceived any man, the most acute and enlightened observer. No one could have looked into that face and seen blackness in the heart of that woman. Everyone must have trusted her. Many must have loved her. Her appearance inspired more than confidence—reverence; there was something angelic in its purity. There was something religious in its quiet gravity. His heart grew heavy as he looked at her, heavy with a horror far more great than any that had overcome him as he examined the bestial company around. And when he came away, and long afterwards, Catherine Sirrett's face remained in his memory as the most horrible face in all that silent, watchful crowd of beings who had wrought violence upon the earth. For it was dressed in deceit. The other faces were naked. So he thought. He did not know Catherine Sirrett's story, though he remembered that a woman of her name had been hanged in England some years before, when he was in India, and that she had gained many sympathisers by her bearing and roused some newspaper discussion by her fate.

This is her story, the inner story which the world never knew.

Catherine Sirrett's mother was an intensely, even a morbidly, religious woman. Her father was an atheist and an æsthete. Yet her parents were fond of each other at first and made common cause in spoiling their only child. Sometimes the mother would whisper in the little girl's ear that she must pray for poor father who was blind to the true light and deaf to the beautiful voice. Sometimes the father would tell her that if she would worship she must worship genius, the poet, the painter, the musician; that if she would pray she must pray to Nature, the sea, the sunset and the springtime. But as a rule these two loving antagonists thought it was enough for their baby, their treasure, to develop quietly, steadily, in an atmosphere of adoration, in which arose no mist of theories, no war of words. Till she was ten years old Catherine was untroubled. At that age a parental contest began to rage—at first furtively—about her. With the years her mother's morbidity waxed, her father's restraint waned. The one became more intensely and frantically devout, the other more frankly pagan. And now, as the child grew, and her mind and heart stood up to meet life and girlhood, each of her parents began to feel towards her the desire of sole possession. She had been brought up a Christian. The father had permitted that. So long as she was an ignorant infant he had felt no anxiety to attach her to his theories. But when he saw the intelligence growing in her eyes, the dawn of her soul deepening, there stirred within him a strong desire that she should face existence as he faced it, free from trammels of superstition. The mother, with the quick intuition of woman, soon understood his unexpressed feeling and thrilled with religious fear.

Although—or indeed because—she loved her husband so much she was tortured by his lack of faith. And now she was alarmed at the thought of the effect his influence might have upon Catherine. She was roused to an intense activity of the soul. She said nothing to her husband of her fear and horror. He said nothing to her of his secret determination that his only child should grow up in his own faithless faith. But a silent and determined battle began to rage between them for the possession of Catherine's soul. And, at last, this battle turned the former love of the parents into a sort of uneasy hatred. The child did not fully comprehend what was going on around her, but she dimly felt it. And it influenced her whole nature.

Her mother, who was given over to religious forms, who was ritualistic and sentimental as well as really devout and fervent, at first gained the ascendancy over Catherine. Holy but narrow-minded, she compressed the girl's naturally expansive temperament, and taught her something of the hideous and brooding melancholy of the bigot and the fanatic. Then the father, quick-sighted, and roused to an almost angry activity by his appreciation of Catherine's danger, threw himself into the combat, and endeavoured to imbue the girl with his own comprehension of life's meaning, exaggerating all his theories in the endeavour to make them seem sufficiently vital and impressive. Catherine lived in the centre of this battle, which became continually more fierce, until she was eighteen. Then she fell in love with Mark Sirrett, married him, and left her parents alone with their mutual hostility, now complicated by a sort of paralysis of surprise and sense of mutual failure. They had forgotten that their child's future might hold a lover, a husband. Now they found themselves in the rather absurd position of enemies who have quarrelled over a shadow which suddenly vanishes away. They had lost their love for each other, they had lost Catherine. But her soul, though it was given to Mark Sirrett, had not lost their impress. Both the Puritanism of her mother and the paganism of her father were destined to play their parts in the guidance of her strange and terrible destiny.

Mark Sirrett, when he married Catherine, was twenty-five, dark, handsome, warmhearted and rich. It seemed that he had an exceptionally sweet and attractive nature. He had been an affectionate son, a kind brother in his home, a generous comrade at school and college. Everybody had a good word for him; his family, his tutors, his friends, his servants. Like most young and ardent men he had had some follies. At least they were never mean or ungenerous. He entered upon married life with an unusually good record. Those who knew him casually, even many who knew him well, considered that he was easily read, that he was transparently frank, that, though highly intelligent, he was not particularly subtle, and that no still waters ran deep in Mark Sirrett. All these people were utterly wrong. Mark had a very curious side to his nature, which remained almost unsuspected until after his marriage with Catherine, but which eventually was to make a name very well known to the world. He was, although apparently so open, in reality full of reserve. He was full of ambition. And he had an exceptionally peculiar, and exceptionally riotous, imagination. And this imagination he was quite determined to express in an art—the art of literature. But his reserve kept him inactive until he had left Oxford, when he went to live in London, where eventually he met Catherine.

His reserve, and his artistic hesitation to work until he felt able to do good work, held Mark's imagination in check as a dam holds water in check. He sometimes wrote, but nobody knew that he wrote except one friend, Frederic Berrand. And Berrand could be a silent man. Even to Catherine, when he fell in love with her and wooed her, Mark did not reveal his desire for fame, or his intention to win it. The girl loved her lover for what he was, but not for all he was. Of the still water that ran deep she as yet knew nothing. She thought her husband, who was rich, who appeared gay, who had lived so far, as it seemed, idly enough, would continue to live with her, as he had apparently lived without her, brightly, honestly, a little thoughtlessly, a little vainly.

She had no sort of suspicion that she had married that very curious phenomenon—a born artist. Had her mother suspected it she would have been shocked. Had her father dreamed it he would have been delighted. And Catherine herself? Well, she was still a child at this time.

She and Mark went to Spain for their honeymoon, and lived in a tiny white villa at Granada. It stood on the edge of the hill whose crown is the exquisite and dreamlike Alhambra. Its long and narrow garden ran along the hillside, a slope of roses and of orange flowers, of thick, hot grass and of tangled green shrubs. The garden wall was white and uneven, and almost hidden by wild, pink flowers. Beneath was spread the plain in which lies the City, bounded by the mountains over which, each evening, the sun sets. And every day the drowsy air hummed in answer to the huge and drowsy voice of the wonderful Cathedral bell, which struck the hours and filled this lovely world with almost terrible vibrations of romance. In the thick woods that steal to the feet of the ethereal Palace the murmur of the streams was ever heard, and the white snows of the Sierra Nevada stared over the yellow and russet plain, and were touched with a blue blush as the night came on.

Catherine, although she loved her parents and had never fully realised the enmity grown up between them, felt a strange happiness, that was more than the happiness of newborn passion, in her emancipation. She was by nature exquisitely sensitive, and she had often been vaguely troubled by the contest between her parents. Their fighting instincts had sometimes set her face to face with a sort of shadowed valley, in whose blackness she faintly heard the far-off clash of weapons. Now she was caught away from this subtle tumult, and as she looked into her husband's vivacious dark eyes she felt that a little weight which had lain long on her heart was lifted from it. She had thought herself happy before, now she knew herself utterly happy. Life seemed to have no dark background. Even love itself was not spoiled by a too great wonder of seriousness. They loved in sunshine and were gay—like grasshoppers in the grass that the sun has filled with a still rapture of warmth. Not till two days before their departure for England was this chirping, grasshopper mood disturbed or dispelled.

At one end of the long and narrow garden there was a little crude pavilion, open to the air on three sides. The domed roof was supported on painted wooden pillars up which red and white roses audaciously climbed. Rugs covered the floor. A wooden railing ran along the front facing the steep hillside. The furniture was simple and homely, a few low basket chairs and an oval table. In this pavilion the newly married pair took tea nearly every afternoon after their expeditions in the neighbourhood, or their strolls through the sunny Moorish Courts. After tea they sat on and watched the sunset, and fancied they could see the birds that flew away above the City towards the distant mountains drop down to their nests in Seville ere the darkness came. This last evening but one was intensely hot; the town at their feet seemed drowning in a dust of gold. Cries, softened and made utterly musical, rose up to them from this golden world, beyond which the sky reddened as the sun sank lower. Sometimes they heard the jingling bells of mules and horses in the hidden streets; they saw the pigeons circling above the house-tops, and doll-like figures moving whimsically in gardens that seemed as small as pocket-handkerchiefs. Thin laughter of playing children stole to them. And then the huge and veiled voice of the Cathedral bell tolled the hour, like Time become articulate.

A voice may have an immense influence over a sensitive nature. This bell of the Cathedral of Granada has one of the most marvellous voices in the world, deep with a depth of old and vanished ages, heavy with the burden of all the long-dead years, and this evening it seemed suddenly to strike away a veil from Catherine's husband. She was leaning her arms on the painted railing and searching the toy city with her happy eyes. Mark, standing behind her, was solicitously winding a shawl round her to protect her from the chill that falls from the Sierra Nevada with the dropping downward of the sun. As the bell tolled, Catherine felt that Mark's hands slipped from her shoulders. She glanced round and up at him. He was standing rigid. His eyes were widely opened. His lips were parted. All the gaiety that usually danced in his face had disappeared. He looked like an entranced man.

"Mark!" Catherine exclaimed. "Mark! why, how strange you look!"

"Do I?" he said, staring out over the wide plain below.

The voice of the bell died reluctantly on the air, but some huge and vague echo of its heavy romance seemed to sway, like a wave, across the little houses to the sunset and faint towards Seville.

"Yes, you look sad and stern. I have never seen your face like this—till now."

He made no answer.

"Are you sad because we are going so soon?" she asked. "But then why should we go? We are perfectly happy here. There is nothing to call us away."

"Kitty, does not that bell give you the lie?" he answered.

"The bell of the Cathedral?" she asked, wondering.

"Yes. Just now when I listened to it, I seemed to hear it whispering of the mysterious things of life, of the hidden currents in the great river, of the sorrows, of the terrors, of the crimes."

"Mark!" said Catherine in amazement.

"Nothing to call us away from our idle happiness here!" he continued. "Do you say—nothing?"

"Why—no. For we are free; we have no ties. You have no profession, Mark. You have no art even to call you back to England. Dear father—how he worships the arts!"

"And you, Kitty—you?"

Mark spoke with a curious pressure of excitement.

"He has taught me to love them too."

"How much, Kitty? As he loves them, more than anything else on earth?"

She had never heard him speak at all like this. She answered:

"Ah no. For my mother—"

She paused.

"My mother has made me understand that there is something greater than any art, more important, more beautiful."

"What can that be?"

"Oh, Mark—religion!"

He leaned over the railing at her side, and the white and red roses that embraced the pillar shook against his thick dark hair in the infant breeze of evening.

"But there are many religions," he said. "A man's art may be his religion."

A troubled look came into her eyes and made them like her mother's.

"Oh no, Mark."

"Yes, Kitty," he said, with growing earnestness, putting aside his reserve for the first time with her. "Indeed it may."

"You mean when he uses it to do good?"

He shook his head. The roses shivered.

"The true artist never thinks of that. To have a definite moral purpose is destructive."

The City at their feet was sinking into shadow now, and the air grew cold, filled with the snowy breath of the Sierra.

"When we go back to England I will teach you the right way to follow an art, to worship it; the way that will be mine."

"Yours, Mark? But I don't understand."

"No," he said. "You don't understand all of me yet, Kitty. Do you want to?"

"Yes," she said.

There was a sound of fear in her voice. Mark sat down beside her and put his arm round her.

"Kitty," he began. "I'm only on the threshold of my life, of my real life, my life with you and with my work."

"You are going to work?" she exclaimed.

"Yes. That bell just now seemed to strike the hour of commencement— to tell me it was time for me to begin. I should like, some day—far in the future, Kitty—to hear it strike that other hour, the hour when I must finish, when the little bit of work that I can do in the world is done. I shan't be afraid of that hour any more than I'm afraid of this one. Perhaps, when you and I are old we shall come here again, and listen to that bell once more, the same, when we are changed."

He pointed towards the Cathedral which was still touched by the sun. Catherine leaned against his shoulder. She said nothing, and did not move.

"Everything in life has its appointed recorder," he continued. "They are a big band, the band of the recorders who strive accurately to write down life as it is. Well, Kitty, I am going to be one of that band."

"You are going to be a writer, Mark?"

"Yes."

"Then, you will record the beauty, the joy, the purity, the goodness of life?"

His usually bright face had become sombre and thoughtful. It looked strangely dark and saturnine in the twilight.

"I shall record what I see most clearly."

"And what is that?"

"Not the things on the surface, but the things beneath the surface, of life."

And then he told Catherine more fully of his ambition and gave her a glimpse of the hidden side of his duplex nature.

She gazed up at him in the gathering twilight and it seemed to her that she was looking at a stranger. The climbing roses still shook against Mark in the wind. While he talked his voice grew almost fierce, and his dark eyes shone like the eyes of a fanatic. When he ceased to speak, Catherine's lips were pursed together, like her mother's when she listened to the pagan rhapsodies of Mr. Ardagh.

Two days later the Sirretts left Granada for England.

On their return they paid a short visit to Catherine's parents, who were living in Eaton Square. Mr. and Mrs. Ardagh received them with a sort of dulled and narcotic affection. In truth, for different reasons, the Puritan and the pagan cherished a certain resentment against the man who had stepped in and robbed them of their cause of warfare. Nevertheless they desired his company in their house. For each was anxious to study him and to discover what influence he was likely to have upon Catherine. During her daughter's absence Mrs. Ardagh had found the emptiness of her childless life insupportable, and she had, therefore, engaged a young girl, called Jenny Levita, to come to her every day as companion. Jenny was intelligent and very poor, bookish and earnest, even ardent in nature. Mrs. Ardagh gained a certain amount of interest and pleasure from forming the pliant mind of her protégée, who was with her always from eleven till six in the evening, who read aloud to her, accompanied her on her charitable missions, and took—so far as a stranger might—the place of Catherine in her life. Catherine met Jenny upon the doorstep of her parents' house on the evening of her arrival, and hastened to ask her mother who the slim girl, with the tall figure, narrow shoulders, fluffy brown hair, and large oriental eyes was.

"My paid daughter," said Mrs. Ardagh, almost bitterly. "But she can't fill the place of my lost Catherine."

Nevertheless, Catherine discovered that her mother was truly attached to Jenny.

"I took her partly because she is easily led," she said, "easily influenced and so very pretty and poor. I want to save her for God, and when I met her there was one who wished to lead her to the devil. She won't see him now. She won't hear his name."

Then she dropped the subject.

Catherine was alternately questioned by her father and by her mother as to the influence of Mark. But something within her prevented her from telling them of the conversation in the Pavilion, when the cries of the toy city died down into the night. Mrs. Ardagh, now sinking in the confusion of a rather dreary middle age, complicated by a natural melancholy, and by incessant confession to a ritualistic clergyman seductive in receptivity, was relieved to think that Mark was harmless.

Art for Art's sake—the motto of her husband—had apparently little meaning for Mark. As Mrs. Ardagh thought it the devil's motto she was glad of this and said so to Catherine. Mr. Ardagh, on the other hand, was vexed to find Mark apparently so frivolous; and he also expressed his feelings to Catherine, who became slightly confused.

"I should like to see your husband doing something," he said. "You have much of me in you, Kit, despite your poor dear mother's extravagant attempts to limit your reading to Frances Ridley Havergal. Why didn't you marry an artist, eh? A painter or an author, somebody who can give us more beauty than we have already, or more truth? You're too good for Frances Ridley Havergal. Leave her to your mother and that girl, Jenny, who is like wax in your mother's hands and the hands of the Reverend Father Grimshaw. Piff!"

Catherine said nothing, but she sought an opportunity of seeing something of Jenny. She found it, just before the day on which she and Mark were to leave London for their country house. Jenny had come as usual one morning, to read aloud to Mrs. Ardagh. They were just then deep in the "Memoirs" of a certain pious divine, whose chief claim upon the attention and gratitude of posterity seemed to be that, during a very long career, he had "confessed" more Anglican notabilities than any of his rivals, and had used up, in his church, an amount of incense that would have put a Roman Catholic priest to shame. On the morning in question the reading was interrupted. Mrs. Ardagh was called away to consult with a lay-worker in the slums upon some scheme for reclaiming the submerged masses, and Catherine, running in to her mother's boudoir after a walk with Mark, found the tall, narrow-shouldered girl with the oriental eyes sitting alone with the apostolic memoirs lying open upon her knees. Catherine was not sorry. She took off her fur coat and sat down.

"What are you and my mother reading, Miss Levita?" she asked.

Jenny told her.

"Is it interesting?"

"I suppose it ought to be," Jenny answered, thoughtlessly.

Then a flush ran over her thin cheeks, on which there were a great many little freckles.

"I mean that it is very interesting," she added. "Your mother will tell you so, Mrs. Sirrett."

"Perhaps. But I was asking your opinion."

It struck Catherine that Jenny had her opinion and was scarcely as compliant as Mr. Ardagh evidently supposed her to be. At Catherine's last remark Jenny glanced up. The two girls looked into each other's eyes, and, in Jenny's, Catherine thought she saw a flickering defiance.

"I was asking your opinion," she repeated.

"Well, Mrs. Sirrett," Jenny said, more hardily, "I don't know why it is. I admire and love goodness, yes, as your mother—who's a saint, I think—does. But I'll tell you frankly that I think it's often very dull to read about. Don't you think so?"

She blushed again, and let the heavy white lids droop over her eyes, which had glittered almost like the eyes of a fever patient while she was speaking.

"Only when dull people write about it, surely," said Catherine.

"I don't know," Jenny said, twisting her black stuff dress with nervous fingers. "I often think that in the books of the cleverest authors there are dull moments, and that those dull moments are nearly always when the good, the really excellent, characters are being written about."

"And in real life, Miss Levita?" asked Catherine. "Do you find the good people duller, less interesting, than the bad ones in real life?"

"I haven't known many very bad ones, Mrs. Sirrett."

"Well—but those you have known!"

Jenny hesitated. She was obviously embarrassed. She even shifted, like an awkward child, in her chair. But there was something of obstinate honesty in her that would have its way.

"If you must know—I mean, if you care to know, please," she said at length, "the most interesting person I ever met was—yes, I suppose he was a wicked man."

Her curious, sharp-featured, yet attractive, face was hot all over as she finished. Catherine divined at once that she was speaking of the person who, according to Mrs. Ardagh, had wished "to lead her to the devil." At this moment, while the two girls were silent, Mrs. Ardagh returned to the room. As Catherine left it she heard the soft and high voice of Jenny taking up once more the parable of the highly-honoured divine.

Catherine was not altogether sorry when she and her husband left Eaton Square for the house in Surrey which Mark had rented for the summer months.

In this house the young couple were to face for the first time the reality of married life. Hitherto they had only faced its romance.

The house was beautiful in an old-fashioned way. Its rooms were low and rather dark. A wood stood round it. The garden was a wild clearing, fringed with enormous clumps of rhododendron. Wood doves cooed in the trees like invisible lovers unable to cease from gushing. Under the trees ferns grew in masses. Squirrels swarmed, and in the huge rhododendron flowers the bees lost themselves in an ecstasy of sipping sensuality. It was a fine summer, and this house was made to be a summer house. In winter it must have been but a dreary hermitage.

The servants greeted them respectfully. The horses neighed in the stables. The dogs barked, and leaped up in welcome, then, when they were noticed and patted, depressed their backs in joyous humility, and, lifting their flexible lips, grinned amorously, glancing sideways from the hands that they desired. It was an eminently unvulgar, and ought to have been a very sweet, homecoming.

But was it sweet to Catherine?

She asked herself that question, and the fact that she did so proved that it was not wholly sweet. Already the future oppressed her. In this house, which seemed full of the smell of the country, of the very odour of peace, she felt that the stranger, the second Mark—scarcely known to her as yet—was to be born, was to gain strength and grow. She feared him. She watched for him. But, for the first few days, he did not show himself. The grasshoppers chirped and revelled in the grass. Mark and Catherine sat in the wood, wandered on the hills, rode in the valleys, cooed a little even, like the doves hidden in the green shadows of the glades, and making ceaseless music. The lovers—for they were still lovers at this time—made a gay dreamland for themselves. But dreams cannot and ought not to last. If they did they would become painfully enervating. One day, in the wood, Mark resumed the conversation of the Pavilion.

"Because I am rich I must not be idle, Kitty," he said.

And into his dark eyes there crept that look of the stranger man.

"Thank God that I am rich," he added.

"Why, Mark dear?"

"Because I can dare to do what sort of work I choose," he answered. "The pot boils without my labour. So I am independent of the public, whom I will win in my own way. If I have to wait it will not matter."

And then, speaking with growing enthusiasm, he gave Kitty a sketch of a book he had projected. The doves cooed all through the plot, which was a sad and terrible one, very uncommon and very unlike Mark. Catherine listened to it with, alternately, the mind of her father and the mind of her mother. It was the old antagonism of the Puritan and the pagan. But now it raged in one person instead of in two, as the girl sat under the soft darkness of the trees, listening to the eager voice of her boy husband, who was beginning at last to cast the skin of his reserve. The voice went on and on, interrupted only by the doves. But sometimes Catherine felt as if she leaned upon the painted railing of the Pavilion, and heard the distant cries of the golden City. At last Mark said, "Kitty, that is what I mean to do."

"It is terrible," she said.

And she pursed her lips like her mother.

"Yes," Mark answered, with enthusiasm. "It is terrible. It is ghastly."

Catherine looked at him with an intense and growing surprise. She was wondering how the conception of such horrors could take place in a man so gay as Mark.

At last she said, "Mark, you feel your own power, do you not?"

"Kitty," he replied quietly, almost modestly, yet with a firm gravity that was strong, "I do feel that I have something to say and that I shall be able to say it in my book. I have waited a long while. Now I believe that I am ready, that it is time for me to begin."

"Then, Mark, if you feel that you have this power, don't you feel a desire to conquer the greatest difficulties in your art, to show that you can succeed where others have failed?"

He looked at her curiously, realising that she had something to say to him, and that she was trying to prepare the way before it.

"Come, Kitty," he said. "Say what you wish to say. You have the right. What is it?"

Catherine told him of her conversation with Jenny.

"That little thin girl," he said. "So she thinks wickedness more interesting, more many-sided than virtue, more dramatic in its possibilities. Well, she and I are agreed. But what was it you wanted?"

"Mark, I want you to prove to her—to everyone—that it is not so."

"How?"

"By writing a different kind of book—a noble book. You can do it. Where others have failed, you can succeed."

He laughed at her, gaily.

"Perhaps, someday, I'll try," he said. "But I can only write at present what I have conceived. Till this book is done, I can think of nothing else. I see you are interested, Kitty. I must tell you all I am intending to do."

He continued, until it was quite evening, expatiating on the force with which he intended to realise in literature the terrors that trooped in his imagination. And by the time he had finished and darkness stood under the trees, Catherine was carried away by the pagan spirit. She thought no more of the possible harm the projected book might work in sensitive natures. She thought only of its power, which she acclaimed.

Mark kissed her with a solemnity of passion he had never shown before, and they went back to the house.

It was an immense relief to Mark to open his book of revelation and to allow Catherine to read these pages in it. But he could not be continuously unreserved to any human being. And that evening he subsided into his former light-hearted gaiety, and shrouded the stranger man in an impenetrable veil. Catherine sat with him in wonderment, while the moon came up behind the trees and shone over the clearing before the house. She did not yet understand the inflexible secrecies of genius. A nightingale sang. Its voice was so sweet that Catherine felt as if the whole world were full of tenderness and of sympathy. She said so to Mark, just as she was turning from him to go to bed.

"Ah, Kitty," he said, "there are other things in the world besides tenderness and sympathy, thank Heaven. There are terrors, there are crimes, there are strange and fearful things both within us and outside of us."

"How sad that is, Mark!" said Catherine.

He smiled at her gaily—cruelly, she thought a moment afterwards when she was alone in her bedroom.

"Sad?" he said. "I don't think so, for I love drama. Life is dramatic. If it were not it would be intolerable."

And still the nightingale sang. But he did not hear it. Catherine heard it till she fell asleep.

Now Mark began to write with assiduity. Catherine busied herself with her household duties, with the garden and with charities in the neighbouring Parish. Her mother's rather hysterical beliefs lost their hysteria in her, at this period, and were softened and rendered large hearted. Catherine's sympathy with the world was indeed a living thing, not simply a fine idea. While Mark was shut up every morning with his writing she visited the poor, sat by the sick, and played with the village children. The Parish—this came out forcibly at her trial—grew to love her. She was the prettiest Lady Bountiful. The impress made upon her by her mother was visible in all this. For Mrs. Ardagh, rigid, melancholy as she was sometimes, was genuinely charitable, genuinely dutiful. If she adored the forms of religion she loved also its essence—the doing of good. In these many mornings Catherine was like her mother—improved. But in the evenings she no longer resembled Mrs. Ardagh, but rather, in a degree, echoed her father, and responded to his vehement, if furtive, teachings. For in the evenings Mark read to her what he had written during the day and discussed it with her in all its bearings. He recognised the clear quickness of Catherine's intellect. Yet she very soon noticed that he was exceedingly inflexible with regard to his work. He liked to discuss, he did not like to alter, it.

One night, when he had finished the last completed chapter, he laid down the manuscript and said,

"Well, Kitty?"

Catherine was lying on a couch near the open French window. She did not speak until Mark repeated, "Well?"

Then she said, "I think that far the finest chapter of your book—"

Mark smiled triumphantly.

"But it seems to me terribly immoral," she finished.

"Oh, that's all right, dear. So long as it is properly worked out, inevitable."

"It teaches—"

"Nothing, Kitty—nothing. It merely describes what is."

"But surely it may do harm."

"Not if it is truly artistic. And you think—"

"It that? Yes, I do. But, Mark, art is not all."

"Your father would say so."

"My father—yes."

"And he is right. I neither inculcate nor do I condemn. I only produce, or try to produce, a work of art. You admire the chapter? You think it truly dramatic?"

"Indeed I do—that's just why I am afraid of it."

"Little timorous bird."

He came over to the sofa and kissed her tenderly. She shivered. She thought his lips had never been dry and cold like that before.

The book was finished by the end of the summer. It was published in November and created a considerable sensation. Mark issued it under the name of "William Foster." Only Catherine and his friend Frederic Berrand knew who William Foster really was. The newspapers praised the workmanship of the book almost universally. But many of them severely condemned it as dangerous, morbidly imaginative, horrible in subject, and likely to do great mischief because of its undoubted power and charm. It was forbidden at some libraries.

Mark was delighted with its reception. Now, that he had brought forth his child, he seemed more light-hearted, gay and boyish than ever. His too vivid imagination had been toiling. It rested now. Catherine and he came up to town for the winter. They meant to spend only their summers in Surrey. They took a house in Chester Street, and often dined with the Ardaghs in Eaton Square. At one of these dinners Jenny Levita was present. Mark, remembering what Catherine had told him about her in Surrey, looked at her with some interest, and talked to her a little in his most lighthearted way. She replied briefly and without much apparent animation, seeming indeed rather absent-minded and distraite.

Presently Mr. Ardagh said, "This new man, William Foster, is that very rare thing in England—a pitiless artist. He has the audacity of genius and the fine impersonality."

Catherine started and flushed violently. As she did so she saw Jenny's long dark eyes fixed earnestly upon her. Mark smiled slightly. Mrs. Ardagh looked pained.

"His book is doing frightful harm, I am sure," she said.

"Nonsense, my dear," said her husband. "Nothing so absolutely right, so absolutely artistic, can do harm."

An obstinate expression came into Mrs. Ardagh's face, but she said nothing. Catherine looked down at her plate. She felt as if small needles were pricking her all over.

"Have you read the book?" said Mr. Ardagh to his wife.

"Yes," she replied. "It was recommended to me, I began it not knowing what sort of book it was."

"And did you finish it?" asked her husband, with rather a satirical smile.

"Yes. I confess I could not leave off reading it. That is why it is so dangerous. It is both powerful and evil."

Then the subject dropped. Mark was still smiling quietly, but Catherine's face was grave. When she and her mother and Jenny went up into the drawing room, leaving the men to their cigarettes, Catherine recurred to the subject of "William Foster's" book.

"Do you really think that a novel can do serious harm, mother?" she began. "After all, it is only a work of the imagination. Surely people read it and forget it, as they would not forget an actual fact."

Mrs. Ardagh sighed wearily. She was a pale woman with feverish eyes. The expression in them grew almost fierce as she answered,

"It is the black imagination of this William Foster that will come like a suffocating cloud upon the imaginations of others, especially of—" She suddenly broke off. Catherine, wondering why, glanced up at her mother and saw that she was looking towards the far end of the big drawing room. Jenny was sitting there, under a shaded lamp. She had some work in her hands but her hands were still. Her head was turned away, but her attitude, the curve of her soft, long, white throat, the absolute immobility of her thin body betrayed the fact that she was listening attentively.

"I would not let that child read William Foster's book for the world," Mrs. Ardagh whispered to Catherine.

Then she changed the subject, and spoke of some charity that she was interested in at the East End of London. Jenny's hands instantly began to move about her embroidery.

That night Catherine spoke to Mark of what her mother had said.

He only laughed.

"I cannot write for any one person, Kitty," he said, "or if I do it must be—"

"For whom?" she asked quickly.

"Myself," he replied.

Catherine slept very badly that night. She was thinking of William Foster and of Mark. They seemed to her two different men. And she had married—which?

Mark did no work in London. He knew too many people, he said, and besides, he wanted to rest. Catherine and he went out a great deal into society. At Christmas they ran over to Paris and spent three weeks there. During this holiday William Foster, it almost seemed, had ceased to exist. Mark Sirrett was light-hearted, gay, and the kindest, most thoughtful husband in the world. When they came back to London, Catherine went at once to see her mother. Mr. Ardagh had gone to the Riviera and Catherine found Mrs. Ardagh quite alone in the big house in Eaton Square.

"Why, where is Jenny Levita?" she asked.

Mrs. Ardagh made no reply for a moment. Her face, which was rather straw-colour than white, worked grotesquely as if under the influence of some strong emotion that she was trying to suppress. At length she said, in a chill, husky voice,

"Jenny has left me."

"Left you—why?"

"She was taken away from me. She was taken back to the sin from which I hoped I had rescued her."

"Oh, mother! By whom?"

Mrs. Ardagh put her handkerchief to her eyes.

"William Foster," she answered.

Catherine felt cold and numb.

"William Foster—I don't understand," she said slowly.

Mrs. Ardagh rolled and unrolled her handkerchief with trembling fingers.

"She got hold of that book—that black, wicked book," she said, and there was a sort of fury in her voice. "It upset her faith. It tarnished her moral sense. It reminded her of the—the man from whose influence I had drawn her. All her imagination was set in a flame by that hateful chapter."

"Which one?" Catherine asked.

Mrs. Ardagh mentioned the chapter which Catherine had most hated, most admired, and most feared.

"I fought with William Foster for Jenny's soul," she said, passionately. "But I am not clever. I have no power. I am getting old and tired. She cried. She said she loved me, but that goodness was not for her, that she must go, that life was calling her, that she must live—live! William

Foster had shown her death and she thought it life. I always knew that in Jenny good and evil were fighting, that her fate was trembling in the balance. That book turned the scale."

She sobbed heavily, then with a catch of her breath, she added, "William Foster is a very wicked man."

Catherine flushed all over her face. But she said nothing. That night she told Mark of Jenny's fate. She expected him to be grieved. But he was not.

"An author who respects his art cannot consider every hysterical girl while he is writing," he said. "And, besides, it is only your mother's idea that she was influenced by my book. Long ago she showed you the bent of her mind."

"But, Mark, don't you remember how that chapter struck me when you first read it to me?"

"I remember that you thought it the finest chapter in the book, and you were right, Kitty. You've got artistic discernment, like your father. Berrand and you would get on together. Directly he comes back I'll introduce you to each other."

Catherine said no more. From that time she devoted herself more than ever to her mother, who now, under the influence of sorrow, allowed her nature to come to its full flower. Abandoning the pleasures of society, which had long wearied her, she gave herself up to services, charities and good works in the poor parts of London. She carried Catherine with her on many of her expeditions, and there can be no doubt that her fervour and curious exaltation had a marked effect upon the girl. Catherine had always been highly susceptible to influence, but she had been during most of her life attacked perpetually by two absolutely opposite influences. Now one of these, her father's, was removed from her. She came more than ever before under her mother's domination. For Mark, when he was not "William Foster," was simply a high-spirited and happy youth, full of energy and of apparently normal desires and intentions. He had that sort of genius which can be long asleep in the dark, while its possessor dances, like a mote, in sunshine.

In the spring the Sirretts made ready to leave London. As the day drew near for their departure Mark's manner changed, and he displayed symptoms of restlessness and of impatience. Catherine noticed them and asked their reason.

"I am longing to return to 'William Foster,' Kitty," he said.

She felt a sharp pain at her heart, but she only smiled and replied,

"I almost thought you had forgotten him."

"On the contrary, I have been preparing to meet him again all these months."

His dark eyes shone as he spoke. And once again that stranger stood before Catherine. She turned and went upstairs, saying that she must see to her packing. But when she was alone in her bedroom she shed some tears. That afternoon she went to Eaton Square to bid her mother goodbye. Mrs. Ardagh was looking unhappy.

"Your father returns from Italy on Wednesday," she said. "You'll just miss him."

"I am so sorry, mother," Catherine said.

Mrs. Ardagh looked at her in silence for a moment. Then she said in a low voice,

"I am not."

"Mother—but why?"

"I think you are better away from him. My heart tells me so. Oh, Kitty, I thank God every day of my life that Mark is—is such a good fellow, without those terrible ideas and theories of your poor father. You cannot think what I suffer."

It was the first time she had ever spoken so plainly on the subject, and even now she quickly changed to another topic. Mark had never introduced poor Mrs. Ardagh to "William Foster." And Catherine would not add another burden to those she already had to bear.

Surrey was looking very lovely in the spring weather. The trees were just beginning to let out the tips of their green secrets. The ground was dashed with blue and with yellow, where bloomed those flowers that are the sweetest of the year because they come the first, and whisper wonderful promises in the ears of all who love them. There had been some rain and the grass of lawns and hillsides was exquisite in the startling freshness of its vivid colour. Nature seemed uneasy with delight, like a child on a birthday morning. The tender beauty of everything around her reassured Catherine, who had come from town in a mood of strange apprehension. As she looked at the expectant woods awaiting their lovely costume in fragile nudity, at the violets that seemed to sing in odours, at that pale and shallow sky which is a herald of the deeper skies to come, it seemed to her impossible that Mark, who could be so blithe, so radiant, could turn to dark imaginings in such an atmosphere of exquisite enterprise. She was filled with hope and with a species of religious optimism. Some days passed, Catherine and Mark spent them in a renewal of friendship with their domain. They were like two children and were gayer than the spring. Then one evening Mark said, "And now, Kitty, I am going to start work again. Berrand has written that he will be in England next week and will come on here at once. But he won't disturb me. And my scheme is ready."

Catherine felt the breath fluttering in her throat as she murmured, "Your scheme is ready?"

"Yes. It's a great one. Berrand thinks so. I have written something of it to him. I am going to trace the downfall of a nature from nobility to utter degradation."

His eyes sparkled with enthusiasm, as he repeated in thrilling tones, "Utter degradation."

Catherine thought of the spring night, in which such holy preparations for joy were silently being carried on, of all the youthful things just coming into life. An inspiration came to her. She caught her husband's hand and drew him to the window.

"Pull up the blind, Mark," she said.

He obeyed, smiling at her as if in wonder at this freak.

"Now open the window."

"Yes, dear. There! What next?"

In front of the window there was a riband of pavement protected by an overhanging section of roof. Catherine stepped out on this pavement. Mark followed her. They stood together facing the spring night. There was no moon, but the sky was clear and starlit. Nature seemed breathing quietly, like a thing alive but asleep. The surrounding woods were a dusky wall. The clearing was a vague sea of dew. And the air was full of that wonderful scent that all things seem to have in spring. It is like the perfume of life, of life that God has consecrated, of life that might have been in Eden. It is odorous with hope. It stings and embraces. It stirs the imagination to magic. It stirs the heart to tears. For it is ineffably beautiful and expectant.

"How delicious!" Mark said.

Catherine's hand tightened on his arm.

"The trees are talking," he said. "That damp scent comes from their roots, and the flowers and grasses round them."

He drew in his breath with a gasp of pleasure.

"Yes?" Catherine said.

He bent down and touched the lawn with his hand.

"What a dew! Look, Kitty, there goes a rabbit!"

A hunched shadow suddenly flattened and vanished.

"Little beggar! He's gone into the wood. What a jolly time he and his relations must have."

"Yes, Mark. Isn't the night happy, and the spring?"

He drew in his breath again.

"Yes."

"Mark!"

"Well, dear?"

"Mark—don't write this book."

Mark started slightly with surprise.

"Kitty! what are you saying?"

"Write a happy book."

"My dear babe—how uninteresting!"

"Write a good book, a book to make people better and happier."

"A book with a purpose! No, Kitty."

"Well then, a spring book. This night isn't a night with a purpose, because it's lovely."

He laughed quite gaily.

"Humorist! Why did you bring me out into it?"

"To influence you against that book."

He was silent.

"Are you angry, Mark?"

"No, dear."

"Will you do what I ask?"

"No, Kitty."

He spoke very quietly and gently, then changed the subject, talked of the coming summer, the garden, prospective pleasures. But he talked no more of his work. Next day he shut himself up in his study, and thenceforward his life became a repetition of his life during the previous summer. A fortnight later Frederic Berrand arrived.

Catherine had long felt an eager desire to see this one intimate friend of Mark's. She expected him to be no ordinary man, and she was not mistaken. Berrand was much older than Mark. He looked about forty. He was thin, sallow, eager in manner, with shining eyes—almost toad-like—a yellowish-white complexion, and coal-black hair. His vivacity was un-English, yet at the back of his nature there lay surely a stagnant reservoir of melancholy. He was a pessimist, full of ardour. He revelled, intellectually, in the sorrows and in the evils that afflict the world.

It was easy to see that he had a great influence over Mark. And it was easy to see also that the dismal genius of "William Foster" appealed to all the peculiarities of his nature with intense force. He was at once on friendly terms with Catherine, to whom he spoke openly of his admiration of her husband.

"Mrs. Sirrett," he said one evening, when Mark was working—he had taken to working at night now as well as in the morning—"your husband will do great things. He will found a school. The young men will be captivated by his sombre genius, and we shall have less of the thoughtless rubbish that the journalist loves and calls sane, healthy, and all the rest of it."

"But surely sanity and health—"

"My dear Mrs. Sirrett, we want originality and imagination."

"Yes, indeed. But can't they be sane and healthy?"

"Was Gautier healthy when he wrote of the Priest and of the Vampire? This book Mark is writing will be awful in its intensity. It will make the world turn cold. It is terrible. People will shudder at it."

He walked about the room enthusiastically.

"And its terror is the true terror—mental. How the papers will hate it, and how everyone will read it!"

"May it—may it not do a great deal of harm?" said Catherine, slowly.

"What if it does? Nothing can prevent it from being a great book."

And he broke out into a dissertation on art that would have delighted Mr. Ardagh.

Catherine listened to him in silence, but when he had finished she said, "But you are one-sided, Mr. Berrand."

"I!" he cried. "How so?"

"You see only the horrible in life, even in love. You care only for the horrible in art."

"The truth is more often horrible than not," he answered. "We dress it in pink paper as we dress a burning lamp. We fear its light will hurt our weak eyes. Almost all the pretty theories of future states, happy hunting grounds, and so forth, almost all the fallacies of life to which we are inclined to cling, are only pink paper shades which we make to save ourselves from blinking at the light."

"You call it light?" she said.

And she felt a profound pity for him. There was no need of that. Berrand was one of those strange men who are happy in the contemplation of misery.

While Berrand was staying with the Sirretts, Mrs. Ardagh came to them on a visit. She was now in very poor health, and her mind was greatly set, in consequence, on that other world of which the healthy scarcely think, unless they wake at night or lose a near relation unexpectedly. Mr. Berrand immediately horrified her. Of course he did not speak of "William Foster." "William Foster's" existence in the house was a secret. But he freely aired his sentiments on all other subjects, and each sentiment went like a sword through Mrs. Ardagh's soul.

"How can Mark make a friend of such a man," she said to Catherine. "Like your father, he has no religious belief. He worships art instead of God. He loves, he positively loves, the evil of the world. Such men are a curse. They go to people hell."

Her feverish eyes glowed with fanaticism.

"Oh, mother!" said Catherine, thinking of "William Foster."

"They do not care to do good, they do not fear to do harm," continued Mrs. Ardagh. "Why are they not cut off?"

She made her daughter kneel down with her and pray against such men.

Then they went down to dinner, and dined with "William Foster."

Catherine felt like one in a fever. She knew that her mother had an exaggerated mind. Nevertheless, she was deeply moved by it, recognising that it exaggerated truth, not a lie.

At dinner Mrs. Ardagh, by some ill-chance, was led to mention "William Foster's" book. Mark raised gay eyebrows at Berrand and Catherine grew hot. For Mrs. Ardagh denounced the author as she had denounced him in London, but with more excitement.

"I trust," she said, "that he will never live to write another."

Catherine felt as if a knife were thrust into her breast, and even Mark started slightly and looked almost uneasy, as if he fancied that the force of Mrs. Ardagh's desire might accomplish its fulfilment. Only Berrand was undismayed. There was a devil of mischief in him. His eyes of a toad gleamed as he said, turning to Mrs. Ardagh, "I happen to know that 'William Foster' is writing another book at this very time."

Catherine bent her eyes on her plate. She was tingling with nervous excitement.

"Do you know him, then?" said Mrs. Ardagh, in her fervid, and yet dreary, voice.

"Slightly."

"Then tell him of the dreadful harm he has done."

"What harm?"

Mrs. Ardagh spoke of Jenny Levita. It seemed that she had now fallen into an evil way of life.

"But why should you attribute the folly of a weak girl to William Foster's influence?" said Berrand.

"Her soul was trembling in the balance," said Mrs. Ardagh, striking her thin hand excitedly on the table. "That book turned the scale. She went down. Tell him of her, Mr. Berrand, tell him of the ruin of that poor child. It may influence him."

"I'm afraid not," said Berrand, with a glance at Mark. "William Foster is an artist."

"It is terrible that he should be permitted to work such evil," said Mrs. Ardagh.

During that summer a vague and hollow darkness seemed to brood round the life of Catherine. It stood behind the glory of the golden days. She felt night even at noontide, and a damp mist floated mysteriously to her out of the very heart of the sun. Yet she had some happy, or at least some feverishly excited, moments, for Berrand was generally staying with them, and Catherine—abnormally sensitive as she always was to her undoing—came under his curious influence and caught some of his enthusiasm for the talent of "William Foster."

Once again Mark began to speak to her of his work, to read parts of it aloud to both his companions. And there were evenings when Catherine, carried away by the intellectual joy of the two men, exulted with them in the horrible fascination of the book and in the intensity of its dramatic force. But, when these moments were over, and she was gone, she brooded darkly over her mother's words. For she knew that the book was evil. Like a snake it carried poison with it, and, presently, it was going to carry that poison out from this house in the woods, out into the world. Ah! the poor world, on which a thousand things preyed, in which a thousand snakes set their poisoned fangs!

And then she wept. Mark and Berrand were eagerly talking of the snake, praising its lustrous skin, marvelling at its jewelled eyes, foretelling its lithe progress through Society. She heard the murmur of their voices until far into the night. And sometimes she thought that distant murmur sounded like the hum of evil, or like the furtive whisper of conspirators.

Berrand did not leave them until the new book was nearly finished. As he pressed Catherine's hand in farewell he said, "You will have a sensational autumn, Mrs. Sirrett."

"Sensational. Why?" she asked.

"London will ring with William Foster's name. My word how the Journalists will curse! They protect the morality of the nation you know—on paper."

He was gone. As the carriage drove away Catherine saw his beautiful, and yet rather dreadful, eyes gleaming with mischievous excitement. Suddenly she felt heavy-hearted. Those last words of his cleared away any mist of doubt that lingered about her own terror. She recognised fully for the first time the essential difference between Mark and Berrand. Mark was really possessed by the spirit of the artist, was driven by something strange and dominating within him to do what he did. Berrand was possessed by a spirit of mischievous devilry, by the poor and degrading desire to shock and startle the world at whatever cost. For the moment Catherine mentally saw Mark in a light of nobility; Berrand in a darkness of degradation.

Yet—this thought followed in a moment—Berrand was harmless to the world, while Mark—

"Kitty, come in here," called her husband's voice from the study. "I want to consult you about this last chapter."

In the Autumn "William Foster's" new book was issued by an "advanced" publisher, who loved to hear his wares called dangerous, and who walked on air when the reviewers said that such men as he were a curse to Society—as they occasionally did when there was nothing special to write about.

In the autumn also Mrs. Ardagh's illness grew worse and it appeared that she could not live much longer. Catherine was terribly grieved, and was for a time so much engaged with her mother that she scarcely heeded what was going on in the world around. Incessantly immured in the sickroom she did not trace the progress of the snake through Society until—as Berrand had foretold—the cries of the Journalists rose to Heaven like cries from a burning city. "William Foster" was held up to execration so universal that his book could hardly be printed in sufficient quantities to satisfy the demands of a public frantically eager to be harmed. In her sickroom Mrs. Ardagh, now not far from death, yet still religiously interested in the well-being of the world she was leaving, heard the echoes of the journalistic cries. Some friend, perhaps, conveyed them. For Catherine was silent on the matter, keeping a silence of fear and of shame. And these echoes stayed with the dying woman, as stay the voices in the hills.

One night, when Catherine came into her mother's room, Mrs. Ardagh was crying feebly. On the sheet of the bed lay a letter which she had crumpled in her pale hands and then tried, vainly, to fling away from her. Catherine leaned over the bed.

"What is it, mother?" she said. "You are not in pain?"

Mrs. Ardagh shifted in the bed. There was a suggestion of almost intolerable uneasiness in the movement.

"I am in pain, horrible pain," she answered. "No—no," as Catherine was about to ring for the nurse, "not in the body—not that."

Catherine sat down by the bed and clasped her mother's hot hand.

"What is it?" she whispered.

Mrs. Ardagh was silent for a moment. She blinked her heavy eyelids to stop the tears from falling on her wasted cheeks. At length she said,

"William Foster has done more evil."

Catherine did not speak. Her heart beat irregularly, and then seemed to stop, and then beat with unnatural force again.

"Catherine," her mother continued, "Jenny is utterly lost."

"No, mother, no!" Catherine said. "I will go to her. Let me go. I will rescue her. I will make her see—"

"Hush—you can't. She is dead and she died in shame."

She paused. Catherine did not speak.

"And now," Mrs. Ardagh continued feebly, "that man is spreading the net for others. Do you know, Catherine, I often pray for him?"

"Do you, mother?"

"Yes. He has great powers. I never let your father know it, but that first book of his made an impression upon me that has never faded. That's why I think of him even now—that and the fate of poor Jenny."

She lifted herself up a little in the bed.

"His last book, I am told, is much more terrible, much more deadly than the first."

"Is it?"

"You haven't read it?"

Catherine hesitated a moment, then she said, "I know something about it."

Mrs. Ardagh lay still for a while, as if thinking. Presently she said, "Catherine, such an odd, foolish idea keeps coming to me."

"What is it, mother?"

"That I should like to see 'William Foster' and—and try to make him understand what he is doing. Perhaps he doesn't know, doesn't realise. God often lets the devil blind us, you know. If I told him about Jenny, told him all about her, he might see—he might understand. Don't you think so?"

Catherine was holding her mother's hand. She pressed it vehemently.

"Oh, mother, perhaps he might!"

Mrs. Ardagh sat up still more among her pillows.

"You don't think it's a silly fancy?"

"I don't know. I wonder."

Catherine was crying quietly.

"It keeps coming," said Mrs. Ardagh, "as if God sent it to me. What can I do? How can I send to William Foster? I don't know where he is. Could that Mr. Berrand—"

"Mother," Catherine said. "Leave it to me, I will bring William Foster to you."

She was trembling. But the invalid, exhausted with the excitement of the conversation, was growing drowsy. She sank down again in her pillows.

"Yes," she murmured. "I—might—tell—him—William Foster."

She slept heavily.

"Mark," Catherine said to her husband the next day. "Mother is dying. She can only live a very few days."

"Oh, Kitty! How grieved I am!"

His face was full of the most tender sympathy. He took her hand gently and kissed her.

"My Kitty, how will you bear this great sorrow?"

"Mark," Catherine said, and her voice sounded curiously strained. "Mother wants very much to see you, before she dies. She has something to say to you. I think she cares more about seeing you than about anything else in the world."

Mark looked surprised.

"I will go to her at once," he said. "What can it be? Ah, it must be something about you."

"No, I don't think so."

"What then?"

"She will tell you, Mark. It is better she should tell you herself."

"I will go to her then. I will go now."

"Wait a moment"—Catherine was very pale—"Promise me, Mark, that you won't—you won't be angry if—if mother—you will—"

She stopped. Her emotion was painful. Mark was more and more puzzled.

"Angry with your mother? At such a time!" he said.

"No—you wouldn't. I am upset. I am foolish. Let me go first to tell her you are coming. Follow me in a few minutes."

She went out leaving her husband amazed. When she arrived in Eaton Square Mr. Ardagh met her in the hall.

"She is worse," he said. "Much worse. The end cannot be far off."

"The beginning," Catherine said, looking him straight in the eyes.

He understood then which parental spirit had conquered the spirit of the child, and he smiled—sadly or gladly? He hardly knew. So strangely does death play with us all. Catherine went upstairs into her mother's room, which was dim and very hot. She shut the door, sent away the nurse, and went up to the bedside.

"Mother," she said, "William Foster is coming. Do you feel that you can see him?"

Mrs. Ardagh was perfectly conscious, although so near death.

"Yes," she said. "God means me to give him a message—God means me."

She lay silent; Catherine sat by her. Presently she spoke again.

"I shall convince him," she said quietly. "That is meant. If I did not God would strike him down. He would be cut off. But I shall make him know himself."

And then she repeated, with a sort of feeble but intense conviction, "If I did not God would strike him down—yes—yes."

Something—perhaps the fact that her mother was so near death, so close to that great secret—made her words, faltering though they were, go home to Catherine with the most extraordinary poignancy, as words had never gone before. She felt that it was true, that there was no alternative. Either Mark must be convinced now, by this bedside, in this hot, dark room from which a soul was passing, or he would, by some accident, by some sudden means, be swept away from the world that he was injuring, that he was poisoning.

Mrs. Ardagh seemed to grow more feeble with every moment that passed. And suddenly a great fear overtook Catherine, the dread that Mark would come too late, and then—God's other means! She trembled, and strained her ears to catch the sound of wheels. Mrs. Ardagh now seemed to be sinking into sleep—Catherine strove to rouse her. She stirred and said, "What is it?" in a voice that sounded peevish.

Just then there was a gentle tap on the door. Catherine sprang up, and hastened to it with a fast-beating heart. Mr. Ardagh stood there.

"How is she?" he whispered.

"I think she is not in pain. She is just resting. Has Mark come?"

"No."

"Please send him up directly he comes."

She spoke with a hushed, but with an intense, excitement.

"I want him to—to say goodbye to her," she added.

Mr. Ardagh nodded, and went softly downstairs.

"Is that he—is that William Foster?" said Mrs. Ardagh feebly from the bed.

"No, mother. But he will be here directly."

"I'm very tired," said the sick woman in reply. And again her thin voice sounded irritable.

Catherine sat down by her and held her hand tightly, as if that grasp could keep her in this life. A few minutes passed. Then there was the sound of a cab in the Square. It ceased in front of the house. Catherine could scarcely breathe. She bent down to the dying woman.

"Mother!"

"Well?"

"Mother, he has come—but I want to tell you something—are you listening?"

"Move the pillow."

Catherine did so.

"Mother, I want to tell you. William Foster is—"

The bedroom door opened and Mark entered softly. Catherine stood up, still holding her mother's hand, which was now very cold. Mark came to the bed on tiptoe.

"Mother," Catherine said, "William Foster"—Mark started—"is here. Tell him—tell him."

There was no reply from the bed.

"Kitty," Mark whispered, "what is this?"

"Hush!" she said. "Mother—mother, don't you hear me?"

Again there was no reply. Then Catherine bent down and cast a hard, staring glance of enquiry on her mother.

Mrs. Ardagh was dead.

Catherine looked up at Mark.

"God's other means," she thought.

The death of her mother left a strong and terrible impression upon Catherine. She brooded over it continually and over Mrs. Ardagh's last words. The last words of the dying often dwell in the memories of the living. Faltering, feeble, sometimes apparently inconsequent, they appear nevertheless prophetic, touched with the dignity of Eternal truths. Lives have been moulded by such last words. Natures have been diverted into new and curious paths. So it was now. For the future Mr. Ardagh's influence had no force over his daughter. An influence from the grave dominated her. Mr. Ardagh recognised the fact, shrugged his shoulders and travelled. His philosophy taught him to accept the inevitable with the fortitude of the Stoic. From henceforward the

Sirretts saw little of him. As to Mark, with his habitual tenderness he set about consoling his wife for her loss. He was kindness itself. Catherine seemed grateful, was indeed grateful to him. Nevertheless, after the death of Mrs. Ardagh, something seemed to stand between her and her husband, dividing them. Mark did not know what this was. For some time he was unconscious of this thin veil dropped between them. Even when he became aware of it he could not tell why it was there. He strove to put it aside, but in vain. Then he strove not to see it, not to think of it. He forgot it in his work. But Catherine always knew what set her apart from her husband. It was that influence from the grave. It was the memory of her mother's last words. She recognised them from the first, blindly, as words of prophecy. Yet the days went by. "William Foster" sat in his study in the Surrey home once more, while the spring grew, imitative of last year's spring. And there was no sign from God. Catherine never doubted that the dying woman had been inspired. She never doubted that "William Foster" would be stayed, however tragically, from working fresh evil in the world. Indeed she waited, as one assured of some particular future, breathless in expectation of its approach. Sometimes she strove to picture precisely what it might be, and, fancifully, she set two men before her—Mark and "William Foster." Even in real life they seemed two different men. Why not in the life of the imagination? And that was sweeter, for then she could look forward to the one standing fast, to the other being stricken. Might not his genius die in a man while the man lived on? There had been instances of men who had written one or two brilliant books and had seemed to exhaust themselves in that effort. And she dreamed of her husband's gift being stolen from him—divinely—of the stranger being slain. Yet this dreaming was idle and fantastic, the image which greets closed eyes. For Mark's energy and enthusiasm were growing. The fury of the papers fed him. The cries of pious fear emboldened his dogged and dreary talent. His genius grew darker as its darkness became recognised.

This third book of his promised to be more powerful, more deadly, than either of its forerunners. He did not speak much of it to Catherine. But now and then, carried away by excitement and by the need of sympathy, he dropped a hint of what he was doing. She listened attentively but said little. Mark noticed her lack of responsiveness, and one night he said rather bitterly, "You no longer care for your husband's achievements, Catherine."

He did not call her Kitty.

"I fear them, Mark," Catherine replied.

"Fear them! Why?"

"They are doing great harm in the world."

Mark uttered an impatient exclamation. As a man he was kind and gentle, but as an artist he was wilful and intolerant. Soon after this he wrote to Berrand and invited him to stay. Berrand came. This time Catherine shuddered at his coming. She began to look upon him as her husband's evil genius. Berrand did not apparently notice any change in her, for he treated her as usual, and spoke much to her of Mark. And Catherine was too reserved to express the feelings which tortured her to a comparative stranger. For this reason Berrand did not understand the terrible conflict that was raging within her as "William Foster's" new work grew, and he often spoke to her about the book, and described, with mischievous intellectual delight, its terror, its immorality and its pain. Catherine listened with apparent calm. She was waiting for that interruption from heaven. She was wondering why it did not come.

One night in summer it chanced that she and Berrand spoke of Fate. Catherine, dominated by her fixed idea that God would intervene in some strange and abrupt way to interrupt the activities of Mark, spoke of Fate as something inevitably ordained, certain as the rising of the sun or the dropping down of the darkness. Berrand laughed.

"There is no Fate," he said. "There is man, there is woman. Man and woman make circumstance. We fashion our own lives and the lives of others."

"And our deaths?" said Catherine.

"We die when we've done enough, when we've done our best or worst, when we've pushed our energy as far as it will go—that is, if we die what is called a natural death. But of course now and then some other human being chooses to think for us, and to think we have lived long enough or too long. And then—"

He paused with a smile.

"Then—?" said Catherine, leaning slightly forward.

"Then that human being may cut our thread prematurely, and down we go to death."

Catherine drew in her breath sharply.

"But that again," continued Berrand. "Is man—or woman—not the fantasy you call Fate?"

"Perhaps Fate can take possession of a man or a woman," Catherine said slowly and thoughtfully, "govern them, act through them."

"That's a dangerous doctrine. You believe that criminals are irresponsible then?"

"I don't know," she said. "I suppose there must be an agent. Yes, I suppose there must."

She spoke as one who is thinking out a problem.

"God," she continued, after a moment of silence, "may choose to use a man or woman as an agent instead of a disease."

"Oh, well," said Berrand, with his odd, high laugh, "I cannot go with you on that road of thought, Mrs. Sirrett. I am not afflicted with a religion. Oh, here's Mark. How have you been getting on, Mr. William Foster?"

"Grandly," he replied.

His dark eyes were blazing with excitement. Catherine suddenly turned very cold. She got up and left the room. The two men scarcely noticed her departure. They plunged into an eager discussion on the book. They debated it till the night waned and the melancholy breath of dawn stole in at the open window.

Meanwhile, Catherine, who had gone to bed, lay awake. This summer was so like last summer. Now, as then, she was sleepless, and heard the distant, excited voices rising and falling, murmuring on and on hour after hour. Now, as then, they accompanied activity. Now, as then, the activity was deadly, harmful to an invisible multitude, hidden out in the great world. But there was a difference between last year and this, so like in many ways. Mark's power had grown in the interval. He had become more dangerous. And Catherine had developed also. Circumstance—spoken of by Berrand—had changed, twisted into a different shape by dying hands, twisted again by the hands—all unconscious—of that man who talked downstairs, of Berrand. Was he, too, an agent of Fate, at which he scornfully laughed? Why not?

Oh, those everlasting voices! They rang hatefully in the sleepless woman's ears. Their eagerness, their enthusiasm, were terrible to her. For now their joy seemed to summon her to a great darkness. Their sound seemed to call her to the making of a great silence. She put her hands over her ears, but she still heard them till it was dawn. She still heard them when they were no more speaking.

From this time Catherine waited indeed, but with a patience quite different from that which possessed her formerly. Then she was expectant, almost superstitiously expectant, of an abrupt interposition of Fate. Now she waited, but with less expectancy, and with a strange and growing sense of personal obligation which had been totally absent from her before the issue lay between the thing invisible and herself. And each day that passed brought the issue a step nearer to her. How pathetical seemed to her the ignorance of the two men who were her companions in the cloistered house at this time. Tears rose in her eyes at the thought of her secret and their impotence to know it. But then she thought of her mother's deathbed and the tears ran dry. For the spirit of her mother surely was with her in the dark, the spirit that knew all now and that could inspire and direct her.

The book grew and Catherine waited. Would Mark be allowed to complete it? that was the great question. If he was, then the burden of action was laid upon her by the will of God. She had quite made up her mind on that. She had even prayed, and believed that an answer had been given to her prayer, and that the answer was—"In the event you anticipate it is God's will that you should act." She was fully resolved to do God's will. And so she waited, with a strong, but how anxious, patience. The growth of the book was now become ironical to her as the growth of a plant which must die when it attains a certain height; the labour spent upon it, the discussion that raged around it, the decisions that were arrived at as to its course—all these things were now most pitifully pathetic to Catherine. As she watched Mark and Berrand, as she listened to them, she seemed to watch and listen to children, playing idly, chattering idly, on the edge of events that must stop their play, their chatter—perhaps forever.

For this book would never see the light. No one would ever read it. No one would ever speak of it but these two men, whose lives seemed bound up in it. And Catherine alone knew this.

Sometimes she had a longing to tell them of this knowledge, to say to Mark, "Do not waste yourself in this useless energy!" To say to Berrand, "Do not rejoice over the future of that which has no future." But she refrained, knowing that to speak would be to give the lie to what she spoke. For such revelation must frustrate her contemplated action. So nobody knew what she knew, except the spirit that stood by her in the night. She waited, and the book drew slowly towards its climax and its close. As Berrand grew more excited about it he spoke more of it to Catherine. But Mark—conscious of that veil dropped between him and his wife—scarcely mentioned it to her, and declined to read any passages from it aloud. Catherine understood that he distrusted her and knew her utterly unsympathetic and adverse to his labours. The sign for which she had hoped, which she had once most confidently expected, did not come. And at length she almost ceased to think of it, and was inclined to put the idea from her as a foolish dream.

The burden of action was, it seemed, to be laid upon her. She would accept it calmly, dutifully. So the summer waned, drawing towards autumn. The atmosphere grew heavy and mellow. The garden was languid with its weight of bearing plants and with its fruits. Mists rose at evening in the woods, clouding the trunks of the trees, and spreading melancholy as a sad tale that floats, like a mist, over those who hear it. And, one day, the book was finished.

Berrand came to tell Catherine. He was radiant. While he spoke he never noticed that she closed her hands tightly as one who prepares to face an enemy.

"We are going to London this afternoon," he added. "Mark must see his publisher."

"He is taking up the manuscript?" said Catherine hastily.

"No, no. There are one or two finishing touches to be put. But he must arrange about the date of publishing. He will return by the midnight train, but I shall stay in town for the night."

Mark locked up the manuscript in a drawer of his writing table, the key of which he carried about him on a chain. And the two men took their departure, leaving Catherine alone.

So the time of her duty was fully come. She had waited till now, because, till now, she had not been absolutely sure that she was to be the agent through whom Fate was to work. But she could no longer dare to doubt. The book was finished. Mark had been allowed to finish it. But its deadly work was not accomplished till it was given to the world. It must never be given to the world.

The day was not cold. Yet Catherine ordered the footman to light a fire in Mark's study. When he had done so she told him not to allow her to be disturbed. Then she went into the room and shut the door behind her. She walked up to the writing table, at which Mark had spent so many hours, labouring, thinking, imagining, working out, fashioning that shell which was to burst and maim a world. The silence in the room seemed curiously intense. The fire gleamed, and the sun gleamed too; though already it was slanting to the West. Catherine stood for some time by the table. Then she tried the drawer in which Mark kept his manuscript and found it locked. The resistance of the drawer to her hand roused her.

Two or three minutes later one of the maids in the servant's hall said,

"Whatever's that?"

"What?" said the footman who had lit the study fire.

"Listen!" said the maid.

They listened and heard a sound like a blow struck on some hard substance.

"There it is again," said the maid. "What ever can it be?"

The footman didn't know, but they both agreed that the noise seemed to come from the study. While they were still gossiping about it Catherine stood at Mark's writing table, and drew out from an open drawer the manuscript of the book. She lifted it in her hands slowly and her face was hard and set. Then she turned and carried it to the hearth, where the fire was blazing. By the hearth she paused. She meant to destroy the book in the fire. But now that she saw the book, now that she held it in her hands, the deed seemed so horribly merciless that she hesitated. Then she knelt down on the hearth and leaned towards the flames. Their light played upon her face, their heat scorched her skin. She held the book towards them, over them. The flames flew up towards it eagerly, seeming to desire it. Catherine tantalised them by withholding from them their prey. For now, in this crisis of action, doubts assailed her. She remembered that she had never read the book, though she had heard much of it from Berrand. He was imaginative and essentially mischievous. Perhaps he had exaggerated its tendency, drawn too lurid a picture of its horrible power. Catherine turned a page or two and glanced at the clear, even writing. It fascinated her eyes.

At eight the footman opened the door, announcing dinner.

Catherine started as if from a dream. Her face was white and her eyes were ablaze with excitement. She put the manuscript back in the drawer, went into the dining room and made a pretence of dining. But very soon she was back again in the study. She sat down under a lamp by the fire and went on reading the book. She knew that Mark would not be home till midnight; there was plenty of time. She turned the leaves one by one, and presently she forgot the passing of time, she forgot everything in the evil fascination of the book. She was enthralled. She was horror-stricken. But she could not cease from reading. Only when she had finished she meant to burn the book. No one else should ever come under its spell. She never heard the clock striking the hours. She never heard the sound of carriage wheels on the gravel of the drive. She never heard a step in the hall, the opening of the study door. Only when Mark stood before her with an exclamation of keen surprise did she start up. The manuscript dropped from her hands on to the hearth. The drawer in the writing table, broken open, gaped wide.

"Catherine," Mark said, and he bent hastily and picked up the book. "Catherine, what is the meaning of this? You have—you have—"

He stopped, struck dumb by flooding astonishment. She stared up at him without a word and with a dazed expression in her eyes. He looked towards the drawer.

"You have dared to break open my writing table!"

"Yes," she said, finding a voice. "I have dared."

"And to read—to read—"

She nodded. Mark seemed utterly confused by surprise. He looked almost sheepish, as men do in blank amazement. She got up and stood before him and laid her hands on his, which held the book.

"You see that fire?" she said in a low voice.

He looked at it, as if he had not noticed it before.

"What's it for?" he said, also in a low voice.

"Don't you know?"

They looked into each other's eyes for a moment.

"To—to—you intended to burn—"

She nodded again, and closed her hands tightly on the book.

"Mark," she said solemnly. "It's an evil thing. Let it go."

His face changed. Astonishment died in fierce excitement.

"You're mad!" he said brutally.

And he struck her hands away from the book with his clenched fist. She did not cry out, but her face became utterly dogged. He saw that.

"D'you hear me?" he said.

"Yes."

His passion rose, as he began fully to grasp the enormity of the deed that his coming had prevented.

"You would destroy my labour, my very soul," he said hoarsely. "You who pretended to love me!"

"Because I love you," she said.

He laughed aloud.

"You hate me," he cried.

"I hate to see you do evil," she said.

"This is fanaticism," he muttered, looking at her obstinate white face, and steady eyes. "Sheer fanaticism."

It began almost to frighten him.

"You shall not do this evil," she said. "You shall not."

Mark stared at her for a moment. Then he turned away.

"I'll not argue with you," he said. "But, if you had done what you meant to do, if you had destroyed my labour, I would have recreated it, every sentence, every word."

"No, Mark!"

"I would, I would," he said. "The world shall have it, the world should have had it even then. Go to your room."

She left him. But her face had not changed or lost its expression.

She went upstairs slowly. And the spirit of her mother went with her. She felt sure of that.

When two days afterwards, late in the evening, Mark Sirrett suddenly died—from poison, as was proved at Catherine's trial—she had no feeling that Mark was dead. That only came to her afterwards, as she sat by the body, awaiting the useless arrival of the doctor. She only knew that the stranger was gone, the stranger into whose wild eyes she had gazed for the first time in the Pavilion of Granada, when the world was golden beneath them and the roses touched his hair. She looked at the body, and she seemed to hear again the bell of the cathedral, filling the drowsy valley with terrible vibrations of romance. It was a passing bell. For God had stricken down "William Foster."

THE INN

I

I met her when I was staying near the frontier of Tunisia at Hammam-Ziloutine. I had gone there from Europe to take the sulphur baths, and stayed in the hotel at the edge of the boiling springs, which throw up their wandering columns of smoke among the silver-green olive trees. The worst of it was that I struck a patch of bad weather. Generally between December and March there are several weeks of rain in that part of North Africa. I came in for some of those weeks. When I arrived there were dark, swollen clouds drifting over the hills which surround the pastoral valley made famous by the healing waters. As I drove from the wayside station to the hotel I saw a mournful vision of camels slipping on the greasy high road, and dreary Arabs shrouded in sacking or exposed to the downpour in rags. And when I got to the hotel the courtyard was streaming, the tennis court of hard earth was diapered with puddles of rainwater, the melodious voice of the springs was almost drowned by the sound of the rain.

I had asked for a sitting room as well as a bedroom. They had improvised one for me in the long wing which runs out from the main building, at the edge of the narrow grove where the Israelites from Constantine love to picnic during the Jews' season in April; a table, a couple of chairs which pretended to be armchairs, a larger piece of furniture which pretended to be a sofa, two ordinary chairs, a wardrobe lingering on in spite of the changes and chances of life. My bedroom was next door and opened into my sitting room. In both rooms there were fireplaces, and in the sitting room, by the hearth, there was a small pile of firewood cut from the olive trees which abound in that district. Promptly I ordered a fire to be lighted. This was done by the French servant, Raoul, a pale, willing fellow who had suffered many things in the war. Meanwhile I unpacked and transferred my books and papers and photographs to the sitting room, settling in to the accompaniment of the beating rain and the loudly shivering eucalyptus trees.

In the evening at dinner I saw her for the first time.

In spite of her obvious and unmistakable good looks, what struck me first was not her beauty, but her expression. Hopelessness seemed carved upon her face. Cynicism stared from her large, deep eyes. Her mouth was the home of bitterness. This expression of hers tried surely to destroy her beauty. But it could not. She had to be beautiful, and her beauty was clear, white, black, red, full of sharp contrasts; the complexion radiant white, the hair very black, the lips very red. Her figure was tall and slim. She was like a dark Atalanta who had known many tragedies and had learnt disbelief in joy.

After dinner I saw her go across the tiled lobby in front of the bureau into the *salle de lecture*, a small room full of old copies of *L'Illustration* and cane armchairs. A log fire had been made there, and when I followed I found her sitting in front of it smoking and reading a French translation of a book by Ibanez, *Les Morts Commandent*. When we got into talk I remember that I asked her whether she thought that statement about the dead was true. She paused, and looked at me with a sort of hostile interrogation, as if she suspected a trap. Perhaps I showed innocence and surprise, for she suddenly smiled that bitter smile of hers, and said, in her curious soft voice, with the extremely clear, almost sharp, enunciation that was characteristic of her:

"Yes, if we are fools enough to let them!"

We got into talk that first evening. She was not anxious to talk, nor determined not to talk unless it couldn't be helped. It seemed to me that she was a woman who just didn't care; didn't care whether she was alone or in company, whether she talked or was silent, whether she interested you or bored you, whether you wanted her or didn't want her. Similarly, I don't think she really cared whether the rain poured or the sun shone, whether the trees stood silent and erect under a glory of blue, or shuddered and bent in the wind beneath blackness. So many things didn't seem able to get at her, to touch her. There was about her an independence that was terrible, because it didn't seem natural, didn't seem thoroughly human.

I remember thinking about her, "That woman has gone over the edge!"

I don't believe I ever interested her at all, but she interested me immensely. And she told me things. Somehow I made her tell me things. Or—no, I didn't make her. I don't think anyone could have made her do anything against her will. So I suppose she just chose to tell me because I was there, and interested in her, and we got to know each other rather well in that damp solitude among the African hills. Or, perhaps, she was more thoroughly human than she generally seemed, and really needed an outlet. Who can tell? I can't.

That very first night, after we'd had a talk in the *salle de lecture*, and she got up—I supposed to go to her bedroom—things moved. I got up, too, and went out with her into the dark, rainy night, a soaking wet night smelling of Africa, and down the steps to the arcade of the wing where my two rooms were.

"I sleep down here," she said, "on the ground floor. Good night."

And then I suggested further talk by the fire in my improvised sitting room above, and she "didn't mind." And we went there and talked.

That was how it began. She didn't care whether she came to my room, whether we talked or not. And so she came and we talked.

II

The rain went on and on. How it rained! The beautiful country round the hotel—Arcadia in the fine African weather—ceased to exist. That was my feeling about it. The persistent rain seemed just to do away with it, to wipe it off the face of the earth. Day by day I took my baths, creeping down in the rain over the steps running with water to the bathhouse. And then I read by the fire among the pretending chairs, and the pretending sofa, and the lingering wardrobe. And I walked and talked with her. It seemed monstrous for Africa to be like that. When I leave Europe for Africa I always feel that I have a right to magnificent weather there. And when I don't get it I am put out and angry, and feel like a cheated man. But I don't think she cared. And we used to walk out in the rain together, up the valley towards the frontier, or down the valley towards Jemmapes. And sometimes we went through the wet myrtle bushes and the wild oleanders along the stream, where the Arabs love to bathe and lie in the sun smoking their carefully rolled cigarettes. But there were no Arabs; and the ground seemed to "give" under our feet, and the stream was swollen into a turbulent muddy river.

She wasn't taking the baths, and I didn't know why she was there, or how long she was going to stay, till one day she told me.

"I'm here because I may as well be here as anywhere else, and I shall stay on here till something moves me."

"Something?" I said.

"Things happen or don't happen. I may be jerked out of here. If I'm not I shall stay till the hotel shuts for the summer."

"And then?"

"I haven't the least idea where I shall go."

And I knew she hadn't, and, moreover, I knew she didn't care where she went.

"The people of the hotel want me to go to Provence with them. That's where they go for the summer. Perhaps I shall."

"It would be interesting to explore the country of Mistral," I said.

"Do you think so?" she said, with profound indifference.

We had come back from an unusually long walk on the high road towards the frontier. The weather had cleared a little. For the moment the rain had stopped. But I felt it in the air. The country smelt of it. The clouds overhead looked like crazy sacks full of it. And in the reek of the damp there was cold.

"You'll come up to my room to tea?" I said, when we reached the arcade.

"Yes; why not?"

She turned round and went into her bedroom.

"I'll change," her voice said from within. "You go up and I'll join you."

I went up. The fire was burning; not fiercely but glowing gently and steadily. I rang for Raoul and ordered tea for two. Then I cleared the books and papers from the table and drew up the pretending chairs. Raoul brought a large japanned tray, with tea, slightly sour toast, very yellow butter, and thick, cloudy honey.

"Will you tell Madame it's ready?"

"*Oui, Monsieur.*"

She was Madame, not Mademoiselle. I had found that out long ago. But I had never heard mention of any husband or, indeed, of any man in connection with her.

My room opened on to the corridor by means of French windows; soon I heard her step coming towards it. She had a firm, unhurried step, and walked well with a sort of unconscious dignity.

"Do come in!" I said.

She had taken off her round hat, and her thick black hair waved round her broad white forehead. The rain had just begun again. I could hear it falling on the pavement below. I could see the wet oranges shining on the trees just beyond the glass of the corridor. The short day was already closing in. They looked like little round lamps, decorations for some festival, in the rainy dusk.

"Let's forget outside!" I said to her.

And I shut the French windows.

"Shall I turn on the light or shall we only have the fire?"

"I don't mind."

I didn't turn on the light. We sat down by the fire and I gave her tea. It was a cosy hour. The chairs weren't really comfortable, but they might have been worse. The little room was warm and looked almost interesting because of the firelight. The tea, at any rate, was steaming hot. And we were prepared for it all, prepared for enjoyment of it, by a long damp walk. Just then I felt that we ought to feel as children say, "good all over." And then I looked at her—we were sitting opposite to each other, on either side of the fire, each using an end of the table— and I saw the hopelessness carved on her face, the cynicism in her eyes, the bitterness about her lips. And a sort of impotent anger which was, I know, very unreasonable rose in me, and I said:

"Can't you enjoy *anything?* Can't you enjoy even an hour like this, sitting down after a long walk, resting in the warm, drinking hot tea? Would you as soon be in a cold, fireless room, alone—"

I stopped. I remember I felt intense irritation.

"What's the matter?" she said.

"Can't you enjoy *anything?*" I repeated angrily.

"Enjoy?" She paused. "No! There are things I can't do without. My body needs certain things, of course, at certain times, and I suppose having those things at the appropriate times gives me—what shall I call it?—gives me physical relief. But as to enjoying anything, no, I don't. Do you mean to say that you are *enjoying* this?"

"No—not now! But I could have enjoyed it if you had given me the chance. Why can't you be natural?"

"That's just what I am. You'd like me to pretend. But I can't. Perhaps someday I may be able to. I don't know. But I certainly can't now. I'm impotent to pretend. Almost everybody does pretend and so almost everybody expects pretence from others. I surprise you and irritate you by being perfectly natural. That's your affair. You needn't ask me up to your room."

"If I never did again you wouldn't mind."

She said nothing.

"Would you?" I said.

"If you insist upon it—no, I shouldn't."

It was very stupid of me, but I felt hurt. Perhaps it was the male conceit most men have which resented her truth-telling. And I was fool enough to exclaim:

"Sorry I bore you!"

"Now you are being absurd," she said.

I expected her to add the woman's cliché, "What children all you men are!" But she didn't. She looked at me and said:

"Would you rather I went?"

"No, no, no!"

I suddenly realised at that moment that I was getting to like her very much, that I was becoming profoundly interested in her, and that that was the reason why she irritated me.

"Don't go!" I said. "My being with you makes no difference to you, but your being with me makes all the difference to me. I suppose that's why I've been rude. Forgive me!"

"Of course! What does it matter?"

My irritation flamed up again, but I checked expression of it. There was a sarcastic look in her eyes which I was getting to know very well.

"I wish you'd tell me why you are so infernally indifferent about everything," I said. "I've no right to ask you to, of course. Still, in a way we're friends now, I hope. At any rate I feel friendship for you."

"I don't mind telling you," she said. "I used to be rather a proud woman, but I'm not proud now. Pride's no good to one. It doesn't win love, of course, but it doesn't even gain you respect. So what's the use of it?"

She pushed away her cup and her plate. I moved the tray. We had finished.

"Shall I close the shutters?" I said.

"Yes, if you like."

I got up and drew them together and latched them. Then I put two more logs on the fire and sat down again.

III

"Have you been long in Africa?" she asked.

"No; I've only just come over. Why?"

"I was only wondering whether you'd seen things about me in the Algerian or French papers. I dare say there was something in the English papers, too. But I haven't seen them for ages."

"If Colegate is your own name, I haven't seen anything."

"It is my married name. I didn't bother to change it."

"Then I haven't seen."

"It was some time ago. I've been away from England a good while now. My husband wanted to show me North Africa. He was fond of it. He was a man who'd travelled a great deal, and found Europe rather small and cramped and niggling. He was an Australian, and came over to Europe, for the fourth or fifth time, to fight in the war with the Australian contingent. That's how I came to meet him. He was one of the Australian giants."

"Yes?"

"Tremendous fellows they were—weren't they?"

"Yes. A bit wild, but good fighters."

"Exactly! Good fighters—but a bit wild."

She changed the order of my words with a sort of tragic deliberation, and I heard her sigh. Then she said: "I paint—portraits."

The abruptness of this unexpected statement surprised me. I wondered where she was going now.

"You'll understand why I tell you that in a moment."

"Yes?"

"Or, rather I used to paint portraits. I don't now. I've given, it up. But I was very interested in painting, and I've got some talent. When my husband and I had married, after the war, we came over to North Africa. We went first by Spain to Morocco. He wanted to be in the wilds. We camped and rode. He shot. That was a passion with him— shooting. He was a thorough outdoor man, like so many Australians. And so we went through Morocco. From there we came by way of Oran to Algiers. But we didn't stay there long. It wasn't at all the sort of place that suited him. And we went away, meaning to go to Touggourt, and on to Ouargla, and other places. But we had plenty of time. We weren't in a hurry. Presently we came to a place that took my fancy tremendously, and that he liked, or seemed to like, too. One gets very tired of hotels. There was an Inn, what I call an Inn. No smart public rooms, no hall porter, no formal bureau, no bowing parasites showing their teeth for tips. It was 'run' by a French family—father, mother, a son, daughters. A grandmother was there too. It was patriarchal. They had come to Africa long ago, and settled down in this lonely place amongst rocks near some native villages, and started the Inn, and made some money, and built on, and bought some land, and grown crops, and got richer, and improved the Inn until it was, oh! such an attractive place. But they had never tried to make it smart. They didn't know anything about smartness. But it was beautifully clean, with good beds and excellent cooking, and smiling faces and interest. They loved their Inn, and made you love it too. It stood by the road, between a river and the road. And the road led through a gap in a gigantic wall of red rocks into the desert. And the gap was the only outlet from the desert thereabouts. To escape from the desert you had to pass by the Inn."

"To escape?"

"Yes! We settled down there for a while, and I began painting a portrait of my husband. I had an easel in the little dining room—you can tell by that how primitive it was—and painted there when he was patient enough to sit to me. But he was an impatient, restless man and was seldom quite happy unless he was out of doors. Still, I made progress, and presently, even when he was away, he was there on the easel in the little dining room."

"Was he away much, then?" I found myself asking, prompted, I believe, by something in the sound of her low and very clear voice when she said those words, "even when he was away."

"Yes, a good deal. He went out shooting in the mountains near the Inn. That was at first. And then he heard that gazelle were often found in the desert near an oasis called El-Djer. And he went there. And when he went there he had to sleep out—it was a considerable distance off—in an auberge. I didn't go with him. He said I should be too uncomfortable and have nothing to do. And I loved the place where we were staying so much that I didn't mind occasionally being alone. Besides, I had a theory about men"—she smiled, and her smile was intensely bitter—"I thought that men, real men, needed a good deal of liberty, and that the women who gave it them freely were the women who kept them. I didn't believe in a chain, even if it were made of flowers. I loved my husband. I trusted him absolutely. How could I try to chain him? And he was a splendid, wild man. That's why I loved him. Tameness in men has never attracted me."

I looked at her dark beauty in the firelight, and realised that very thoroughly.

"He went several times to El-Djer, staying away two or three nights each time. He was lucky and brought back gazelle. Meanwhile, I painted, strolled in the palm gardens by the river and through the native villages, made friends with the Arab women and children, and thought I was very happy."

"I wonder what you looked like then," was my thought.

She must have read it, for she said:

"You can hardly imagine me happy, can you? I was a different woman then. *Then* I was interested in everything. All the little things delighted me. When the heart's at ease the mind goes its butterfly way. And every flower is a flower of Paradise. I know that and yet, now, I can scarcely believe it. How it's raining again!"

Beyond the closed windows and shutters, beyond the corridor and its windows, I heard a wide but faint rustling sound. I bent and put another log on the fire.

"There it was always fine. The sun seemed always to be shining down on the Inn. It was shining on the morning one when he went away for—it shone when he went away again one morning to El-Djer. Now I must just tell you something about the Inn, if you really care to hear all this."

"Please go on."

"Give me a little piece of paper, will you?"

I brought her some paper and a pencil.

"It was built like this."

She leaned over the table and drew. She might have been an architect coldly drawing a plan.

"Here was the part for the guests, the part where we lived, with an upper story, and a large terrace—like that! The kitchen was at the end—there, straight on from the dining room, with windows looking on to the courtyard, a row of Judas trees, a well, and the road beyond a green railing with a gate in it. Caravans continually went by on the road under the shadow of the rocks. Now here, quite separate from the main building, was a second smaller building in the same courtyard. The landlord and all his family lived in that, with the three Arab servants who helped in the work of the Inn. So that at night any travellers staying there were separated from the servants and the family once the doors were locked at bedtime."

"I understand."

She pushed the bit of paper away and laid the pencil down.

"When my husband left me for El-Djer *that* time it happened that nobody was staying at the Inn except ourselves. So that at night I was entirely alone in the main building. I didn't mind. It wasn't large and it was very cheerful. Besides, the family were close by. And it wasn't a dangerous place. I thought nothing of it—I mean of being alone. He was to be away for two nights that time. The two nights passed, and I was expecting him back at any moment, when a *petit bleu* was put into my hand. It was from him, and was signed 'Colin,' which was his first Christian name. It told me that sport was so good that he was staying on at El-Djer for a night or two longer. I was rather disappointed. I wanted him back. But it couldn't be helped. The telegram came in the evening just before dinner. I had to sit down to dinner by myself.

Before I did that I remember going to the portrait of my husband which stood on the easel and looking at it. While I was looking the Arab servant, Smain, came up behind me, and said something about my husband's eyes. They were steel-grey. Smain stared at them and said to me:

"No Arab has eyes like that!"

She repeated the words. Then she added:

"Australian far-seeing eyes they were!"

And she was silent. But suddenly she roused herself.

"I sat down to dinner. It was cold there at night among the rocks, and I had the fire lighted. There was no other sitting room. I meant to spend the evening by the fire. But I had the dining room windows left open because some Arabs were playing native music in the distance, and I wanted to hear it. And so it happened that when a horse came galloping on the high road that led from the desert I heard the sound clearly in the night. I heard it first in the distance, but it came nearer rapidly, right up to the Inn, and stopped abruptly, and then I heard a man's rough voice shouting to the servants, and I saw a tall man in riding boots, and covered with dust, walking rather unsteadily in the little courtyard of the Inn. He glanced through the window at me sitting at my table lit up by an oil lamp, and I saw that he was young, about thirty I should think, and looked fierce, strange, and exhausted. He gave me a stare that seemed both piercing and wavering, and I heard him enter the Inn and go up the uncarpeted stairs heavily.

"A minute later, Smain, who had gone out, came back, and I asked him to shut the windows. I had begun to feel rather cold. He shut them, and then said he would have to get supper for 'Monsieur Henri,' the man who had just galloped up, and who, he informed me, must have ridden all the way from El-Djer, the place where my husband was staying to shoot gazelle. I asked one or two questions about this man, who had made—I scarcely knew why—a very strong and not pleasant impression upon me, and Smain told me that he owned the Inn where my husband was staying, that he was a gentleman of a good French family, but that he had been very wild, had run away from home, had served for a time in the French Foreign Legion, and had finally married an Algerian girl 'with eyes like the moon,' and settled down at El-Djer, where he cultivated date palms, grew crops, and, with his wife, looked after the Inn, which my husband had described to me as a 'one-horse' auberge quite unfit for me to stay in, but which Smain said was *une bien belle maison.*

"While Smain was talking I heard the man coming down the wooden stairs. When he came in I saw that he had brushed his clothes. But he still looked haggard and extraordinary, and, I thought, like a man who had been drinking heavily. Without glancing at me he ordered supper and a bottle of champagne. Smain went to fetch them, and I sat down by the fire, while the man went to one of the windows and looked out into the night with his face close to the glass. His attitude at the window, the way he almost pressed his face to it, made me wonder what was the matter. The man remained by the window till Smain came in with his supper and the champagne. Then he turned round sharply and muttered something—I could not hear what. I believe he must have spoken in Arabic. He went to sit down at the table, and Smain told him that room Number 3 was ready for him. 'Who told you I was going to stop the night?' he said ferociously. Smain replied that the last train had gone, that there were no horses to be got, and that his own horse had gone dead lame from being overridden. At that he started up and hurried out of the room, followed by Smain. He came back in a few minutes. While he was away I went to look again at the portrait of my husband. When I heard him coming in I dropped a covering over it and went back to the fire, while he sat down to his supper. I noticed that he had a black look on his face.

"Presently I felt a strange urge to speak to the man. I disliked being with him in total silence. I had to say something to him, and I asked how his horse was. He looked up, stared at me, and then told me the animal had gone lame. 'You overrode him!' I said. He laughed and let the champagne cork fly. And just then I heard Smain shutting up the Inn for the night. The man heard it, too, and looked startled. 'What's that?' he asked. I was going to tell him, when Smain closed the dining room shutters. Immediately afterwards he came in and bade us good night. His soft steps died away down the passage that led to the kitchen and the back door. I realised that I was now shut up for the night alone with this stranger. I wasn't afraid. I'm not at all a nervous woman. But I felt almost sure the man had been drinking. There was an extraordinary wildness about him, and I thought I'd go up to my room. But when I got up to go he got up, too, and said he hoped he wasn't driving me away. I told him I often went early to bed, like the Arabs. But he pointed to the recently lit fire, shook his head, and then abruptly asked me if I was afraid of him. That was like a challenge to me, and I told him I wasn't afraid of any man. Apparently he didn't believe me, for he said something to the effect that I knew nothing about him, and so didn't choose to talk to him. Thereupon I said I did know something about him. He seemed astonished and asked what I knew, and I gave him Smain's information, even to the fact of his being married to a girl with 'eyes like the moon.' When I said the last words a dreadful look distorted his face for an instant. He seemed, I thought, struggling with himself. Finally, he got control—that was how I felt it—and begged me to sit down again by the fire while he finished his supper. And, somehow, I had to do it. There was an occult reason. I had to do it. I couldn't leave that man."

She paused, then added as if to herself:

"And he couldn't let me go."

Then she sat quite still, staring into the fire, till at last I said:

"Did you stay up with him long?"

"Yes; and the more I was with him the more strongly I felt that there was some reason, some strange, hidden, powerful reason why I had to be with him. I have never felt like that with any man before. I shall never feel like that with any man again. He sat down once more at the supper table and ate voraciously, and drank till the bottle was empty; and he talked; but all the time he seemed to be listening for sounds from outside the Inn. And he often turned and looked at the shuttered windows. I knew he was attentive. I knew he was afraid, or expectant, of something. But I didn't know what it was. As he drank he became more and more communicative, and I realised that I had been right in my suspicion. Before he arrived at the Inn he had certainly been drinking, and the champagne increased his carelessness. For there was in him, and about him like an atmosphere, a sort of wild, savage carelessness. And yet underneath it I seemed to feel attention, and a horrible secret alertness. With me he could be careless, even reckless; but not with what was outside. It seemed like that somehow, but it's difficult to make another understand it.

"At last the bottle was empty, and he lit a black cigar, and came over to the fire, where I was, and began to talk more volubly. Some of his fatigue had worn off under the influence of food and wine. He was, I think, in that mood when a man longs to 'open out,' to be confidential, talk about himself, explain himself to another. Too much drink had brought egoism well to the surface. But all the time underneath he was afraid. And that mixture of egoism and fear interested me that night, even fascinated me, and roused my curiosity. I can't tell you all we talked about by the fire. But this was how it was in the end. He began to speak about treachery, and said human beings could never be trusted. He said he knew life down to the bottom, and that at the bottom there were always dregs. I told him I didn't agree with him. He laughed and jeered at me when I said I could trust, and did trust. And, finally, he told me that he had once had a friend who had trusted, as I did, and who had been betrayed in the basest possible way. I asked how that was, and he began to tell me. It was an ordinary tale enough; of a man who worshipped a woman, and who believed in her absolutely, and who was betrayed by her with another man. Nothing could be more ordinary than that—could it?"

She looked at me from the other side of the fire.

"I suppose not," I said. "At any rate, it can't be called a new sort of story, can it?"

"No; but it interested me. No story has ever interested me as that one did. He began to describe the betrayer presently. It seemed that— he described him as an outdoor man, the sort of man who can't stay long cooped up between walls, a big athlete of a man, very physical and strong, a man with a passion for hunting and shooting. He was a hunter, that man, and when he wasn't hunting gazelle he was after women."

Something in me seemed to go suddenly cold when she said the last sentence.

"Please go on!" I heard myself saying.

"I knew by this time somehow that my companion was telling me his own story. I knew that the woman in it was his own wife. But, nevertheless, I fished for facts, and he gave them to me. Among them were these. The man who had betrayed him was a traveller. The house where the woman and her husband lived was an Inn. The man came to stay at the Inn to go after gazelle. That was how they had come to know him."

She told me this quietly. There was no sound of emotion in her voice. Her face had its curious, fixed look of bitter calmness. But the cold within me persisted and grew. I don't know whether she realised that. But I think she did. She kept her eyes on me as she continued, and was evidently sharply aware of me, whereas before she had given me the impression that she was gazing back into the past.

"When I had got these facts I asked the man to tell me what had come of it all, what was the end of the story."

"And what was it?" I asked.

For she had stopped again and seemed, I thought, held up by something or reluctant to go on.

"Oh—well, the end was ordinary enough too. There was really nothing original about it. But, then, you see it happened to be *true*. And life isn't too full of originality, is it? It keeps on repeating and repeating itself, and always will to the end, I suppose."

"Yes—but this business you were telling me of?"

"Oh!"

Had she suddenly lost interest, or what was it? A sort of white indifference seemed to have settled upon her. It seemed that she roused herself out of pure politeness.

"Oh—well, the end of the story was this. The husband went away from the Inn on business connected with his date palms—a day's ride away. While he was doing his business an Arab arrived from El-Djer and gave him a certain piece of information. He gave the Arab a thrashing for saying such a thing. But then he went back by night—in the usual way, you know, of husbands on such occasions. And he found that for once an Arab had spoken the truth. It wasn't a matter of surmising. He saw. We may be liars, many of us, but Providence has at any rate provided each of our bodies with a couple of truth-tellers. He didn't disturb the lovers—let them know he was there. Evidently he was a man with self-control in difficult moments. So he let them alone. But on the following morning, when the lover started off at dawn after gazelle—to be lucky with gazelle you have to get up and be out at dawn—the husband met him in the desert, caught him alone, when his two native hunters were off at work for him, and knifed him. That was his end."

She said the last words stolidly, coldly, with what I can only call a stubborn lack of emotion. And then she sat with her arm on the table looking at me. I felt a kind of mental paralysis in me just then. What she had just told me, her manner of telling it, the hideous surmise which the incidents related had brought to birth in me, and now this staring silence, this nearly dull fixity of gaze, and this unnatural bodily stillness, had somehow, in combination, an overwhelming effect upon me. I don't know how long it was before I managed to say:

"And the Epilogue?"

"The Epilogue?"

She seemed with difficulty to rouse herself.

"The Epilogue, if you like to call it so, was rather more original than the story itself. When the man said that the seducer had died under the knife of the husband, I told him that I had realised that *he* was the husband. He didn't deny it. I suppose by then he saw that to deny would be useless. I asked him when the murder had been committed. I insisted. He seemed astonished at my insistence. I saw suspicion growing in him. He wanted to know why it mattered to me—such a thing. I told him that I had a reason, a good one"—she smiled as she said the word 'good'—"for wishing to know. But, as I was saying that, I happened to make a gesture. I touched my breast, and my fingers felt a thin bit of paper which I had pushed into the front of my gown. It was the *petit bleu* I had had that evening from my husband. It had been despatched that day in the afternoon. When I realised that I think I began to laugh. Can you guess why?"

I nodded. I didn't feel like speaking just then.

"When I began to laugh, and had the *petit bleu* in my hand, he seemed startled. He sprang at me, pulled the paper away, and read it. When he got to the last word he said it aloud, pronouncing it as if it were French. 'Colin!' he said. 'Colin!' I told him it was my husband's name. I told him my husband was at the hotel at El-Djer, had gone there for gazelle shooting. If he was half drunk—and I know he was—that sobered him. Do you guess why?"

Again I nodded and did not speak.

"That's the most original thing in the matter, isn't it, that he should have come upon me, related the story to me, without knowing who I was! When I had told him he went very white under the colour the sun of Africa had set on his face, and he muttered 'Good night,' and shrank off from me as if to get out of the room. But I stopped him. I caught his arm. I made him come in front of the portrait I'd been painting, I pulled away the covering that hung over it, and asked the man if he knew the face. He tried to deny that he knew it, but he couldn't look at it. After one glance he couldn't look anymore. In a moment he'd have bolted out of the room, leaving me and that painted man together to stare at each other. But just then there came a loud knocking on the outer door of the Inn. The murder had been discovered. The gendarmes were after him.

"When we heard the knocking we stood still by the portrait. We three were silent in the room, and it seemed to me that the painted man was listening, holding his breath, as we were. Then the knocking came again. 'It's the police!' he said. He caught hold of my wrist. 'I killed him. But he betrayed you. Will you give me up?'"

Again she was silent. And now she seemed absorbed in thought and unconscious that I was with her in the room. At last I couldn't stand her silence any longer, and I said, rather sharply, for my nerves were all on edge:

"What did you do?"

She looked up, as if startled.

"Do? Oh, about him! I showed him how to get away through a window at the back of the Inn, and when he was gone I opened the door to the gendarmes. And then I lied to them. I said no one had been there. They asked me lots of questions. I kept them as long as I could. I told them that I had been supping, that I had been drinking champagne. I even"—she smiled—"I even let them think I had drunk a little too much. Anything—to hold their attention; to keep them with me! At last they left me."

"And didn't they—"

"Oh, yes! It was a forlorn hope. When they left me they knocked up the landlord, and then, of course, the game was up, as they say."

"And—what happened?"

"They caught him eventually. And he was tried by a French jury and, naturally, acquitted. He's still living at El-Djer."

"With—with the woman?"

"Oh, no! She bolted. She's probably in the Kasbah at Algiers by now, earning her living as such women do."

Just then there came a tap on the shutter. I started violently.

She smiled.

"It's only Raoul, I expect, come to take away the tea."

It was Raoul. When he had carried the tray out she got up.

"It will soon be dinnertime. I must go to my room."

She went to the now open French window.

"Still raining!" she said. "But I don't mind."

She looked round at me.

"Now you know why I don't care where I am, and why I don't think it would be especially interesting to explore the country of Mistral."

And then she went out of the room, and I heard her footsteps dying away down the corridor.

I remember that I said to myself:

"Ibanez is right. The dead command."

THE VILLA BY THE SEA

In a country house where I was staying some months ago I met a man whom I will call Arthur Pierce. He had with him a very charming wife. We became in a few days almost intimate, as sometimes happens when people are thrown closely together in country houses. We talked of many things under the sun and, when the time came for saying goodbye to our hostess, we agreed to meet again. Shortly afterwards I received an invitation from the Pierces to visit them at their house in Surrey, not far from Farnham, on the edge almost of Tilford Common. While I was there Pierce and his wife between them—for she often charmingly "put in her oar," sometimes appealed to, sometimes unasked—told me a story.

We had been talking about lingering influences, and how they mysteriously affect sensitive persons, like beings almost, invisible, inarticulate, laying frail hands on our sleeves as if trying to attract and hold our attention, anxious to give us knowledge of the past. Why? We seldom know. It is as if they suffered under a burden and desired to rid themselves of it, or as if they were pushed to an attempt at revelation by some secret power. Many of us have been vaguely, or even sharply, aware of such influences at certain moments in our lives; in a certain room of a house, in a certain corner of a garden, near a door in a dark alley, by an old well, on a moss-covered terrace before a blind and deserted building—in one place or another. In the Pierces' studio drawing room on a summer night, when the owls were hooting in the pine woods outside, after a long talk on this mystery—for a mystery it still is to me, despite the many debates and the profuse writings on the subject—they told me this story, the story of the villa by the sea.

"We came upon it by chance," Pierce said, "some years ago when Elaine and I were on our honeymoon. We were motoring for a few days in North Africa on our way from the baths of Hammam Meskoutine to Tunis. Rather late in the afternoon, when we were nearing a small seaside town where we intended to pass the night, I saw a white gleam of walls and cup-shaped cupolas on a height above, and close to, the sea, a white gleam showing enticingly through a sort of jungle of pine trees and palms, which suggested to my mind a garden on the French Riviera. No other house was in sight. The road was deserted. On that day I saw no smoke of a steamer, no sail of a fishing boat, upon the tempestuous sea. For though the African sun was still strong there was a wind blowing, sirocco, I think, which roared through the trees, and dashed clouds of spray on the rocks below the bluff on which the villa was perched in its sheltering garden. It looked to me like a thing in hiding, yet half inquisitive, unable to resist a peep at the world below it, at the ocean, the rocks, the narrow winding highway, at Elaine and me flying by. The villa peeped down at us and I looked up at it. A white gleam, a faint thrill of interest on my part, and it was gone. But a moment later, as we swung round the point, I saw low down, close to the road, a board with *A Louer* in big black letters upon it. There were other words too, but I had not time to decipher them. The Arab chauffeur drove fast. We had had a long day, and he was no doubt in a hurry to reach the next stopping-place.

"The little town which was our destination proved to be not far off, though the villa was completely isolated. Some fifteen minutes of fast going and the first houses were upon us. We extricated ourselves from our impedimenta before the colonnade of the only inn, the Hotel de Paris. And Elaine's voice was almost immediately raised in the delightfully English demand for *une tasse de thé*."

"And what about your voice, Arthur?" said Mrs. Pierce. "If you are going into these details—"

"Details make a story live, dear!"

"Then—he passionately demanded a whisky and soda."

"And got it—to my damnation," said Pierce. "But to return to our villa. We had meant to leave the next morning after breakfast, but Fate was against us—"

"Or for us, perhaps," interjected his wife. "Don't you think so, Arthur?"

"Well—yes. For the more of interest and of strangeness you cram into your life the better. Anything, anything but the banal! Our chauffeur came to us while we were at breakfast with a tale of grave interior damage to his car. It was, I think, a fifth-hand Ford, or something of that nature. He said he couldn't get it to move that day, and perhaps not the next. It was apparently very sick indeed. What was to be done? We could have taken a slow train to Tunis, but we wanted to see the country. The inn wasn't bad. We were not in a hurry. We decided to wait till the car got better. Mohammed left us changed. The sense of motion which never seems quite to abandon one on a motor trip of the day-by-day kind had suddenly slipped from us. We were enveloped by a sensation of stagnant calm."

"Not stagnant, Arthur!"

"Wasn't it, dear? I remember you lethargically ordered a boiled egg as Mohammed left the room."

"That was my way of expressing serenity of mind, but not stagnation."

"And a very charming way too! The egg eventually came, was disposed of, and then the empty day lay before us. What were we going to do in Sidi Barka? It was then that a white gleam of walls, the snowy purity of little cupolas emerging, or rather half emerging, from the green of pines and palms enticed my imagination, and I asked Elaine whether on the previous day she had noticed in passing the villa by the sea. She hadn't. I told her of it, told her it was like a white secret that seemed almost anxious to be unveiled. I added that it was to let, and suggested we should go in a carriage, lunch in its Riviera-like garden, and have a look at it. She agreed."

"Yes, but I remember wondering at your eagerness, Arthur."

"I wondered at it too. But the villa enticed me."

"Enticed you—yes!" said Mrs. Pierce, with a sort of imaginative gravity, and for a moment her large grey eyes rested upon me with still intensity. "It had called to you as we went by, but not to me. I suppose," she added, speaking to me, "I am less sensitive than he is, in spite of being a woman."

"That is against the usually accepted theory," I said non-committally. "But I have noticed again and again that what are generally called occult influences rather break than conform to rules."

"You are right," said Pierce. "Well, we ordered lunch and a carriage, and then I got hold of the landlord to enquire about the villa. I wanted to procure an order to 'view' it. The landlord, a Frenchman, at first seemed rather vague, but when I became precise in my description he exclaimed:

"'*Ah, oui, monsieur! La Villa Persane! En effet, c'est vide.*'

"And he added that since the abrupt departure of Monsieur and Madame Ormely no one had occupied it. He could easily get me an order to see the villa, and in fact he did so. He sent into the town, and when the carriage came round he handed me a card on which was written in French a permission to go over the house and grounds.

"'But the key?' I said.

"'Monsieur will get the key on the way. I have told the driver.'

"Well and good! The luncheon basket was put into the victoria; we followed; the Maltese driver cracked his whip; the two horses trotted, jingling their bells. We were *en route* for the villa by the sea.

"The key! When and where should we get the key? I wondered as we drew near to the outskirts of the town, and when we had left the last mean little house behind I inquired of the driver. In tragic French he replied that the key was waiting for us at the house of Monsieur Bonnivard, the great vine grower, to whom the villa belonged. This gentleman lived 'out there.' The whip was pointed towards the mountainside on our left. In the distance I saw a large white square house standing in vineyards. As we drew near I could make out two stone posts, and a gate of wrought iron, and a hedge of thorny cactus surrounding a small domain. We stopped before the gate, I gave the driver the card 'to view,' and he disappeared up the stony private road to the house. In about five minutes he returned with a good-sized key and the card in his hand. He gave both to me, heaved himself up to his box, whistled to his horses, and again we were off. And this time we did not stop till, after what seemed to me a long and somewhat desolate drive, we came in sight of the villa, or rather of those sections of it which were visible from the road.

"'There it is!' I remember exclaiming to Elaine."

"Yes," said his wife, "and then you made me get out and walk. You wouldn't let the carriage drive up to the house."

"I didn't want a Maltese atmosphere in that delicious place. For already then I knew it was delicious. And—wasn't it, Elaine?"

"Yes. How we loved it!"

Again she turned her grey eyes on me with a still intensity.

"You know we took it," she said. "We had to."

"Yes," said her husband. "It made us take it. Oh, it had a will of its own, the villa by the sea!"

"What was it like?" I asked.

"Well, in the first place it was modern. You're disappointed? He's disappointed, Elaine!"

"I'm sorry!" she said. "But we can't help it, can we? We have to tell the truth. And it was modern, fantastic-modern, but oh, so clever and delicious! It was as white as snow, with cupolas, and edgings of Moorish tiles, and little outside tiled stairways, and morsels of terraces, and doors of cedar wood, and deep-set windows with round arches, and Moorish pillars, and a dear flat roof, or rather roofs, for bits were higher than other bits, and there were narrow steps up and down. The man who made it had imagination and subtlety. And I am sure he had read

The Arabian Nights after being at Monte Carlo. For there were touches of the Riviera mixed up with the African touches. Indeed, the whole thing simply smelt of the Mediterranean. Didn't it, Arthur?"

"Yes. And the sea sang in every corner of the house and the garden, and yet, in some odd way, the villa seemed remote from the sea. There were so many trees. The luxuriance of foliage was so great. And the gardens seemed climbing about the house and stretching out arms to hide it away from the sea. It was a retreat, a hiding place, and yet it was cheerful. In its remoteness from the world there was nothing sad. We called it a radiant hiding place where no one would ever come, or even dream of coming. The nearest town—Sidi Barka! Now who, I ask you, has ever heard of Sidi Barka?"

I had to acknowledge that the words Sidi Barka conveyed very little to me.

"But who," I added, "was the strange being who had built such a delicious house in such a remote place?"

"We found out eventually," said Pierce. "It was a French eccentric. God bless all eccentrics, say I! They flavour this world in a rut. They put in the spices. We curse them, or laugh at them, but we should be duller without them. Our Frenchman spent unnumbered francs on the villa by the sea, lived in it for two or three months, got sick of his lonely Paradise—we heard he had a mistress who deserted him—and finally sold it for next to nothing to the vine grower who handed us over the key. The vine grower bought the villa as a speculation, and eventually let it to a Mr. and Mrs. Eardsley."

"Mr. and Mrs. Eardsley!" repeated Mrs. Pierce in a dreamy, almost mysterious, voice.

Both husband and wife had—it seemed to me—pronounced these words with a peculiar significance. I was alert to know more about the Eardsleys.

"English?" I asked. "Americans?"

The Pierces exchanged glances. Then Pierce replied:

"They were—Eardsleys. Now let me get on. We are examining the irregular, the fantastic exterior of the villa with delight. And the sound of the sea is in our ears all the time, and the sound of whirring pine trees, and of rustling swishing palms, and of many birds. But we are sheltered from the wind. That day it was not really strong. It just gave a stir to everything and filled the garden with sounds. I remember we said it set the garden conversing."

"Yes," said his wife with a smile. "Everything big was talking."

"But the bougainvillea which decorated the house theatrically, and the jasmine, and the masses of geraniums, and the roses, and the hibiscus were very discreet. They left the talking to the trees. Well, we were like children that day. We saved up the house. We didn't go in for quite a long time. First we explored the gardens. I call them gardens because they were so broken up, so diversified, so 'rummagy' almost. They climbed to the top of a steep hill, from the summit of which at a distance one could see the town of Sidi Barka lying at the edge of its harbour. They were terraced gardens, with winding narrow paths, and masses of trees. There was a certain wildness in them mingled with a certain fragmentary formality. And they were full of hiding places which seemed deliberately made for two people. Seats—dark green and white—were dotted about here and there. But the most definite feature of the gardens was the palm avenue. This was, I should say, almost in the centre of the little property, and quite near to the house. It stretched away from an oval space sheltered by Lebbek trees—we called it the *salon vert*, and took coffee there after lunch and dinner— and was long and exquisitely harmonious. The palms on either side of the broad sandy alley must all have been planted about the same time. They matched almost perfectly in size. Their fan-like glossy leaves formed a roof overhead, but the sunlight trickled through in many places. Shadows and sun shafts made patterns on the sand. Two hedges of red geraniums flanked the wrinkled trunks of the palms. It was a romantic place, with a silence, and a softness of warmth which seemed peculiarly its own. 'Hide here and love!' it seemed to say. That was Elaine's expression of its meaning. But we were on our honeymoon then."

"I still think I found the right meaning," said Mrs. Pierce gravely.

"'The Eardsleys must often have walked in this avenue,' Elaine said that day. Already we began to take an interest in that unknown couple who had been the last tenants of this now deserted Paradise. And, having wandered all over the gardens—except on one terrace—we ate our lunch under the palms."

Pierce turned to his wife.

"I think it was there that in both our minds was born a desire to be eccentric, wasn't it, Elaine?"

"In mine at least!" she replied.

"And in mine, I believe. I remember thinking: 'How delightful to be absurd for once and to take this for our own!' And presently I thought: 'Why not? Life is short. Why let it be dull? Why not put out a hand and catch at the firefly—romance?' And I looked at Elaine. But I didn't say anything then. And at last it was time to enjoy what we had both been saving up. I felt for the key, and we got up and went towards the house."

Pierce paused for a moment, and Mrs. Pierce, after waiting as if fearing to interrupt his thought, said: "Then came a surprise upon us. We found that the house was furnished and all in perfect order. Till we unlocked the door and went in we supposed it to be unfurnished. But the vine grower had bought it just as it was and, so, the Eardsleys had taken it."

"Was it pretty?" I asked.

"Tell him!" said Mrs. Pierce to her husband.

And Pierce spoke again.

"Heaven knows what other English people would have thought of it," he said. "We, perhaps, were biased in its favour. The furnishing was undoubtedly eccentric. There was—who could expect it?—no homely English comfort. Instead there were a fantasy, a daintiness, an amusingness, a mingling of Africa and the Riviera. There was a black and sealing wax red room, and there was an orange and silver room. And there was a room that suggested spring, all blue and daffodil yellow and misty green. There were divans with multicoloured cushions. And there were Louis Quinze cabinets and chairs. Rugs from Tunis lay on the parquet floors. In one room there was an alabaster vase with an electric light hidden in it. The bedrooms had huge painted Arab bedsteads, and painted and brass clamped coffers such as the Ouled Nail women use to hold their finery. There was no subtle harmony in the house, but there were many surprises. And some of them were delightful. No doubt our taste ought to have been outraged by what we saw. But I'm afraid it wasn't. I'm afraid we were delighted almost like children. Evidently the present owner took care of his property, sent someone frequently to look after it, to open the windows to the sea, to keep it clean and fresh. There was in it none of that fustiness peculiar to most shut-up and abandoned houses. And, as I said, even the rugs were spread on the floors. We wandered everywhere, examined everything, and at last sat down on a divan in a room upstairs. In this room there was a glass door which opened to a small white terrace surrounded by low, foot-high walls. From the terrace, through a gap in the trees, there was a view of the sea.

"We sat down to rest and *feel* the house. And it was soon afterwards that, for the first time, I felt an influence in the house. Elaine had left me and had gone out upon the terrace I mentioned. From where I was sitting I could not see her. I was not expecting anything. I was simply sitting there and imagining that the villa by the sea was my home, and Elaine's, that we were living there in a wonderful isolation, far away from our own country, our usual pursuits, our relations and friends. I heard through the window-space the sound of the sea, the whisper—the wind had lowered—of the innumerable trees. In a way I was dreaming, I suppose, as sometimes one dreams in daylight. I think I had let go of my mind just then, and perhaps, because of that—I don't know—the influence was able to approach me, to slip in as it were through an open door. Anyhow—it came then.

"I seemed suddenly and mysteriously to become aware that in this room where I was sitting something tremendous had once taken place. I knew this. The walls, the floor, the furniture, and the draperies seemed suddenly and quite definitely to tell me so. 'Here, in this small enclosed space,' I said to myself, I remember, 'something extraordinary has happened in the past, something such as has happened in very few chambers of men.'"

"Was it a sitting room?" I asked.

And I don't know why I was moved to ask that question.

"It was like the charming sitting room of a woman—not English. But there was a big Arab bed in a recess to the left of the window. And opening out of the room there was a bath and dressing room. Elaine remained outside on the terrace."

"I was feeling the villa in my way," said his wife, "and imagining all sorts of things, pleasant things, romantic, wonderful things."

"I was glad of that," said Pierce. "I wanted to give myself up to the influence which I had suddenly felt so strongly. I remember that I sat very still, and that I tried to empty myself of thought, tried to leave plenty of room for anything that wanted to come in."

"And what happened then?" I asked, as he paused.

"This happened. I seemed to realize a woman standing outside alone on the terrace who was not Elaine, who was not at all like Elaine, and a man in the room not myself, not at all like me. Something, I felt, had once occurred in that room between two people, a woman and a man, something so strange and tremendous—for them—that it had somehow affected the room in which it had happened. I could not tell what it was."

"Did you feel that it was connected with a crime, or that it was a crime?" I said. "Was there physical violence in it?"

"That I couldn't tell. But I felt that it had been very sad, even that there must have been something like terror in it. As I sat there I began to feel a sort of moral fear. There was nothing definitely physical in it. No; it was moral fear, fear of the soul, such fear as might come upon a man expectant of punishment, but not of physical punishment. Presently Elaine must have shifted her foot upon the terrace. I heard a dry, slightly scraping, sound. I thought: 'She is coming in!' and with the thought a sort of interior tremor seemed to shake me. An instant later she did come back into the room, and I got up quickly to meet her. And then, with the movement, the whole thing left me as suddenly as it had come, but not before Elaine had had time to notice something."

"And what was that?" I said to Mrs. Pierce. "What did you notice?"

"Simply that Arthur looked very peculiar," she answered, "strained, I thought, and unusually grave. I even—but it may have been merely imagination—fancied he had become very pale. I spoke about it, didn't I, Arthur?"

"Yes. But I didn't tell you what I had been feeling."

"No," said Mrs. Pierce to me. "He didn't tell me, although we were on our honeymoon."

"Ah, but I had a very good reason for my silence! I didn't want to give the influence away. Such things are shy birds. They have to be encouraged, like the curious robin which longs to approach you, which hops all round you, but at a brusque movement flutters away. Already I thought of the influence as one thinks of a living thing. And I didn't want to *brusquer les choses*. So I said nothing to Elaine."

"But then," I said, "had you already made up your mind to come back to the villa?"

"I could hardly say that. The exact truth, I think, was that I already knew that I was going to be familiar with the villa. I knew that this short visit was going to be repeated, that I should see again, and often, and intimately, the curious, fantastic little rooms, that I should often stand upon the terraces and stroll through the hidden ways of the climbing gardens. Without definitely making up my mind to anything just then, I knew all this. Elaine came in and seemed to wonder a little. But as I said nothing she, incurious as are few women—"

"Say rather discreet, Arthur!"

"Discreet, then—didn't press the matter. And soon we were outside the house and I was turning the key in the door. When I had drawn the key out Elaine's eyes met mine, and she said—do you remember what you said, Elaine?"

"Yes. I said: 'Well, Arthur?' And you said: 'But how can we?' And I said: 'I don't know, but—don't you think we shall?' And then we both looked at the white walls and the cupolas. And we listened to the sound of the sea in the trees. And then, in silence, we went back to the palm avenue, and stood there breathing in the peace and the remoteness and gazing at the patterns on the sand. And all the time we were living there. The villa was ours, and the garden was ours, and the sound of the sea in the trees was ours. We had done with our usual life. We had become two eccentrics and had decided that we would be happy."

"Yes," said Pierce, "that was it. And then we went back to the carriage, and found the Maltese coachman lying on his back on the grass near it, sending his snores to Heaven. And we woke him and drove back to the vine grower's house near the mountain. And, but not immediately— for we really did struggle against eccentricity, and made a feeble attempt to be dull and ordinary and strictly conventional—we took the villa by the sea."

"But not till we had been back in England for some time," said Mrs. Pierce. "We were living in London then, in Wilton Place. And there came a whole week of yellow fog. Arthur had found out before we left Africa how much a year the villa would cost. And in the fog I kept saying to him: '*Only* three hundred a year! *Only* three hundred a year!' And at last he couldn't bear it any longer. And he rushed almost frantically to his writing table and began to write with desperation. I said to him: 'What are you writing?' And he said: 'Something—it all! A cheque for the first quarter.' And I nearly cried with joy."

"Yes," Pierce said. "That was how we gave in and became, in a moment, in the twinkling of an eye, two eccentrics."

"One thing strikes me," I said to Pierce. "What you had felt in that room with the terrace. I should have thought that the sensation you had there might have set you against the villa."

"On the contrary, it drew me back to the villa. I was intrigued by it. I longed to feel more, to know more. When I thought of that room I was fascinated and longed to be in it again."

"And while you were in London you never mentioned the matter to your wife?"

"No, never."

"I suppose I ought to owe him a grudge for that," said Mrs. Pierce. "But really I sometimes think in these voluble and all-revealing days a human being who can hold his tongue, even to his wife, is deserving of astonished respect. So—I forgive him."

"You see what one gains by silence!" said Pierce. "The priceless blessing of a wife's forgiveness. And now—soon after Christmas we set out for Tunisia; we arrived at Sidi Barka and descended at the inn. We had brought no servants with us. No English servant who respects him or herself—and they all do that when they are bored or cross—would remain long in the neighbourhood of Sidi Barka. We were too wise to attempt the impossible. We would get our servants—two or three at most—at Sidi Barka. We got them, and they didn't turn out at all badly. Peace be with them! As soon as we had engaged them we settled in at the villa by the sea. Elaine had the terrace room as her bedroom. You know the—"

"Yes," I said.

"Other rooms had terraces, of course. But I call that the terrace room. She chose it. Didn't you, Elaine?"

"Yes," said his wife. "I had no feeling about it then, except that it was the bedroom I liked best."

"I had a room close by. It was odd—that settling down in remoteness, with no friends or acquaintances near, no ties, no definite duties. It was odd settling down to the eccentric life. Of course I had my painter's work when I chose to do it. Indeed, there would have been nothing strange in our staying for a few weeks anywhere, in however remote a place. But we were living in our own house. That made all the difference. We had taken the villa by the sea as home.

"Just at first we were occupied in finding out things, things about the house and gardens, special charms, special oddities, special eccentricities. We were discovering hiding places. We were getting to know. And we found a terrace we had not noticed before we came to live at the villa.

"This terrace was at the very bottom of the property, and had no sheltering trees, no flowers or plants to decorated it. It ran along by a wall which divided the garden from the high road, and at the far end of it there was a large isolated room built against the rock. The outside walls of this room were stone-coloured. Perhaps that was why I had not noticed it before I came to live in the villa. From this terrace we looked right upon the sea. It was, so to speak, out in the world. Walking upon it you could be seen—the upper part of you, that is—from the highway. In the room at the end of the terrace, which had plain whitewashed walls, there was a rummage of furniture. Apparently things not wanted in the house had been put in there. Among them was a writing table with drawers. An inkstand with dried ink in it stood on the table, with some penholders lying beside it. There were two or three chairs. There was a large sofa, a bookcase. But all was in a certain disorder. A roll of carpet stood on end in a corner. The room looked rather dismal. Why it had been built there we never knew. It had a big window, which looked out over the sea. Elaine suggested that perhaps I could use it as a studio. Later I did a little painting there.

"The weather when we were first at the villa was rather rainy and stormy. Nevertheless we were not disappointed with our new home. We both loved it from the first. It certainly was very strange having absolutely no acquaintances, no engagements, no ties of any sort, seeing no one, except the servants and a few fisherfolk who dwelt in a little village some ten minutes' walk from the house. Few people passed on the highway that ran by the sea. Now and then we saw from some nook in the garden, unseen ourselves, a horseman go by, a string of carts, or, very occasionally this, a hurrying motor which was gone in a moment. Scarcely any English or American tourists, it seems, visit Sidi Barka. There is no travellers' season there. Only those few people who explore Tunisia by motor go there, and even they never stay more than one night. The place is in very truth out of the world.

"What did we do there? I scarcely know what we did at first, but when the weather cheered up, and the sun shone brilliantly, and the sea put on glorious colours, the days were too short for us. Never have I known days to slip by so swiftly as they did in the villa by the sea."

"And—the lingering influence?" I asked.

"Ah! Well, now!" said Pierce. "Elaine, you see, had the room. I was often in and out of it, but I seldom sat in it for long."

"Even in Africa you had said nothing—"

"To her? Not a word. I wondered whether she would notice anything. I was resolved to suggest nothing to her. We had been told all about the Frenchman who built and furnished the house. He had, of course, done it for a woman. And, almost equally of course, after a short time in that very complete isolation, he and the woman had quarrelled and parted. Knowing that, I might well have supposed that there had been the final, and perhaps terrible, quarrel in Elaine's room, and that that had been the something tremendous which had mysteriously left its influence behind like a dweller in the otherwise deserted villa. That would, I think, have been very natural. But it was not so.

"I felt no interest whatever in the Frenchman and his mistress; on the other hand—why, I can't tell you—I often secretly longed to know something about Mr. and Mrs. Eardsley. And presently I realized that Elaine was also becoming interested in our immediate predecessors in the villa by the sea. Several times she spoke of the Eardsleys in a way which made me certain that they were very often in her mind. And one evening, when we were sitting late in the open space which gave on to the palm avenue under the Lebbek trees, she said:

"'I wonder what the Eardsleys were like. I wish we knew.'

"'Why?' I said.

"'Well, they used to be here.'

"'Yes, but so were that Frenchman and his lady love. Do you wonder about them?'

"'No,' she said, 'I feel no interest whatever in them.'

"'Why?' I said again.

"'I don't know. I don't think there can have been very much in them.'

"'Well, but it was he who planned the house, and had it built, and furnished it so fantastically.'

"'Yes, that's true. But it is the Eardsleys I want to know something about.'

"So Elaine—as I then knew—was feeling as I was. That seemed to me strange—strange that both of us should, as it were, skip the undoubtedly clever and imaginative man who had made what we both delighted in, and come to the Eardsleys about whom we knew nothing but the name.

"'I really wish you continued, Elaine—'"

"Yes, I remember."

"'I really wish you would try to find out something about them. I am sure that you could. Ask someone, the fishermen, or the landlord of the hotel at Sidi Barka. They must know something.'

"I said I would make some inquiries, and on the following morning— you see, I am an obedient husband, especially when my curiosity marches hand in hand with my wife's—I set out for the fishing village I have mentioned. As yet I knew none of the people there, though I had nodded and wished 'good day' to the few I had seen from time to time when walking by the sea. Elaine did not accompany me that day. She was hidden away somewhere in the garden with a book and her dreams. She developed a terrible capacity for daytime dreaming in the villa by the sea.

"When I reached the village—it is built on the edge of a long curving stretch of sand—some boats had just returned from the fishing, and were being hauled up on the beach by swarthy and wild-looking men and boys. I stood and watched them for a while. I was trying to pick my man. Presently I decided to address myself to an oldish fellow, whose straggling beard was streaked with grey, and who seemed, I thought, to have a certain authority over the others. He soon saw that my eyes were upon him, and cast from time to time fiery glances at me. He was probably suspicious of the stranger and wondered what I was up to.

"Presently his work was done, and he threw a rough sort of jacket over his broad shoulders, without putting his bare brown arms into the sleeves, and turned, apparently to go up to his house in the village. And as he turned he again sent a sharp inquiring glance at me. Thereupon I went up to him and said 'good morning' in French. He replied gruffly and with a markedly foreign accent. I asked him about the fishing. He answered in bad French. I spoke then in Italian. Immediately his face lighted up and, speaking that language, or rather a mixture of Italian and a dialect which certainly had its origin in Sicily, he told me he was a native of Catania, but had left there with his family when he was a boy to settle in Tunis, and now lived where I had found him with his wife and family. In return I told him that I was living nearby, at the Villa Persane. This was evidently no news to him, for he jerked his head and exclaimed: '*Si, si,*' with the manner of one who is told what he already knows.

"'I should like to go out fishing now and then,' I went on. And I asked him if I might go in his boat. He scented money at once. I knew that by the hawk-like look that came into his large dark eyes, and a sideways lifting of his upper lip that was characteristic of Sicily. We were soon good friends, and presently, feeling that I could not keep him much longer from the meal which was probably awaiting him in one of the cottages up yonder, I asked if my predecessor at the villa, Signor Eardsley, had ever gone fishing. He jerked up his strong blue chin and clicked his tongue against his teeth.

"'Was the *Signore* here long?' I asked.

"'*Si,* for many months,' said he.

"'Did you know him?'

"'He never spoke to us fishermen.'

"'What sort of man was he?' I said.

"I felt I could be blatant with my new friend. What did it matter if he were intrigued by my obvious curiosity?

"'Tall, very tall, with white hair,' said the fisherman.

"'Oh—an old man!'

"'They said he was young, *Signore*, but he had the snow on his head.'

"'Young, with white hair!'

"'*Ma si!* "Sorrow hair" the women call it.'

"'Prematurely white! Was he English?'

"'*Si, Signore*. The white *Inglese* we called him. He was hiding here.'

"'Hiding?' I said.

"'That's what we all thought. Why should an Englishman come to live here?'

"'Well, I am English!' I said with a smile. Do you think—'

"'*Non, Signore!* But the white Englishman was different from you.'

"'And his wife?'

"'She was a beautiful woman'—*una bellissima donna*, he said—'but she ran away from him. One day she was gone and she never came back.'

"When I heard the man say that I immediately felt sure that he was mixing up in his mind the Frenchman and his mistress with the Eardsleys.

"'But that was the lady who lived with the Frenchman, the man who built the Villa Persane,' I said.

"'*Non, Signore!*' said the fisherman obstinately. It was the wife of the white *Inglese*. She left him. She ran away. He stayed up there'—he threw out his right arm in a large reckless gesture—'for weeks after, all alone. And then one day he was gone. He had been something bad in his own country. That is what we all thought. He had come here to hide.'

"'Now tell me,' I said, 'don't you think I am hiding here, too?'

"The man stared into my face with a lack of self-consciousness that seemed to me animal. Then he jerked up his chin.

"'*Non, Signore!* You are different.'

"I gave him something, promised to go out one day in his boat, and left him."

Pierce stopped at this point in his narrative to light a cigar. He blew out some smoke, watched it rise and evaporate, travelling in most delicate curves till we lost it, then said to me:

"One thinks about, meditates over, a lot of things—anyhow things," he said. "Doesn't one?"

"Yes," I said.

"Have you ever wondered what becomes of the people who disappear, of the perhaps well-known people who get mixed up publicly in horrible scandals, who are accused of offences and crimes, whose names are thrown to the greedy public like offal to hungry dogs? Some of them aren't sent to prison, but they are done for all the same. Others are condemned and go to prison, and eventually come out. All these people, or nearly all, disappear. Have you ever wondered what becomes of them, where they go to live—they must live somewhere—what they do for the rest of their days, what human beings they dwell among and know? For instance—"

And he mentioned two or three well-known names of men of our time who had "gone under" after terrible public scandals.

"Have you ever wondered where they are now?"

I answered that now and then I had thought about that, and with a peculiar sort of pain and almost horror. For such thoughts bring with them a dreadfully intimate realization of the ugly mysteries of life.

"Well," pursued Pierce, "that day, as I walked away from the fisherman, I pondered over the fates of the disappeared. Might not one of them, Eardsley, have disappeared to the villa by the sea? I could not remember having ever heard of a scandal, or a crime, connected with the name of Eardsley. But I supposed that those unfortunate people who disappeared dropped, with their former lives, former associations, their former names, the names which had become infamous through their own misdoings, or misfortunes. If Eardsley had really, as the fisherfolk supposed, sought the Villa Persane as a hiding place, the chances were that his real name wasn't Eardsley at all.

"A sudden storm came up that evening, one of those abrupt and amazing storms which sometimes attack the North African world. A wild wind smothered the sea with white horses, and thrashed mercilessly through the trees of our garden. All the windows had to be shut. The persiennes were fast closed beyond them. While we were dining I suggested to Elaine that we should have a wood fire lighted in her bed-sitting-room and go up there after dinner.

"'But what about the wind?' she said. 'Perhaps the fire will smoke.'

"'Let's try it,' I answered. 'I feel I should like to sit there tonight, and in this storm something living and warm will give us a cosy feeling.'

"She agreed, gave the order. The fire was lighted and luckily burned well. We shut ourselves in with it, and settled down to an unusual evening. By this time the rain was coming down in torrents, such rain as we never know in England. It seemed to us almost as if the sea were being miraculously emptied upon the villa from the sky. The roar of the sea filled the house, mingled with the voices of wind and rain.

We were enclosed in fury.

"I had not yet told Elaine of my colloquy with the Sicilian fisherman. I thought I would wait and see whether she returned to the subject of the Eardsleys.

"She was doing some embroidery that night and I was smoking a cigar. Presently she laid the embroidery down—do you remember, Elaine?"

"Yes. And I said how dreadful it would be if two people, who had deliberately gone away from all their world, and who were entirely isolated by their own action, were to quarrel."

"Yes. And then we discussed what the misery and the terror of such a quarrel in complete isolation would be like, with no one to appeal to, no one to judge the rights of the case—if judgment were desired—no one to put in the word of common sense, or of harsh kindness, which sometimes has power to bring angry people back to a normal state. And if the quarrel were irreparable! You kept harping on that, Elaine."

"I know. And the storm was all about us, making everything seem black and desolate in spite of the fire."

"At last," said Pierce, "I asked Elaine why her thoughts had turned on the ugly subject we were discussing so exhaustively, and with so much painful detail, and why she kept using that beastly word— irreparable. But she evaded giving me an answer and, instead, said to me:

"'I wonder whether the Eardsleys ever quarrelled when they were living here.'

"That was my cue. I took it and said:

"'I am told that they did. Or rather I have been told something which implies that they did.'

"Then naturally, at once, Elaine was all interest and eager curiosity, and I told her fully what I have just told you, what the fisherman had said to me on the sands that day. I even told her what my subsequent thoughts had been. When I had finished she said:

"'And so those people think the Eardsleys were hiding here!'

"'Evidently they do. But most of them, I expect, are Sicilians, and my experience of Sicilians of that class tells me that they have wild, and usually evil, imaginings about most strangers and foreigners within their gates.'

"That was my reply. And then Elaine startled me by saying that she believed the fishermen were right, that she believed the Eardsleys had quarrelled in our villa irreparably. Of course, I asked her why she believed this, knowing absolutely nothing about the Eardsleys. And that led to two avowals, one from Elaine, the other from me. Elaine!"

Pierce's way of saying his wife's name was a call to her to speak, and she answered it without hesitation.

"My avowal amounted to this, that I had gradually been infected—it seemed like that—with a curious impression of intense mental anguish, which came to me in my bedroom and upon the terrace outside my window. This impression did not connect itself in my mind with two people. It's rather difficult to describe. It was as if in living at the villa, and being, of course, often in my bedroom, I gradually came to realize, as I had never realized before, how intense, how extraordinary, the mental anguish of a woman might be in certain circumstances."

"Ah—the mental anguish of a woman!" I said.

"Yes. Of course I, like others, have had sad moments in my life. But it seemed to me that I had never at all realized sorrow and pain till I came to live in that room in the villa. The room had given me, I had come at last to think, that intimate realization. And so I told Arthur."

"But then weren't you miserable in the villa?"

"No. That was the odd thing. I knew I was very happy. My feeling was: 'this awful unhappiness is possible; it exists; it has been experienced; it has been experienced here'—for I got to that. 'But I am happy. I know this horrible grief as if it were mine, but it is not mine. It is outside me.' I seemed to have a power, quite beyond the power of the imagination, to realize this frightful devastating misery and horror—there was horror in it—and yet *I* was still happy. For it wasn't my grief. I told Arthur this."

"And it was the grief of a woman?"

"I never thought of it as anything else."

"And the impression was perpetually with you?"

"Oh, no! Only now and then. It came and went. Sometimes days passed without my feeling it at all. But each time it returned it seemed to be more acute. And before the night of the storm I had begun to connect it with Mrs. Eardsley. I don't know why. So, when Arthur told me what the fisherman had said, I felt certain that something terrible had really happened between Mr. and Mrs. Eardsley, something so terrible that vestiges of it—what am I to call them? I scarcely know— still clung to my room in the villa and affected me. And then Arthur told me of the curious impression he had had."

"Yes," said Pierce, "and we talked it over for a long time. The storm did not abate. On the contrary, it increased as the night grew deep.

What a talk we had by the fire! We discussed what type of sorrow, coming suddenly on a human being, would be the most terrible, the most difficult to endure. There are so many different types of sorrow, aren't there? We ranged over them that night. There is death, of course, sudden, absolutely unexpected death. But there are so many others. Elaine and I tried to come to a decision as to which would be the most unendurable. Here we were, two people who loved each other, far away from the world, wholly dependent for our happiness upon one another. Here we were—Eardsleys, let us suppose! What terrible thing, suddenly revealed or discovered, would most certainly and irreparably smash our happiness to pieces?"

"And drive me away from you!" interposed Mrs. Pierce.

"Yes, as—according to the fisherman—Mrs. Eardsley was driven away from the man she was with in the villa, her husband probably, anyhow the man she was closely linked to."

"Did you come to any conclusion?" I asked.

"Elaine said that she thought the most terrible discovery a woman could make about a man would be that she had never known him."

"Never known him!" I said.

"That she had lived with him in the most intimate relation possible between two human beings without ever being really intimate with him at all, without ever knowing him at all as in essence he was. She thought that the sudden discovery that your lover had always been to you a stranger would be the most shocking she could conceive of."

"I still think so," said Mrs. Pierce.

"But," I said, "is that possible? Do you think any woman could live with a man in that relation, isolated, and not know him as he was?"

"Yes, I do."

"You think you could?"

"I think some women could."

"Ah!" said Pierce.

And I believe we both smiled at that moment.

"Perhaps I could—even the marvellous I! Anyhow, I am sure it has happened, that awful discovery of a long and complete ignorance in love."

"And what was your conclusion?" I asked of Pierce.

"I thought the most awful discovery, the most terrible thing that could come upon a human being in that relation, would be to find out that you were not loved where you had felt absolutely certain that you were loved."

"I confess," I said then to Mrs. Pierce, "that I should have thought a woman would have been almost certain to pitch upon that very thing."

"In a way I did," she said. "For to discover that would be like the discovery that one had been living with a stranger. Wouldn't it?"

"To be sure—yes. Well, then, I suppose you and your husband were really agreed."

"No. For I think I meant more than he did by what I said," she answered. "I meant by stranger a man whom you had not only never known as he really was in relation to yourself, but also in relation to others. For instance, suppose a woman married to a man she believes to be tender, merciful, kindhearted. She discovers he does not love her. That would be terrible. But suppose in addition she discovers him horribly ill-treating a child. That would be much more terrible."

"I understand," I said.

"We women are not quite so personal, so crassly individual, as men seem often to suppose," she added. "We can value virtues in men, hate and shrink from vices, which do not directly affect our own personal happiness. I knew a woman—probably you won't believe it, but it is true—who loved, and was loved by, a man. One day, by chance, she caught him brutally ill-treating a dog. That made her hate him. I happen to know it. She was never able after that to feel towards him as she had felt before. When he came into the room—she saw the dog."

"Mysteries!" I said. "And—the end of that night's strange discussion?"

"We sat still and silent," said Pierce, "and tried mutually to feel the Eardsleys, to feel what had happened in that room in the villa by the sea. And, of course, we were able to feel nothing. No influence made its presence known to us. But before we went to bed, very late, Elaine said to me:

"'Only two sets of people have lived here before us, it seems.'

"'Yes, I believe so,' I answered.

"'The Frenchman and his companion, and the Eardsleys. It's rather strange if in both cases the associations ended in disaster, isn't it?'

"'Yes. Do you think you and I shall quarrel irreparably if we stay on in the villa?'

"'I can't imagine such a thing. And yet—'

"I remember then I felt we were on the edge of becoming very morbid. Africa—the storm—our isolation—just then things were getting on our nerves. I decided it was time for bed.

"From that night Elaine and I gave the villa by the sea a new name. We called it 'The Hiding-Place.' Urged by Elaine, who began to seem almost obsessed by the desire to know something more definite about Mr. and Mrs. Eardsley, went to Sidi Barka to make some, if possible, discreet inquiries about them. I called at the Hotel de Paris, lunched there alone, and got into conversation afterwards with the landlord. I offered him a good cigar and asked him to join me over my coffee and to take a liqueur with me. He accepted and we had a talk. At first we discussed the sporting possibilities of the neighbourhood. I said it was a pity more travellers did not come to Sidi Barka, which lies at the edge of a tract of country attractive to sportsmen. In the forests nearby wild boar abound. There is excellent wild duck shooting in the marshy land near the sea to the south of the town. The landlord, an ardent lover of *la chasse*, grew eloquent on the resources of his native place. For I found he had been born in Sidi Barka. We agreed to go out after boar together later on. And presently I suggested that probably my predecessor in the Villa Persane had been a sportsman, had come to live there for *la chasse*.

"'Monsieur Eardsley!' said the landlord, raising his eyebrows and throwing up his square, thick-fingered hands.

"And he proceeded to tell me that never, during the whole time of his residence in the villa, did Monsieur Eardsley take a gun in his hands. Although he was English, young—

"'Young, with white hair!' I interjected at this point.

"'Monsieur knows he had white hair?' said the landlord, apparently surprised.

"'Yes, the fishermen at the village near us said so.'

"'Monsieur Eardsley was quite young, m'sieu,' said the landlord. 'His hair had gone white, God knows why! We think—my wife and I'—he leaned forward over the table towards me—'that he had had to leave his own country.'

"'Why?' said I carelessly. What makes you think that?'

"'He would never come into the town. He never had anything to do with anyone here. He never spoke to a soul who lives, except, of course, his poor wife and the servants. There were two of them, a Frenchwoman and a Jewess, both from Tunis.'

"'Why d'you call his wife poor?' I said. 'This is excellent benedictine.'

"'Yes, m'sieu. Another glass?'

"'Thank you.'

"'His wife left him suddenly and came away here, to take the train. I saw her for a moment. She looked terrible, m'sieu—terrible. She had been pretty, young, one of the fair English women all the world admires.

But then she was like one gone suddenly old. That day she was ugly. She had a tic, too. Her face went like this.'

"He twitched his face violently sideways.

"'Her left hand was trembling. She could hardly walk. She came in here for a minute and asked for some brandy. And she kept on saying: "When's the next train? When's the next train?" She was told—in two hours. But she went at once to the station. It was raining, m'sieu, but she walked up and down by herself in the rain till the train came in. The last I saw of her an Arab porter was helping her up into a carriage as you help a sick person. And she had no luggage—nothing with her.'

"'And her husband stayed on?'

"'For some weeks. I was away when he went. I did not see him go. They told me that after his wife left he was never seen outside the garden till the day he went away. But the fishermen used to see him sometimes walking up and down on the bottom terrace, where there is a room.'

"'I know it, of course.'

"'They had never seen him there before his wife left. They think he slept there too, because they used to see a light in the window very late. The French servant left the day after Madame, and only the Jewess stayed on. She was one of those Orientals from Tunis, wore a pointed cap—you know!'

"'Yes.'

"'It was she who got in the food and things. And—she didn't talk! Think of that, m'sieu!'

"'Extraordinary! An Oriental Jewess and not talk!'

"'She was old and heavy. But we think he paid her to—'

"And the landlord shut his big mouth and pressed his hand on it.

"Such was his report on the matter which interested us, and I conveyed it to Elaine. Two or three days later she said that she wanted to move into another bedroom, and she confessed that since she had heard the account of Mrs. Eardsley's flight, and of her condition when she was last seen in Sidi Barka, she had conceived a distaste for the room, pretty though it was.

"'For I am sure,' she said to me, 'Mrs. Eardsley got to know the thing that drove her away from the villa in that room. Let us shut it up and forget it. It is only there that we have felt—well, I think it must be her misery, her horror.'

"'And his!' I said.

"'His?' she said.

"'Yes.'

"'I have only felt hers!' said Elaine decisively. 'We will lock the room up. And then we can give ourselves happily to the rest of this darling house and delicious garden. There is only sorrow for me in that one room.'

"Elaine moved the same day and we locked the room up."

"But we did not forget it, did we, Elaine?"

"No. Though I never did what you did."

"What was that?" I asked, as Pierce said nothing.

"He kept the key of the room, and several times unlocked the door and shut himself in there at night when I was innocently asleep all unsuspecting. His curiosity was greater than mine."

"Or was it rather that your recollection of the room was more painful than mine?" said Pierce.

"Perhaps really it was that," said Mrs. Pierce. "My impression of grief had been terrible there. I can never put into words exactly what I felt—perhaps I ought to say was aware of in that room. It—it was like a spiritual foundering, as if a soul went under. Ever since then I have prayed every night that I may never have to endure a terrific moral shock. We happy people as a rule have absolutely no real understanding of deep moral misery. That is why we talk so airily of people 'getting over' things, and blame them so often for 'giving way' to their griefs. The reason the world has so little genuine sympathy to spare is because it possesses such a feeble imagination. But I had been given insight. Something had—told me, and in such a way that I could not help understanding. And because of that, I suppose, I had had enough of that room."

"And you were happy in the villa after you had moved from it?" I said.

"Yes, very happy. The influence did not follow me. It seemed to be locked in. But, of course, I still often thought of the Eardsleys and wished very much to know what had happened to them."

I turned towards Pierce.

"It's true," he said, "that I couldn't keep out of the room. But I didn't wish Elaine to know that I went there. And she didn't know at the time. I chose the night hours when, as she said, she was asleep."

"And the result?"

"Not remarkable. And I attribute that to the fact of my mind being far too self-conscious, far too definitely anxious to get on the trail.

These lingering influences, I am sure, are shy of the bloodhound mind. What they are I don't know, and don't suppose I shall ever know. How they succeed in remaining in a place, by what means they convey a knowledge of themselves to certain perhaps peculiarly constituted people, I cannot tell. They seem to me to be ultrasensitive, to come only when they are not sought for, but to retreat to a distance when pursued. They will have no dealings with a detective. When I was shut up in the room at night, when I stood upon the little terrace under the stars, or under the darkness of a clouded sky, I sometimes imagined that I felt something near me, or about me, something of the past that emanated—as smoke from a fire—from the destinies, as it were, of my predecessors in the villa by the sea. But I am inclined to think now, indeed I have long thought, that really my imagination was at work then, prompted by what I knew. I have no genuine confidence in my own *bona fides* at that time. 'Ask, and it shall be given unto you,' certainly does not hold good when one comes to deal with the mysteries which are like those faint and floating mists one half-sees by twilight in the shadowy woods of autumn. It is much better not to ask.

"The springtide was now upon us; the weather was radiant; the garden was brilliant with flowers; and the noonday heat of the sun was so powerful that we felt Africa in it. The tourist season of Northern Africa was in full activity. Tunis and Algiers, we read, were crammed. Beds were at a premium in Biskra. Constantine was full of sightseers, Hammam-Meskoutine of bathers in sulphur springs. El-Kantara had more than its normal number of sportsmen. Even Touggourt and Làghouat, and, in Tunisia, Kairouan and Nefta were not neglected by eager travellers. But Sidi Barka preserved its usual aspect of busy, but strictly colonial, cheerfulness. No English and Americans walked its streets. There was no booking ahead at its one hotel. I knew this because more than once I had been out shooting with the landlord, and had listened to his complaints about the universal neglect of Sidi Barka. Elaine and I did not share his patriotic indignation. We were thankful that our little scrap of the northern coast of Africa made no appeal to travellers, that the beautiful season brought no invasion to our doors. Mischievously we revelled in the thought of all that was going on elsewhere in what might almost be called our neighbourhood, while we were wrapped in radiant peace, and congratulated ourselves on our eccentric choice of a home. Sometimes even, in order to emphasize to ourselves our own felicity, Elaine would read aloud passages from the *New York Herald*, or the *Daily Mail* of Paris, dealing with the travel season in our part of Africa.

"One glorious morning the post had just arrived, and Elaine unfolded a paper. We were sitting in the palm avenue, with our feet in white shoes on the warm caressing sand, hatless and contented, guarded by red geraniums, and with the faint sound of the quiet sea in our ears.

"'Biskra has never been so full before,' said Elaine with her eyes on the paper.

"'Poor Biskra!' I said.

"'People are sleeping on mattresses laid on the floor and on billiard tables.'

"'Poor devils! And I suppose they imagine they are getting to understand the Garden of Allah!'

"There was a brief silence, during which I lit a cigarette, felt gloriously warm and thought about nothing in particular.

"'Tunis is thronged with Americans,' observed Elaine, still reading the paper. 'But there are a few English too, and many are expected.'

"She was silent for a minute reading.

"'Lady Cathcart is at the Tunisia Palace, the Home Secretary and one of his daughters, and the Begum of some place I can't pronounce. Oh!'

"'What is the matter?'

"Elaine was looking at me over the top of the paper. Do you know your eyes were very expressive just then, Elaine?"

"Were they? I remember that I felt quite startled at that moment."

"Why?" I asked.

"There was a paragraph in the paper about a small new hotel just opened in Tunis by an Armenian. It described the clever Eastern decorations, and advised visitors who liked something out of the common to go there. At the end it gave a very short list of the people who had already found this hotel out. What do you think was the first name on the list?"

After barely a second's hesitation I said:

"Eardsley?"

"Mrs. Eardsley."

"Ah—Mrs. Eardsley only!"

"Yes. I told Arthur, and then I remember I said immediately: 'Do you think she is coming here?' Didn't I, Arthur?"

"You did. And I suggested that there were no doubt various Mrs. Eardsleys, and that the lady whose name was in the list of travellers at the Armenian's hotel was probably not the Mrs. Eardsley of the

Villa Persane."

"Yes. But you felt sure that she was, just as I did."

"I confess that. I took the paper from Elaine and looked at the printed name, Mrs. Eardsley, and as I looked, and afterwards when I was speaking to Elaine, I thought: 'It is she. It is the woman who has lived here.'"

"And yet he tried to pretend that it might be anybody, and when I said again: 'Do you think she is coming here?' he said: 'Of course not!'"

"But," I said to Pierce, "did you think that she was coming to the villa?"

"Strangely enough," he answered, "I did think so. I even felt sure of it. Through my mind there passed the thought: 'She has come to Tunis on her way here.' But I didn't acknowledge what I was thinking to Elaine just then. I couldn't. I felt obliged to be reserved. There are moments when we can't be strictly truthful, when our wish to keep something intimate to ourselves is irresistible. I'm sure you both know that."

I acknowledged that I did. Mrs. Pierce only smiled slightly with, I fancied, a delicate indulgence.

"Besides, I think at the moment I was trying secretly to be superior. I was trying to give Elaine the impression that I, a man, was not the victim of convictions based on nothing, of wild fancies no doubt quite suitable to, and to be looked for in, a woman, but alien to the strong brain and firm common sense of a man."

"I think that was it," murmured Mrs. Pierce, still smiling slightly. "We women are so much more honest in our sillinesses than you men are in yours. To Arthur's feigned superiorities I gave an honest answer. I told him I knew the woman at the Armenian's hotel was our Mrs. Eardsley, and that she was coming to the villa."

"And he—"

"He continued to say: 'What nonsense!' And to think as I did."

"But was it likely that Mrs. Eardsley, if it were the woman who had lived at the villa, would come back to it long after her husband had abandoned it?" I said.

"She might not know that," said Pierce.

"That's true."

"Presently I left Elaine under the palms," he went on, "and I wandered through the garden till I came to the lowest terrace, where the room was built against the rock. I had had the carpet laid, and the furniture put in order, and had from time to time done a little painting in it. But

I had never spent much of my abundant leisure there. I preferred the boskiness of the rest of the garden to this bare unsheltered bit, the cosy fantasy of the house to this solitary room confronting the sea.

"The sun was blazing down on the terrace. The sea was calm, and strongly, almost fiercely blue. I stood still for a moment to look at it. Here the fishermen had sometimes seen Eardsley alone. Why, I wondered, had he apparently only frequented this exposed bit of the garden after his wife had left him? For the landlord of the Hotel de Paris had made no mention of his having been seen on the terrace till then.

"I looked towards the room built against the rock at the far end of the terrace. There, again after Mrs. Eardsley's abrupt departure, a light had been seen in the window when darkness had fallen. Eardsley no doubt had been there alone in the night. The fishermen thought he had slept there. Had the house then become horrible to him? Yet he had stayed on in it for some time. Could he have had any hope of his wife's return? For a moment I imagined a man deserted by one he loved coming to this terrace because from it the highway could be plainly seen, because from it the sound of approaching wheels could be heard before they could be heard from the house or from the more distant parts of the garden.

"The great blue sea stretched almost at my feet, sparkling in the fierce light of Africa. Away to the left, at a long distance, I saw a black moving speck, presently, very faintly, a thin trail of dark smoke blurring the gold of the sunshine. A steamer was on its way, probably one of those coasting steamers which carry passengers to the various North African ports, voyaging from Morocco towards Tripoli. I watched it for a moment with that peculiar interest, almost mystic, which any small object moving through vastness creates in the mind. Then I walked towards the room at the end of the terrace and entered it.

"As I did so I looked round, and I felt that I looked inquiringly. A green folding blind was let down over three-quarters of the great window. There was a pleasant shadow in the room. The deep sofa stood against the whitewashed wall exactly opposite to the writing table. I lay down on it, stretched out my legs, put my hands behind my head, and fell into a daydream.

"The steamer was in it, voyaging between blue and blue in a mist of gold, voyaging towards Tripoli. Perhaps not so long ago it had passed before Carthage and Sidi-Bou-Said. And in my dream, too, were the mysterious Eardsleys with their unknown, but suspected, sorrows, and the Villa Persane, and Elaine and myself, and life with its multitude of secrets, its tangle of hidden things. And I dreamed and dreamed into sleep.

"When I woke and opened my eyes the first thing I saw was the writing table. I had never used it. The inkstand holding dried ink still stood on it. Nearby lay the penholders I had noticed when for the first time I had entered the room. I lay still for a few minutes. Then I got up and went to the writing table. There were five drawers in it, a middle drawer and two drawers on either side. I pulled at the middle drawer. It came out with some difficulty, sticking fast once or twice. Evidently it had been out of use for a considerable time. In it were some scattered fragments of paper. I turned them over, and saw writing, a large and, I thought, violent calligraphy. Presently, while idly dispersing these fragments, I found a sheet of foolscap with blue lines, and two words written on it in a large, oddly distorted hand. These words were: '*She knows.*' The strange thing was that they had been written again and again, and at all sorts of angles, and on both sides of the sheet. Wherever I looked I saw them: '*She knows—she knows.*'

"I pulled a chair up to the table, and sat down, keeping the sheet of paper in my hand. I wanted to study it, to get, if possible, a right impression from it. And after sitting there for two or three minutes I seemed to see—in imagination—a human being, obsessed by some thought, scrawling words upon paper without being aware that he was doing it, as an absent-minded man will sometimes idly draw lines, or faces, or even elaborate patterns upon paper. So, I felt, had those words been written while the writer had been plunged in thought.

"*She knows.* The words seemed to stare at me from every part of the blue-lined sheet: *She knows—she knows.*

"Presently I laid the sheet back in the drawer. I did not read any of the words written on the torn scraps of paper. To have done that would have been—I thought then—a deliberate attempt on my part to get to know something that neither I, nor anyone else, had been meant to know. Writing torn up is not intended to be read. I resolved to get presently a wastepaper basket, and to convey the scraps of paper to the rubbish heap. I shut the drawer and got up, meaning to leave the room. And I was just about to go when—I don't know why—I tried the top drawer on the left-hand side of the table. It resisted my pull. I tugged at the handle. The drawer didn't move. It was fast locked. Then I tried all the other drawers. None was locked; all were empty.

"I went to the house, came back with a wastepaper basket, and emptied the middle drawer, tearing up the sheet of foolscap and throwing it away with the other fragments of paper. Then I looked at the locked drawer. I wanted to force that drawer open. I had a right to, for when I had acquired the Villa Persane the understanding was that I was to have the full use and benefit of all the furniture it contained. This room was, of course, legally a part of the villa. I had the right to use that locked drawer. But I couldn't exercise my right unless I found the key to it or, failing that, prised it open with some instrument. Where the key was I didn't know. I examined the room carefully but failed to discover it. Possibly the last tenant of the villa had carried it off when he left, either deliberately or—more probably—by accident.

"I didn't force the drawer that day. Something—perhaps a certain delicacy—held me back. I remember distinctly that I felt a reluctance to do violence even to a bit of furniture in that room, though the writing table was not a fine 'piece,' but, on the contrary, was an ordinary enough affair in walnut wood, useful but of no particular value.

"But though I let the drawer alone just then, so changeable is man that on the morrow I overcame my reluctance in that matter. In the evening of the day I've been telling you about Elaine talked persistently of the Eardsleys at dinner. After dinner—what a night that was, Elaine!"

"Yes, hot almost, and breathing perfumes, and carrying to us only the faintest sighing of the sea."

"After dinner we sat out till very late, and still Elaine's mind was busy about our predecessors in Paradise. She imagined all sorts of things about them, constructed dramatic scenes which might, or might not, have taken place within the precincts of the hiding place, and finally declared that she was certain that 'Eardsley thoughts,' as she whimsically called them, were still busy about the villa. I remember she said: 'The Eardsleys have left it, but they have not finally done with it. It has meant too much to them for that. It pulls at them still. I am sure of it.'

"I replied that these remarks were really the result of Elaine's glance at the morning paper. She had seen the name of a Mrs. Eardsley, and had jumped to conclusions, one conclusion being that the Mrs. Eardsley who had arrived at Tunis was *en route* to Sidi Barka. If she was able to believe that, naturally she must suppose that the Mrs. Eardsley was being pulled at by the villa, in the sense that she was thinking about the villa with an intention of returning to it.

"'But when no Mrs. Eardsley comes here,' I added, 'your present feeling about Eardsley-thoughts and the influence of the villa will die away.'

"'Mrs. Eardsley will come here!' Elaine said obstinately.

"'When?' I said.

"'Very soon. I am certain of it. I feel that she is coming.'

"'Do you think she is actually on the way?' I asked.

"And I remember that just then I thought of the steamer I had seen that day from the lowest terrace. In the night I seemed to see the smoke from its funnel rising up and evaporating in the gold and the blue. Perhaps that steamer had been steering for the port of Sidi Barka.

"'I don't know whether she is on the way,' Elaine answered. 'But I know she is coming here. That is why she came to Tunis.'

"And then, Elaine, we both laughed, and we agreed that sensible *terre-à-terre* people, if they could know of our thoughts and talk, of our locking up the terrace room, and of our extraordinary preoccupation about the Eardsleys, would think us very foolish. And I believe we tried to believe we were foolish."

"But we didn't succeed."

"No. And indeed it ended in a confession from me."

"Yes, Arthur confessed that he was of my opinion. He confessed that he also had believed from the first that the Mrs. Eardsley in Tunis was the Mrs. Eardsley who had formerly lived in the Villa Persane, and that he also believed she would, while in North Africa, revisit the house and garden from which she had fled so abruptly. He told me, too, about the steamer he had seen that day voyaging along our coast, and also about his little adventure with the writing table. And I begged him to open the locked drawer."

"Elaine even wanted to get a lamp and to visit the room on the terrace there and then," said Pierce. "But I was firm in my refusal. I said I must 'sleep on it' before I finally decided whether or not I would force open that drawer."

"Did he tell you the whole of the writing table adventure?" I asked Mrs. Pierce.

"Yes. And I constructed quite a drama upon the evidence of the sheet of foolscap. I told Arthur that Mr. Eardsley must have married his wife under false pretences, that is allowing her, or perhaps inducing her deliberately by trickery or deceit, to believe that he was quite other than the man he really was; that they had come to live in the villa by the sea while Mrs. Eardsley was still happily under this false impression; that they had spent months together in isolation without her finding out the truth. But at last the suspended sword had fallen, and all the happiness had been slain in a moment. Mrs. Eardsley, suffering under the acute shock of some nameless horror, had fled from the villa and from the man who had deceived her. He had been left alone. And while alone, and brooding over the ruin of his life in the solitary room at the edge of the terrace, he had mechanically traced over and over again the two words which summed up the destruction of his happiness."

"And until very late in the night," said Pierce, "we sat discussing what Mrs. Eardsley had learnt, and how she had learnt it, whether by some hideous accident, through some oversight on the part of her husband, or in a romantic way which Elaine suggested."

"What way was that?" I asked.

"I said that possibly, after being married for some time to his young wife, and living with her in perfect happiness, Eardsley might have made a tragic mistake. He might have come to think that he and his wife were indeed one, so completely one that he might dare to trust her absolutely. Do you understand?"

"You mean that perhaps he confessed of his own accord? Told the truth of himself to one who was not great enough to be able to bear it?"

"Yes," she said.

"It's terribly dangerous," said Pierce, "to trust anyone absolutely. It's the most dangerous thing you can do in life."

"I suggested that Eardsley had done that driven by an intense love," said Mrs. Pierce. "And that he had been terribly punished."

"Such a tragedy as that would be, I think, the greatest of all tragedies," I said.

"Yes," said Mrs. Pierce. "To have a secret that was not suspected, to tell it purely out of love, and then to be loathed because of it! I remember feeling a sudden hatred against Mrs. Eardsley when I thought that perhaps something of that kind had happened in the villa by the sea. I believe I even expressed it."

"You did!" said Pierce, " and I laughed at you and reminded you—I had to remind her—that all this was only supposition. And then I said that really we were getting Eardsleys on the brain, and that we simply must pull up. And I recounted coldly what we knew about them, so that we might realize how very little it was. And even what we knew was only hearsay. A fisherman had told. The landlord of the Hotel de Paris had told—"

"And the sheet of foolscap!" I said.

"Yes, that wasn't hearsay. But what did it prove? She knows! And what does she know? Perhaps merely that it is tea-time! Our sensations in the terrace room I ruled out that night. I wanted to soothe dear, excited Elaine."

"Thank you for your solicitude, Arthur!"

"I feared lest she might lie awake. And besides, I was quite hurt by her merciless attack upon poor Mrs. Eardsley."

"I merely said that if Arthur told me, out of affection for me, and trust in me, a secret about himself which I had never suspected, I should love him all the more for having been able to do it," said Mrs. Pierce.

"Admirable!" I said, and I spoke without any sarcasm.

"And I told her I had no secrets. And at last, still arguing, I'm afraid, we went to bed.

"On the following day two things worth recording in connection with our stay in the villa by the sea happened. One was absolutely unexpected. The other I have hinted at. I forced open the drawer in the writing table. And Elaine received a telegram summoning her to England. Her mother had been seized with a sudden and dangerous illness. The telegram arrived at noon, after I had succeeded in opening the writing table drawer. By the evening Elaine had started on her journey to England. She would not allow me to accompany her."

"No," said Mrs. Pierce. "Women really have wonderful instincts. I acted on mine. I knew Mrs. Eardsley was coming to the Villa Persane, and I wanted Arthur to be there to receive her. I was forced to go away. He was not. And I made him stay on."

"And did Mrs. Eardsley really come?" I asked.

"First let me tell you what I found in the writing table drawer," said Pierce. "Elaine was with me when I opened it. As it was she who had urged me to the deed, I insisted that she must be present. No! Wait a moment! I believe it was she who demanded—"

"That will do, Arthur!" said Mrs. Pierce with a delicate dryness. "I don't think our guest is at all interested in your cruel thrusts at a wife whose only fault is that she has spoilt what might possibly, but for her, have been a moderately estimable character."

There was a moment of silence in the long room. I heard the owls hooting outside in the darkness of the pine woods. And suddenly I realized Surrey, and for a moment was away from the villa by the sea. Then Pierce said: "I forgive you, Elaine " and continued his story.

"After some difficulty I got the drawer open. Both Elaine and I had felt almost certain that we should find something in it. If there were documents or letters we meant to seal them up, and keep them till we discovered Mr. Eardsley's address, or till—if Elaine's instinct proved to be a true one—Mrs. Eardsley presented herself at the Villa Persane. If the drawer contained anything else, we would see what we would do. Well, as I say, I got the drawer open, and it seemed to be empty. In the first moment we both thought it was empty. But I had not drawn it quite out. Elaine noticed that, and pulled it. And a little oblong box of pink cardboard came into our view. It lay in the right-hand corner at the back of the drawer. I took it up. On the top of it was printed in dull red lettering something of this kind: 'W. Smithson and Co., Ltd., Heraldic Stationers, Manufacturing Silversmiths, and Makers of High-Class Leather Goods.' And an address in New Bond Street, London. Then there was a thick red line, and below it was printed an announcement that visiting, wedding, at-home, and all kinds of invitation cards could be supplied at the shortest notice. I shook the little box, which was fairly heavy for its size. Then I said to Elaine: 'It is only a box of visiting cards which the Eardsleys must have forgotten when they went away.'

"'Open it!' she said.

"After a little trouble—for the cards were tightly packed in the box, and the box was closely fitted into a cover from which it had to be drawn out—I was able to get at the wonderful secret of the drawer. Out came a packet of visiting cards, wrapped up in grey paper and tied up with twine. On the top of the packet, under a sheet of transparent tissue paper, one card was laid with the name outwards. I read the name aloud. It wasn't Eardsley."

"Not Eardsley!" I said, surprised.

"No!" said Pierce. "It was the name of a man, and in the left-hand bottom corner of the card was printed the name of a well-known London Club."

I looked from Pierce to his wife.

"Did you know the name?" I asked.

"Yes," said Mrs. Pierce. "We both knew it—from the newspapers."

"Oh!—some public man?"

"The name on the card had become public property through a sensational case which had made a great stir in England some time before," said Pierce. "It was the name of a man who had been tried for murder and who had been acquitted by the jury. The judge who had tried the case, one of the greatest judges on the bench, had entirely concurred in the verdict. The prisoner had, of course, been discharged without a stain on his character. On leaving the court he had been greeted by the huge crowd which had assembled outside the Old Bailey with frantic cheering. He had with difficulty made his way to a taxicab, and had been driven away—to his future. All this Elaine and I had read in the newspapers. I must tell you that both of us—we were unmarried at the time—had followed the case with a deep interest, which had no doubt been shared by hundreds of thousands of English people, that both of us had felt convinced of the innocence of the accused man, that both of us had rejoiced at his acquittal. He was a gentleman, a man of very good birth. We had discussed the case together. At the time the trial took place we were already engaged to be married. Our engagement, for various reasons, was a long one. I need not trouble you with the whole history of the case. But this I must tell you. The man was accused of the murder of a woman considerably older than himself, who had apparently troubled his life by her imperious devotion to him—a devotion which had evidently taken very disagreeable forms. She must have made the man's life an almost intolerable burden. The prosecution was very strong on that. It was necessary, of course, to prove motive. And this tormenting passion of an elderly woman was put forward as an adequate motive for the commission of a crime by the man who had suffered from it. But linked with this suggested motive there was another. The accused man, it was said, was deeply in love with another woman, a girl, and the entanglement with the woman who died, as was proved, through an overdose of a dangerous drug, was—so the prosecution insisted—a serious obstacle in the way of his marriage with this girl."

"Then the accused man wasn't married—hadn't, I mean, been married to the dead woman?" I said.

"No. She was a married woman separated from her husband."

"Had he been her lover?"

"Evidently. But she had probably taken him as a prey. He was a young man. That was our idea, wasn't it, Elaine?"

"Yes."

"One other thing about this matter I must tell you. Very soon after the acquittal an announcement appeared in the 'Morning Post,' and subsequently in other papers. It was the announcement of the accused man's marriage to the girl whose name had been mentioned in the case."

"Did she give evidence?"

"No. She wasn't called. We had heard—I forget how; everyone seemed to know it—that all through she had passionately asserted her belief in her lover's innocence. She was a girl whose character was beyond reproach. Not a word was said, or even hinted, against her. But—her name was mentioned in the case."

"Horrible for her!"

"Yes. Well, those two married—and disappeared!"

"Disappeared!"

"From the public eye, from the public ken. The man had been in official employment. He had had a good post. He gave it up. He didn't what is sometimes called 'stick it out.' Instead he married the girl he loved, quietly at a registry office. And then she and he were no more heard of. Evidently they had had enough, and more than enough, of the horrors of publicity. Evidently they wished to live at peace far from those—too many—who were familiar with their names. And so they had carried their love away—where?"

Pierce fixed his eyes on me as he said that last word.

"To the villa by the sea?" I said.

"When I read the name on that card aloud to Elaine," said Pierce, "we were both of one mind. We both felt that it had been given to us at that moment to know who Mr. and Mrs. Eardsley really were. We felt certain that Mr. Eardsley was the man who had been accused of murder and triumphantly acquitted, that Mrs. Eardsley was the girl who had believed in his innocence all through and who had married him. Why the box of visiting cards had been left locked up in that writing table we didn't know. We don't know now. That didn't, and doesn't, matter. It had served its purpose to us. It had given us what we felt to be knowledge, although, strictly speaking, it was, of course, only supposition. Well, we carried off the box of cards. And then the other important incident of that day happened. Elaine got her telegram, and in the afternoon she started for Tunis on her way to England, leaving me alone—except for the servants—in the villa by the sea."

"Had you time to talk the whole thing—you know what I mean by that—over thoroughly before the telegram came and you had to leave?" I asked Mrs. Pierce.

"We were talking it over when the summons for me to go to England arrived," she answered. "We had both come to a horrible conclusion about the matter of the Eardsleys."

"We may as well call them by that name to the end," said Pierce.

"I suppose," Mrs. Pierce added, "you have guessed what that conclusion was?"

"Did the sheet of foolscap found in the middle drawer of the writing table help you to it?" I said, in my turn asking a question.

"Yes, it did."

"I suppose I have guessed," I said. "But it's very terrible. I can scarcely conceive of a more terrible situation than the one I am thinking of."

"Tell us what it is," said Mrs. Pierce.

"I suppose this was in your minds: that Eardsley had been wrongly acquitted, that he was really a murderer, that Mrs. Eardsley married him absolutely convinced of his innocence and lived with him for months happily in that conviction—"

"Lived with him in our villa by the sea!" interposed Mrs. Pierce.

"And that one day —" I hesitated. "Did you think that she found out the truth?" I asked.

"No," said Pierce.

"You thought that he, driven perhaps by conscience, or even perhaps, more strangely, moved to be absolutely sincere with the woman who loved him because of his very great love for her, told her of his own accord the naked truth of himself that she had never suspected?"

"We thought that he told her of his own accord," said Pierce.

"And that in her horror she fled from him—abandoned him?"

"Yes. We were inclined to differ as to his probable reason for the confession we believed him to have made to his wife. I thought that in all probability a tortured conscience had moved him to tell the truth. That seemed to me, thinking of the matter as coldly as I could, the most likely prompting motive. Elaine, more romantic than I, stuck to her original idea, that Eardsley had loved his wife so much, had grown to believe so absolutely in the depth of her love for him, that he had not only felt obliged to trust her with his unsuspected secret, but had convinced himself that he might dare to trust her with it, that she would be able still to love him when she knew it."

"And there she had been wrong!"

"Undoubtedly. She had been unable to bear the truth with any sort of fortitude, and had fled from the man who had told it to her."

"It occurs to me," I said, "that in the truth there might have been a last, as it were a finishing touch, of horror."

"Yes?" said Mrs. Pierce.

And her eyes fixed upon me were full of a shining eagerness.

"Suppose the motive of the murder to have been Eardsley's love for the girl who became his wife? And suppose he told her that?"

"That is what I believe," said Mrs. Pierce.

"Then, indeed, her flight was explicable," I said. "A highly sensitive girl learns not only that she has married a murderer, but also that she was the cause of his murder! If that was what happened in the villa by the sea—"

"In the terrace room!" said Pierce.

"—no wonder she fled!"

"I am sure I should have stayed!" said Mrs. Pierce.

"That is what she reiterates!" said Pierce. "She will not forgive Mrs. Eardsley."

"If a man who loves you tells you such a thing as I am sure Eardsley told his wife, tells you of his own accord—don't forget that—out of his immense trust in your love for him, aren't you a coward, aren't you a cruel, selfish egoist, concentrated on yourself, if you abandon him? I could not have done it."

"She should have married a criminal!" said Pierce, smiling, but sending a deeply affectionate glance to his wife. "I give her no chance to prove what is in her."

"Go on, Arthur!" said Mrs. Pierce rather brusquely, touched, I thought, by a sudden reserve. "I am sure our very patient friend wants to know the rest of the story. And I have nothing to do with it. For Fate removed me at the most critical moment."

"Pitiless," said Pierce, "you were taken away. And the merciful one was left."

"We all know that men are made up of mercy where women are concerned," said Mrs. Pierce. "Now—merciful one!"

"That day," continued Pierce, "when I returned to the villa after seeing Elaine off by the train from Sidi Barka, I was conquered by the strangeness of the abrupt. It seemed almost incredible that she was gone, that she would not, at the best, be back for some weeks. I had seen the train go out of the station with her in it. Nevertheless I could scarcely believe that she was not still about the villa, that I should not see her face at one of the windows, see her standing on a terrace, hear her voice calling to me from some nook in the gardens. That evening I felt reaction as I have seldom felt it either before or since. I strolled vaguely about the garden. I went down to the lower terrace. I visited the solitary room. I came out again and, standing by the low wall, I stared out to sea. And the sun declined in the heavens, and my world changed magically, and the night came, with many stars, but without a moon.

"I shan't easily forget that night."

Perhaps Pierce saw at this moment an alertly expectant look in my eyes, for he hastened to add:

"Oh, it was entirely uneventful! I dined. The servants supped. I sat in the garden and smoked. They sat in the servants' hall and probably gossiped. They went to bed and presently I went to bed. Nothing happened. It was what I felt that will always give that night a special place in my memory."

"You didn't go into the locked-up room?" I said.

"No. I thought of doing so. I even wanted to go there. But I felt that, after what had happened, and in the condition I was in just then, certainly not a strictly normal condition, I had better not go. If I had gone I should not have been able to empty my mind. I should have been full of thoughts, and surmises, even, perhaps, of convictions about Eardsley and his wife. No influence, suppose any strange influence were still lingering there, would have had a chance to get at me in its own time, and in its own way. I should have been metaphorically clamouring for it, thrusting forward to meet it. That is no good. I am not like those spiritualists who will have a manifestation when they attend a 'sitting.' Besides, if I had gone to that room, being a conscientious sort of fellow in my way, I should have made a violent effort to get back to normal, to cold-douche my rather blazing imagination, and to knock on the head the energy of my dark-hour mind. I didn't want to make a violent effort. On the contrary I wanted to let myself go. So I stayed alone in the garden under the stars, and let myself go.

"Have you ever deliberately given yourself, thrown yourself as a prey, to your imagination?"

"Oh yes!" I said.

"I did that then in my startling solitude. I brooded over all that had happened in the villa—it wasn't very much; still there was something to go on—and over my discussion with Elaine of that day, before the telegram came. I imagined that Elaine's supposition was right. I needn't tell you again what it was. And then—it's almost voluptuous sometimes, isn't it, that giving yourself to your imagination—I imagined that the woman who had gone away from the Villa Persane that day was not Elaine Pierce, but Mrs. Eardsley, and that the man left behind, and now sitting in the dark and lonely garden, and listening to the sound of the sea, and the faint, surreptitious voices of the trees about the villa, was not myself but Eardsley. In imagination I became Eardsley deserted, Eardsley on the night of the day of revelation, Eardsley facing his new and loveless life absolutely alone. He had not dared to try to keep his wife with him. There are some things no man can dare. We knew, from the evidence of the landlord of the Hotel de Paris, that Mrs. Eardsley had arrived in Sidi Barka quite alone, had been there for some two hours alone walking in the station, had been hoisted up into the train by—an Arab porter. So Eardsley had not followed her, had not attempted to detain her. He must have realized in a flash the irrevocable. Abruptly, when he told her, she had fled from him in soul. He let her flee from him in body. After all, once the soul has gone, what does it matter—in love—what the body does?

"The crash of a life, absolute, final, beyond hope of recovery—Eardsley had probably had to face that in the garden of the villa by the sea, in the white house Elaine and I loved. I faced it that night in imagination, and realized, I think, at any rate partially, our tremendous ignorance of ourselves and each other, even in the closest relation. We don't know what we can bear—what we can 'stand,' as the phrase goes. We don't know what others can stand. We don't trust when we might. We trust when to do so brings ruin. We hide truths that might safely be told. We tell truths—less often though, much less often—that it were better for us never to tell. If Elaine were right, Eardsley had done a great thing. At least I think so. And the doing of it had brought him terrific punishment. I was punished that night. In imagination I felt his abandonment; I cursed myself for what he had done in the terrace room of the villa by the sea; I faced his appalling future; I saw the last ray of hope die out in his heart; I knew the last extremity of his loneliness. The garden was horrible to me—because she had gone. The house was the most terrible house in the world. And the voices about me, soft, delicate, whispering voices of Nature in a night of perfection, were the voices of Hell. For I had done the maddest thing a man can do; I had told the truth of myself to one whom I loved and who was too small to carry its burden.

"It must have been towards dawn when I went into the terrible house."

"Did you sleep?" I asked.

"Yes, profoundly. I think I was tremendously tired. I think I was tired out.

"When I woke in the morning an absolute calm enfolded the land. It was an intensely hot day. No airs were stirring in the garden, which had become a breathless Paradise. For a moment I did not realize the absence of Elaine. When I did realize it I faced the emptiness of my life with the regretful common sense of Arthur Pierce, not with the spiritual agony of Eardsley. My imagination had, as it were, worked overtime the night before. Now it was taking a rest.

"I got up and plunged into a cold bath. I had breakfast out of doors. I thought of Elaine on her journey and wished that she were with me to greet this wonderful African day. Then I lit a pipe and wandered through the garden, wondering at its exquisite, its almost magic, stillness. I mounted to the top of the hill, and looked down on Sidi Barka sleeping in the distance beside the painted blue water of its harbour. For the water there looked like a coating of paint spread upon the land that day.

"It was extraordinary being quite alone."

"He felt—I know it—a wonderful sense of freedom," said Mrs. Pierce. "But he has never acknowledged that to me."

"There are some truths no woman can bear to be told," said Pierce quietly. "Now, while I was up there on the hilltop looking over the wide country to Sidi Barka, I remembered why Elaine had wished me to remain in the villa while she travelled to England. Perhaps she had thought of sparing me a long and tedious journey. That would have been like her. But she had told me that she knew Mrs. Eardsley would one day come to the villa, that she wanted me to be there when Mrs. Eardsley came. Would Mrs. Eardsley come? Again I thought of the steamer I had seen. If she had been on her way to Sidi Barka, she must have been in the port since the day before yesterday. I gazed towards the harbour. I could distinguish shipping lying there, a blur of darkness at the edge of the blue. But Mrs. Eardsley would not come. Elaine and I had been absurd. Besides, even if Mrs. Eardsley did come, she would surely not travel by sea on a coasting steamer. There was the train. It was certainly a very tedious journey from Tunis to Sidi Barka. But still—nevertheless I continued to gaze towards the distant harbour, and to think of Mrs. Eardsley at sea, voyaging towards the white house where, perhaps, she had learnt such a fearful truth.

"Presently the sun became fierce up there on the hilltop, and I descended into the shadows of the trees. I thought of Eardsley walking on the terrace close to the sea after his wife's departure. Had he been listening for the sound of wheels? Had he still been able to cherish any hope of his wife's eventual return? Surely not. And yet he had often been seen there after she had left him.

"Although I had descended the hill to get out of the sun, I did not stay in the pleasant shadows under the motionless palms. I went down to the terrace by the wall, stood there and listened attentively. From that place I could just hear the sea lapping at the foot of the rocks on the other side of the road, sucking at the land with soft lips. But I was listening for another sound. I think I listened for a long time. But I only heard the sea. And at last I went into the room built against the rock. I had an unfinished picture on an easel there, and I began to do something to it. After a little while I became engrossed in my work and forgot all about the Eardsleys. I don't know how long I had been working when I became aware of something which vaguely disturbed me. What was it? I listened. I heard a fly buzzing against the great window in the heat, and there seemed to be heat in the sound. After an instant I bent down once more towards my canvas. But—there was something. I stood absolutely still. The fly buzzed again. Then I heard a very faint sound that was thin and cheerful, the sound of a jingle of bells at a distance. The bells were on the necks of horses. I laid down my brush. And almost immediately I heard the noise of trotting hooves on the hard white road, the bells more clearly, and carriage wheels. I went to the door of the room, and I saw a carriage—a hired victoria from the town—pass by rapidly beneath me in the shadow of my wall. It was covered with a light-coloured awning. From where I was standing I could not see the whole carriage. Nor could I see whether there was anyone in it besides the coachman. In a moment it was beyond me and out of sight. The noise of the bells, of the horses' hooves and the wheels died away.

"The garden of the Villa Persane is a long one. The high road makes a rather sharp curve beneath it. The entrance gate lies well beyond the curve, and is on the opposite side of the house from the side on which is the sea terrace with its solitary room.

"When I lost the sounds which had disturbed me, I returned to my easel. But the mood for work had entirely left me. Nevertheless I was obstinate and tried to force myself back into it. I stared at my picture, strove to feel interested in it, put in a touch here and there. But my thoughts were with the carriage which had just passed below me. Where was it going? Who was in it? A traveller, or some inhabitant of the town of Sidi Barka out for an airing? It was a very hot day to choose for an excursion. I looked at my watch. It was nearly noon. I was returning the watch to my pocket when I heard in the distance a long and wailing call. It was repeated almost instantly.

"*Sig—nor—re! Sig—nor—re!*'

"Our house parlour maid in the villa was an Italian. I recognized her somewhat strident voice. I went to the door and shouted in reply to her summons. Soon I saw her broad figure at the end of the terrace. A large folded handkerchief was laid on the top of her blue-black hair to protect her head from the sun. She came towards me swinging her wide hips.

"'What is it, Maria?'

"'A lady has called in a carriage, *signore*. She gave me this for you.'

"And she handed me a note.

"'Wait a moment!' I said.

"I tore the envelope quickly, opened the paper inside and, before reading the note written on it, looked at the end. I was in a hurry to see the signature. My eyes rested on the words 'Evelyn Eardsley.'

"So it was she!

"The note was short. I don't pretend to remember the exact wording of it, but it was almost exactly like this:

> DEAR SIR,— I am a complete stranger to you, but I used to live in the house you are occupying at present. I was very fond of it. Happening to be in this part of the country, I thought I should like just to see it again, and to walk through the garden. They told me at the hotel that you had taken it and were in residence. I did not know before that it had been re-let. I hear Mrs. Pierce is away and you are here alone. If it would not disturb you very much, and be inconvenient, might I just glance into the rooms I once knew so well, and walk for a few minutes in the garden? With my apologies for troubling you,
>
> Believe me, yours faithfully,
> EVELYN EARDSLEY.

"I think I've got the note almost exactly as it was. The envelope was addressed to 'Arthur Pierce, Esq., Villa Persane.'

"Now I suppose that it would have been natural if I had gone at once to answer this note in person. That was what I wanted to do. In fact, I was longing to do it. But something held me back. Had I known and suspected nothing about my visitor, I should certainly have gone to her and played the part of a courteous host. But I did know something about her, and I suspected a great deal. And this made me hesitate. My curiosity was like a chain upon me holding me where I was. There seemed to me to be something guilty in it. And an interior voice whispered within me: 'You must leave her to do what she wishes to do—alone.'

"Maria's large eyes questioned me. She put up her brown hands to the folded handkerchief which lay on her head.

"'*Santo Dio, the caldo!*' she murmured.

"'Wait a minute, Maria! I'll write—no, I haven't a pen! Stay—a pencil will do!'

"I hurried into the room, and on a sheet of drawing paper I wrote in pencil a brief note cordially begging Mrs. Eardsley to visit the house and garden, and to stay in both as long as she liked. I added that I was painting in the room on the lower terrace and should not be in her way. This note I twisted up. Then I wrote on it: 'Mrs. Eardsley,' and told Maria to take it to the lady who was waiting.

"'By the way, where is she?' I asked.

"Maria replied that she was sitting in the carriage, waiting for my answer.

"'She wishes to visit the house and garden. She used to live here,' I said.

"'*Veramente?*'

"'Yes. Let her see all she wishes to see. You need not go with her if she prefers to be alone.'

"'*Va bene!*'

"And Maria went away, rocking on her hips, and with one hand pressed to the sheltering handkerchief.

"Then I returned to my painting room—but not to paint. I think I was half angry with myself for what I had, or rather, I suppose I ought to say, for what I had not done. Mrs. Eardsley was actually in the villa, and I was not going to see her. What would Elaine say to me when eventually I told her of my preposterous conduct? For she would surely think it preposterous. Had I not stayed on in the villa to see the mysterious Mrs. Eardsley if she put in an appearance, if she justified Elaine's instinct? And now I should not see her. I should be obliged to say that she had been and that she had gone away unseen by me! Yes, I was half angry with myself. But for the life of me I could not change my line of conduct. Something imperious told me to leave Mrs. Eardsley alone with her memories in the villa by the sea. Surely they were mingled of sweetness and horror. I could not intrude upon them. I simply dared not. But I was quite unable to paint. And presently I took up a book—it was Pierre Loti's '*Roman d'un Spahi*,' I remember—sat down on the sofa and tried to read.

"A long time passed—it seemed at least very long to me. Mrs. Eardsley's visit to her old home was evidently being a thorough one. Certainly she was not hurrying herself. I knew that she could not have gone away yet. When she did go I should hear the bells on the horses' necks, the horses trotting and the roll of wheels on the highway close to me. I listened for those sounds, but I didn't hear them. Noon was surely long past. It must be lunchtime. As I thought this I heard a bell rung in the garden. That was a summons to me. But I did not obey it. I could not go to the house while Mrs. Eardsley was in the villa or garden. I knew, or thought I knew, too much about her to do that. It seemed to me just then that if I were to meet her, if I were to look even for an instant into her eyes, she would know of my terrible suspicions, which were indeed almost certainties, about the events which had driven her from the villa. I felt that I could not face her naturally, as one faces a total stranger about whom one knows nothing, or scarcely anything. Had I been a woman I dare say I might have done so. But I was a man, and somehow I felt guilty.

"So I tried to go on reading, and when the bell sounded again insistently I did not obey the summons.

"A few minutes went by. Then I heard the sound of a footstep. No doubt poor Maria was once more facing the blaze of the sun in my service. But the footstep sounded light. It was slow, but it was certainly oddly light—for Maria's. It was not Maria's footstep. As I realized that I got up. An instant later a woman I had never seen before appeared in the doorway."

"She was tall, about five foot eight or so, I should think, and very thin. In the first moment of seeing her I thought her middle-aged. But she was a young woman who, through bad health, or cruel circumstances, or both, had aged prematurely. Her hair was very fair, almost flaxen fair. She had eyes which probably had been of a very bright, keen blue once, but which now looked faded. They were surrounded by crow's feet. Her pale face was wasted and scored with many little lines. It must have been beautiful, for the features were fine and harmonious, and had the stamp of distinction upon them. But all bloom had left it. The complexion was unhealthy; the mouth was haggard with very pale lips. A tic frequently distorted her face on the left side, causing the left eye to shut sharply, and drawing her features askew. She was simply dressed in a thin grey gown, wore a small grey hat and white suede gloves, and carried a parasol, dark in colour. I think it was dark blue.

"'Please forgive me!' she said. 'I am Mrs. Eardsley.'

"I asked her to come in. She stepped into the room.

"'I ought not to disturb you,' she said. 'It is very kind of you to let me see the house and garden. I lived here once.'

"'Yes. Do sit down.'

"She hesitated, then sat down on the sofa.

"'I heard a bell. I think it must have been for your lunch.'

"'Probably it was,' I said. 'May I hope that, as you are here—'

"But she interrupted me.

"'No. Thank you very much. But I am not hungry.'

"Her eyes were travelling round the room. She looked at everything, earnestly.

"'I wanted to ask you,' she said. 'I went into the house. One of the rooms was locked up.'

"'Oh—yes!' I said.

"'That used to be my bedroom.'

"She now looked at me and I thought there was intense inquiry in her eyes.

"'Don't you ever use it?'

"'No; not now,' I said uncomfortably.

"I had forgotten the locked room unaccountably when I gave permission for Mrs. Eardsley to see the house.

"'Oh!' she said.

"There was a pause.

"'I dare say you want to see that room again,' I said, still with discomfort. 'I can easily find the key. Was that—'

"'It was partly that,' she said. 'But—but I don't think it matters. I have seen all the other rooms.'

"She looked down, and seemed to be hesitating. Her tic just then was very noticeable. Finally, seeming to make up her mind, she looked at me again, and said:

"'Are you and your wife happy here?'

"'Yes,' I said. 'We are very fond of the villa.'

"'May I, although I am a stranger to you, ask you to do something for me if ever you should have the opportunity?'

"'Please do!' I said, wondering very much what was coming.

"'I left—I had to leave here very suddenly.'

"'Yes?'

"'This is the first time I have been back. I did not think I should ever come back. But—I was led here again. I did not know till I arrived at the hotel in Sidi Barka that the villa had been given up.'

"'No?' I said, as she paused.

"'I thought possibly my husband still had it.'

"'I believe he left it a long time ago,' I said as casually as I could.

"'Yes. Are you staying on here?'

"'As far as I know. I shall go to England presently.'

"'But you intend to come back?'

"'Oh, yes.'

"'What I want to ask you is this. If I send you a letter addressed to my husband, and he should ever come back here, will you kindly give it to him?'

"'Certainly; with pleasure.'

"'Thank you. I dare say he won't ever come. Still, he might. And I don't care to leave the letter with the landlord of the hotel. But, if you will allow me, I will tell the landlord, before I leave tomorrow, what I have done. Then, if my husband should come when you are away, the landlord can tell him there—'

"Her voice faltered for the first time. But she recovered herself instantly and continued:

"'—there is a letter waiting for him. You will leave your English address, I dare say?'

"'Yes.'

"'Thank you very much. My husband and I have lost sight of one another. Otherwise I would not trouble you.'

"She got up to go.

"'May I accompany you?' I asked.

"'Thank you—as your lunch is waiting,' she said.

"And we walked together to the house without saying another word. When we reached it, I said:

"'Shall I get the key of that bedroom?'

"Mrs. Eardsley hesitated. She was obviously doubtful what to do, was considering the matter deeply. I heard her sigh. Then she said:

"'No, thank you. It doesn't matter.'

"We skirted the house, and reached the short drive which leads up from the high road. I saw the carriage waiting outside the gate in the sunshine. Mrs. Eardsley stopped.

"'Please don't trouble to come any further,' she said. 'I have kept you much too long.'

"She held out her hand. I took it. I saw 'goodbye' on her lips, but—

they did not utter it. Some thought checked them.

"'Why do you keep that room locked?'

"I did not know what to answer. I believe my face flushed. Probably I looked like a guilty man.

"'My wife,' I said—'It was her room at first—my wife felt as if there were sadness, a sad influence that is, in that room. So—so she left it for another, and then we locked it up.'

"'Ah!' said Mrs. Eardsley.

"She seemed about to say something more, but apparently decided not to, and gently withdrew her hand from mine.

"'You came here by train?' I said.

"It was a question I had been wishing to ask for some time.

"'No; I took a steamer from Tunis.'

"There was a look of faint surprise in her face as she answered me.

"'Goodbye,' she added, 'and thank you very much.'

"Then she walked to the carriage, got in and drove away.

"Next morning a note came:

DEAR MR. PIERCE,— Here is the letter I spoke about yesterday. It will be very kind of you to give it if you should ever have the opportunity. Thank you very much for your promise and for letting me see again a place where I, too, was once very happy.
Yours sincerely,
EVELYN EARDSLEY.

"And—there was an end!"

Pierce was silent.

I looked from him to his wife.

"And the letter?" I said.

"Oh—yes!" said Pierce. "There was an enclosure, addressed simply: 'John Eardsley.' I have it still."

"He never came?"

"No, never."

"And eventually you gave up the villa?"

"Yes; we had to. Work claimed me. The children came, and Elaine and I agreed that a father and mother must not be eccentric."

"But I've left our address," said Mrs. Pierce. "If John Eardsley should ever go to Sidi Barka he is certain to visit the Hotel de Paris, and the landlord will tell him at once. We have arranged it all. There is no fear that— We have taken care."

"I am glad of that," I said.

Pierce got up.

"I've often told Elaine," he said, "that if the gods would grant me the fulfilment of a desire, I should say to them: 'Let it be granted to me to give to the man who is now called John Eardsley—a letter.' Haven't I, Elaine?"

"Yes. But the gods take no heed! Nevertheless, perhaps someday—" She broke off and looked wistfully out to the night. And Pierce echoed: "Perhaps!"

THE ADDRESS BOOK

I

I may be a snob. In fact I suppose I am a snob. But isn't it natural to wish to be "in it" if one lives in a great City? Being out of it in the depths of the country is really quite bearable. One doesn't know anyone, but there's no one to know. Now I have never lived in the depths of the country. My destiny has obliged me to live mainly in London. I was born in the wilds of Hampstead certainly, but when I was only some three years old my parents descended the hill and established themselves—very foolishly, as I realised years ago—in Bayswater. So I may almost claim to be a Londoner, and I do lay that claim. I consider myself a Londoner. My parents—my dear father was a doctor and I am his only son, in fact, his only child—were completely out of it in Bayswater. They knew only my father's patients, which was equivalent to knowing nobody. But they were quite satisfied with that state of affairs. Where I got my strong social ambition from I don't know, but it certainly wasn't from them. They had none. It never occurred to them that there existed in London a marvellous organisation called "Society," complex, desirable, attainable—by some remarkable and fortunate people, even though they have had the dangerous misfortune to have been brought up in Bayswater.

I can prove what I say. In fact I am going to prove it by the career of Effie Smith, later Mrs. Burden, now Lady Burden, wife of Sir Larchmont Burden, Knight, and no doubt, in process of time, Lady Burden wife of Sir Larchmont Burden, Baronet, and eventually Lady Burden wife of Lord Burden of somewhere or other. I know it will come to that in the end. For Effie has decreed it. And what Effie decrees in regard to social ambitions must come to pass inevitably sooner or later. She has a secret power like the power of the tides. A marvellous woman! But I and my darling cornered her once and she will never forget it.

We, my Father, Mother and I, knew the Smiths in Bayswater, because Mr. Josiah Smith, Effie's Father, called my Father in when Mrs. Smith, the Mother of Effie, got the yellow jaundice. (All this is many years ago, but I have to explain it.) The acquaintance of the two families was made over the yellow jaundice, and ripened into familiarity if not into friendship. In fact in those days—she may try to deny it now, but I am speaking by the book—I called her Effie and she called me Dick.

I was educated in Bayswater and she was educated in Bayswater. I know she talks airily of Brighton now, but it won't do. Others may be deceived. In fact they are. But I, the only son of Doctor Cradgett formerly of Bouncefield Gardens, Bayswater, just simply know.

And now we come to it.

Effie Smith was born greedy. Before the first tooth came, not lingering on its way either, she must have made up her mind not only to get into society but to be a power there. Her Father—he was an "importer of Japanese goods," whatever that may imply—made a good deal of money. Her Mother looked important in a freckled sort of way. Effie would have something eventually. She knew it, and gave herself millionaire airs about it before she was ten. At seventeen, released from the Bayswater school—she never was at school at Brighton; I could prove that if necessary—she started on that wonderful climb which has never ceased till this day, when she is known to all London as Effie Burden of Burden House, Knightsbridge, and Sprotcombe Park, Mullingate, Barkston, Sussex.

That wonderful climb of Effie's, from Bayswater to Knightsbridge, from Miss Smith, the importer of Japanese goods' daughter, to Lady Burden who entertains not everybody—she's far too clever to do that now—but only the most remarkable people, who shall describe it adequately, describe the heroism of it, the agility of it, the acrobatic daringness of it, the cold-blooded cruelty of it, its persistence, its thrilling patience, its contempt of exhaustion, its astounding staying power? Harold Lloyd going up the outside of a New York skyscraper was as nothing compared with Effie on her way to the topmost heights of the wicked world.

All through that climb Effie has been shedding old friends. She began by shedding Bayswater, which incidentally included me. When she was twenty-one she had already quite done with Bayswater. Bayswater tried to hang on to her, scenting the glories of her future, but she wouldn't have it. From the moment she married Larchmont—I still believe she chose him as her husband partly because of his Christian name—she kicked Bayswater out of her life. She wouldn't even be married there. Already she had found out that a marriage at a church in Bayswater would be a fatal mistake at the beginning of a career such as she had designed for herself. So she was married in the country, and quite quietly, practically nobody there, no bridesmaids, no fuss, no reporters. This astonished some people who knew Effie, or rather who thought that they knew her. But her reason was subtle and extraordinarily characteristic of her. The Smiths didn't know anybody who could make a "show" in the papers, so Effie wouldn't have anybody asked to her wedding. She said marriage was far too sacred to be made a spectacle of. What she meant was that she didn't care to have a list of names in the papers without a single good title among them.

Larchmont, now Sir Larchmont, was then apparently quite an ordinary young man and by no means rich. But Effie hadn't married him without having her reasons. He had one great asset. He had been educated at Eton and was able to talk, and did talk perpetually of "the dear old Eton days." His father was a merchant of some kind, but he had an enormous family to devour his money, and couldn't give Larchmont a big allowance. When Effie made Larchmont think he was in love with her he was eating his dinners for the Bar. But she hawked him out of that, and got him first into the Japanese business, and then later into the great Marling, Prendergast and Samson firm, which deals with the selling of big houses and estates all over the country. During her climb she somehow manoeuvred Samson into obscurity and put Larchmont in his place, so now, as everyone knows, the firm is Marling, Prendergast and Burden.

Larchmont had been to Eton, he had a somewhat Roman appearance and he was essentially malleable. On these three assets Effie boldly staked, and from the moment she was married she took complete control of Larchmont and set out to turn him into a successful snob. The world knows whether she has attained her aim. Larchmont now looks exactly like a slightly damaged Roman Emperor who, by some strange freak of destiny, has strong affiliations with the middle classes of England. When he talks he talks with weighty importance, when he is silent his silence is impressive. And he has a faculty of not seeing old friends on the lower rungs of the ladder which is only equalled by the ardent blindness of Effie herself.

Also he has been in Parliament.

Effie got him in, and a damned fellow from the mines of Whitehaven got him out, but not before Effie had persuaded a Conservative Premier that Larchmont's services to the party were deserving of the reward of a title. As a matter of fact Larchmont is a K.C.V.O., which looks very well on the outside of an envelope. And he won't bother to stand again as there is every reason to suppose a Baronetcy will shortly come his way without his contesting another election. Effie has made him contribute very handsomely, and in a very public manner, to the Hospitals Sustainment Fund.

There is practically no doubt that it will be all right when the New Year's Honours are distributed.

Effie's first married home was far away from Bayswater. She swept Larchmont with her to the other side of the Park and established him and herself in a discreet neighbourhood on the South side of the interminable Cromwell Road. There they shed Bayswater, including my humble self. Since then they have shed South Kensington and gone to Buckingham Gate. From Buckingham Gate they have migrated to Queen Anne Street, from Queen Anne Street to Cadogan Gardens, and from Cadogan Gardens to Burden House, Knightsbridge, a lordly mansion with a side-view of the Park. I am told, but I'm not certain it is true, that Effie is now in treaty for a corner house in Grosvenor Square. If she gets it their wanderings ever upwards will probably come to an end, as really the traffic makes Park Lane so very noisy nowadays.

I'm very sorry but I must now say a few words about myself, though I don't wish to appear as an egoist.

My name, as I've explained, is Cradgett. This of course is a misfortune. Effie's was Smith, but being a woman she has been able to conceal that fact under the married name of Burden, and very few of her now innumerable smart and celebrated friends have any idea who she was. But Cradgett I am, and though, in a laudable effort to get the better of circumstances, I have long ago added my Mother's maiden name to it, and now invariably call myself Cole-Cradgett, there's no doubt that I labour under a very heavy handicap. Then there's the Bayswater business. That of course tells against me, though I am now established in Beckford Gardens which is close to Queen's Gate, and am shortly moving to Queen Street—yes, really, I assure you—to Queen Street, Mayfair.

Like Effie I was born with strong social ambitions, but unlike her I lacked the subtle power which is hers in so marked a degree, the power to bend everything to the one great purpose of getting on and getting up. The consequence of this lack has been that while Effie has soared like the eagle I have only fluttered like a sparrow with the pip. And yet I did my best. And if I had trusted only to myself I might possibly now be nearer to the Peaks.

I began by utterly refusing to be a doctor, and by going on the Stock Exchange. I then fled, like Effie, from Bayswater and added the name of Cole to my other name of Cradgett. Established in Kensington I sought to fortify myself for raids upon the aristocracy of my beloved country by a clever marriage. I chose a Miss Mount, the daughter of a civil Engineer, who had a little money of her own and a strong desire to shine in the social world. Unfortunately my darling proved not to be an Effie. She wanted to be at the top, she wanted it so much that I have seen her dear brow beaded with perspiration as the legendary cry "Excelsior!" broke from her panting lips. But—she didn't know how to get there. She cut the wrong people. She shed old friends too quickly, before we had consolidated the friendship of the new ones. She bluffed on twos and threes and let her bluff be seen through. In short, she made a muddle of it, and we were left panting in the middle distance while Effie scaled the heights.

I must tell you that my darling and I, after our marriage, had called upon the Burdens, then living close to the Cromwell Road, and had been received—we got in through the ignorance of a new parlourmaid who was afterwards dismissed—with cold politeness, although I presented myself as the old crony, Dick, and frequently murmured "Effie" in the course of the brief conversation. Our visit was "returned" by a presentation of cards by a commissionaire, and then the acquaintance practically ceased. We asked the Burdens to dinner and received a polite refusal. No invitation came to us, though my darling lived in expectation of one for nearly a year, and only gave up hope when Effie didn't remember her, or wouldn't see her, at the Private View of the Royal Academy for which I had somehow managed to scrape up a couple of cards.

There is nothing, as you probably know, so mortal as the hatred of a woman for a woman who has ignored her socially. After this my wife didn't like Mrs. Burden, and when Larchmont was made Sir Larchmont, and Effie became "my lady," my wife was—well, not pleased. Nevertheless we called again—this time in Cadogan Gardens—to offer our congratulations, and were refused admittance by a butler and two footmen, though we knew it was Effie's "at home" day. (Since then she has entirely given up being publicly "at home" for fear of the wrong people getting in. So we had lost our last chance until the great thing happened.)

From that moment my darling confessed herself conquered, and we settled down to the husks of society, while Effie stuffed herself full on the fatted calf.

And then the great thing happened!

It came about in this most extraordinary way. It's all very well to jeer at coincidences in popular fiction and plays. I contend that coincidences are continually occurring, and I can now cite my own case as an example. But wait one moment! I must just explain first where Effie had got to by this time.

She had got to the top, where she is now. Having passed through South Kensington Society she had left it for a Melbury Road sort of set, in which painters abounded. Then she had got to know a few minor poets, a few novelists. Later on a dramatist or two, a pianist or two, some actors and actresses had gathered about her. A fairly well-known historian and a grave authority from the British Museum had presently fallen victims to her excellent cook. In their train had come some serious literary lights. Money coming increasingly to Larchmont, now in the big estate agency, Effie had been enabled to rent a house in the country, next door to the famous Countess of Marchmont who has, as everyone knows, kicked up her heels in all worlds, and is as popular with Labour as she is with Royalty. Effie somehow managed to become intimate with her. After that it was easy sailing. She drove with the swiftness of the racing yacht *Britannia* before a favouring gale right into the great world. She got to know the Peerage. She was presented at Court. She entertained a minor Royalty and gave satisfaction. Then she bought Sprotcombe Park, cut practically everyone whom she had formerly been friends with, and started afresh, carefully covering up her tracks, burning her boats and leaving the Rubicon behind her.

She now knew "everybody." And to say this is not a mere *facon de parley*. It is on the contrary the announcement of a solemn and tremendous fact. For Effie is a prodigious labourer in the vineyard of society. However late she stays up at night—and she goes to everything, first nights, dinners, Charity fêtes, balls, nightclubs, supper parties, cabarets—soon after seven in the morning she is up writing invitations and working with her private Secretary, Miss Bromhead, on cards, on the arrangement of visits, on the settlement of house parties—she entertains every weekend at Sprotcombe Park—on the judicious elimination from her visiting list of those whom she has "got beyond," on schemes of fashionable charity, etc., etc. Later, after an early breakfast, she usually receives her "publicity agent," whose business it is to keep her name perpetually in the papers, and to arrange for the chronicling of all her movements and pursuits, for the descriptions of her dresses and hats and jewels, for the announcement of her hobbies, her subscriptions to charities, her efforts at Bazaars and Matinées, and for the publication of the names of all the important people whom she is in touch with.

(I know about all this because I know Miss Bromhead, and am quite "thick" with Snipson, the publicity agent in question.)

After these hours of strenuous labour Effie's "day" begins. And it lasts until well into the small hours of the succeeding morning.

And now for the great event which gave Effie for a time into what I may humorously call the hands of Bayswater.

II

I had known for some time, through Miss Bromhead, that Effie possessed a social Bible, in which were inscribed the names and addresses of all her important and celebrated friends, with comments on their different values, hints as to the probable best ways to "hold" them, notes on their characters, tiny essays about their habits, their tastes, their inclinations, guesses as to the amount of money they were likely to possess and the amount of social influence they exercised, and elaborate calculations under the title "*Whom should be asked with whom.*"

Miss Bromhead—of course unsuspected by Effie—had become quite "chummy" with my darling, who fed her with muffins at the Savoy, and even on one occasion comforted her with caviare and lobster at the Berkeley. She was one of those women who are apt to become expansive when carefully nourished on the food they care most for, and sedulously filled up, like some precious vase, with the liquids their natures crave. Apparently reticent and subdued, though practical, under the subtle influence of the appropriate viands, and the special brands she had a liking for, she rapidly developed into the most indiscreet of women. After the caviare and lobster she babbled almost wildly to my darling about this marvellous "Bible" of Effie's, which though always called "The Address Book" was in fact the fruit of Effie's now vast social knowledge, a record of her patient and successful labours in the vineyard, a careful guide to the future, a minutely thought-out warning against false social steps, an elaborate means adapted to the greatly desired end, the solving of all social problems, however complex, however difficult. Without this wonderful book, as Miss Bromhead, under the combined and subtle influence of caviare, lobster and Chateau Lafitte—she couldn't digest the other Chateau wines—almost frantically assured my darling, "Lady Burden would be *lost*."

Now this is what happened.

On a certain day, just when the London season was beginning with all its multifarious social activities, I left the City soon after five o'clock and went to my Club, the Royal Automobile. I stayed there until seven o'clock playing bridge—my darling was away from home visiting her Mother at Bexhill-on-Sea—and then walked a little way down Pall Mall and hailed a passing taxicab not far from the corner of St. James's Street. I gave the chauffeur my address, stepped in, and was confronted by a rather unusually large, and very expensive-looking bag—a woman's bag. In the middle of one side of it were engraved in some green substance—jade, I afterwards knew—the initials E. B.

I picked it up, sat down and—mechanically, I seem to remember—opened it.

Inside in tiny but plain silver lettering, I read these remarkable words: *Stolen from Effie Burden, Burden House, Knightsbridge, S.W.*

Really! Really! I stared at the cheeky inscription. It was so like Effie to call herself Effie Burden, instead of Lady Burden. She had, I knew, arrived at that social altitude where all titles are dropped, where Duchesses are familiarly called Jenny so-and-so, where even Princesses are given nicknames, and Queens are spoken of as "Tata Central Europe," "Marmozet Scandinavia," and so on and so forth.

Effie's bag in my possession! Remarkable!

I suppose I ought to have shut it. Let me be truthful. I didn't. On the contrary I explored it, as Stanley explored the pathless jungles of Africa. What did I find? Face things, perfume, powder puff, visiting cards, a mirror engraved with "Effie" in sparkling stones, and *The Address Book.*

When I reached my home in Beckford Gardens I was, as the servants used to say, and for all I know say still, "all of a tremble." I hid the bag under an overcoat which, being liable to bronchial colds, I was fortunately wearing, paid the cabman and sneaked rapidly into my house.

And that night, alone, and immured in my library, with whisky, Perrier, and plenty of Havana cigars, I read every word of Effie's marvellous social *vade-mecum.*

It was a wonderful book. Effie's whole social soul and brain were in it complete. It was, as it were, the record of her climb laid bare. I don't believe there's anything exactly like it to be found in the whole world. It wasn't only a record. In it were the addresses and telephone numbers of all Effie's important friends with comments and hints attached. Just to give you an instance. One entry was as follows:

"Corisande, Duchess of Barnstaple. 22 E Park Lane.
Remember the Duchess is very touchy about precedence. Has a strong temper. Very High Church views. Is fond of young men, especially of the dark, South American type. A bad bridge player. No knowledge of music. Hates books. Never ask her with a literary man. Hunting, racing, ritualism of the Halifax type, her principal topics. Passionately fond of gossip, pâté-de-foie-gras, pineapples, and old port. Likes -65 brandy and good-looking professional dancers. *Never ask her with the Marchioness of Cumberland, and never let Lady Cumberland be mentioned in her presence. Never speak of illegitimate children before her.* Be sure to have -65 brandy when she dines and to put a dark young man next to her."

This remarkable paragraph will give you a clear notion of what the book was like and of the amount of brain and social knowledge Effie had put into it. It will also give you an idea of what the loss of the book meant to Effie.

I realized that directly I had finished exploring.

It was of course my bounden duty to return "The Address Book" to Effie on the following day. But I didn't do that. Something held me back. I decided to await the return of my darling before taking any measures.

A couple of nights passed while the book lay locked up in my library. Then I saw in the Agony Column of *The Times*, which I am in the habit of reading regularly at breakfast, the following announcement:

Twenty pounds reward. Left in a taxicab, number unknown, in Piccadilly on Wednesday last, the twenty-seventh of April, a *Lady's Bag*, engraved with the monogram E.B. in jade. Inside the bag inscribed in silver the following announcement: *Stolen from Effie Burden, Burden House, Knightsbridge, S.W.* Bag contains among other contents an *Address Book* bound in white and gold. Anyone bringing the Bag, or merely the *Address Book*, to Burden House, Knightsbridge, S.W. will receive the above reward. Anyone found retaining the Bag after this notice will be *Prosecuted.*

The agony of Effie seemed to glare out at me from this advertisement.

I'm afraid, being human, this agony entertained me. In fact the vulgar thought went through my mind, "Serve her right." You see I stood for Bayswater rejected.

This "serve her right" mood persisted in spite of the ominous *"Prosecuted"* at the end of Effie's advertisement. I knew I ought to go at once to Burden House, Knightsbridge, with the bag, but I couldn't, simply couldn't, bring myself to do it. Being a very much married man—my darling is a remarkable specimen of the dominant female species in spite of her social shortcomings—I felt I must consult her before taking any decisive step. And she wasn't due to return for ten days. During that interval I saw three more advertisements from Effie in the Agony Column of *The Times*. In the first of them the reward offered had mounted to thirty pounds, in the second to forty pounds, and in the last to fifty pounds. The wording of the last advertisement was also more poignant. It read thus, after the usual beginning:

> Lady Burden does not care about the *Bag*, but she implores the person who has found it to return to her the *Address Book* it contained. No questions will be asked, the reward will be paid on the spot, and no fear need be entertained of any *Legal Proceedings*.

On the day that this passionate plea made *The Times* for once really interesting, my darling returned just as twilight was failing.

The first thing she said to me was,

"I'm shingled! What do you think of it?"

And, taking off her helmet-like hat, she exposed her orange-coloured head for my inspection.

I warmly approved. To tell the truth I didn't dare to do anything else. And then, leading her apart into the remotest recess of my small library, I told her the news. As she listened I noticed that under her coating of paint she flushed with excitement.

When I had finished she simply said, "The book!" and stretched out her carefully manicured hand.

Of course I gave it to her.

She didn't come down to dinner. She didn't speak to me again for I should think at least three hours. Something—I believe it was a fried sole—was carried up to her on a tray with a half bottle of champagne. It was eleven o'clock at night when she finished the book. Her maid—

she had always insisted on having "my maid," like all self-respecting women whether they can afford it or not—then summoned me to her bedroom, where I found her reclining on a sofa in a maze of pink draperies.

"Well?" I said, as I entered.

"Shut the door, Percy."

(My full name is Richard Percy Cole-Cradgett.)

I obeyed, and then again uttered a significant "Well?"

"Well," she said. "This is our chance."

I sat down on something that my darling always calls "The Tuft."

"Our chance for what?" I enquired.

"Our chance to get into Society at last!" she exclaimed. "Are you blind?"

"I don't think so."

"Well, then, can't you see? The Burden woman is in our hands. We can make our own terms with her."

"But the terms she offers are fifty pounds."

"Fifty pounds! What do we want with her money?"

"But the bag isn't ours, and we've no right to —"

"That's just like a man!" she observed. "Pray why have you kept it ten days?"

"I wanted to consult you."

"What about, pray?"

When my darling says "pray" I know my duty.

"About what it would be best to do," I murmured with becoming meekness.

"Well, I'm telling you!" she snorted.

She has a way of speaking through her nose at critical moments which is very impressive.

I sat back on "The Tuft" and replied, soothingly, "And I am here to listen."

It was a disarming answer and it seemed to have its effect, for she continued in a much less nasal manner, but nevertheless with the decision of a woman who is resolved not to spare.

"We shall hold the Burden woman to ransom. We shall bring her to her knees at last."

"But how can we—"

"If you will only listen I will tell you."

From that moment I listened on "The Tuft," speechless, all ears.

"We shall make a bargain with her and it will be this. She will only have this"—she struck her bright coral-coloured nails on the Book—"back when she has launched us in her set. I shall manage it through Eleanora Bromhead. She is on our side already. I am the only living person"—I found the qualification superabundant—"who has ever lavished caviare, lobster and Château Lafitte on her. She will never find another to do as much for her, or half as much, and she knows it. Tomorrow I shall take her out to—to—" she rolled her fine eyes, and seemed to be calling on the Heavens for a sign—"to Claridge's and give her lunch there. You can leave the rest to me."

I left the rest to her and this is what happened.

My darling took Eleanora Bromhead to Claridge's and there gave her of the best, regardless of expense as I very well know, for I paid the bill. Even -65 brandy was added to the programme, with the following result. Eleanora, while dealing faithfully with a hothouse peach near the end of all things, revealed to my darling a hitherto unsuspected hatred of her employer, Effie, and swore later, over a glass of the -65, that she would like nothing better than to see her "humbled in the dust." My darling having pointed out that the humbling in the dust of her ladyship would do no good to our social prospects, Eleanora offered to do anything—*anything*—that her hostess desired in connection with Lady Burden. She even used these striking words, as my darling reported to me later, "I am ready to go through fire and water for you. Only tell me what to do."

Fire and water having been ruled out as having no immediate bearing upon our social aspirations, the following plan was suggested to Miss Bromhead by my darling, and was passionately agreed to by her over a second glass of the -65 tempered by Turkish coffee.

Miss Bromhead was to go to Effie and to tell her that she,

Miss Bromhead, had "got on the track" of the lost address book, and of course incidentally of the bag, that they were in "safe keeping," that no offer of money, however great the amount, would lead to their restoration, but that they would be given up on terms.

The terms were as follows. Effie was to sign a document pledging her word of honour to take no proceedings in connection with the restoration of the bag and its contents. She was to undertake to ask no questions. She was furthermore to promise, and to keep the promise, to ask my darling and myself to every party of whatever kind, be it lunch, tea, dinner, supper, musical, or what not, and to every "at home," reception and ball which she gave during the remainder of the London season, and to invite us on at least four occasions to spend "weekends" at

Sprotcombe Park, Mullingsgate, Barkston, Sussex. In addition we were to be numbered among her guests for Ascot week, if she took a house for the week, as was her usual custom. If all this were duly done, without enquiry, and without jibbing, the bag with its contents would be restored to her by the person now in possession of it through Miss Bromhead on the ensuing first of August. If, however, all this were not duly done, and if there were the slightest attempt to find out what had become of the bag, the Address Book would be instantly destroyed, after certain portions of its contents had been accurately copied out with a view to immediate publication in a prominent Sunday paper.

When my darling informed me of these decisions I confess to being terrified. Visions of prosecution, even of hard labour, opened up before me, and I was so wrought upon that I uttered such words as "actionable" and even "blackmail," and trembled on "The Tuft."

"Are you a coward?" she asked.

For once I was strictly honest, and without hesitation I spoke the truth.

"Yes," was my answer.

"What are you afraid of?" she said.

My reply lasted, I should judge, for about ten minutes. When I had exhausted the catalogue, she remarked,

"Percy, you're a fool!"

I didn't deny it. She might be right. How was I to know?

"Shall I tell you what the Burden woman will do?"

"Yes, if you know it."

"Of course I know it. She'll sign the agreement—it's drawn up already—and she'll keep to it."

"But suppose she doesn't? Suppose she—"

"Then the book will be destroyed after all the incriminating portions have been given to the Sunday press."

At that moment I realised fully, perhaps for the first time, that the world is ruled, and always will be ruled, by women.

"But will any paper print them?"

"Will any pa—" she stopped short.

Her contempt would not allow her to proceed. After a moment of bleak silence she was able to continue.

"Is it possible you don't realise that we have it in our power to drive the Burden woman out of Society forever?"

"But it seems to me that she has it in her power to put us both in prison."

"And what earthly good would it do her to know we were picking oakum if she hadn't a friend left in the world?"

"Do they pick oakum?"

"Of course they do! Wherever were you brought up not to be aware of it?"

"In Bayswater, like Effie," I replied.

"Well, I wasn't. *I* was brought up in North Ealing and my head is screwed on the right way."

"And isn't Effie's?" I couldn't help saying.

My darling's fine eyes flashed.

"You will very soon see whether your Effie is such a marvel as people think her!" she exclaimed. "If Eleanora Bromhead does as I tell her I'll undertake to say that you and I will go everywhere—*everywhere*—this season. I've already ordered a dozen new dresses from Reville's. That will prove to you whether I have faith in myself or not."

I was aghast, but I dared not show it. A dozen new dresses! And how many hats? I was too terrified to ask. All I could do was to speculate—and pay. And speculate I did, in rubber and oil, with surprisingly fortunate results. I also had a flutter in Swedish matches which brought me in quite a nice little sum.

Meanwhile Eleanora Bromhead did as my darling "told her," and then rushed over to Beckford Gardens to report progress and to be rewarded with a nice little dinner and a bottle of Pommery (the only champagne she can drink without ill effects).

The scene with Effie must have been tremendous. It seemed that at first Effie fell into transports of indignation, and was for communicating at once with the police, and going with them "in person" to Beckford Gardens to demand the instant return of "the Address Book." But Miss Bromhead had sat so firm and lied so sedulously that gradually Effie had been reduced to a different mood. The address book, she was told, was not with us. It had been found in the cab by an adherent of ours, who, indignant at the cruel way in which Effie had treated a childhood friend—myself—had made the conditions for its return on our behalf but without any prompting from us. Miss Bromhead had represented this mythical personage as resolute in the lists against snobbery and absolutely determined to blow Effie's social reputation to smithereens unless she instantly complied with the demands made upon her. Extracts from the Book, Miss Bromhead obstinately asserted, were already copied out, and would be handed at once to the Editor of *The Populace* for immediate publication in the event of Effie showing fight.

Of course Effie replied that she would prosecute the paper. Miss Bromhead had her answer ready. It was this:

"Think of the scandal!"

These simple, yet sublimely effective words were, it seems, her answer to every threat made by Effie. Whatever Effie said she would do, to Miss Bromhead, to us, to our mythical adherent, to the Editor of *The Populace*, was met by the inexorable Miss Bromhead with that one piece of terse and excellent English,

"Think of the scandal!"

And in the end Effie did think of the scandal and capitulated. The document drawn up by my darling, with the cunning assistance of a clever lawyer who happened to be her godfather and devoted to her, was signed by Effie and held in our possession. A copy, signed by an old, and totally unknown friend, who was under obligations to me and whose name I shall never divulge to the public, was duly deposited with Effie. And the fact of her complete capitulation was conveyed to us by the following card:

Sir Larchmont and Lady Burden
request the pleasure of the company of
Mr and Mrs Cole-Cradgett
at dinner—at 8 o'clock—
on Friday, May 4th.

R.S.V.P.

Burden House
Knightsbridge, S.W.

That dinner was the beginning of our season, I may even say of our first season in London. At it we met, among a galaxy of other celebrities, Corisande, Duchess of Barnstaple, and were edified to find that though of course Sir Larchmont sat on one side of her Grace on the other side sat a young Brazilian, with lustrous black eyes, glittering teeth and a skin of the softest, most delicate brown. Illegitimate children were carefully banished from the conversation, we noted. At dinner there was an abundance of pâté-de-foie-gras, followed eventually by pineapples, old port, and –65 brandy. Later on the Tango was danced on a specially erected stage by two professional dancers, one of whom, the man, was only twenty-one years of age and had just arrived hot-foot from the Argentine.

Our greeting by Effie and her subsequent behaviour to us at the dinners, lunches, musical parties, receptions and so forth which she gave profusely during the ensuing weeks, and at Sprotcombe Park where my darling and myself were included in house parties as per contract, showed her to be an accomplished woman of the world. Although of course her soul abhorred us she concealed her abhorrence in a masterly manner. Her first reception of us gave us an indication of the line she had decided on taking with us. When we entered the drawing room at Burden House on the occasion of that first dinner party she came forward, smiling with a detached sweetness which was perfect in its isolation, its lack of all real humanity, and, just touching our eager hands, remarked to my darling,

"So glad to see you! Just a few intimate friends! If there's anyone here you don't happen to know do tell me."

Need I say that we knew not a single person of all those present? But my darling didn't choose to say so, and the consequence was that we passed an evening which could hardly be designated as jolly. Later on, however, as party succeeded party, and people became more accustomed to the sight of us, we found ourselves on bowing terms with quite a choice selection of the great. The weekend parties at Mullingsgate— Effie cancelled her lease of a house at Ascot for the "week," undoubtedly on our account—were the greatest trial to me. My darling somehow didn't "go down" with Effie's terrifically smart and critical friends. The dresses from Reville were of course in evidence, together with marvellous hats from Paris and elsewhere which cost me a pretty penny. I was even let in for jewels from Cartier's, including a diamond tiara which I only managed to pay for by selling out at a heavy loss a lot of Selukwes. But in spite of it all my darling didn't "go down."

And of course Effie "spotted" it.

We endeavoured to give a smart dinner. I say endeavoured, for all those whom we asked, including of course Sir Larchmont and Effie, unfortunately happened to be engaged for the night we selected. And now we are moving to Mayfair. But I don't believe the move will advance us very much. There seems to be something in my darling which doesn't fit in with the notions of the best people. They find me fairly right. At least I think so. But somehow she *won't* "go down."

And Effie knows it.

How my darling hates Effie! Her hatred is such that when the first of August came round and Miss Bromhead called for the Address Book (according to contract), my darling at first refused to give it up.

"She shan't have it!" my darling exclaimed. "Not if she comes to me for it on her bended knees."

It was then that for the first time since our marriage I was forced to play the man. Sheer terror of criminal proceedings drove me to a show of determination, and eventually, after a domestic scene which I shall never describe, Miss Bromhead departed with the Address Book, and the knowledge that the only person who had ever ministered to the needs of her capricious palate would minister to them no more.

Since that day the Burdens have given us the cut direct, and my darling and I are scarcely on speaking terms with each other.

Being from Bayswater I don't like the sin of unfaithfulness even in thought, but really there are moments now when I can't help wondering whether things mightn't have gone better for me if I hadn't married my darling. There's something about her that—but I mustn't brood over that.

Still it isn't much good to keep on shrieking "Excelsior," if you don't "go down" with the Duchesses, is it?

THE CRY OF THE CHILD

Part I
The Dead Child

The peasants going homeward at evening, when the last sunbeams slanted over the mountains and struck the ruffled surface of the river, did not hear the cry. The children, picking violets and primroses in the hedgerow by the small white house, did not hear it. The occasional tourists who trudged sturdily onward to the rugged pass at the head of the valley did not hear it.

Only Maurice Dale heard it, and grew white and shivered.

Even to him it had been at first as faint as an echo pulsing through a dream. He had said to himself that it was a fancy of his brain. And then he had pulled himself together and listened. And again, as if from very far off, the little cry had stolen to his ear and faded away. Then he had said to himself that it was the night wind caught in some cranny of the house, and striving to get free. He had thrown open his window and leaned out, and trembled, when he found that the hot night was breathless, airless, that no leaf danced in the elm that shaded his study, that the ivy climbing beneath the sill did not stir as he gazed down at it with straining eyes.

It was not the cry of the wind then. Yet it must be. Or if not that it must be some voice of nature. But the river had no such thrill of pain, of reproach in its song. Then he thought it was some night bird, haunting the eaves of his cottage, or the tangle of wood the country people called his garden. And he put on his clothes eagerly, descended the narrow staircase, and let himself out on to the path that curved to the white gate. But, in the garden there was no sound of birds.

This was a year ago. Maurice remembered very well his long vigil in the garden, and how he had prayed that he might hear one note, one only, of a night-jar, or the hoot of an owl in the forest, so that the black thought just born in his mind might be strangled, and the shadow driven out of his heart. But his prayer had not been granted. And he knew he had not deserved that it should be. Towards dawn he went back into his house again, and on the threshold, just as a pallor glimmered up as if out of the grass at his feet, he heard the cry again.

And he knew that it came from within the house.

Then the sweat stood on his forehead, and he said to himself, with pale lips, "It is the cry of the child!"

All the people of Brayfield by the sea were agreed on one point. The new doctor, Maurice Dale, young as he looked, was clever. He had done wonders for Mrs. Bird, the rich old lady at Ocean View. He had performed a quite brilliant amputation on Tommy Lyne, the poor little boy who had been run down by a demon bicyclist. And then he was well born. It got about that his father was an Honourable, and all the young ladies of Brayfield trembled at the thought that he was a bachelor. His looks were also in his favour. Maurice was pale and tall, with black, smooth hair parted in the middle, regular features, and large black eyes. The expression he assumed suited him. It was curiously sad. But, at first, this apparent pathos was a great success in Brayfield. It was only at a later period that it was the cause of unkind tittle-tattle. In the beginning of Maurice's residence at Brayfield eulogy attended it and applause was never far off. People said that Maurice was impressionable, and that the vision of pain upon which the medical student's eyes must look so closely had robbed him of the natural buoyancy of youth. Poor young man, they thought enthusiastically, he suffers with those who suffer. And this was considered—and rightly considered—a very touching trait in Maurice.

Brayfield was well satisfied with its new doctor, and set itself to be ill for his benefit with a fine perseverance. But, as time went on, the satisfaction of Brayfield became mingled with curiosity. The new doctor was almost too melancholy. It would not be true to say that he never smiled, but his smile was even sadder than his gravity. There was a chill in it, as there is a chill in the first light of dawn. One or two particularly impressionable people declared that it frightened them, that it was uncanny. This idea, once started, developed. It went from house to house. And so, gradually, a spirit of whispering awe arose in the little town, and the vision of human pain ceased to be altogether accountable for the pale sorrow of the young doctor. It was decided that his habitual depression must take its rise from some more personal cause, and, upon this decision, gossip naturally ran a wild course. Since nobody knew anything about Maurice Dale except that his father was an Honourable, rumour had plenty of elbow room. It took advantage of the situation, and Maurice was more talked about than anybody in Brayfield. And Lily Alston, the daughter of Canon Alston, Rector of Brayfield, launched out into surmises which, however, she kept to herself.

Lily, at this time, was a curious mixture of romance and religion, of flightiness and faith. She read French novels all night and went to early service in the morning. She studied Swinburne and taught in the Sunday School with almost equal ardour, and did her duty and pursued a thousand things outside of her duty with such enthusiasm that she was continually knocked up. On these continual occasions Maurice Dale was invariably sent for, and so an intimacy grew up between him and the Rectory, which contained the Canon, his daughter, and the servants. For Mrs. Alston was dead, and Lily was an only child. Real intimacy with a Rectory means, above all things, Sunday suppers after evening church, and, in time, it became an unalterable custom for Maurice Dale to spend the twilight of his Sabbaths with the Canon and his daughter. The Canon, who was intellectual and desolate, despite his daughter, since his wife's death, liked a talk with Maurice; and Lily, without having fallen in love with the young doctor, thought him, as she said to herself, "a wonderfully interesting study."

Lily's wild surmises, already alluded to, were born on one of these Sabbath evenings in winter, when she, the Canon, and Maurice, were gathered round the fire after supper.

The sea could be heard rolling upon the pebbly beach at a distance, and the wind played about the skirts of the darkness. The Canon, happily at ease after his hard day's work, rested in his red armchair puffing at his well-seasoned pipe. Lily was lying on a big old-fashioned sofa drawn before the flames, a Persian cat, grave in its cloud of fur, nestling against her and singing its song of comfort. Maurice Dale sat upright, pulling at a cigar. It chanced that Lily had been away the week before, paying a visit in London, and naturally the conversation turned idly upon her doings.

"I used to love London," the Canon said, with a half sigh. "In the old days, when I shocked one or two good people here, Lily, by taking your mother to the playhouses. Somehow I don't care for these modern plays. I don't think she would have liked them."

"I love London, too," Lily said, in her enthusiastic voice, "but I think modern plays are intensely interesting, especially Ibsen's."

"They're cruel," the Canon said.

"Yes, father, but not more cruel than some of the older pieces."

"Such as—?"

"I was thinking of *The Bells*. I saw Irving in it on Friday for the first time. You've seen it, of course, Mr. Dale?"

Maurice, who had been gazing into the fire, looked up. His lips tightened for a moment, then he said:

"No, never!"

"What! Though you lived in London all those years when you were a medical student?"

"I had opportunities of seeing it, of course, but somehow I never took them—and I dislike the subject of the play greatly now."

There was a certain vehemence in his voice.

"Why?" the Canon asked. "I remember my wife was very fond of it."

"I think it morbid and dangerous. There are troubles enough in life without adding to them such a hateful notion as a—a haunting; a horrible thing that—" he looked round with a sort of questioning gaze in his dark eyes—"that must be an impossibility."

"I don't know," the Canon said, without observing the glance. "I don't know. A sin may well haunt a man."

"Perhaps. But only as a memory, not as a jingle of bells, not as a definite noise, like a noise a man may hear in the street any day. That must be impossible. Now—don't you say so?"

Lily, on her sofa, had noticed the very peculiar excitement of the young doctor's manner, and that his denial was really delivered in the form of an ardent interrogation. But the Canon's mind was not so alert after the strain of pulpit oratory. He was calmly unaware of any personal thrill in the discussion.

"I would not be sure," he said. "God may have what men would call supernatural ways of punishment as well as natural ones."

"I decline to believe in the supernatural," Maurice said, rather harshly.

"Granted that these bells might ring in a man's mind, so that he believed that his ears actually heard them. That would be just as bad for him."

"Then, I suppose, he is a madman," Lily said.

Maurice started round on his chair.

"That's a—a rather shocking presumption, isn't it?" he exclaimed.

"Well," the Canon said, knocking the ashes slowly out of his pipe, "if you exclude the supernatural in such a case, and come upon the natural, I must say I think Lily is not far wrong. The man who hears perpetually a nonexistent sound connected with some incident of his past will at any rate soon be on the highway to insanity, I fancy."

Maurice said nothing for a moment, but Lily noticed that he looked deeply disturbed. His lips were pressed together. His eyes shone with excitement, and his pale forehead frowned. In the short silence that followed on the Canon's remark, he seemed to be thinking steadfastly. At last he lifted up his head with a jerk and said:

"A man may have a strong imagination, without being a madman, Canon. He may choose to translate a mere memory into a sound-companion, just as men often choose to play with their fancies in various ways. He may elect to say to himself, I remember vividly the cry of—" He stopped abruptly, then went on hastily, "the sound of bells. My mind hears them. Let me—for my amusement—push on my imagination a step further and see what will happen. Hark! It's done. My ears can hear now what a moment ago only my mind could hear. Yes, my ears hear it now."

He spoke with such conviction, and the gesture which he linked with his words, was so dramatic, that Lily pushed herself up on the pillows of the sofa, and even the Canon involuntarily assumed an attitude of keen attention.

"Why, Dale," the latter said after a moment, "you should have been an actor, not a doctor. Really you led me to anticipate bells, and I only hear the wind. Lily, didn't you feel as I did, eh?"

Lily had gone a little pale. She looked across at Maurice.

"I don't know that I expected to hear bells, father," she said slowly.

As she said those words, Maurice Dale, for the first time, felt as if a human being drew very near to his secret. Lily's glance at him asked him a question. "What was it that pierced through the wind so faintly?" it seemed to say.

"What then?" the Canon asked.

"I don't know," she replied.

Maurice got up.

"I must go now," he said.

The Canon protested. It was early. They must have one more smoke. But Maurice could not be induced to stay. As he walked rapidly homeward in the darkness he told himself again and again that he was a fool. How could it be? How could she hear the cry? The cry of the child?

That night Lily did not read a French novel. She lay awake. Her fancy was set on fire by the evening's talk. Her girlish imagination was kindled. In those dark and silent hours she first began to weave a web of romance round Maurice, to see him set in a cloud of looming tragedy. He looked more beautiful to her in this cloud than he had looked before. Lily thought it might be wicked, but somehow she could not help loving mental suffering—in others. And the face of Maurice gazed at her in the blackness beneath a shadowy crown of thorns.

Next day, at the early service, she was inattentive to the ministrations of religion. Her father seemed a puppet at its prayers, the choir a row of surpliced dolls, the organ an empty voice. Only at the end, when silence fell on the kneeling worshippers, did she wake with a start of contrition to the knowledge of her impiety, and blush between her little hands at her concentration upon the suspected sorrow of the young doctor. But in that night and that morning Lily ran forward towards Maurice, set her feet upon the line that divides men from women. She knew that she had done so only when she next encountered him. Then, as their eyes met she was seized with a painful idea of guilt, bred by an absurd feeling that he could see into her mind, and know how all her thoughts had been crowding about him. It is a dangerous symptom that sensation of one's mind being visible to another as a thing observed through glass. Lily did not understand her danger, but she was full of a turmoil of uneasiness. Maurice noticed it and felt conscious also, as if some secret understanding existed between him and Lily, yet there was none, there could be none.

In conclave the individually stupid can sometimes almost touch cleverness. Brayfield only began to talk steadily about Lily and the young doctor from the day of this meeting of self-consciousnesses which had, as it chanced, taken place on the pavement of the curved parade by the sea. Till that day the little town had attributed to Maurice hopelessness, to Lily simply friendship for a sad young man. Now its members talked the usual gossip that attends the flirtations of the sincere, but added to it a considerable divergence of opinions as to the likelihood of Maurice's conversion from despair. Lily, they were all decided, began to love Maurice. But some believed and some denied, that Maurice began to love Lily. This would have been hard for Lily had she noticed it, but her fanciful and enthusiastic mind was concentrated on one thing only and her range of vision was consequently narrowed. She was incessantly engaged in trying to trace the footsteps of the doctor's misery, of which she was now fully convinced. And indeed, since that Sabbath evening already described, Maurice had scarcely endeavoured to play any part of ordinary happiness to her. Her partial penetration of his secret quickly brought a sense of relief to him. There was something consoling in the idea that this little girl divined his loneliness of soul, if not its reason.

By degrees they grew quietly so accustomed to the silent familiarity existing between their ebbing and flowing thoughts; they were—

without a word spoken—so thoroughly certain of the language their minds were uttering to each other, that when their lips did speak at length, the words that came were like a continuance of an already long conversation.

Lily was, once more, knocked up, and the Canon called in Maurice to prescribe. He arrived in the late afternoon and was taken by the Canon into Lily's little sitting room, where she lay on a couch by the fire. A small, shaded, reading lamp defined the shadows craftily.

"Now, Dale," the Canon said, "for goodness' sake tell her to be more orderly and to do less—mind and body. She behaves as if life was a whirlpool. She swims stupendously, tell her to float—and give her a tonic."

And he went out of the room shaking his head at the culprit on the couch.

When the door had shut upon him, Maurice came up to the fire in silence and looked at Lily. She smiled at him rather hopelessly, and then suddenly she said:

"Poor dear father! To ask you to make me take life so easily!"

That remark was the first onward gliding of their minds in speech, the uttered continuance of the hitherto silent colloquy between them. Maurice sat down. He accepted the irony of the situation suggested by the Canon without attempt at a protest.

"Life can never be easy, if one thinks," he said. Then, trying to adopt the medical tone, he added:

"But you think too much. I have often felt that lately."

"Yes," she said.

Her eyes were bent on him with a scrutiny that was nearly ungirlish. Maurice tried not to see it as he put his fingers on her wrist. She added:

"I have felt that about you too."

Maurice had taken out his watch. Without speaking he timed the fluttering pulsation of her life, then, dropping her hand and returning the watch to his pocket:

"Your too eager thoughts were of me?" he asked.

"Yes, but yours were not of me."

"Not always," he said, with an honesty that pleased her.

And again Lily saw above his face the shadowy crown of thorns. She was really unwell and ready to be unstrung. Perhaps this made her say hastily, as she shifted lower on her cushions:

"I'm partly ill today because you let me see how horribly you are suffering."

"Yes," Maurice said heavily. "I let you see it. Why's that?"

There was nothing like a shock to either of them in the directness of their words. They seemed spoken rightly at the inevitable time. No thought of question, of denial, was entertained by them. Maurice sat there by her and dropped his mask utterly.

"Miss Alston, I am a haunted man," he said.

And, in a moment, as he spoke, he seemed to be old. Lily said nothing. She twisted between her little fingers the thin rug that covered her, and was angry with herself because, all of a sudden, she wanted to cry.

"And I am beginning to wonder," Maurice went on, "how much longer I can bear it, just how long."

Lily cleared her throat. It struck her as odd that she did not feel strange with this man who looked so old in the thin light from the lamp. Indeed, now that the mask had entirely fallen from him, he seemed more familiar to her than ever before.

"I suppose we must bear everything so long as God chooses," she said.

"No, so long as we choose."

"But how?"

"To live to bear it. I cannot be haunted after I am dead. That can't be."

He lifted his head and looked at her with a sort of pale defiance, as if he would dare her to contradict him. Lily confronted the horror of his eyes, and a shudder ran over her. The thorns had pierced more deeply even than she had believed as she lay awake in the night. Just then a door banged and a footstep approached on the landing.

"Hush, it's father," Lily whispered.

And the Canon entered to ask the condition of the patient. Maurice prescribed and went away. In the windy evening as he walked, he was conscious of a large change dawning over his life. Either the spirit of prophecy—which comes to many men even in modern days—was upon him, or hope, which he believed quite dead in him, stirred faintly in his dream. In either event he saw that on the black walk of his life there was the irregular, and as yet paltry, line of some writing, some inscription. He could not read the words. He only knew that there were some words to be read. And one of them was surely Lily's name.

He did not meet her until the evening of the following Sunday when, as usual, he went to supper at the Rectory. Lily was better and had been to church. The Canon was delighted and thanked Maurice for his skill in diagnosis and in treatment.

"You cure everyone," he said.

Lily and Maurice exchanged a glance. He saw how well she understood that he felt the words to be an irony though they were uttered so innocently. After supper, just as the Canon, with his habitual Sunday sigh of satisfaction, was beginning to light his pipe, Sarah, the parlour maid, came in with a note. The Canon read it and his sigh moved onwards to something not unlike a groan. He put his filled pipe down on the mantelpiece.

"What is it, father?" asked Lily.

"Miss Bigelow," he replied laconically.

"On a Sunday. Oh, it's too bad!"

"It can't be helped," the Canon said. "Excuse me, Dale, I have to go out. But—stay—I shall be back in half an hour."

And he went out into the hall, took his coat and hat and left the house. Miss Bigelow was his cross. She was a rich invalid, portentously delicate, full of benefactions to the parish and fears for the welfare of her soul. She kept the Canon's charities going royally, but, in return, she claimed the Canon's ghostly ministrations at odd times to an extent that sometimes caused the good man's saintly equanimity to totter. Hating doctors and loving clergymen, Miss Bigelow was forever summoning her distracted father confessor to speed that parting guest—her soul, which however, never departed. She remarked in confidence to those about her, that she had endured "a dozen deathbeds." The Canon had sat beside them all. He must now take his way to the thirteenth.

As soon as the hall door banged Maurice looked up at Lily.

"Poor, dear father," she murmured.

"I am glad," Maurice said abruptly.

The remark might have been called rude, but it was so simply made that it had the dignity belonging to any statement of plain truth. Neither rude nor polite, it was merely a cry of fact from an overburdened human soul. Lily felt that the words were forced from the young doctor by some strange agitation that fought to find expression.

"You wish—you wish—" she began.

Then she stopped. The flood of expression that welled up in her companion's face frightened her. She trembled at the thought of the hidden thing, the force, that could loose such a sea.

"What is it?" she said like a schoolgirl—or so, a moment afterwards, she feared.

"I ought not to tell you," Maurice said, "I ought not, but I must—I must."

He had got up and was standing before her. His back was to the fire, and a shadow was over his face.

"I want to tell you. You have made me want to. Why is that?"

He spoke as if he were questioning his own intellect for the reason, not asking it of her. And she did not try to answer his question.

"I suppose," he continued, "it is because you are the only human being who has partially understood that there is something with me that sets me apart from all my kind, from all the others."

"With you?" Lily said.

She felt horribly frightened and yet strong and earnest.

"Yes, with me," he answered. "I told you that I was a haunted man. Miss Alston, can you, will you bear to hear what it is that is with me, and why it comes. It is a story that, perhaps, your father might forbid you to read. I don't know. And, if it was fiction, perhaps he would be right. But—but—I think—I wonder—you might help me. I can't see how, but—I feel—"

He faltered suddenly, and seemed for the first time to become self-conscious and confused.

"Tell me, please," Lily said.

She felt rather as if she were beginning to read some strange French story by night. Maurice still stood on the hearth.

"It is a sound that is with me," he said. "Only that; never anything else but that."

"A sound," she repeated.

She thought of their conversation about *The Bells*.

"Yes, it is a cry—the cry of a child."

"Yes?"

"That's nothing—you think? Absurd for a man to heed such a trifle?"

"Why do you think it comes?"

Maurice hesitated. His eyes searched the face of the little girl with an almost hard gaze of scrutiny, as if he were trying to sum up the details of her nature.

"Long ago—before I came here, before I was qualified, I was cruel, bitterly cruel to a child," he said at last, speaking now very coldly and distinctly.

His eyes were on Lily. Had she made just then any movement of horror or of disgust, had an expression betokening fear of him come into her eyes, Maurice knew that his lips would be sealed, that he would bid her good night and leave her. But she only looked more intent, more expectant. He went on.

"I was bitterly cruel to my own child," he said.

Then Lily moved suddenly. Maurice thought she was going to start up. If she had intended to she choked the impulse. Was she shocked? He could not tell. She had turned her face away from him. He wondered why, but he did not know that those last words had given to Lily an abrupt and fiery insight into the depths of her heart.

"At that time," Maurice said, still speaking very distinctly and quietly, "I was desperately ambitious. I was bitten by the viper whose poison, stealing through all a man's veins, is emulation. My only desire, my only aim in life was to beat all the men of my year, to astonish all the authorities of the hospital to which I was attached by the brilliance of my attainments and my achievements, I was ambition incarnate, and such mad ambition is the most cruel thing in the world. And my child interfered with my ambition. It cried, how it cried!"

He was becoming less definitely calm.

"It cried through my dreams, my thoughts, my endeavours, my determinations. Do you know what a weapon a sound can be, Miss Alston? Perhaps not. A sound can be like a sword and pierce you, like a bludgeon and strike you down. A little sound can nestle in your life, and change all the colour and all the meaning of it. The cry of the living child was terrible to me, I thought then. But—then—I had never heard the cry of the dead child. You see I wanted to forget something. And the tiny cry of the child recalled it. There were no words in the cry, and yet there were words,—so it seemed to me—telling over a past history. This history—well, I want to say to you—"

Lily had now put a guard on watch over her impulsive nature. When Maurice stopped speaking she was able to look towards him again and murmur:

"Say all you want to."

"Thank you," he said, almost eagerly. "If you knew—Miss Alston, before this time, when I was a very young student, I had fallen into one of the most fatal confusions of youth. I had made a mistake as to the greatest need of my own nature. I had, for a flash of time, thought my greatest need was love."

"And it wasn't," the girl said, with a note of wonder in her voice.

"No, it was success, to outstrip my fellows. But I thought it was love, and I followed my thought and I sacrificed another to my thought. My child's mother died almost in giving her to me, and, in dying, made me promise to keep the child always with me. I kept that promise. I was a young student, very poor. My love had been secret. Now I was alone with this helpless child. I left my own lodgings and took others. I brought it there, and its presence obliged me to shut my doors against my own family and against my friends. To keep the door shut I put forward the excuse of my ambition. I said that I was giving myself up to work and I shut myself in with the child. I was its nurse as well as its father. I thought I should be sufficient for it. But it missed—her, whom I scarcely missed."

"You had not loved her?"

Maurice bent his head.

"I had made a mistake, as I said. I had only thought so. Long before she died I had almost hated her for crippling my ambition. She was swept out of my path. But the child was left crying for her."

"Yes. I know."

"Its wail came eternally between me and my great desire. When I sat down to work the sound—which I could not quiet—perplexed my brain. When I lay down to get, in sleep, power for fresh work, it struck through my dreams. I heard it when the stars were out over London, and in the dawn, when from my lodging windows I could see the first light on the Thames. Miss Alston, at last it maddened me."

Lily was pale. She scarcely knew of what she was expectant.

"I had tried to comfort the child. I had failed. Now I determined to forget it, to shut it out from my working life. At last, by force of will, I almost succeeded. I read, I wrote, I analysed the causes of disease, the results of certain treatments as opposed to the results of others. And sometimes I no longer heard my child, no longer knew whether it wailed and wept or whether it was silent. But one evening—"

Maurice stopped. His face was very white and his eyes burned with excitement.

"One evening," he repeated, speaking almost with difficulty, and with the obstinate note in his voice of one telling a secret half against his will and better judgement, "I could not work. The wail of the child was so loud, so alarmed, so full of a fear that seemed to my imagination intelligent, and based on a knowledge of something I did not know, that my professional instinct was aroused. At first I listened, sitting at my writing table. Then I got up and softly approached the folding doors. Beyond them, in the dark, the child lamented like one to whom a nameless horror draws near. Never had I known it to weep like this; for this was no cry after a mother, no cry of desire, no cry even of sorrow. It was a half-strangled scream of terror, I did not go into the room, but as I listened, I knew—"

He faltered.

"Yes," Lily said.

"As I listened I knew what the cry meant. Miss Alston, is it not strange that even a baby who scarcely knows life knows so well—death?"

"Death!"

"Yes, recognises its coming, shrinks from it, fears it with the terror of a clear intelligence. Is it not very strange?"

"Death!" Lily repeated.

She too was pale. Maurice continued in a low voice.

"I understood the meaning of the cry, and I did not enter the inner room. No, I walked back to my writing table, put my hands over my ears—to deaden the cry—and gave myself again to work. How long I worked I don't know, but presently I heard a loud knocking at the door of my room. I sprang up and opened it. My landlady stood outside.

"'What do you want?' I asked.

"The good woman's face was grave.

"'Sir, I know that child must be ill,' she said.

"'Ill—why? What do you mean?'

"'Oh, sir, its crying is awful. It goes right through me.'

"I pushed the woman out almost roughly.

"'It is not ill,' I said. 'It is only restless. Leave me. Don't you see I am working?'

"And I shut the door sharply. I sat down again at my table and toiled till dawn. I remember that dawn so well. At last my brain had utterly tired. I could work no longer. I pushed away my papers and got up. The room was misty—so I thought—with a flickering grey light. The dirty white blind was drawn half up. I looked out over the river, and from it I heard the dull shout of a man on a black barge. This shout recalled to me my child and the noise of its lament. I listened. All was silent. There was no murmur from the inner room. And then I remember that suddenly the silence, for which I had so often longed and prayed, frightened me. It seemed full of a dreadful meaning. I waited a moment. Then I walked softly across the room to the folding doors. They were closed, I opened them furtively and looked into the bedroom. It was nearly dark. Approaching the bed I could scarcely discern the tiny white heap which marked where the child lay among the tumbled bedclothes. I bent down to listen to the sound of its breathing. I could not hear the sound. Then I caught the child in my arms and carried it over to the sitting room window so that the dawn might strike upon its little face. The face was discoloured. The heart was not beating. Miss Alston, while I worked, my child had died in a convulsion. It had striven against death, poor feeble baby, and had had no help from its father. My medical skill might have eased its sufferings. Might have saved it. But I had deliberately closed my ears to its appeal for love, for assistance. I had let it go. I should never hear it again."

Maurice had spoken the last words with excitement. Now he paused. With an obvious effort he controlled himself and added calmly:

"I buried my child and gave myself again to work. My examination was close at hand. I passed it brilliantly. But I shuddered at my success. Those lodgings by the river had become horrible to me. I left them, took a practice in a remote Cumberland valley, and withdrew myself from the world, from all who had known me. In this retirement, however, I had a companion of whose presence at first I was unaware. The dead child followed me, the child of whom now I feel myself to have been the murderer."

"No—no—not that!" Lily whispered. But he did not seem to hear her.

"One night," he continued, "in my lonely house in the valley I was awakened by some sound. I sat up in bed and listened. All was black around me, and at first all was quiet too. I lay down again to sleep. But as I touched the pillow I heard a faint murmur that seemed to come from far away. I said to myself that it was a fancy of my mind but again it came. Then I thought it was the wind caught in some cranny of my house. I opened my window and leaned out. But there was no wind in the trees. What was the noise then? The cry of a bird perhaps. Yes, it must be that. Yet did any note of a bird have a thrill of pain in it? I hurried on some clothes and let myself out into the garden. I would hear that bird again. I would convince myself of its presence. But in the garden I could hear nothing save the thin murmur of the stream that threaded the valley. So I returned to the house, and at the door I was greeted by a little cry from within. Miss Alston, it was the cry of my dead child, full of pain and of eternal reproach. I shut the door, closing myself in with my fate, and since that night I have been a haunted man. Scarcely a day has passed since then, scarcely a night has gone by without my hearing that appeal for help which once I disregarded, which now I can never reply to. I fled from the valley, in a vain hope of leaving that voice behind me. I came here. But the child's spirit is here too. It is forever with me."

He stopped abruptly, then he added, "I can even hear it now, while I look at you, while I touch your hand."

His burning eyes were fixed on Lily's face. His burning hand closed on hers as if seeking assistance.

"What am I to do?" he said, and for the first time his voice broke and failed.

"Pray!" she whispered.

"I have prayed. But God forgives only those who reverse their evil acts. Mine can never be reversed. I can never be kind to my child to whom I have been bitterly cruel. There is no help for me, none. Yet I had a feeling that—that you might help me."

"If I could!" the girl cried with a blaze of sudden eagerness. Her heart leaped up at the words, leaped up from its depth of pity for Maurice to a height of almost fiery enthusiasm.

"But how?" he said.

Then his face hardened and grew stern.

"No," he said, "there can be no help for me, none in this world."

The drawing room door opened and the Canon appeared.

"Miss Bigelow has not died for the thirteenth time," he said, coming up to the fire.

When the Canon kissed his daughter that night, after Maurice Dale had gone home, he seemed struck by a new expression in her face.

"Why, how excited you look, child!" he said, "what is it?"

But Lily returned his kiss hastily and ran away without a word. Once in her room she locked the door—for no reason except that she must mark the night by some unwonted action—put on her dressing gown and threw herself down on her bed. Her mind was alive with thoughts. Her imagination was in flames. For so much had come upon her that evening. In the first place she understood that she loved Maurice. She knew that, when he spoke the words, "My child," and jealousy of an unknown woman struck like some sharp weapon to her heart. She realised that he did not love her, yet so great was her simple unselfishness, that she did not dwell on the knowledge, or blame for an instant the selfishness which concentrated Maurice's mind so entirely upon himself and his own sorrow. Her only anxiety was how to help him. Her only feeling was one of tender pity for his agony. And yet, for Lily was a girl of many fancies and full of the wilful side-thoughts of women, she found room in her nature for a high-flown sense of personal romance which now wrapped her round in a certain luxury of complacency. She moved in a strange story that was true, a story that she might have read with a quickening of the pulses. She and Maurice, whom she loved, moved in it together heroine and hero of it. And none knew the story but themselves. And then she burst into silent tears, calling herself cruel for having this moment of half joy in the tragedy of another. She pushed down into the depths of Maurice's misery. And then, with a clearer mind, she sat up on the bed. It was dead of night now. Was he listening in the silence to that haunting cry that was destroying him? She wondered breathlessly. And she recalled the conversation about *The Bells*. Was Mathias truly haunted? or was he mad? She asked herself that, putting Maurice eventually behind footlights in his place. Was there really a veritable cry, allowed to come out of the other world to Maurice? or did his diseased brain work out his retribution? She could not tell. Indeed she scarcely cared just then. In either event, the result upon him was the same and was terrible. In either event, the outcome might be what she dared not name even to herself. And, though he did not love her, he turned to her for help. Lily flushed in the thought of this. Almost more than if she had his heart it seemed to have his cry for assistance. She must answer it effectually. She must. But how? And then she sprang up and began to pace the room. How to help him. Slowly, and with a minute examination, she went in memory through his story, with its egoism, its cruelty, its ambition, its punishment, its childlike helplessness of tonight, and of many nights. She recalled each word that he had spoken until she came to almost the last, "I have prayed. But God forgives only those who reverse their evil acts. Mine can never be reversed. I can never be kind to my child—" Just there she stopped. Maurice's words flew against what Lily's religion taught her of the Great Being who can pardon simply and fully so long only as the sinner entirely and deeply repents. But she accepted them as true for Maurice. There was the point to be faced. She felt that his nature, haunted indeed or betrayed by its own weakness, but still loved by her, could only be restored to peace if he could fulfil the impossible, reverse—as he expressed it— that act of his past. Ah, that cry of the little dying, helpless child, of his little child. Lily could almost hear it too, the tears came into her eyes. How could she still it? How could she lay the little spirit to rest forever? Peace for child, peace for father, sinned against and sinner—she felt she would gladly sacrifice her own life, her own peace, to work the miracle of comfort on dead and living. Yes, she could give up her love— if— Suddenly Lily threw herself down on her bed and buried her burning face deep in the pillows. A thought had come to her, so strange that she wondered whether it were not wicked. The hot red colour surged over her with this thought, and all the woman in her quivered as she asked herself whether, in this life of sorrows and of abnegations, it could ever be that the grief and the terror of another could be swept away by one who, in the endeavour to bring solace, must obtain intense personal happiness. In books it is ever self-sacrifice that purges and persuades, martyrdom of the senses that renews and relieves. Lily was ready indeed to be a martyr for the man she loved. But the strange way she saw of being his possible saviour lay only in a light of the sun forever on herself.

She wept and saw the light, herself and Maurice walking in it together, till the church bell chimed in the morning, and the tide came up in the sunshine to murmur that it was day.

Maurice Dale was puzzled. He noticed a change in Lily so marked that even his self-centred nature could not fail to observe it. This girl, whom he had thought pretty, fanciful, tenderhearted and gently sympathetic, who had attracted his confession by her quick and feminine receptiveness, now seemed developed into a woman of strength and purpose, full of calm and of dignity. Her shining eyes were more steadfast than of old, her manner was less changeful, less enthusiastic, but more reliant. Brayfield wondered what had come to Miss Alston. Maurice wondered too, dating the transformation accurately from the night when he unburdened his soul in search of the help, which, after all, no human being could give to him. It was strange, he thought, that a man's terror, a man's weakness, should endow a weak girl with confidence and with power. It was too strange, and he laughed at himself for supposing that he had anything to do with the new manifestation of Lily's nature. Nevertheless she began to attract him more than he had believed possible. The nightmare in which his life was encircled grew less real when he was with her. There was virtue in her that went out to him. He came to desire always to be with her and yet he could not say to himself that he loved her with the passion of man for woman. Rather was the desire that he felt for her like that of a criminal towards a place of refuge, of a coward towards an asylum of safety. Sometimes he longed that she might share his trouble, selfishly longed that in her ears might ring the cry of pain that tormented his.

One day, when they were together on a down that overlooked the sea, he told her this.

"I wish it too," she answered softly.

"You are all unselfishness, as I am all selfishness," he said, condemning himself, and nearer to loving her than ever before.

The sails went by along the wintry sea, and the short afternoon faded quickly into a twilight that was cold in its beauty like a pale primrose in frost. They were descending slowly towards the little town that lay beneath them in the shadows.

"I have no voice to trouble my life—no dead voice, that is," Lily said.

"No dead voice?" Maurice asked. "And the living?"

"Oh, in most lives there is some one voice that means almost too much," Lily answered slowly.

Maurice stopped.

"Whose voice means so much to you?" he said.

"Why do you care to ask?"

"Is it mine?"

The girl had stopped too. Her face was set towards the sea and its great sincerity, which murmurs against the lies and the deceptions of many lives that defile the land, and takes so many more to itself that they may persist no longer in their evil doing. And perhaps it was her vision of the sea that swept from Lily any desire to be a coquette, or to be maidenly—that is, false. She looked from the sea into Maurice's eyes.

"Yes," she answered. "It is yours."

"You love me then, Lily?"

"Yes, I love you, Maurice."

There was no tremor in her voice. There was no shame in her eyes. Alone in her chamber on the night of Maurice's confession she had flushed and trembled. Now she stood before him and made this great acknowledgement simply and fearlessly. And yet she knew that he did not love her with the desire of man to the woman whom he chooses out of the world to be his companion. She was moved by a resolve that was very great to ignore all that girls think most of at such a moment. Maurice took a step towards her. How true and how strong she looked.

"I dare not ask you to share my life," he said. "It is too shadowed, too sad. I have not the right."

"If you will ask me, I will share it."

She put her hand into his. He felt as if her soul lay in it. They walked on. Already the evening was dark around them.

Canon Alston was a little surprised, merely because he was a father, and fathers are always a little surprised when men love their children. But he liked Maurice heartily and gave his consent to the marriage. Miss Bigelow ordered a valuable wedding present, and resolved to live until over the marriage day at least. And Brayfield gossiped and gloried in possessing a legitimate cause for excitement.

As for Lily, she was strangely happy with a happiness far different from that of the usual betrothed young girl. She loved Maurice deeply. Nevertheless she did not blind herself to the fact that he was still unhappy, restless, self-engrossed and often terror-stricken, although he tried to appear more confident than of old, and to assume a gaiety suitable to his situation in the eyes of the world. She knew he could never be entirely free to love so long as the cry of the child rang in his ears. And he told her that, strangely enough, since their engagement it had become more importunate. Once he even tried to break their contract.

"I cannot link my life with another's," he said desperately. "Who knows—when you are one with me, you may be haunted as I am. That would be too horrible."

It was a flash of real and heartfelt unselfishness. Lily felt herself thrill with gratitude. But she only said:

"I am not afraid."

On another occasion—this was about a month after they became engaged—Maurice said:

"Lily, when shall we be married?"

She glanced up at him, and saw that he was paler even than usual, and that his face looked drawn with fatigue.

"Whenever you wish," she answered.

"Let it be soon," he said. And then he broke out almost despairingly:

"I cannot bear this much longer. Lily, what can it mean? There is something too strange. Ever since you and I have been betrothed the curse that is laid upon me has been heavier, the cry of the child has been more incessantly with me. I hear it more plainly. It is nearer to me. It is close to me. In the night sometimes I start up thinking the child is even beside me on the pillow, complaining to me in the darkness. I stretch out my hand. I feel for its little body. But there is nothing— nothing but that cry of fear, of pain, of eternal reproach. Why does the spirit persecute me now as it never persecuted me before? Is it because it believes that you will make me happier? Is it because it wishes to deny me all earthly joy? Sometimes I think that, once we are actually husband and wife the cry will die away. Sometimes I think that then it will never leave me even for a moment. If that were so, Lily, I should die, or I should lose my reason."

He covered his face with his hands. He was trembling. Lily put her soft hand against his hands. A great light had come into her eyes as he spoke.

"Let us be married, Maurice," she said. "Perhaps the little child wants me."

He looked up at her and his dark eyes seemed to pierce her, hungry for help.

"Wants you?" he said. "How can that be? No, no. It cries against my thought of happiness, against my desire for peace."

"We must give it peace. We must lay it to rest."

"No one can do that. If I have not the power to redeem my deed of wickedness, how can you, how can anyone living redeem it for me?"

Lily looked away from him. Her cheeks were burning with a blush. A tingling fire seemed to run through all her veins and her pulses beat.

"There is some way of redemption for everyone," she said.

But he answered gloomily:

"Your religion teaches you to say that, Lily, perhaps to believe it. But there is no way. The dead cannot return to earth that we may give them tenderness instead of our former cruelty. No—no!"

"Maurice—trust me. Let us be married—soon."

That night, before she went to bed, Lily knelt down and prayed until the night was old. She asked what thousands of women have asked since the world was young. But surely never woman before had so strange a reason for her request. And when at length she rose from her knees she felt that time must bring the gift she had prayed for, unselfishly, and with her whole heart.

A month afterwards, on a bright spring morning, Maurice and Lily were married. It was a great occasion for Brayfield. The church was elaborately decorated by the many young ladies who had secretly longed to be the brides of the interesting doctor. Crowds assembled within and without the building. Miss Bigelow rose from her fourteenth deathbed in a purple satin gown and a bonnet prodigious with feathers and testified to the possibility of modern resurrection in a front pew. Flowers, rice, wedding marches filled the air. But people remarked that the bridegroom looked like a man who went in fear. Even when he was on the doorstep of the church in the throng of curious sightseers he moved almost as one whom a dream attends, who sees the pale figures, who hears the faint voices that inhabit and make musical a vision of the night. The bride too, had no radiant air of a young girl fulfilling her girlish destiny and giving herself up to a protector, to one stronger, more able to fight the world than a woman who loves and fears. Her face, too, was pale and grave, even—some thought—a little stern. As she passed up the church she glanced at no one, smiled at no friend. Her eyes were set steadfastly towards the altar where Maurice waited. And when, after the ceremony, she came down the church to the sound of music her eyes were fixed on her husband. She took no heed of anyone else, for her hand pressed upon his arm, felt that he was trembling. And her ears seemed to hear through all the jubilant music, through all the murmur of the gazing crowd, a cry, far away, yet more distinct than any sound of earth, thin, piercing, full of appeal to her—the spirit-cry of the child.

Part II
The Living Child

The honeymoon of Lily and Maurice was short, and many would have called it sad, could they have known how different it was from the marriage holiday of most young couples. Maurice had looked forward to the wedding as a desperate man looks forward to a new point of departure in his life. He had fixed all his hopes of possible peace upon it. He had dated new days of calm, if not of brightness, from it. He had sometimes vaguely, sometimes desperately, looked to it as to a miracle day, on which—how or why he knew not—the shadow would be lifted from his life. The man who is doomed to death has a moment of acute expectation when some new doctor places him under a fresh mode of treatment. For a few days the increased vitality of his anxious mind sheds a dawn of apparent life through his body. But the mind collapses. The dawn fades. The darkness increases, death steals on. So it was with Maurice. Immediately after the wedding, Lily noticed that he fell into a strangely watchful condition of abstraction. He was full of tenderness to her, full of cares for her comfort, but even in his moments of obvious solicitude he seemed to be on the alert to catch the stir of some remote activity, or to be listening for the sound of some distant voice. His own fate engrossed him even in this first period of novel companionship with another soul. The monomania of the haunted man gripped him and would not release him. He thought of Lily, but he thought more, and with a deeper passion, of himself.

The girl divined this, but she did not for an instant rebel. She had set up a beautiful unselfishness in her heart and had consecrated it. Purpose does much for a woman, helps her sometimes to rise higher than perhaps man can ever rise, to the pale and vacant peaks of an inactive martyrdom. And Lily was full of a passion of purpose known only to herself. She loved Maurice not merely as a girl loves a man, but also as the protective woman loves the being dependent upon her. His secret was hers, but hers was not his. She had her beautiful loneliness of silent hope, and that sustained her.

They went away together. In the train Maurice said to her suddenly, with a sort of blaze of hungry eagerness:

"Lily—Lily—today there is a silence for me. Oh, Lily, if you have brought me silence."

He seized her hand and his was hot like fire.

"Will it last—can it last?" he whispered.

And he glanced all around the carriage like one anticipating an answer to his question from some unknown quarter, then he said:

"The noise of the train is so loud, perhaps—"

"Hush!" Lily said. "Don't fight your own peace, Maurice."

"Fight it—no, but I can scarcely believe in it. Lately the—it has been so ceaseless, so poignant. Lily, I have had a fancy that you alone could be my saviour. If it is so! Ah, but how can that be?"

She gave him a strange answer.

"Maurice," she said, "it may be so, but do not despair if the cry comes again."

"What!" he exclaimed almost fiercely, "you—do you hear it then?"

"No, no, but it may come."

"It shall not. The silence is so beautiful."

He put his arms around her. The tears had sprung into his eyes.

"How weak I am," he said, with a fury against his own condition, "you must despise me."

"I love you," she said.

He looked at her with a creeping astonishment.

"I wonder why," he said, slowly. "How can you love a man who has been so miserable that he has almost ceased to be a man?"

"I love even your misery. Don't think me selfish, Maurice. But it was your sorrow, you see, that first taught you to think of me."

He leaned from her suddenly towards the window which was open and pulled it sharply up.

"Why do you do that?" Lily said quickly.

"One hears such noises in the air when one travels at this speed," he answered. "With the window down one might fancy anything. I must shut out fancy. There are voices in the wind that passes, in the rustling woods that we rush through. I won't hear them."

The train sped on.

Their destination was an inland village set in the midst of a rolling purple moor, isolated in a heather-clad gold of the land, distant from the sea, distant from the murmur of modern life; a sleepy, self-contented and serene abode of quiet women and ruminant men, living, loving, and dying with a greater calm than often pervades our modern life. A lazy divinity seemed to preside over the place, in springtime at least. Men strolled about their work as if Time waited on them, not they on Time. The children—so Maurice thought—played more drowsily than the children of towns. The youths were contemplative. Even the girls often forgot to giggle as they thought of wedding rings and Sunday lovemaking. Little dogs lay blinking before the low-browed doors of the cottages, and cats reposed upon the garden walls round-eyed in sober dreams. If Maurice sought a home of silence surely he had it here. Lily and he put up at a small inn on the skirt of the village and facing the rippling emptiness of the moor. Before going to bed they stepped out into the night and the wide air. Stars were bright in the sky. Cottage lights twinkled here and there behind them in the village. They heard a stream running away into the heart of the long solitude that lay beyond them. Lily was very quiet. Her heart was full. Thoughts, strange and beautiful, overflowed in her mind. She felt just then how much bigger the human soul is than the human body, how much stronger the prisoner is than the prison in which nevertheless it is dedicated to dwell for a time. Her hand just touched the arm of Maurice as she looked across the soft darkness of the moor. He, too, felt curiously happy and safe. Taking off his cap he passed his hand over his hair.

"Lily," he said, "peace is here for me, in this place with you. My brain has been playing me tricks because I have been so much alone, the devil dwells in a man's loneliness. Listen to the silence of these moors. What a music it is!"

The lights in the cottages were extinguished one by one, as bed claimed their owners. But Maurice and Lily, sitting on the dry fringe of the heather, remained out under the stars. Her hand lay in his and suddenly she felt his quiver.

"What is it, Maurice?" she asked.

He got up and made a step forward.

"Lily," he said, "there is—there must be someone near us, a child lost on the moor, or forgotten by its mother. I hear it crying close to us. Say you hear it too. No, no, it is not the old sound. Don't think that. It can't be. There's a natural explanation of this—I'll swear there is. Come with me."

He pulled her hastily up and pressed forward some steps, stumbling among the bushes. Then he stopped, listening.

"It is somewhere just here, by us," he said. "I must see. Wait a moment. I'll strike a light."

He drew out his matchbox and struck a match, protecting the tiny flame between his hands. Then he bent down, searching the uneven ground at their feet. The flame went out.

"I wish I had a lantern," he muttered.

"Maurice," Lily said, "let us go back to the inn."

"What! and leave this child out here in the night. I tell you there is a child crying near us."

He spoke almost angrily.

"Let us go back, Maurice."

He stood for a moment as if uncertain.

"You think—" he began, then he stopped. She took his hand and led him towards the village in silence. As they reached the inn door, the faint light from the coffee-room encircled them. Maurice was white to the lips. He looked at Lily without speaking, and he was trembling.

"Wasn't there anything?" he whispered. "Is it here too? Can't you keep it away?"

Lily said nothing. She opened the inn door. Maurice stepped into the passage, heavily, almost like a drunken man. And this was the first night of their honeymoon.

The incident of the moor threw Maurice back into the old misery from which he had emerged for a brief moment, and, indeed, plunged him into an abyss of despair such as he had never known before. For now he had sincerely hoped for salvation, and his hope had been frustrated. He had clung to a belief that Lily's love, Lily's companionship might avail to rescue him from the phantom, or the reality, that was destroying his power, shattering his manhood. The belief was dashed from him, and he sank deeper in the sea of terror. They stayed on for a while in this Sleepy Hollow, but Maurice no longer felt its peace. Remote as it was, cloistered in the rolling moors, the cry of the child penetrated to it, making it the very centre, the very core of all things hideous and terrible. Even the silence of the village, its aloofness from the world, became hateful to Maurice. For they seemed to emphasise and to concentrate the voice that pierced more keenly in silence, that sounded more horrible in solitude.

"I cannot stay here," he said to Lily. "Let us go back. I will take up my work again. I will try to throw myself into it as I did when I was a student. I shut out the living cry then, I will shut out the dead cry now. For you—you cannot help me."

He looked at her while he spoke almost contemptuously, almost as one looks at some woman whose courage or whose faith one has tried and found wanting.

"You cannot help me," he repeated.

Secretly he felt a cruel desire to sting Lily into passion, to rouse her to some demonstration of anger against his cowardice in thus taunting her love and devotion. But she said nothing, only looked at him with eyes that had become strangely steadfast, and full of the quiet light of a great calm and patience.

"D'you say nothing?" he said.

"If you wish to go, Maurice, let us go."

He had got up and was standing by the low window that looked across the moor.

"Don't you see," he said, "that I am going mad in this place? And you do nothing. Why did I ever think that you could help me?"

"Try to think so still."

She, too, got up, followed him to the window and put her two hands on his shoulders.

"Perhaps the time has not come yet," she said.

Suddenly he took her hands in his and pushed her a little way from him, so that he could look clearly into her face.

"What do you mean? What can you mean?" he said. "Sometimes I think you have some secret that you keep from me, some purpose that I know nothing of. You look as if—as if you were waiting for something; were expectant; I don't know—" he broke off. "After all what does it matter? Only let us go from here. Let us get home. I hate that stretch of moorland. At night it is full of bewailing and misery."

He shuddered although the warm spring sunshine was pouring in at the window. Then he turned and left the room without another word. Lily stood still for a moment, with her eyes turned in the direction of the door. Her cheeks burned with a slight blush and her lips were half opened.

"If he only knew what I am waiting for!" she murmured to herself. "Will it ever come?"

She sank down on the broad, old-fashioned window seat, and leaned her cheek against the leaded panes of glass. The bees were humming outside. She listened to their music. It was dull and dreamy, heavy like a golden noon in summer time. And then the white lids fell over her eyes, and the hum of the bees faded from her ears, and she heard another music that made her woman's heart leap up, she heard the first tiny murmur of a newborn child.

It was sweeter than the hum of bees. It was sweeter than the soul the lute gave up to the ears of Nature when Orpheus touched the strings. It was so sweet that tears came stealing from under Lily's eyelids and dropped down upon her clasped hands. She sat there motionless till the twilight came over the moor, and Maurice entered, white and weary, to ask impatiently of what she was dreaming.

As Maurice wished it, they returned the next day to Brayfield and settled into the house that was to be their home. It stood on a low cliff overlooking the sea; a broad green lawn, on which during the season a band played and people promenaded, lay in front of it. Beyond, the waves danced in the sunshine. The situation of the house was almost absurdly cheerful, and the house itself was new and prettily furnished. But the life into which Lily entered was strangely at variance with the surroundings, strangely antagonistic to the brightness of the sea, the sweetness of the air, the holiday gaiety that pervaded the little town in the summer. For work did not abolish, did not even lull the sound of the voice that pursued Maurice with an inexorable persistence. It was obvious that on his return home after the honeymoon, he made a tremendous effort to get the better of his enemy. He called up all his manhood, all his strength of character. He refused to hear the voice. When it cried in his ears, he went to sit with Lily, and plunged into conversation on subjects that interested them both. He made her play to him, or sing to him in the twilight. He read aloud to her. This was at night. By day he worked unremittingly. When he was not driving to see patients he laboured to increase his knowledge of medicine. He pursued the most subtle investigations into the causes of obscure diseases, and specially directed his enquiries towards the pathology of the brain. He analysed the multitudinous developments of madness and traced them back to their beginnings; and when, as was often the case, he discovered that the mad man or woman whose malady was laid bare to him had inherited this curse of humanity, he smiled with a momentary thrill of joy. His ancestors on both sides of the family had been sane. Yet one of the commonest, most invariable delusions of the insane was the imaginary idea that they were pursued by voices, ordering them to do this or that, suggesting crimes to them or weeping in their ears over some tragedy of the past. Maurice knew that the mind which does not inherit a legacy of insanity may yet be overturned by some terrible incident, by a great shock, or by an unexpected bereavement. But surely such a mind would be aware of its transformation, even as a man who, from an accident, becomes disfigured is aware of the alteration of his face from beauty to desolation. Maurice was not aware that his mind had been transformed. Deliberately, calmly, he asked himself, "Am I insane?" Deliberately, calmly, his soul answered, "No." Yet the cry of the child rang in his ears, pursued his goings out and comings in, filled his days with lamentation, and his nights with horror.

Then, leaving the subject of madness, Maurice began to institute a close investigation into the subject of alleged hauntings of human beings by apparitions and by sounds. He read of the actress, whose lover, who had slain himself in despair at her cruelty, remained forever with her, manifesting his presence, although invisible, by cries, curses, and clappings of the hands. He read of the clergyman who was haunted by the footsteps of his murdered sweetheart, which even ascended the pulpit stairs behind him, and pattered furtively about him when he knelt to pray for pardon of his sin. He filled his mind with visionary terrors, but they seemed remote or even ridiculous to him, and he said to himself that they were the clever inventions of imaginative people. They were worked up. They were moulded into conventional stories. They pleased the magazines of their time. He alone was really haunted of all men in the world, so far as he knew. And then a great and greedy desire came upon him to meet some other man in a like case, to hear from live lips the true and undecorated history of a despair like his own, one of those bald and terse narratives which pierce the imagination of the hearer like a sword, with no tinselled scabbard of exaggeration and of lies. He wondered whether upon the earth a man walked in a darkness similar to that which fell round him like a veil. He wondered whether he was unique, even as he felt. Sometimes he caught himself looking furtively at a harmless stranger, a bright girl tanned by the sea, or a lad just back from a fishing excursion to Raynor's Bay, and saying to himself low and drearily: "Does any spirit trouble you, I wonder? Does any spirit cry to you in the night?" But neither his work, his excursions of the imagination, nor the presence of Lily in his house, availed to cleanse the life of Maurice from the stain of sound, that ever widened and spread upon it. He fought for freedom for a while, strenuously, with all his heart and soul. But the lost battle left him with his energies exhausted, his courage broken. One night he said to Lily:

"Do you know all I have been doing since we came back here?"

"Yes, Maurice, I know."

"And that it has all been in vain," he said, with a passion of bitterness that he could not try to conceal.

"That too I understand, Maurice—I knew it would be in vain."

He looked at her almost as at an enemy, for his heart was so full of misery, his mind was so worn with weariness, that he began to lose the true appreciation of human relations, and to confuse the beauty near him with the ugliness that companioned him so closely.

"You knew it? What do you mean?" he said. "How could you know it?"

"I felt it, Maurice; do not try any longer to work out alone your own redemption."

"You can say that to me?"

"Yes, for I believe that it is useless—you will fail."

He set his lips together and said nothing. But a frown distorted his face slowly.

"Leave your redemption to God. Oh, Maurice, leave it," Lily said, and there were tears in her eyes. "If this cry of the dead child is his punishment to you it must—it will—endure so long as he pleases. Your efforts cannot still it now. You yourself told me so once."

"I told you?"

"Yes—for the dead are beyond our hands and our lips. We cannot clasp them. We cannot kiss them. We cannot speak to them."

"But they can speak to us and mock us. You are right. I can't still the cry—I can't! Then it's all over with me!"

Suddenly, with a sob, Maurice flung himself down. He felt as if something within him snapped, and as if straightway a dissolution of all the man in him succeeded this rupture of the spirit. Careless of the pride of man, before the world and even in his own home, he gave himself up to a despair that was too weak to be frantic, too complete to be angry; a despair that no longer strove but yielded, that lay down in the dust and wept. Then, presently, raising his head and seeing Lily, in whose eyes were tears of pity, Maurice was seized with an enmity against her, unreasonably wicked, but suddenly so vehement that he did not try to resist it.

"You have broken me," he said. "You have told me that there is no redemption, that I am in the hands of God, who persecutes me. You have told me the truth and made me hate you."

"Maurice!"

The cry came from her lips faintly, but there was the ring of anguish in it.

"It is so," he repeated doggedly. "And, indeed, I believe that you have added to the weight of my burden. Since we have been married the persecution has increased. Once, when I was alone, I could bear it. Now you are here I cannot bear it. The child hates you. When you are near—in the night—its cry is so intense that I wonder you can sleep. Yet I hear your quiet breathing. You say you love me. Then why are you so calm? Why do you tell me to trust? Why do you hint that I may yet find peace, and then tell me to cease from working for my own peace? You don't love me, you laugh at my trouble. You despise me."

He burst out of the room almost like a man demented.

It might be supposed that Lily, who loved him, would have been overwhelmed by this ecstasy of anger against her. But there was something that sheathed her heart from death. She might be wounded, she might suffer; but she looked beyond the present time, over the desert of her fate to roses of a future that Maurice, in his misery, could not see, in his self-engrossment could not divine. There is no living thing that understands how to wait, that can feel the beauty of patience, as a woman understands and feels. The curious depth of calm in Lily which irritated Maurice was created by a faith, half religious, half unreasoning, wholly strong and determined, such as no man ever knows in quite the same fullness as a woman. It is such a perfection of faith which gilds the silences in which the souls of many women wait, surrounded by the clouds of apparently shattered lives, but conscious that there is a great outcome, obscure and remote, but certain as the purpose which beats forever in Creation.

From that day Maurice no longer kept up a pretence of energy, or a simulation of even tolerable happiness in his home. The idea that the spirit of the dead child was stirred to an intense disquietude by his connection with Lily, and that, consequently, his marriage had deepened his punishment, grew in him until at length it became fixed. He brooded over it for hours together, his ears full of that eternal complaining. He began to feel that by linking himself with Lily he had added to his original sin, that his wedding had been a ceremony almost criminal, and that if he had scourged himself by living ascetically, and by putting rigorously away from him all earthly happiness, he might at last have laid the child to rest and found peace and forgiveness himself. And this fixed idea led him to shut Lily entirely out from his heart. He looked upon the fate of her being with him in the house as irrevocable. But he resolved that he ought to disassociate himself from her as far as possible, and, without explaining further to her the thought that now possessed him, he ceased to sit with her, ceased to walk out with her.

After dinner at night he retired to his study leaving her alone in the drawing room. He let her go up to bed without bidding her good night. When he was obliged to be with her at meals he maintained for the most part an obstinate silence.

Yet the cry of the child grew louder. The spirit of the child was not mollified. Its persecution continued and seemed to him to grow more persistent with each passing day.

What else could he do? How could he separate himself more completely from Lily?

Canon Alston came one day to solve this problem for him. The Canon had resolved on taking a holiday, and being no lover of solitude in his pleasures, he wished to persuade Maurice to become a grass widower for three weeks.

"Can you let Lily go?" he said. "I know it is a shame to leave you alone, but—"

He stopped, surprised at the sudden brightness that had come into Maurice's usually pale and grave face. Maurice saw his astonishment and hastened to allay it.

"I shall miss Lily of course," he began. "Still, if you want her, and she is anxious to go—"

"I have not mentioned it to her," the Canon said.

And at this moment Lily came into the room. The project was laid before her. She hesitated, looking from her father to her husband. Her perplexity seemed to both the men curiously acute, even to Maurice who was on fire to hear her decision. The prospect of solitude was sweet to his tormented heart now that he was possessed by the fancy that Lily's presence intensified his martyrdom. Yet Lily's obvious disturbance of mind surprised him. The two courses open to her were really so simple that there seemed no possible reason why she should look upon the taking of one of them as a momentous matter.

"Well, Lily, what do you say?" the Canon asked, after a pause. "Will you come with me?"

"But Maurice—"

"Maurice permits it, and I want you."

"I—I had not meant to leave home at present, father, not till after—"

She stopped abruptly.

"Till after what, my dear?" enquired the Canon.

She made no answer.

"Lily," Maurice said, trying to make his voice cool and indifferent, "I think you ought to go. It will do you good. Do not mind me. I shall manage very well for a little while."

"You would rather I went, Maurice?"

"I think we ought not to let your father go on his holiday alone."

"I will go," she said quietly.

So it was arranged. The Canon was jubilant at the prospect of his daughter's company, and asked her where they should travel.

"What do you say to the English Lakes, Lily?" he asked. "They are lovely at this time of year, and the rush of the tourist season has scarcely begun. Shall we go there?"

"Wherever you like, father," she said.

The Canon was feeling too gay to notice the preoccupation of her manner, the ungirlish gravity of her voice. That day, in the evening, when she was at dinner with Maurice, Lily said:

"You lived near the Lakes once, didn't you, Maurice?"

"Yes," he said.

"What was the name of the valley?"

He told her.

"And the house?"

"End Cottage. It was close to the waterfall. I hate it," he added almost fiercely. "It was there that I first heard—but I have told you."

He relapsed into silence and sent away the food on his plate untasted. Lily glanced across at him. But she said nothing more. And Maurice was struck by the consciousness that she took his strangeness strangely, with a lack of curiosity, a lack of protestation unlike a woman; almost for the first time since they were married he was moved to wonder how much she loved him, indeed whether she still loved him at all. He had got up from the dinner table and stood with one hand leaning upon it as he looked steadily, with his heavy and hunted eyes, across at Lily.

"Are you glad to go with the Canon?" he asked.

"I am quite ready to go," she said quietly.

"You don't mind leaving me?"

"I think you wish me to leave you—"

"Perhaps I do," he said, watching her to see if she winced at the words.

But her face was still and calm.

"What then?"

"Then it is better for me to go for a little while than to stay."

"For a little while," he repeated, "yes."

He turned and went slowly out of the room, and suddenly his face was distorted. For, in the darkness of the hall, he heard the child crying and lamenting. He stopped and listened to it like a man who resolutely faces his destruction. And, as so many times, he asked himself; "Is this a freak of my imagination, a trick of my nerves?" No, the sound was surely real, was close to him. It thrilled in his ears keenly. He could not doubt its reality. Yet he acknowledged to himself that he could not actually locate it. Only in that respect did it differ from other sounds of earth. As he stood in the half darkness, listening, a horror, greater than he had ever felt before, came over him. The cry seemed to him menacing, no longer merely a cry for sympathy, for assistance, no longer merely the cry of a helpless creature in pain. He turned white and sick, and clapped his two hands to his ears. And just as he did so the dining room door opened and Lily came out, a thin stream of light following her and falling upon Maurice. He started at the vision of her and at the revealing illumination. His nerves were quivering. His whole body seemed to vibrate.

"Don't come near me," he cried out to Lily. "It is worse since you are with me. Your presence makes my danger. Ah!"

And with a cry he dashed into his study, banging the door behind him, as if he fled from her.

A few days later Maurice stood at the garden gate and helped Lily into the carriage that was to take her to the station. A summons to a patient prevented him from seeing her and the Canon off on their journey northwards. Just before Lily put her foot on the step she stopped and wavered.

"Wait a moment," she said.

She ran back into the little house which had been her home since she was married. Maurice supposed that she had forgotten something. But she only peeped into her bedroom, into the gay drawing room, into Maurice's den. And as she looked at this last little chamber, at the books, the ruffled writing table, the pipes ranged against the wall, her photograph standing in a silver frame upon the mantelpiece, her eyes filled with tears, and there was a stricken feeling at her heart.

"Lily, you will miss the train," Maurice called to her.

She hurried out, got into the carriage and was driven away, wondering why she had gone back to take a last glance at her home, why she had scarcely been able to see it for her tears.

That evening Maurice returned from his round of visits in a curious state of excitement and of anticipation, mingled with nervous dread. He felt as if the eyes of the dead child were upon all his doings, as if the mind of the dead child pondered every act of his, as if the brain of the dead child were busy about his life, as if the soul of the dead child concerned itself for ever with his soul, which it had secretly dedicated to a loneliness assured now by the departure of Lily. By living alone, even for a few weeks, was he not in a measure obeying the desire of the little spirit, which possessed his fate like some inexorable Providence? If so, dare he not hope for an interval of peace, for that stillness after which he longed with an anxiety that was like a physical pain?

He entered his house. Twilight was falling, and the hall, in which on the previous night the child had complained in so grievous a manner, was shadowy. He stood there and listened. He heard the distant wash of the sea, the voices of two servants talking together behind the swing door that led to the kitchen. No sound mingled with the sea, or with the chattering voices. Slowly he ascended the stairs and entered the bedroom, in which Lily had slept quietly, while he, by her side, endured the persecution of the child. The blinds were up. The dying daylight crept slowly from the room, making an exit as furtive and suppressed as that of one who steals from a death chamber. Maurice sat down upon the bed and again listened for a long time.

He was conscious of the sense of relief which comes upon a man who, through some sudden act, has removed from his shoulders a terrible burden. He took this present silence to himself as a reward. But would it last? Opening the window he leaned out to hear the sea more plainly. All living voices, whether of Nature or of man, were beautiful to him, they had come to make his silence.

A servant knocked at the door. Maurice went down to dine. He passed the late evening as usual in his study. He slept calmly. He woke—to silence. Did not this silence confirm his fixed idea that his marriage with Lily had vexed that wakeful spirit, had troubled that unquiet soul of the child? Maurice, wrapped in a beautiful peace, felt that it did. And, as the silent lovely days, the silent lovely nights passed on he came gradually to a fixed resolve.

Lily must not return to him, must not live with him again.

He pondered for a long time how he was to compass their further separation. And, at length, he sat down and wrote a letter to Lily telling her the exact truth.

"Think me cruel, selfish," he wrote at the end of his letter. "I am cruel. I am selfish. Despair has made me so. The fear of madness has made me so. I must have peace. I must and will have it, at whatever cost."

He sent this letter to the *poste restante* at Windermere, as Lily had directed. She and her father were moving about in the Lake district, and did not know from day to day where they might be. He received a reply within a week. It reached him at breakfast time, and, happening to glance at the postmark before he opened it, his face suddenly flushed and his heart beat with violence. For the letter came from that lonely village in that sequestered mountain valley in which he had once lived, in which he had first heard the cry of the child. What chance had led Lily's steps there? Maurice read the letter eagerly. It was very gentle, very submissive. And there was one strange passage in it:

"I understand that you are at peace," Lily wrote. "Yet the child is not at peace. It is crying still. You will ask me how I know that. Do not ask me now. Someday I shall send for you and tell you. When I send for you, if it is by day or night, promise that you will come to me. I claim this promise from you. And now goodbye for a time. My father is very unhappy about us. But he trusts me completely, and I have told him that you and I must be apart, but only for a time. I shall not write to you again till I send for you. Even my letter may disturb your peace and I would give up my life to give you peace."

There was no allusion in the letter to the reason which had led Lily and her father to the out-of-the-way valley which had seen the dawn of Maurice's despair. And Maurice was greatly puzzled. Again there came over him a curious conviction that Lily had some secret from him, some secret connected with his fate, and that she was waiting for the arrival of some day, fixed in her mind, on which to make a revelation of her knowledge to him. This mention of an eventual summons, "by day or night." What could it mean otherwise? Maurice read the letter again and again. Its last words touched him by their perfect unselfishness and also by their feminine romance. He had a moment's thought of the many emotional stories Lily had read. "She lives in one now," he said to himself. And then, as usual, he became self-engrossed, saw only his own life, possibly touched forever with a light of peace.

The Canon returned alone. He met Maurice gravely, almost sternly.

"I trust my child entirely," he said. "She has told me that for a time you must live apart. She has made me promise not to ask you the reason of this separation. I don't ask it, but if you—"

His voice broke and he turned away for a moment. Then he said:

"Lily remains in the place from which she wrote to you."

"She is going to live there!" Maurice exclaimed.

"For the present, I could not persuade her otherwise. Her old nurse, Mrs. Whitehead, is going up to be with her. I cannot understand all this."

The old man cast his eyes searchingly upon Maurice.

"What—?" he began, then, remembering his promise to his daughter, he stopped short.

"We will talk no more about this," he said slowly. "No more."

He bade Maurice goodbye and returned, sorrowful, to the Rectory.

Lily kept her word. Maurice had no more letters from her. He only heard of her from the Canon, and knew that she remained in that beautiful and terrible valley, which he remembered so vividly and hated so ardently. Meanwhile he dwelt in a peace that was strange to him. The little voice had gone out of his life. The cry of the child was hushed. Often, in the past, Maurice had contemplated the coming of this exquisite silence, but he had always imagined it as a gradual approach. He had fancied that if the lamentation of the child ever died out of his haunted life it would fade away as the sound of the sea fades on a long strand when the whispering tide goes down. Day by day, night by night, her crying would grow less poignant, less distinct in a long diminuendo, as if the restless spirit withdrew slowly farther and farther away, till the cry became a whisper, then a broken murmur, then—nothing. This abrupt cessation of persecution, this violent change from something that had seemed like menace to perfect immunity from trouble, was a fact that Maurice had never thought of as a possibility. He had grown to believe that Lily's presence in his home intensified the terror from which he suffered, certainly. But he had never supposed that her removal from him would lay the spirit entirely to rest. And she said that it was not at rest. How could she know that? And if it were not at rest, in what region was it pursuing its weird activity? Whither had it gone? He wondered long and deeply. And then he resolved to wonder no more. Peace had come to him at last. He would not break it by questioning the reason of it. He would accept it blindly, joyfully. Man blots the sunshine out of life by asking "Why?"

Time passed on. Brayfield had gossiped, marvelled and sunk into a sort of apathy of unrewarded and quiescent curiosity. The Canon pursued his life at the Rectory. Maurice visited his patients and continued unremittingly his medical researches. The immunity he now enjoyed gradually wrought a great change in him. He emerged from prison into the outer air. His health rapidly improved. His heavy eyes grew bright. His mind was active and alert. He was a new man. The darkness faded round him. He saw the light at last. For the silence endured. And at last he even forgot to listen, at dawn or in the silent hours of the night, for the cry of the child. Even the memory of it began to grow faint within his heart. So rapidly does man forget his troubles when he still has youth and the years are not heavy on him.

Yet Maurice often thought of Lily. And now that he was no longer bowed under the tyranny of a shattered nervous system he felt a new tenderness for her. He recalled her devotion and no longer linked her with his persecution. He remembered her unselfishness. He wished her back again. And then—he remembered all his misery, and that, with her, it went. And his selfishness said to him—it is better so. And his mental cowardice whispered to him—your safety is in your solitude. And he put the memory of Lily's love and of the beauty of her nature from him.

So his silent autumn passed by. And his silent winter came. One day, in a December frost, he met the Canon, muffled up to the chin and on his way to see Miss Bigelow, who professed herself once again *in extremis*. They stopped in the snow and spoke a few commonplace words, but Maurice thought he observed a peculiar furtiveness in the old man's manner, a hint of some suppressed excitement in his voice.

"How is Lily?" Maurice asked.

"Fairly well," the Canon said.

"She is still at the inn?"

"No, she lately moved into a little house further up the valley."

"Further up the valley," Maurice said. "But there's only one other house in that direction. I have been there you know," he added hastily.

"Lily told me you had stayed there."

"Well, but—" Maurice persisted, "there is only one house, a private house."

"They have been building up there," the Canon said evasively. "Houses are springing up. It is a pity. Good night."

And he turned and walked away. Maurice stood looking after him. So they had been building in the valley, and End Cottage no longer possessed the distinction of being the finale of man in that Arcadia of woods and streams, and rugged hills on which the clouds brooded, from which the rain came like a mournful pilgrim, to weep over the gentle shrine of nature.

So they had been building in the valley.

Maurice made his way home. His mind was full of memories.

The close of the year drew on. It was a bad season, a cruel season for the poor. Men went about saying to one another that it was a hard winter. The papers were full of reports of abnormal frosts, of tremendous falls of snow, of ice-bound rivers and trains delayed. There were deaths from cold. The starving died off like flies, under hedges by roadsides, in the fireless attics of towns. Comfortable and well-to-do persons talked vigorously of the delights of an old-fashioned Christmas. The doctors had many patients. Among them Maurice was very busy. His talent had monopolised Brayfield and his time was incessantly occupied. He scarcely noticed Christmas. For even on that day he was full of work. Several people managed to be very ill among the plum puddings. The year died and was buried. The New Year dawned, and still the evil weather continued. In early January Maurice came down one morning to find by his plate a letter written in a hand of old age, straggling and complicated. It proved to be from Mrs. Whitehead, Lily's old nurse; and it contained that summons of which Lily had spoken long ago in her letter to her husband. Lily was ill and wished to see Maurice at once. The letter, though involved, was urgent.

Maurice laid it down. There was a date on it but no name of a house. By the date Maurice saw that the letter had been delayed in transit. Blizzards, snowstorms, had been responsible for many such delays. He got up from the table. At that moment there was no hesitation in his mind. He would go to Lily at once, as fast as rail could carry him. In a few moments his luggage was packed. Within an hour he was on his way to the station. He stopped the carriage at the Rectory and asked to see the Canon for a moment. The servant, looking reproachful, told him her master had started three days before to see "Miss Lily," who was ill.

"Miss Lily," Maurice said. "You mean Mrs. Dale. I am on my way to see her too. What is the matter? They do not tell me."

"I don't know, sir," the servant said, softening a little on learning that Maurice was going north to his wife.

Maurice drove on to the station.

In all his afterlife he never could forget his white journey. It seemed to him as if nature gathered herself together to delay him, to turn him from his purpose of obeying the summons of Lily. Even the line from

Brayfield to London was blocked, and when at length Maurice reached London he found the great city staggering under a burden of snow that rendered its features unrecognisable. All traffic was practically suspended. He missed train after train, and when he drove at last into Euston Station and expressed his intention of going north by the night mail the porter shook his head and drew a terrible picture of that arctic region.

"Most of the lines are blocked, sir," he said, "or will be. It's a-coming on for more snow."

"I can't help that," Maurice said. "I must go. Label my luggage."

The train was due to start at midnight. Maurice had a lonely dinner at the station hotel. While he ate in the gaily lighted coffee-room he thought of Lily and of his coming journey. The influence of the weather had surrounded it with a curious romance such as English travel seldom affords. Maurice was very susceptible to the mental atmosphere engendered by outward circumstances, and yielded more readily than the average man to the wayward promptings of the faithful spirit that nestles somewhere in almost every intellect. He began to regard this white journey to the ice-bound and rugged north with something of a child's wide-eyed, half-delighted, half-alarmed anticipation. He thought of the darkness, of the dangers by the way, of the multitudes of lonely snow-wreathed miles the train would have to cover; of the increasing cold as they went higher and higher up the land, of the early dawn over fells and stone walls, of the grey light on the grey sea. Then he listened to the strangely muffled roar of a London hoarse with cold. And he shivered and had feelings of a man bound on some tremendous and novel quest. As he came out of the hotel the wintry air met him and embraced him. He entered the station, dull and sinister in the night, with its haggard gas-lamps and arches yawning to the snow. There were few passengers, and they looked anxious. The train drew in. Maurice had his carriage to himself. The porter wished him good luck on his journey with the voice and manner of one clearly foreseeing imminent disaster and death. The whistle sounded, and the train glided, a long black and orange snake, into the white wonder of the clouded night. Snow beat upon the windows, incrusted with the filagree work of frost, and as the speed of the train increased the carriage filled with the persistent music of an intense and sustained activity. This music, and the thoughts of Maurice fought against sleep. He leaned back with open eyes and listened to the song of the train. Its monotony was like the monotony of an irritable man, he thought, always angry, always expressing his anger. Beneath bridges, in tunnels, the anger was dashed with ripples of fury, with spurts of brutalising passion. And then the normal current of dull temper flowed on again as before. Maurice wished that the windows were not merely thick white blinds completely shutting out the night. He longed to see the storm in which they fled towards greater storms, the country which they spurned as they sprang northwards! Northwards! And to that valley!

His thoughts went to his old life alone there, to the coming into it of the haunting voice, to his terror, his struggle, his flight southward. He had never thought to return there. Yet now he fled towards that place of memories, calm, sane, cleansed of persecution, with his mind fortified, and his heart steadily and calmly beating, unshaken by the agonies of old. Was he the same man? It seemed almost impossible. And now Maurice said to himself again that perhaps after all the cry of the child had been imagination, a symptom of illness in him from which he had—perhaps even through some obscure physical change— recovered completely. Yet Lily had believed in the cry and believed in the unquiet spirit behind it. But women are romantic, credulous—

The train rocked in a rapture of motion. Maurice drew his rugs more closely round him. With the advance of night the cold grew more deadly.

Towards morning the pace of the train incessantly decreased. Huge masses of snow had drifted upon the line. For a rising wind drove it together under hedgerows and walls until expanding upon the track, it impeded the progress of the engines. Maurice let down a window and peered out. He saw only snow, stationary or floating, at rest in shadowy heaps that fled back in the darkness, or falling in a veil before his eyes. It seemed to him now as if a hand were stretched out to stay his impetuous advance to Lily. The train went slower and slower. At last, towards morning, it stopped. A long and distracted whistling pierced the air. There was a jerk, a movement forward, then another stoppage. They were snowed-up in the middle of a desolate stretch of country, with a blizzard raging round them.

How many hours passed before they were released Maurice never knew. He lay wrapped up to the eyes, numbed and passive, of body, but mentally travelling with an extraordinary rapidity. At first he was in the valley. He saw it, as he had seen it in old days, in snow, its river ice- bound, its waterfall arrested in the midst of an army of crystal spears. White mountains rose round it to a low sky, curved, like a bosom, in grey cloud shapes. The air was sharp and silent, clearer than southern air, a thing that seemed to hold itself alert in its narrow prison on the edge of solitude. He heard the bark of a dog on the hills, in search of the starving sheep.

Then he came to one of those new houses of which the Canon had spoken, and in it he found Lily. She was pale, but he scarcely noticed that, engrossed in the strangeness of finding her there. For in the south he had never fully realised Lily at home in the valley, walking on the desolate narrow roads by day, sleeping in the shadow of the hills by night. Now he began to realise her there. Where would the house be? Near End Cottage, perhaps in sight of the garden to which he had stolen on that evil night to listen for the voice of a bird!

After many hours the train was dug out of the snow, and sped forward again in daylight. Maurice slept a little, but uneasily. And now, when he was awake, he began to be filled with an unreasonable apprehension, for which he accounted by taking stock of the low temperature of his body, and of the loss of vitality occasioned by want of food and rest. He was seized with fear as he came up into the north and saw vaguely the moors around him, the snowy waves where the white woods rippled up the flanks of the white hills. He began to realise again his former condition when his life was full of the lamentation of the child. He began to feel as if he drew near to that lamentation once more. Perhaps the little sorrowful spirit had only deserted him to return to the valley in which it first greeted him. Perhaps it would come again to him there. He might hear the cry from the garden of the cottage as he hastened past.

He shuddered and cursed his wild fancies. But they stayed with him through all the rest of the journey, through all the delays and periods of numb patience. And they increased upon him. When at last he reached the dreary station by the flat sandbanks, at which he changed into the valley train, he was pale and careworn, and full of alarm.

Very slowly the tiny train crawled up into the heart of the hills as the darkness of the second night came down. Maurice was the only passenger in it. He felt like one alone in a lonely world, fearing inhabitants unseen, but whose distant presence he was aware of. Could Lily indeed be here, beyond him in this desolation? It seemed impossible. But the child might be here, wandering, a lost spirit, in this unutterable winter. That would not be strange to him. And his soul grew colder than his body. He could see nothing from the window, but occasionally he heard the dry tapping of twigs upon the glass, as the train crept among the leafless woods. And this tapping seemed to him to be the tiny fingers of the child, feebly endeavouring to attract his attention.

He shrank away from the window to the centre of the carriage.

At the last station in the valley the train stopped. Maurice got out into the darkness, and asked the guard the name of the house in which Mrs. Dale lived.

"Mrs. Dale," he said, in the broad Cumberland dialect, "Oh, she bides at End Cottage."

Maurice stared at his rugged face peering above the round lamp which he held.

"End Cottage?"

"Yes, sir. The poor lady took it on a six months' lease, but I hear she's—"

But Maurice had turned away with a muttered:

"I'll send up for the luggage."

He stumbled out into the white lane and through the little village. One or two lads, roughly dressed and sprinkled with snowflakes, eyed him from the shelter of the inn porch. As he moved past them, he heard their muttered comments. He left the houses behind and found himself among snow-laden trees. End Cottage was hidden in this narrow wood which was generally full of the sound of the waterfall.

Now the waterfall was silent, motionless, a dead thing in a rocky grave. Maurice saw a faint and misty light among the bare trees. It came from his old home, and now his hand touched the white garden gate, prickly with ice. He pushed it open and stole up the path till he reached the little porch of the cottage. As he stood there his heart beat hard and his breath fluttered in his throat. It seemed to him that there must be some strange and terrible meaning in Lily's presence here. With a shaking hand he pulled at the bell. He waited. No one came. He heard no step. The silence was dense, even appalling. After a long pause he turned the handle of the door, opened it, and stood on the threshold of the cottage. Instead of entering at once he waited, listening for any sound of life within the house, for the voices or footsteps of those inhabiting it.

Just so had he waited on a summer night long ago, with the moon behind him and leaf-laden trees. He listened, and, after a moment of profound stillness, he heard—as he had heard in that very place so long ago—the faint cry of a child. It came from within the house, clear and distinct though frail and feeble.

Involuntarily Maurice moved a step backward into the snow. Horror overwhelmed him. The dead child was here then with Lily, in his old abode. The spirit was not laid to rest. It had only deserted him for a while to greet him again here, to take up again here its eternal persecution; and this resurrection appalled and unmanned him more than all the persistent haunting of the past. He was dashed from confidence to despair. The little cry paralysed him, and he leaned against the wall of the porch almost like a dying man.

And again he heard the cry of the child.

How live and how real it was! Maurice remembered that he had said to himself that the cry was a phantasy of the brain, an imaginary sound vibrating from an afflicted body. And now his intellect denied such a supposition; the cry came from a thing that lived, although it lived in another world. It seemed to summon him with a strange insistence. Against his will, and walking slowly as one in a trance, he moved forward up the narrow stairway till he reached the room that had been his old bedroom.

The cry came surely from within that room. The dead child was shut in there. Yes, never before had Maurice been able to locate the cry precisely. Now he could locate it. With shaking fingers he grasped the handle of the door. He stood in a faint illumination, and the cry of the child came louder to his ears. But there mingled with it another cry, faint yet thrilling with joy:

"Maurice!"

He looked and saw Lily, white as a flower. She was propped on pillows, and, stretching out her thin girl's arms, she held feebly towards Maurice a tiny baby.

"Maurice—it is the child!" she whispered.

"The child!" he repeated hoarsely.

For an instant he believed that his fate was sealed, that the spirit, which for so long had pursued him with its lamenting, now manifested its actual presence to his eyes. Then, in a flash, the truth came upon him. He fell upon his knees by the bedside and put out his arms for the child. He held it. He felt its soft breath against his cheek. A cooing murmur, as if of tiny happiness, came from its parted lips. It turned its little face, flushed like a rose, against the breast of Maurice, and nestled to sleep upon his heart.

And Lily's hand touched him.

"I thought you would not come in time," she said, as the nurse, at a sign from her, stole softly from the room.

"In time?"

"To see me before—they say, you know, that—"

"Lily!" he cried.

"Hush! The child! Listen, dear. If I die, take the child. It is your dead child, I think, come to life through me. Yes, yes, it is the little child that has cried for love so long. Redeem your cruelty, oh, Maurice, redeem it to your child. Give it your love. Give it your life. Give it—"

"Lily!" he said again. And there were tears on his cheeks.

"I gave myself to you for this, Maurice. I was waiting for this. Do you understand me now? You scarcely loved me, Maurice. But I loved you. Let me think—in dying—that I have brought you peace at last."

He could not speak. The mystery of woman, the mystery of child was too near to him. Awe came upon him and the terror of his own unworthiness, rewarded—or punished—which was it?—by such compassion, such self-sacrifice.

"When I left you," Lily murmured, and her voice sounded thin and tired, "it seemed as if the spirit of the child came with me, as if I, too, heard its dead voice in the night, crying for its salvation, for its relief from agony. But, Maurice, you cannot hear it now. You will never hear it again—unless—unless—"

She fixed her eyes on him. They were growing dim.

"God has given the dead to you again through me," she faltered, "that you—may—redeem—redeem—your—sin."

She moved, and leaned against him, as if she would gather him and the sleeping child into her embrace. But she could not. She slipped back softly, almost like a snowflake that falls and is gone.

Maurice Dale is a famous doctor now. He lives with his daughter, who never leaves him and whom he loves passionately. Many patients throng to his consulting room, but not one of them suspects that the grave physician, deep down in his heart, cherishes a strange belief— not based upon science. This belief is connected with his child. Secretly he thinks of her as of one risen from the grave, come back to him from beyond the gates of death.

The cry of the child is silent. Maurice never hears it now. But he believes that could any demon tempt him, even for one moment, to be cruel to his little daughter, he would hear it again. It would lament once more in the darkness, would once more fill the silence with its despair.

And then a dead woman would stir in her grave.

For there are surely cries of earth that even the dead can hear.

THE END

Robert Hichens Bibliography
(1864-1950)

Novels

The Coast Guard's Secret (1886)

The Green Carnation (published anonymously, 1894; republished as by Hitchens, 1948)

An Imaginative Man (1895)

Flames (1897)

The Londoners (1898)

The Daughters of Babylon (1899; with Wilson Barrett)

The Slave (1899)

The Prophet of Berkeley Square (1901)

Felix (1902)

The Garden of Allah (1904)

The Woman With the Fan (1904)

Call of the Blood (1905)

Barbary Sheep (1907)

A Spirit in Prison (1908)

Bella Donna (1909; reprinted as *Temptation*, 1946)

The Dweller on the Threshold (1911)

The Fruitful Vine (1911)

The Way of Ambition (1913)

In the Wilderness (1917)

Mrs. Marden (1919)

The Spirit of the Time (1921)

December Love (1922)

After The Verdict (1924)

The Unearthly (1925; UK as *The God Within Him*)

The Bacchante and the Nun (1926; US as *The Bacchante*)

The First Lady Brendon (1927)

Dr. Artz (1928)

On the Screen (1929)

The Bracelet (1930)

The Gates of Paradise (1930)

The First Lady Brendon (1931)

Mortimer Brice (1932)

The Paradine Case (1933)

The Power to Kill (1934)

Susie's Career (1935)

The Pyramid (1936)

The Sixth of October (1936)

Daniel Airlie (1937)

Secret Information (1938)

The Journey Up (1938)

That Which Is Hidden (1939)

The Million (1940)

Married or Unmarried (1941)

A New Way of Life (1941)

Veils (1943)

Young Mrs. Brand (1944)

Harps in the Wind (1945; U.S. as *The Woman in the House*)

Incognito (1945; Hutchinson)

Too Much Love of Living (1947)

Beneath the Magic (1950; U.S. as *Strange Lady*)

The Mask (1951)

Night Bound (1951)

Collections

After To-Morrow, and the New Love (1895)

The Folly of Eustace and Other Stories (1896)

Bye-Ways (1897)

Tongues of Conscience (1898, 1900)

The Black Spaniel and Other Stories (1905)

Snake-Bite and Other Stories (1919)

The Last Time (1924)

The Streets and Other Stories (1928)

The Gates of Paradise and Other Stories (1930)

My Desert Friend and Other Stories (1931)

The Gardenia, and Other Stories
(1934)

The Afterglow and Other Stories
(1935)

The Man in the Mirror and Other
Stories (1950)

The Return of the Soul and Other
Stories (2001; ed. S. T. Joshi)

Nonfiction

Old Cairo (1908; article)

Egypt and Its Monuments (1908)

The Holy Land (1910)

The Spell of Egypt (1910; orig.
published as *Egypt and Its
Monuments*, 1908)

The Near East (1913)

Yesterday (1947)

Plays

The Medicine Man (1898; with H. D.
Traill)

Becky Sharp (1901; with C. G.
Lennox; U.S. title: *Vanity Fair*)

The Real Woman (1909)

The Garden of Allah (1911; with
Mary Anderson)

The Law of the Sands (1916)

Black Magic (1917)

Press the Button! (1918)

The Voice from the Minaret (1919)

Filmography [based on the novel
unless otherwise noted]

Bella Donna (directed by Edwin S.
Porter and Hugh Ford;1915)

The Garden of Allah (directed by
Colin Campbell; 1916)

Barbary Sheep (directed by Maurice
Tourneur; 1917)

Flames (directed by Maurice Elvey;
UK, 1917)

The Slave (directed by Arrigo Bocchi;
UK, 1918)

Hidden Lives (directed by Maurits
Binger and B. E. Doxat-Pratt;
Netherlands, 1920, based on a play
by Robert Hichens and John
Knittel)

The Call of the Blood (directed by
Louis Mercanton; France, 1920)

The Woman with the Fan (directed
by René Plaissetty; UK, 1921)

The Fruitful Vine (directed by
Maurice Elvey; UK, 1921)

The Voice from the Minaret (directed
by Frank Lloyd; 1923, based on the
play)

Bella Donna (directed by George
Fitzmaurice; 1923)

The Lady Who Lied (directed by
Edwin Carewe; 1925, based on the
story)

The Garden of Allah (directed by Rex
Ingram; 1927)

After the Verdict (directed by Henrik
Galeen; UK, 1929)

Bella Donna (directed by Robert
Milton; UK, 1934)

The Garden of Allah (directed by
Richard Boleslawski; 1936)

Temptation (directed by Irving
Pichel; 1946, based on the novel
Bella Donna)

The Paradine Case (directed by
Alfred Hitchcock; 1947)

Call of the Blood (directed by John
Clements and Ladislao Vajda; UK,
1948)